The Heart of a Sinner

by

Lynn Shurr

A Sinner's Legacy, Book Five

The Heart of a Sinner

Cover Art by *Diana Carlile*

The Wild Rose Press, Inc.
PO Box 708
Adams Basin, NY 14410-0708
Visit us at www.thewildrosepress.com

Publishing History
First Champagne Rose Edition, 2019
Print ISBN 978-1-5092-2378-7
Digital ISBN 978-1-5092-2379-4

A Sinner's Legacy, Book Five
Published in the United States of America

Silently, Matt escorted Annie to her room. All the while, he searched for the right words to put her at ease and take the tears from her eyes, to say what lay deep in his heart. He lacked the facility with language that his mother, the English professor, possessed. He'd had no chance to inherit it from her. Undoubtedly, a big, dumb jock conceived him. He felt it keenly now.

Annie had restored order to her space after Jude ransacked the dresser drawers seeking nightwear before going to bed herself. Only the white silk and black lace nightie lay crumpled on the floor, the single sign of the tempest that had taken place. Annie reached down and balled it into a waste basket.

He spoke the first words that came to him. "Don't do that. I'd like to see you wear it, not Jude."

Annie's eyes grew big. "What?"

"That came out wrong. I meant if you had come to me instead of your sister, we'd be in bed together right now." Everything that came out of his mouth made it worse.

"Really?" Her brows raised. Her cheeks flushed.

"Even without the butterfly tattoo, I knew she wasn't you, the aggressive way she tried to seduce me. You have to believe I didn't encourage her." Still stumbling.

Praise for Lynn Shurr

"Shurr is a wonderful storyteller."

~The Romance Studio

~*~

"Lynn Shurr's delightful New Orleans Sinners series is sure to please both non-sports fans and sports fans alike. Do yourself a favor and dive into the world of the Sinners."

~Farrah Rochon, USA Today best-selling author of the New York Sabers football series

~*~

"The author has created a family full of surprises with the Billodeaux bunch. After reading just one book, I am eager to read more about this colorful family."

~Rachel's Willful Thoughts, The Romance Reviews

~*~

"Very easy reads, well written, combined with conflict, believable plots and secondary characters that make the plot come alive."

~Jane Lange, Romances, Reads and Reviews

~*~

"I love how deep and well-written the characters are."

~Juliette Brandt, Paperbacks and Frosting

Dedication

For the wonderful Oliver Finch Laughlin,
former NICU baby,
and the nurses who take care of the smallest patients

~

Special thanks to Kim McKay Smoak
for her insights on life as a nurse

**The Children of Joe and Nell Billodeaux
who fulfilled the prophecy that they would have
twelve offspring, this way, that way, all ways**

Dean Joseph Billodeaux – Joe's illegitimate son by a one-night stand with a woman who planned to shake him down for money. He is adopted by Nell who believes she cannot have children of her own. Current Sinners quarterback. (*Wish for a Sinner, Son of a Sinner*)

Thomas Cassidy Billodeaux – a redheaded son who enters the family through an open adoption with a teenage mother. His birth father is Joe's no-good cousin. He is a kicker for the Sinners. (*Wish for a Sinner, Kicks for a Sinner, She's a Sinner*)

Jude Emily Billodeaux – twin of Ann, conceived by in vitro fertilization using eggs purchased from Nell's sister, Emily. (*Wish for a Sinner*)

Ann Marie Billodeaux (Annie) – Jude's quiet twin. (*Wish for a Sinner, Heart of a Sinner*)

Lorena Renee Billodeaux (Lori) – First of Nell's little frozen babies to be born, one of the triplets. (*Kicks for a Sinner*)

Mack Coy Christopher Billodeaux – Second of the triplets to be born. (*Kicks for a Sinner*)

Trinity Billodeaux - Youngest of the triplets and named for the Father, Son, and Holy Ghost, smallest of the three and in need of a powerful saintly help to survive. (*Kicks for a Sinner*)

Xochi Maria Billodeaux – child of Joe's no-good cousin by a young Mexican woman. She is Tom's half-sister and is adopted into the family after the terrifying deaths of her parents. Her name means "blossom" in

Aztec. (*Kicks for a Sinner, Sister of a Sinner*)

Teddy Wilkes Billodeaux – a child with spina bifida abandoned by his mother at Nell's health care center and adopted by the family. He believed himself to be Joe's natural son. (*Paradise for a Sinner, Never a Sinner*)

Anastasia Marya Polasky (Stacy) – daughter of Nell's sister, Emily, and a bogus Polish prince. She becomes a ward of the Billodeauxs upon her parents' deaths but is never adopted by her own wish. She arrives on their doorstep the same day as Teddy. (*Paradise for a Sinner, Son of a Sinner*)

Edith Patricia Billodeaux (Edie) – a normally conceived child, twin of Rex. (*Love Letter for a Sinner*)

Rex Worthy Billodeaux (T-Rex) – Edie's twin brother and future Sinner's quarterback, maybe. (*Love Letter for a Sinner*)

Chapter One

Ten p.m. on a Sunday night, the doors to the Neonatal Intensive Care Unit zipped open. Nurse Annie Billodeaux accepted another fragile soul into her care with gentle hands. She weighed in the tiny, bald baby boy delivered by C-section from his mother's womb at twenty-eight weeks of gestation at two pounds, three ounces. Working with the neonatologist, she went about her duties swiftly but carefully: inserting a catheter, hooking up an oxygen feed to the little nose, attaching sensors to the feeble chest, and starting an intravenous line to feed an infant too young to suckle. He'd stay in the warm cocoon of his incubator until large enough to enter a wider world.

She'd done this procedure many times and remembered each child she'd nurtured before turning it over to the parents to take home. Always, Annie called the patient by its name—in this case Daniel Ames Keaton. "There you go, Danny, all safe and sound. Your parents will want to see you soon and make sure you are in good hands. You are."

Now that she had a moment to think instead of simply reacting as trained to the emergency, Annie realized she knew this baby and his parents. Not two weeks ago in early May, she'd had dinner with her mom and dad and other siblings residing in New Orleans before starting her shift. As usual, Joe and Nell

Billodeaux had taken a young couple under their mighty wings, in this case the Sinners football team's new running back, Matthew Keaton and his pregnant wife, Melinda. Her oldest brother, Dean, the quarterback, and his wife had been delegated to help the Keatons find housing in the Crescent City.

Over a shared appetizer of Oysters Rockefeller, or *Huitres en coquille a la Rockefeller* according to the menu at venerable Antoine's, and rejected by Mrs. Keaton who feared contamination even though the oysters were baked, they discussed what features the newcomers wanted in a home: city, suburbs, lakeside, north shore, number of bedrooms, etc. One thing Annie, seated across the table from Melinda, felt certain of— the wife wasn't at all at ease in the Big Easy. She fretted over the traffic and crime, the unhealthy climate, and the quality of the schools she wouldn't need for years.

Hidden by the table, the woman's belly swelled as she neared the seventh month of a pregnancy, though the tall, slim, blue-eyed and beautiful blonde, the type most football players seemed to prefer as wives, carried a rather small bump. Annie knew that meant nothing in the long run. Tall women didn't show as much. If she were lucky enough to become pregnant, with her small stature she'd resemble a pumpkin exactly as her petite mother had. She knew one man who'd gone for short and brunette, her dad. So, maybe someday…

Melinda announced she'd be a stay-at-home mom, subtly dissing Dean's wife, Stacy, who had a part-time nanny that allowed her to continue her interpreting and translating business as well as participate in cultural events. She gave her time to help football players' wives get settled too. As Annie knew well, Stacy, every bit as tall and blonde and better built, seldom backed down. "Good for you. I'd go nuts if I didn't get out of the house for some intellectual stimulation."

Melinda's husband, snatched from Indianapolis as soon as he became a free agent for a forty-million-dollar contract, exuded the confidence of a man who'd made a great move for his career. Matt entirely missed or ignored the byplay in favor of being deep into sports conversation with the Hall-of-Famer quarterback, Joe Billodeaux. Annie couldn't read auras like one of her sisters, but a career in nursing had increased her empathy. Possibly, she could help the situation.

She offered Melinda a confident smile, the one she always wore in the NICU. "Who is your obstetrician? Oh, Dr. Cooper is excellent. Both my sister and I work for Ochsner. It's a great hospital with top notch care. I'd suggest for now you might want to rent a place in the Garden District to be closer to medical care. It's a quiet area with good security." In other words, the realm of the rich.

"So Stacy says since she lives there. Excuse me, I need the ladies' room—again."

"A hazard of your condition," Annie said pleasantly, but none of the Billodeaux women offered to go with her.

Annie's twin, Jude, sitting beside her radiated hostility toward the woman. She whispered to her sister, "Latched onto a husband in college and probably never worked a day in her life." All the Billodeaux girls were expected to live purposeful lives and be able to earn their own way.

"It must be hard on her, coming here pregnant,

losing her support system back home, especially her mother who lived nearby."

"As she mentioned several times already. You know I can't stand nervous Nellies." Jude took no crap from patients or doctors. Suited for the NICU, nope. She'd gone into surgical nursing.

"Yes, if it were one of us in this situation we'd simply squat down and deliver that baby ourselves, wrap it in a blanket, and get back to work."

"Damn right, Sis."

Across the table, their mom gave them the hairy eyeball for whispering at dinner. They stopped. Tiny Nell Billodeaux also took no crap from her grown children. The rules they'd been brought up to obey still held sway. All twelve of them had turned out well so far. Okay, there was Mack, but the family hoped he'd grow out of his antics.

In looks, the twins greatly resembled Nell with her big, brown doe eyes and dark hair, despite having been conceived from eggs donated by her sister. They often regretted having inherited their father's curls and not his impressive stature. But, what could you do about that?

Melinda returned from the restroom just as the impeccable waiters served the entrees. Jude speared the last oyster, the one meant for the squeamish eater, before they took away the tray. "These used to be made with snails, but oysters are easier to get in New Orleans," she said to the expectant mother—and got another glare from her mom.

Nell redirected the conversation. "A pity you don't like seafood, Melinda. It's so very good here."

"The doctor says I'm a little anemic and should eat

more red meat while I'm pregnant. Being from the Midwest, I prefer it to fish, so it all works out," Melinda answered as she accepted her prime tenderloin.

Now, standing by the incubator that held Melinda and Matt's very premature son, Annie wondered what had gone wrong. The mother seemed fine two weeks ago at dinner, but you never knew what might occur in a pregnancy. She asked the neonatal pediatrician also staying near to answer questions, "What happened? Preeclampsia or just one of those things?"

"Accident. The couple strayed into the wrong area of town and drove through a gang shootout. Collateral damage. The mother is still on life support, but she's brain dead. The father is waiting for her family to arrive before pulling the plug."

"Dear God," Annie murmured as Matthew Keaton entered the room, filled it really with his size, his brawn. A powerful six-five, two-hundred-thirty pounds, Annie knew his stats as she did most of the Sinners players. Those substantial shoulders delivered a vicious block and absorbed the same. His long legs ate up the yardage to the goalpost, and just try to knock a ball out of those muscular arms. He'd cultivated a mean, dark-eyed stare for his publicity photos, enhanced by the total lack of a smile in his large, granite jaw.

Someone had garbed him in a blue disposable gown that barely fit, helped him scrub as the sleeves beneath it were rolled up, and tagged him with the ID that paired him with tiny Daniel. Annie wondered if the clothes were blood-spattered. Matt offered no smile now as he stared at his son splayed out like a human sacrifice stuck full of tubes and needles, but the eyes, his eyes, appeared lost and bewildered beneath thick black hair thoroughly raked by frantic fingers.

"Will he live?"

"His chances are excellent. We will nurture his development every step of the way until he is ready to come home," the pediatrician answered. "This is our night nurse practitioner in the NICU, Annie Billodeaux, one of the angels who will be watching over Daniel. She's the best, the heart of the department."

Dear Dr. Brown, always generous with his compliments. All the nurses loved him and dreaded his approaching retirement. Annie produced a gentle smile, but Matthew Keaton didn't seem to notice. "Will he be blind or impaired in some way if he survives?"

She took his question. "Blindness is very rare these days, and he has every chance of being a normal child. Daniel will continue growing right here until he is big enough to go home with you. He might even play football someday. My brothers, Dean and Mack Billodeaux were both preemies. So were Jude and me. Dad delivered us a little early in the back of a wrecked motorhome. All of us grew up just fine."

Her name finally registered on his shell-shocked face. "You're Joe's daughter."

"Yes, we met at dinner a few weeks ago. I am so sorry to hear about Melinda. She very much wanted this child."

"I think so." Matt seemed uncertain. "I hope I did the right thing, letting him be born and not sending him with her."

"You certainly did. You will always have part of Melinda in your life."

"One other item," Dr. Brown said. "We have detected a PDA in your son. That means a duct in his

6

heart is open between the chambers. At this stage of development, it's common and might heal itself as the baby grows. If not, we will reevaluate the situation, consider surgery if necessary. Don't worry for now. If you have any questions, ask me or Annie."

"Thank you, doctor. I must get back to my wife. Her parents are coming in on a redeye flight from Indianapolis. I have to leave to pick them up soon."

Annie intervened. "No, you don't. I'll call Dean. He'll meet them and bring them here if you give me their flight number and time." No sense in having a man in his mental condition cause another accident.

"I'd appreciate that." Matt Keaton dug in his pocket. She took the note jotted on a slip torn from a prescription pad from his outstretched hand. She noticed he took another look at the frail little form in the incubator as if doubting all he'd been told.

"You can watch the baby from Melinda's room on a special monitor. My parents donated enough of them for every NICU unit. The next few days will be hard for you, but please visit your son often. He can hear you and get to know your voice, eventually your touch and scent. It's important for his development."

Half turned away, Keaton simply nodded at her comment and kept walking toward the exit. "Tough one," Dr. Brown remarked. "Maybe the grandparents or a sister will step up to help."

"If not, I'll call in the team wives. And I'll be here for Daniel, too."

Chapter Two

Annie finished her twelve-hour shift, tired but content as usual. After the Keaton baby, none of their tiny charges had coded or experienced other difficulties, a pretty quiet night. She preferred the NICU in the evening when the anxious visiting mothers had gone home, the doctors completed their daily rounds, and the ladies who volunteered to rock the infants left. If she didn't have to rush from one crisis to another, sometimes she rocked the infants herself while offering a small nighttime bottle of breast milk. She didn't mind changing a diaper either. Poop meant progress in their patients' internal growth and dampness functioning kidneys.

For now, she only wanted breakfast in the hospital cafeteria, which had better food than most gave it credit for, before heading home to her apartment over the electronics store on the edge of the French Quarter. No coffee for her, but fresh fruit, a cheese and veggie omelet made on the grill, and a splurge on a large, fluffy biscuit. As she waited on the omelet and ate a few strawberries in the fruit cup, she spied her sister checking out with a large coffee in hand. Too tired for another lecture about her weekend and night hours destroying her social life, Annie ducked her head, but Jude with a twin's sixth sense noticed her and came over to her table.

"Rough night, huh?"

"Not too bad after the C-section baby got settled."

"Matt Keaton's child, it was all over the news last night and this morning. I didn't care for his wife but wouldn't wish that on anyone. Did you know he drove through that hail of bullets and took her straight to the hospital when he saw her slumped in her seat. He had no idea how seriously she'd been hurt and got her into emergency just in time to get her on life support to save the baby."

"He seems like a man of action, wouldn't have made it in pro football if he weren't." Annie accepted her omelet and slathered the healthy spread the hospital provided in lieu of butter on her warm biscuit. "I phoned Dean to pick up her parents at the airport. At least, I could lift a little of his burden. I'm certain he'll blame himself for bringing his wife to New Orleans."

"Yeah, probably. When are you going to ask for a day shift? You missed trying a great new Thai restaurant this weekend, and then, we went over to Mariah's Place and danced with the tourists until all hours since the Sinners they were looking for weren't to be found in the off-season."

Fortunately, Annie did not have to answer her question again, so stale it should be growing mold by now. Jude checked her watch. "I have a surgery at nine. Got to go—but really, we are like those proverbial ships that pass in the night. Get some rest."

"I will."

Annie settled into enjoying her solitary meal as she watched her sister move on.

She'd always let Jude lead the way from adolescent rebellion once they left the rules of the Billodeaux ranch behind to some really poor college choices early on until they settled into nurses' training at LSU. After gaining experience, Jude pushed them on to pursuing rigorous nurse practitioner degrees. There, they'd split with Jude going into the surgical field which offered better hours and lots of adrenaline, and Annie pursuing the treatment of neonates requiring twenty-four-hour care.

When a wonderful job offer came through from Ochsner at the same time Xochi, her aura-seeing sister, decided to give up the apartment in New Orleans in favor of learning to be a *traiteur*, a traditional Cajun healer, Annie seized the chance to live her own life free of her sister's influence. That lasted as long as it took for Jude to find a position at the same hospital and move into the second bedroom.

"Can't survive without my wing woman," her sister claimed. Annie had been that, suffering through many a double date while Jude pursued a guy she wanted, but soon lost interest in having. Men always seemed fascinated by dating twins, building fantasies in their minds and being severely disappointed by the Billodeaux girls.

Working nights gave her some separation and a few hours to herself to find her own way. They still had days off together to shop or go to lunch or return to the luxury of their parents' ranch with its horses for riding and a pool for sunbathing and other spa-like amenities.

She ate the last crumb of her biscuit and scooped a final red grape from the bottom of the fruit cup. Time to go home and sleep away the day in the bedroom secluded from busy Canal Street with its clanging street cars, constant stream of traffic complete with blaring horns, and crowds of boisterous tourists. She happily let Jude have the bigger room with the windows overlooking the hubbub. It suited her sister's personality perfectly.

As she emptied her tray, Dean and Matt entered the cafeteria. They would have stood out even if not handsome and moving with the coordinated grace of athletes. The eyes of every woman in the place from the chunky black lady at checkout to a female doctor in her lab coat tracked them. Dean guided Matt by the elbow as if the man had gone blind. He placed him at a table. "Sit here while I get you something to eat, then you are going home with me." Keaton did not respond. He stared into the shiny metal surface of a napkin holder as if trying to see the future.

Dean veered from the path to the breakfast buffet to head off his sister. "Annie, would you sit with Matt for a few minutes? I know you're exhausted, but you always think of something comforting to say."

Her eldest brother looked fairly tired around the eyes as well. "I can spare the time. Did you stay all night after picking up Melinda's parents?"

Dean nodded. "Mostly out in the waiting room. When I called to let him know they'd arrived on time, he asked if I'd bring him a shirt and slacks to change into before they saw Melinda's blood on him. Jesus, what a tragedy. Anyhow, I caught a few z's, but Matt got nothing, up all night praying with his in-laws who wouldn't let their daughter go. They seemed to be under the impression that he chose the baby's life over their daughter's because he is Catholic, and they are not.

"Blame and denial. It's rare to have to choose between a mother and baby anymore. Weren't they grateful he saved their grandson?"

"I gather not. They asked that the monitor to the nursery be turned off and didn't want to visit the baby after a doctor and hospital psychologist convinced them to let Melinda go around six a.m. They left to make arrangements to have her sent home for burial. Said they'd take a taxi to a hotel afterward and would fly back with the body."

Annie shook her head. "Matt had nothing to say about it?"

"The psychologist came for me and asked me to help, to talk to him. He and Melinda signed on a house in the Garden District, smaller than ours but nice, on Friday. They were out celebrating the new place and drove beneath an overpass on their way home. He didn't recognize the situation until they were in the midst of it. Blames himself big time. Look, I need to get some food into him. Since his in-laws have decamped, I asked him to stay with me and Stacy. He shouldn't go to an empty house. Keep an eye on him for me just a few minutes. I don't want him to take off in a blood-stained car."

"I'd be glad to do that. He's as fragile as one of my infants right now, but no one can see it inside that big body." She moved in Matt's direction, a large man slumped at a small table.

She took a seat across from him. "I heard Melinda has passed, and I am so sorry." Annie gave in to the urge to place her small hand on top of his large, tanned one. His fingers were chilled.

He raised his eyes to hers. "I don't know what to do."

"You don't have to do anything right now. Your

son is safe in our arms and will be for the next three months. He is your focus now. By the time Daniel is mature enough to go home, you'll have a plan. We'll help you with that. Do you have any other family to contact? I could make the calls," she offered even though short on sleep herself. Her hand fell away. He didn't appear to notice.

"No one. I have no one. My folks died in a traffic accident on the way to see me play at Notre Dame. I was adopted as a baby, their only child, their pride and joy. No one could have better parents." Matt scrubbed at his face. "Hard to believe this is worse, but it is."

Annie remembered. That tragedy made the sports pages, too, exactly as this one would. She recalled thinking, "Poor guy, so all alone." Growing up with eleven siblings was often aggravating, but she'd never be without their love and support. Note to self to have more than one child or adopt if she couldn't.

"I have an aunt and uncle, some cousins, in California. Don't know them well. Doubt if they will want to come to the funeral, but I'll get around to calling them. You had a long night too."

"For me, that's normal. What about Melinda's family?"

"The Ames? Plenty of them, a couple of younger brothers in college and a sister still at home. Dozens of cousins Melinda used to say. After I lost my parents, they became my family. Melinda and I had dated only a couple months at the time, but her folks took me in and treated me like a third son. Seemed natural to get married when we graduated and keep things that way. Now I've caused her death. They won't forgive me."

"You did not," Annie said emphatically. "Some out

of control gangbangers did. Focus on the child you saved. He needs you in the days to come. As for family, you've got the support of the team and as many of mine as you can handle."

Dean shoved an overloaded tray of food in front of Matt. Scrambled eggs draped with bacon strips overflowed the plate. They rested on a foundation of sausage patties. He plunked down four biscuits and a bowl of cheese grits as well. A large coffee and an orange juice loomed over all.

Matt reached for the coffee, wrapping his hands around it as if he warmed them. "Thanks, but I'm not hungry. You must be. You eat it, especially those grits. Hoosiers like me don't understand why anyone eats grits."

"Don't mind if I do." Dean topped the bowl of grits with eggs and crumbled a couple of sausage patties into the mix. He split a biscuit and added grape jelly from a packet on the table.

Men the size of Matt and Dean could eat that way, especially when in training, but Annie had to watch every calorie, or she'd go from petite to plump in a minute. Matt made no move to pick up his fork.

"Here, Annie, join us. Have a biscuit." Dean's strategy, obviously, if they ate, maybe Matt would too. Annie accepted a biscuit she didn't want, added jelly, and took a bite. "Good," she said as if encouraging a child.

When that didn't work, Dean issued an order. "As team captain, I'm telling you to eat. You needed to keep up your strength. Voluntary training starts soon. I need you in tiptop condition."

That succeeded, a tough statement from a member

of the Sinners team. Matt shoveled in a few mouthfuls as if he didn't taste a thing but would choke it down anyhow. They were good for the meantime.

Annie stood. "I'll check in with you later." Now to get herself home before she fell asleep behind the wheel.

Chapter Three

Usually when Annie woke in the afternoon around four, her first thoughts were of standing under a hot shower and then scrounging something for dinner. But, as she stood with the water pummeling her shoulders and dripping off her small breasts, her mind kept turning to Matthew Keaton and his tiny child. All parents whose children came into the world so prematurely were stunned, worried, and guilty, though the fault seldom lay with them. To be accused of letting his wife die for the sake of the infant by the in-laws added a whole new layer of emotions. How might she help besides care for Daniel to the best of her ability?

As Annie dried the short, dark curls she could do nothing with as they had a will of their own and settled into a mop atop her head no matter what, she considered the steps she could take. Refreshed and dressed for a quiet recuperative evening at home, she dumped a bag of frozen beef stir fry into a skillet, squeezed the sauce over the top, and turned up the heat. Pushing the mixture around the pan with a wooden spoon, she wondered if Matt had gotten any sleep after Dean took him home.

Setting herself up with a fruit cup of mandarin oranges and a glass of iced tea, she sat at the small table in the kitchen and listened to the TV in the living room blare the five o'clock news. Locally, the commentator led with the Keaton tragedy. Carrying her plate to the sofa, she took a seat in front of the set to learn what happened while she slept.

Matt had issued no statement. The hospital spokesperson took charge of that matter, stating the life of the child had been saved. The mayor declared war on gang violence for the umpteenth time, and the Sinners PR person expressed the team's heartfelt condolences to the family. Some reporter tracked down Mr. and Mrs. Ames at their hotel and recorded a bitter statement from Melinda's mother that if her daughter had stayed in Indiana she'd still be alive. What about their grandson? Only time would tell if he lived or went to join his mother as perhaps God intended. The couple turned and walked away, leaving the interviewer with his mouth momentarily agape. He clamped his jaw back into place and covered his lapse by wishing little Daniel Keaton a full recovery. Daniel had no need to recover as he wasn't ill, but only needed to grow and thrive until he could safely go home. Where would that be?

Annie saved half the meal for Jude when she got off her daytime shift, though knowing her sister she'd probably pick up something more tempting on the way home. Scraping the stir fry into a container and shoving it into the fridge, she made her decision. Picking up her phone, she called her brother, Dean.

Stacy answered. "Hi, Annie."

"How is Matt doing? Did he get any sleep?"

"Yes, the psychologist slipped Dean samples of a sleep aid in case Matt needed them. Dean insisted he take a couple and go to bed. He got up an hour ago. I scrounged up a spare toothbrush and found an extra razor. We want to get him some fresh clothes, but you know the paparazzi will be staking out the new house, so he is wearing some of Dean's right now. Hard to believe Matt is even bigger in the chest, but those Sinners' knit shirts do stretch. They're about the same in the leg. Tomorrow, I plan to go over to the new place and pack his bags."

"Count me in. What time?"

"Nine too early for you?"

"Nope. I'm off until Friday. What is Matt doing now?" Annie twisted one of the curls framing her face around a finger, a bad habit from childhood she'd been unable to break.

"Dean has him outside grilling steaks—red meat, the cure for all things wrong with the world. Shades of Daddy Joe." Stacy laughed, though the sound was tempered with a tinge of sadness for her houseguest. "Our kids are with them, chasing around the fountain, playing with the dog. Maybe Matt will be able to picture a future with his son from watching DJ and Wynn."

"Look, it's important he see the baby again soon for bonding. I'll take him over to the NICU tonight once you've fed him."

"On your first night off? That's generous."

"I love being there. I'll explain the procedures for visiting, and what he can do right now to help his son thrive. Then after a short visit, I'll bring him back to you for more care and feeding. There I go, talking about a two-hundred-pound man as if he were one of my patients."

Stacy laughed a bit more freely this time. "You can't help yourself. Why not come for dinner? I can seldom finish more than half of those gigantic steaks.

We'll have it on the table shortly."

"I already ate. I'll give you an hour before I show up."

"Plan on having dessert with us. It's only ice cream."

"Sure, you tall girls can eat as much ice cream as you want."

"Show up in half an hour and suit yourself when it comes to dessert."

"Be there soon."

Annie hung up. She wrote a note telling Jude where she'd be and ventured out to buy a half-dozen pricey giant chocolate chip cookies at the coffee shop right across busy Canal Street from her apartment. She never knew a time when vehicles weren't crowding the thoroughfare. They'd be her contribution to the meal. The heat of the air inside her subcompact car would warm them up to fresh-baked status by the time she arrived in the Garden District, not far enough away to allow the A/C to kick in full force. Every chance she got, she worked on becoming the favorite aunt to Dean's children since the naturally maternal Xochi spent most of her time with her baby daughter at her big Victorian home in Chapelle. Jude presented no competition as her twin really didn't care for children all that much.

Sliding behind the wheel, Annie slung the bag of cookies into the front seat of her blue Toyota parked in the cul-de-sac alley at the base of the apartment stairs. Parking, always at a premium in the French Quarter, was one of the perks of living over the electronics store. A short drive, walkable when it wasn't so broiling, brought her to the rear gate of Dean's house in the leafy district. She knew they'd be outside at the picnic table amply shaded by venerable crepe myrtles and the more ephemeral banana trees bearing their lovely pink blooms.

Stacy saw her at once and let her inside their sanctuary. Annie found herself engulfed in children hugging her knees and one white, poufy dog that danced on his hind legs to sniff at the cookie bag. "Sorry, chocolate chip, none for you Mati."

Stacy, who had trained the pet, issued a stern, "Off." The Bichon Frise dropped to all fours and the kids unwrapped from Annie's legs as if they, too, had been well-tutored. That allowed her to join the two men who sat at an uncleared table still holding the hollowed skins of baked potatoes, the remains of a wilting salad, a couple of empty beer bottles, and the scraps of steak the dog eyed hopefully.

"How are you doing today, Matt?" Annie asked.

"At little better than yesterday. It's all so hard to believe."

She could tell Stacy didn't approve of her asking such a delicate question under the circumstances. "Annie, how about helping me clear the table and serve the ice cream?"

The last words brought a cheer from the children who clambered onto the bench on either side of their father and grabbed their spoons. The dog followed the women and the leftover steak inside the kitchen. Stacy chopped some of the meat and added it to a bowl of kibble, put it down for Mati to have his dinner. Two cartons of ice cream, plain vanilla and chocolate, the choice of children everywhere, softened on the counter. Taking plastic bowls for the kids and larger glass dishes for the adults from the cupboard, Stacy doled out small scoops topped with chocolate sauce, sprinkles, and a cherry on top for DJ and Wynn, slightly larger amounts for herself and Annie, and what amounted to a banana split without bananas for the men.

"I brought cookies." Annie broke three of the large chocolate chips in half and tucked a piece into the side of each bowl. "I'll leave the rest in here for later."

Stacy shook her head. "There's going to be a sugar high tonight. Put the bag on top of the fridge. Mati gets into everything and jumps pretty high for a dog his size."

Annie followed orders. Stacy and Jude were the bossy ones among the Billodeaux women. They loaded a tray and served the table. The toddler, DJ, devoured most of the cookie before spooning up the melting ice cream. He wore a great deal of it on his Sinners T-shirt, a smaller version of the one with the little red devil worn so well by Matt. Wynn, always the tiny hostess, did not dive in immediately. "Don't you like ice cream, Mr. Matt? Do you want something else?" she asked.

"No, ice cream is really good on a hot day like this." Matt took a mouthful and chased it with a bite of cookie. Wynn's mom and Annie, flanking the guest, rewarded her manners with approving nods and smiles. DJ grubbed for a soggy bit of cookie in the bottom of his bowl. He offered it to Matt in a sticky hand. "More cookie?"

Matt accepted the gift and popped it in his mouth. "Yum."

Annie's fingers strayed to his muscular forearm and gave it a squeeze. "You're going to make a great dad." She felt him go tense and slipped her hand away but wasn't about to abandon her mission. "In fact, why don't we go to visit Daniel after we've finished here?"

"I can do that? Visit any time?"

"Yes, the parents are allowed day or night. We have places you can rest if the child is having surgery or you want to stay for any reason. Do you have your baby ID band?"

"This?" He held up the plastic bracelet on his other wrist. "I guess I forgot to take it off."

"Don't. You'll need it for visits." Annie finished her dessert and blotted her lips with a paper napkin. "I'm ready to go whenever you are." She noticed he dawdled over his bowl, but finally gave DJ the remainder of his cookie and poured the soupy ice cream into the boy's dish. He favored Wynn with the chocolate-covered cherry that had sunk to the bottom of his sundae.

"Are you going to see your tee-tiny baby now? Daddy said you have one so small he can't come home. We aren't allowed to visit either because we have germs. Mom said we mustn't bother you, but I really, really want to see him." Wynn put on her most adorable face: large blue eyes peeping out from a fringe of straight, blonde bangs, and pink pouty lips. It got her nowhere.

Annie rode to the rescue. "Mr. Matt can take a picture with his phone and show it to you later."

"I can?"

"Yes, definitely. Send it to anyone you want."

"There's really no one."

Not about to end on a sad note, Annie quipped, "The paparazzi would pay a fortune for a snap of your son. Let's go now before they figure out where you are.

Quick, escape through the back gate." She tried to make a game of it, grabbed his hand and hurried him across the courtyard. As Stacy buzzed them out, she looked left and right searching for photographers lurking behind the massive trunks of live oaks. "All clear. Run! The blue Toyota."

Annie popped the door locks as they hurried. Nimbly, she slid behind the wheel. "Get in, get in!" She watched Matt contort his body and manage to stuff himself inside the subcompact. His big chin practically rested on his knees. "Oh, sorry, I rarely have riders. Put the seat back as far as you can and stretch out. Seatbelts fastened and away we go. You probably drive one of those big SUVs like most of the players."

He nodded. "It's still on the hospital lot. I should pick it up tonight."

Annie regretted her comment. The slightly bemused expression left his face like melting ice cream replaced by the emptiness of grief. Of course, his wife's blood stained the interior. She'd have to do something about that, but for now she chitchatted about the Garden District and its history.

"This area used to be plantations, but when the Americans moved in, they didn't want to live among the French and bought lots here, built their mansions, and created large gardens to surround them. Hence, the name of the district. Wide Canal Street kept the two factions apart. Over the years, the lots were subdivided and smaller homes built. They are all beautiful."

"That's our house," Matt said, pointing a finger. "It's not nearly as large as Dean's place. We thought we'd start with three bedrooms, two baths and a half, see how things went here before committing to something bigger or going across the lake. Mellie picked it out."

Annie very nearly said, "Obviously," but caught herself in time. Instead she settled on, "I didn't figure you for a little pink palace with a turret on the side kind of guy."

"Nope. My wife wanted the nursery to be in one of the turret rooms. The master bedroom is right beside it with the two windows overlooking that white wrought iron balcony. The third bedroom is on the side of the house. Mellie didn't want to know the sex of the child but had her heart set on a girl. The perfect place for a princess, she said. I told her we had a boy before we let her go. I don't know if she heard."

Most likely not in a brain-dead state, but who knew? People in comas and neonates could hear. If it gave him comfort, let him believe it. After that statement, Annie let the conversation lapse and concentrated on getting them to the hospital and up to the NICU. She'd shown up at the picnic in worn jeans, distressed by use, not the manufacturer, and a very ordinary dark green tee. Outside the door to the unit, she asked Matt to wait while she went to the locker room to change into scrubs and her white nurses' shoes, ugly but supportive. While inside, she made a call to Dean. "Is there any way you can pick up Matt's SUV and have it cleaned?"

"Considering that he forgot his keys, yes. I'll see about getting a service to take it—if the police are done with it, that is. Must be one in this city with all the on-going violence."

"Hadn't thought of that. Whatever you can do. I'll bring him back to your place in my car when we're done."

"That's going to be comfortable for him."

"Hey, I like to be able to reach the pedals and see over the steering wheel when I drive."

"Then, you have the perfect vehicle, Short Stuff."

She hadn't heard that nickname in years. "I'm gonna tell Mom what you called me, you big lout." Stacy gave that sobriquet to Dean as a child. His sisters picked it up with glee. Her big brother merely chuckled and disconnected.

Annie left her cell phone behind in her locker and went to find Matt standing exactly where she'd left him like a mannequin for casual sportswear. He hadn't made a single move toward entering the NICU alone. "Ready to go?"

"No."

Chapter Four

"Ready or not, here we come." Annie grasped his elbow and steered Matt forward. "First, we need to show your ID at the reception desk to get inside."

Access given, they entered her world, the dim, overheated realm of the NICU with its flashing lights and beeping monitors as if they'd been transported aboard an alien spaceship. She led him to a sink.

"Now, we scrub up, three minutes from hands to elbows."

"Sounds like we're going into surgery."

"Pretty much like that." Annie demonstrated, and Matt followed suit.

"No gown or cap?"

"No, only clean clothes and no cologne or other strong odors." Annie inhaled his scent. "Good, just plain soap and water." And testosterone.

"Glad I passed the sniff test." Good, he'd relaxed a little.

"Another thing, if you touch any part of your body or your cell phone, please use the hand gel by each bedside. Cell phones are the worst for germs. Please don't text or call anyone while visiting. In fact, turn off your phone and leave it in a pocket."

"I promised Wynn a picture."

"I can take it for you. In fact, it's great to keep a record of his growth. Each week, you can see how much he's progressed. Okay, here we go. Daniel is right over there waiting for you."

She noticed his skeptical look even before he said, "His eyes aren't open yet. He's like a newborn puppy."

"Yet, a newborn puppy responds to touch, can hear, and find its mother's teat."

"No teats. How is he going to eat? Mellie wanted to nurse. That's off the table."

"Right now, Daniel is getting intravenous nourishment. As soon as his stomach can handle milk, we'll introduce it through a soft tube put through his nose. We have a breast milk bank to draw on since the antigens the baby gets are important. Some mothers are too ill to nurse. Others don't produce enough milk. We see the infant gets what it needs. Shall we say hello to your son? Sit right there near the port in the incubator so he can hear you. Go on, say something."

"Uh, hi, Daniel." The baby showed no response. "Did I do it wrong?"

"No. After a while, he'll know your voice. If he is restless, it might calm him. You'll be able to tell by his heartbeat and other signs since he can't turn his head on his own yet. Would you like to touch him?"

"I guess."

"Put your hand inside but be gentle. His skin is very delicate."

"And really red. It that normal?" Matt, still hesitating, focused on her face instead of his son.

"Absolutely, at this stage. Stroke his arm."

Matt used only one big finger. He ran it from elbow to wrist. The tiny hand starfished open, then clenched into a fist again. He touched the baby's fingers. They didn't grasp. "Shouldn't he be able to

27

hold on?"

"Not yet. He will in time."

Matt stroked the arm again. "He's hairy, red and hairy. I didn't expect that."

Annie grinned. "That's lanugo hair. It will shed eventually. Ready to talk some more?"

"Not really. What did your dad say to his preemies?"

"I was too young to visit when the triplets were born, but Mom said he always started with a prayer, then gave them pep talks. Really, at this point anything in a low, gentle voice is fine. Your tone matters more than your words."

Following her instructions, Matt bowed his head and murmured a brief prayer for the safety of his son, crossed himself, and looked at Annie again for guidance.

Annie helped him out. "Why did you decide on Daniel for his name."

"Oh, Mellie picked it out."

"Tell him, not me."

Matt leaned close to the port. "Your mother chose your name because the prophet Daniel was so brave in the lion's den. Where you are now, it's kind of like being in a lion's den, so you have to be brave, too. Ames is, was, her maiden name. I kind of thought it would be fine to name you Peyton or maybe Montana after some great quarterbacks. Montana Keaton sounds good, but then, your mom said people would call you Monty. Not so hot, right?"

"You're doing well," Annie encouraged.

"Nice hat you got there, Danny. Did the nurses give it to you?"

Annie answered. "Yes, to keep him warm. A lot of heat escapes through the head. Just keep talking. I'll get that picture for you." She wiggled his phone from his snug hip pocket and turned it on.

"Hey, dude. I'm being groped by a nice lady. You should be so lucky, Danny."

"Oh, he'll get tired of my manhandling. I'm the one who pokes and prods and puts tubes down his nose."

"Not sexy at all."

"Nope. Neither is changing a diaper, but it needs to be done." Annie lined up the shot, getting Matt leaning close to the port and his son's pitiful body laid out amid tubes and wires. If all went well, this picture would be a reminder one day of how far the child had come. She turned the phone off again and placed it back in his pocket, a tight fit that warmed her hand against his buttock, so maybe a little sexy. She should be ashamed of herself.

She washed her hands again. "I'm going to see if I can help out anywhere. Just keep talking." As she left, Matt began to tell Daniel what he did for a living. "I play with a ball all day long. Someday, I'll teach you to throw and catch that ball, okay?"

"Sweet," Annie's counterpart in the NICU, Peggy Anderson, whispered. She toiled at the third bassinette, one open to the air and holding a much larger baby, doing a change as Annie passed.

"Yes, he has it in him to be a great father like mine, but he'll need tons of help when football season starts. The players are on the road a lot."

Middle-aged Peggy, who also followed the Sinners avidly, answered, "With that big, fat contract he got he can buy the best care available."

"We were lucky to have our Nurse Shammy and Corazon, but still not the same as a mother. We always had ours nearby."

"Want to help me do a tube feeding?"

"It's what I live for."

They moved to another incubator holding an infant only a trifle larger than Daniel and worked feeding him through a tube left in place in the baby's nose. In the background, Matt murmured on about padding and cleats and what number he'd wear on the field. "I'll ask for number thirty since that's your birthday, May thirtieth."

As Annie started the infusion pump, he glanced her way and ceased talking to his son. "Is that how you're going to feed Daniel? It looks awful."

"Not as cuddly as a mother nursing her child, but really, it doesn't hurt. Might be a little uncomfortable. They sometimes fuss when they get bigger. Eventually, they get a bottle, but you could hold Daniel when we do a tube feeding. He needs to remain upright or inclined afterward to prevent vomiting and what a better way to do that than in his daddy's arms."

Matt shook his head. "I couldn't do it. I'd crush him." He examined his big hands and thick arms as if they were weapons of mass destruction, which in a way they were on the football field.

"You won't. Daniel is tougher than he looks—and you are gentler than you know."

"Don't let Green Bay or the Falcons hear that." There, a small quirk of the lips. Annie returned it with what the staff called her Madonna smile.

"Your secret soft side is safe with me," she assured

him as she stopped the pump and made a notation on the chart of the time and amount of the feeding. When she raised her eyes, Matt still stared at her. A trickle of sweat ran down the side of his strong, rugged face and disappeared into his collar. Annie followed its progress as he made no attempt to wipe it away.

"Hot in here. Can I get some water? Just grab my wallet again and take what you need."

"Not necessary. We have some in the fridge. I'll get a bottle for you."

She returned with chilled water. Matt accepted it gratefully, rolling the cool plastic in his hands, then cracking it open. With his head thrown back, he chugged the entire contents, his Adam's apple bobbing in his thick neck with each swallow. Annie watched.

So did Peggy. "I have to say you drink like a football player, Mr. Keaton." The blue eyes and the smile in her lightly lined face radiated friendliness. Her salt-and-pepper hair gave her a grandmotherly air, but Annie knew Peg had a keen sense of humor that she rarely got to use in the tense atmosphere surrounding them.

"It's all about hydration during training. Where should I put the empty?"

Annie disposed of it. "By the way, you can have covered drinks in here whenever you want, but no food, okay?" Matt nodded. Both gelled their hands again. Matt started another monologue with Danny, this time about the importance of plenty of fluids, and Annie retreated to the second incubator where Peggy changed a diaper so small it might have been intended for a doll.

"I tell you, he just raised the temperature in here another ten degrees. That man can visit my NICU anytime, day or night," Peggy said, sotto voce.

"Peggy, he's a bereaved widower!"

"And I'm a grandmother, but not dead yet. I'll bet you women will bring him casseroles and offer to console him the day he gets back from his wife's funeral. But, I think he might have found his guardian angel in you already. I sense some bonding going on and not just with the baby." If there had been more light in the NICU, her blue eyes might have twinkled.

"You are terrible! I'd better get Matt back to Dean's place before you put the moves on him."

"If you don't want him, tell the guy I'm divorced and eligible on the way home."

"Don't make me whack you with this chart." Annie finished recording the vital signs of baby number three, Arielle Wagner, put the chart back in its place, and returned to Matt's side.

"Ready to leave?" She noted the relief on his face.

"Yeah, I'll save my life story for another night."

"You can come here days, too. Just a few more rules—stay by your child, don't wander around, and don't disturb the other parents. We often have nursing mothers in here. Don't stare. Some of them have a hard enough time coping. Refrain from asking about the health of the other babies. We won't discuss that."

"Got it, no wandering, disturbing, or boob watching."

"Breast would be a better term, but yes, don't watch."

"Right, Nurse Annie." He tagged along like she led him on a leash.

"I'm going to change back into my street clothes. Why don't you wait in the lounge?" She didn't want to find him lingering and lost in the corridor again, and besides, she needed to call Dean about the car.

In the locker room, she contacted her brother. "Did you take care of the SUV?"

"Police towed it away. They wanted to look for slugs and angle of entry. That sort of thing. I guess they need to confirm that Keaton didn't shoot his pregnant wife and make up the story."

"How could they even imagine that?" Annie filled with anger on Matt's behalf.

"Cops are naturally suspicious. They already asked me how he got along with her. I had to say she wasn't happy about the move here and gave him some flack about it."

"You didn't!"

"I can't lie to the law, but I did add that they'd bought a house together and both seemed excited about the baby. You on your way here?"

"Shortly, just don't tell Matt about the police probe. He's got enough problems. See you soon."

Annie discovered Matt studying a rack full of informational pamphlets for the parents of preemies. "Take any you want, then we'll leave."

He searched his pockets for his keys. "I should get my SUV."

"It's no longer here. The police took it to look for evidence against the bad guys, slugs they can match and such." They probably already had the bullet taken from Melinda's brain, the small caliber one that bounced around inside her skull and caused so much damage, but Annie did not volunteer that information.

"I think maybe I'll buy a new car and let that one go."

"A good idea. I'll bet Wynn is waiting up to see the picture of Daniel. Let's show her."

That got him moving in the right direction, though he fell asleep crunched up in the shotgun seat of the Toyota, a feat that seemed impossible. At Dean's house, Annie hated to wake him. She pulled up by the back gate where Stacy waited to let him inside and gently shook his shoulder.

"Mellie?" he said.

That broke her heart. "No, only Annie. We're here. I'll see you tomorrow. Get some more rest."

"You, too. Thanks for taking me over there. I don't think I could have done it alone."

"No need to. You can have one guest with you if you want, and there's always me."

Chapter Five

Annie rose in time to have a quick breakfast with Jude before her sister left for her shift. Only cereal with sliced banana and two cups of coffee, but good enough. She put on jeans, a tee, and sneakers again, good for the excursion to Matt's pink palace to get his clothes. After starting a load of scrubs in the stacked washer/dryer combo in the rear of the kitchen, she headed for Dean's house again and caught his family still at breakfast in the casual, sunny space where they took most of their meals. Easier to clean than the oriental rugs in the formal dining room, Stacy always said.

"I guess I'm really early. Wow, pancakes and sausage." Not typical for Stacy who wasn't the best of cooks and usually pushed fruit, cereal, and yogurt for breakfast. Obviously, she was doing her best to "feed up" her guest.

"Courtesy of Aunt Jemima and Jimmy Dean," her sister-in-law said.

Matt sat between Wynn and DJ with Dean at the head of the table playing *paterfamilias*, a role he took seriously, though Stacy was the true disciplinarian. Dean appeared really happy with the meal considering his half-empty plate. Matt's portion consisted of stacked pancakes dripping syrup and a ring of sausage links swimming in the same. He'd barely touched them as he sat hunched over wearing some of Dean's sweats, not the least bit baggy on his large frame.

"I pour syrup for Mr. Matt," DJ piped up proudly.

"I see you did a very good job of that," Annie told the boy.

"Lots and lots!" More being better, she assumed.

Wynn seemed quieter than usual. Her modest serving of one large pancake with two sausages cut into little pieces by her dad appeared to be pushed around in her puddle of syrup. "Not feeling well, honey?" Annie asked as she took a place at the light oak table.

"No, I'm worried about baby Daniel. He's so small and has things stuck in him. He can't even eat yet, Mr. Matt said."

"Don't worry, we're feeding him. When he's big and strong enough he'll come home, and you can hold him. Not for a long time, though."

"Okay." Wynn picked up her fork with a Disney princess on the handle and began to eat. She paused after a bite. "Mr. Matt, you need to drink your milk and juice to stay strong for football." Wynn showed every sign of being as bossy as her mother.

A slight smile flickered on his tanned face, unshaved this morning. "I guess you're right, Miss Wynn." He gulped the juice down in three swallows and chased it with the milk.

"Sausage?" DJ asked, having eaten his share and clearly wanting more.

Matt forked one of his onto the boy's plastic plate adorned with choo-choo trains and reached to cut it up, but Deej already had the sausage in his mouth via his fingers. "Okay, I guess I need to eat the rest before they're all gone."

The kids were good for him, natural and honest to

the point of being embarrassing, but cute and not easily denied. Annie imagined he might have resented or brushed off an adult cajoling him to eat unless Dean ordered him like yesterday—and that couldn't go on forever.

Still, her brother said, "Load up on those carbs, too. We're going to the training center today for a workout. The women will drive over to your place to get your clothes and anything else you want."

Matt nodded and handed over his door keys to Stacy. "Thanks. Most of my stuff is still in the suitcase. I left my shaving kit in the bathroom." He studied his placemat for a few seconds. "I'll need a dark suit. They're hung in the closet."

For the funeral, of course. It needed to be done, and she and Stacy would take care of the matter.

"The place is pretty messy. We had the furniture in storage and our other things delivered on Saturday, got some of it put away, but then, I convinced Mellie to take a break on Sunday and go out. I didn't want her overdoing because of the baby." His forked clanged against the edge of his plate as he set it down. "I'm ready to go to the training center whenever you are, Dean."

"Let me have a second cup of coffee. My Cajun blood thins without enough of it. Stace, get one for Matt, too. It will help him wash down the rest of those pancakes."

Not a subtle hint, but it worked. Matt shoveled in the rest of his meal while Dean leisurely sipped his coffee. Once done, the men took off for the training center. Stacy and Annie cleaned up the breakfast dishes and scrubbed the kids. "Their nanny will be here soon, then we can go and see what we are able to do at Matt's house. It isn't far from here."

"I know. He showed it to me last night. So terribly sad."

The nanny, a college student who scheduled her classes at Tulane around Stacy's activities for a generous amount of pay being saved for her future medical school expenses, arrived bright and bouncy as a coed should be. The children latched onto her immediately, both shouting out what they wanted to do today, play with rubber dinosaurs or finger paint. With the children in good hands, she and Stacy left.

They approached the pink palace with caution. "Over there," Stacy said. "A car with a paparazzo asleep behind the wheel, another sitting on the curb under the oak tree, and can you believe it, one of them has the nerve to take a seat on the stoop."

"I see them. Are you ready?" Annie said.

Stacy parked directly in front of the house. They got down, strode to the totally inadequate low, white wrought iron fence that matched the small balcony, and sailed in through the gate. The paparazzi came alive like zombies who had only been resting between attacks. The fellow under the oak tree shouted, "Where is Matt Keaton? How's he doing?"

The guy in the car stumbled out with his camera at the ready. "What about the baby? Is it dead?"

The women reached the front door with its beveled glass panels. As Stacy inserted the key, the lurker on the small porch got right in her face. "What do you have to say, Stace?"

She answered immediately. "Get off Mr. Keaton's property before I call the police."

Well-known as Dean's wife, Stacy had at least six inches on him. Though not muscular, she did have an air of command. He backed up. "Off!" she directed as if speaking to her dog. The man stumbled down the four brick steps. "Out!"

The other two crowded the fence but did not venture inside the gate. Their compatriot in an ugly trade joined them. They snapped a bunch of meaningless pictures because they never knew what would sell. "The baby! Matt Keaton!"

Annie didn't have her sister-in-law's height or presence. She threw them a crumb hoping to get rid of them like pesky pigeons. "The baby is stable. Mr. Keaton has no statement to make at this time and would appreciate his privacy during this period of grief and mourning."

Stacy opened the door. They slipped inside and slammed it shut with a rattle of glass.

"We should have brought the men. Or at the very least, Alix," Annie said, referring to their mutual sister-in-law who punted for the Sinners and was often referred to as an Amazon by the press. "She would have kicked that guy's butt across the fence. Too bad she and Tom are visiting Howdy, his mom, and his half-sibs at the Oklahoma ranch."

"I really didn't want Matt to have to face this. He isn't as accustomed as the Billodeaux family to dealing with paparazzi. Press conferences, sure, but not this kind of mess. I gathered he and Melinda led a fairly quiet life. Just look at this place."

Annie surveyed the hallway lined with unpacked boxes. Four rooms filled the downstairs: a parlor across from a sitting room, a formal dining room across from a study or small library where the gentleman of the 1890's might have retired to smoke their cigars and indulge in brandy while the wives enjoyed gossip and tea elsewhere. Each offered a focal point fireplace hardly needed in this climate anymore. The functioning air-conditioning bathed the women in cool air. A kitchen ran across the back of the house, and a fanciful staircase of intricate white spindles spiraled upward toward the second floor. Stacy flipped the switch of a small chandelier hung with strings of crystal drops to illuminate the hall.

Annie peeked into each room. "The furniture is in place but doesn't really fit this house. It cries out for Victorian antiques or maybe modern simplicity, but not Midwestern farmhouse décor. Looks comfy, but not right. Still, I shouldn't be questioning a dead woman's taste."

"Let's go upstairs and bring down what Matt needs. Then, we can take a look at the kitchen and maybe unpack the dishes."

Only the master bedroom possessed all its furniture, which must have been a bear to haul up that staircase, especially the king-sized bed with the big maple newel posts and a mammoth dresser meant to be shared by a couple. Two open suitcases side by side spewed clothing haphazardly. No doubt which one belonged to Melinda, full of maternity wear, while Matt's case held boxer briefs, neatly rolled socks, and a variety of casual clothes. Inside the spacious walk-through closet, they found a row of garment bags hanging on one side along with dress shirts, laundered and pressed, above racks of masculine shoes. The other side displayed row upon row of stylish heels, dresses, and formal gowns as well as coats too warm for the climate.

"Do you think we should put Melinda's clothes into bags or boxes so Matt won't have to face that task?" Annie asked.

"We'd better ask him. It's bound to be a touchy subject. We can come back to do that later."

They unzipped several of the garment bags and selected a custom-made black suit with a silver and ebony striped tie draped around the hanger. A pale gray shirt fresh from the cleaners hung nearby and seemed a good choice. Stacy took care of repacking Matt's suitcase while Annie walked into the bathroom from the closet.

Definitely, not nineteenth century in here, it had the required glassed-in large shower with multiple jets, a graceful tub set on a pedestal in its own nook, double sinks encased in pink-veined marble, large mirrors, and a commode in a private nook. A stained-glass panel of egrets wading among lily pads allowed light into the room yet provided privacy from the next-door neighbors as the bath ran along the side of the house. Annie packed Matt's razor, shaving cream, aftershave, comb, and toothbrush into his kit, a curiously intimate act for a total stranger to perform. She let Melinda's makeup be, only noticing she'd used lily of the valley soap with a delicate scent and owned a large selection of pastel lipsticks.

They moved their finds to the upper hallway and took a moment to explore the remaining rooms: the empty turret chamber and another bedroom containing an unassembled bed, dresser, and night tables in the same Midwestern country style as the other furnishings, but on a smaller scale. Another bathroom sat next to it, not as large and lavish, but very nice. Beside the bath, a dark, narrow staircase led to the kitchen. They decided to lug the suitcase down that way.

"Must have been nice to have servants to do this for you," Annie said, though she carried only the shaving kit and garment bag.

"We had servants at the ranch, but we still had to tote our own bags when we went anywhere."

Annie shrugged. "With twelve children in the family, that is a lot of toting. I remember when you arrived at the ranch and expected Brinsley to carry that huge mound of luggage upstairs for you."

"Well, he was *my* butler, but he became everyone's in a very short time."

"Our Mama Nell at work. We all pulled our weight at the ranch."

Stacy punctuated that remark by dropping the suitcase on the gray flagstone tiles. "Heavy. I'll bet Matt just tucks it under his arm and doesn't use the wheels at all."

"I wouldn't be surprised. He's certainly a big guy. I think he could tuck *me* under his arm and walk a mile with no trouble. I'd be intimidated if I didn't have such large brothers, and if he weren't so totally crushed." Annie surveyed the kitchen with its expanse of pink and brown veined granite counters already cluttered with numerous appliances from a coffeemaker to a convection oven. "Someone sure liked pink." She ran a hand over the tiled backsplash, pink, white, and brown, cool to the touch.

Stacy had the scoop. "The nicest elderly gay couple lived here, Kingston and Ollie. Kingston passed away, and Ollie felt he couldn't bear to live here alone. He sold off the antiques that crammed the place and put the house on the market to fund his move into assisted living. They gave the best small parties, and yes, were very partial to pink. The beverages were always cosmopolitans and pink lemonade, their signature drinks, they said. I'm sorry they're gone, but this was the only house that caught Melinda's fancy after a lot of looking. I think Matt might have preferred Lakeshore or Mandeville, but let his wife have her way."

"She seemed to be good at getting it, but pregnancy does make some women demanding."

"Are you referring to me?" Stacy raised an eyebrow.

"No, you were royally ill with both of yours, and Dean did coddle you because of that. Melinda appeared to be enjoying a normal, healthy pregnancy until the accident. She hadn't gotten to the uncomfortable last trimester yet."

"Upset about the move and being away from her family, I think she took it out on Matt. Melinda wanted a pink house and a daughter exactly like Wynn. I told her to be careful what she wished for as Wynn already has a mind of her own. Mellie got one out of two."

Annie opened a few cupboards. "Looks like they have the dishes and glasses stowed already. She examined a plate banded in gold and Wedgewood blue with a pink cabbage rose in the center. "Wedding china. The everyday stuff is over there. Stainless steel appliances without a fingerprint on them. That will change with a child in the house."

"Nice breakfast area having a view of their little garden. Serene, pretty."

The same flagstone used on the kitchen floor delineated a patio big enough for a table and a few chairs. A mockingbird and a cardinal quarreled over access to a trickle of water cascading into a small pool from a mound of lava rocks on one side. Pink bromeliads with broad green and white strappy leaves were tucked in among the stones. A Japanese magnolia that would of course bloom pink in the spring provided a little shade. Annie spotted some artfully crooked ornamental cherry trees, too, but most of the area held pots of various plants and flowers easy to maintain and move around. Right now, pink and white wax begonias reigned.

"Poor Ollie had to leave his flowers behind. He meditated out there, often in the raw, I heard, but was spared the sight." Stacy's phone sounded. She took it from her shirt pocket. "How's it going at the gym? We'll do that if Matt doesn't want to take care of it. Right after we finish here. Love you, my big lout."

"Dean?"

"Who else would I call that? Bultman's Funeral Home called Matt to ask that he bring clothes for the departed. It shook him. He wants you to pick something out and take it over there. She liked pink."

"No kidding."

Annie and Stacy retraced their steps upstairs and pondered the rack of dresses. They selected a pale pink silk suit that buttoned down one side and bore a faux diamond brooch, star-shaped, on the shoulder. After debating whether shoes were necessary, they added a pair of matching pumps, then searched the suitcase for underwear. Annie held up a pair of maternity panties with a pouch in front and a nursing bra. Stacy shook her head. She opened a drawer in the dresser. "Eureka! A Victoria's Secret stash."

Practical Annie suggested the lacy bra and bikini pants might not fit a formerly pregnant woman. Stacy shook her head again. "If I die young, bury me in something like this, not mom wear. They can always leave it unhooked in the back or slit it up the side. Undertakers have their ways. Anything else? Jewelry, a rosary?"

"Matt is Catholic. Melinda wasn't. I think the pin is enough. Let's go now." Somehow, rummaging through Melinda Keaton's belongings seemed wrong to Annie.

Stacy made a call first to the New Orleans Police Department and asked for a squad car to come to this address and see she and Stacy weren't harassed by the paparazzi. Adding, "This is Mrs. Dean Billodeaux," helped immensely. "Give them ten minutes and they'll be happy to help the wife of the top Sinner."

"It pays to be a Sinner or a Billodeaux in this town. Let's repack her other things and zip it up. Right now, that suitcase reminds me of spilled guts. Matt doesn't need to see it left as it was before they went out."

"Good thinking. We can spend the rest of the time until our escort comes meditating in the garden, but don't take anything off."

"Sick humor, Stace? I get enough of that at the hospital."

"I'll bet you do."

They left Matt's suitcase, shaving kit, and the garment bags with the clothes in the hall and went to sit on the steps leading outside from the kitchen. A brick wall with small ferns growing in the cracks ran across the rear of the garden separating it from a neighbor's yard. A couple of tall palms on the other side rattled their stiff leaves in the breeze. The trickling of the water soothed.

Annie closed her eyes and simply listened for a moment. "I miss having a place like this to destress. On the ranch, there was always some nook or cranny to get away from everyone and everything: the hayloft, up in the boughs of a live oak, behind the palm trees near the pool."

"The rest of us always thought you and Jude were getting into trouble somewhere when you disappeared."

"Not always putting red dye in the swimming pool because we thought it would turn pink and be pretty and not always with Jude. Sometimes, I simply wanted to be on my own for a while. We had to scrub the sides of the pool ourselves by hand after they drained it. It's the Billodeaux way."

"Took me a while to learn that. You hated me when I arrived."

"Yes, we did, Princess, with your mountain of pink luggage, but not your little dog too. She was so cute. Then, you threw a tantrum because Jude and I had the pink bedroom and you had to settle for white and gold. We got over it when you reformed and learned to be a team player as Dad would say."

Stacy glanced back at the house. "I am so over pink."

"Same for me and Jude, but now we live in your old purple and silver apartment."

"Hey, purple and silver is a classy combination, and it matched our Anchi Services uniforms and sign."

They heard the cop car arrive followed by gruff orders to clear the gate and move out of the way. By the time the police arrived at the front door, Stacy and Annie were inside and waiting. A very young officer offered to carry the suitcase for them. He moved out first to clear the way with the women sandwiched between him and the senior officer. Stacy popped the trunk to her car and the door locks. They hustled to stow the clothes and get inside the vehicle. The elder officer asked if they wanted an escort anywhere.

"To the Bultman Funeral Home if it won't be too much trouble. I know you have better things to do." Stacy flashed her movie star smile at them.

"No trouble at all, Mrs. Billodeaux," the younger policeman said.

"Please call me Stacy."

Annie swore the man blushed at being so intimate with the gorgeous woman who slept with the Sinners' quarterback.

"Just follow us, Stacy." He turned on the siren and made the paparazzi trying to encroach leap out of the way.

They cruised effortlessly through traffic and arrived very shortly. The officers offered to help unload but were told only one garment bag was going inside. "Do you need an escort elsewhere?"

"No, I think we lost the photographers. They couldn't get through the red lights. Thank you so much for your service." Stacy shook both hands.

Annie stayed in her shadow. "Just stand next to a tall, beautiful blonde and a short brunette won't be noticed."

"You and Jude were noticed plenty when you were cutting up at college while I studied."

"While you were having an affair with a language

47

professor and lusting after Dean you mean. Not that you didn't get top grades."

"The press lost track of you and Jude once you settled down and went into nursing. You cut off all those dark curls they described as riotous, and now you work nights instead of hitting the clubs. You are under their radar."

Annie ran her fingers through the curls she had left. "More practical in my line of work. I think I prefer quiet to being kidnapped like Xochi."

They entered the lily-scented atmosphere of the funeral home, delivered the clothing for Mrs. Keaton, and accepted condolences to be passed on to Matt. "We will take the best of care of his wife and see to the transfer of her remains to Indianapolis immediately as her family requested," a slim-handed and polite undertaker told them.

"I know she is in good hands. Thank you." Stacy again did the smile and handshake. "So, back to my place—or we could sneak a child-free lunch since my nanny has no classes until two, but I have to be back by one-thirty to let her go."

"I eat all my lunches alone except when Jude is around but sounds good."

"Commander's Palace?"

"I don't think I'm dressed for a place that nice." Annie regarded her worn jeans and plain T-shirt. Stacy wore the same, but somehow it looked great with her long legs, big bust, and high, golden ponytail. Annie checked her phone for information. "Says here no T-shirts, and jeans are discouraged.

"I'd take a Lucky Dog eaten in the shade standing up if I don't have to cut someone's meat and wipe a messy chin. They know our family at the Palace. They will seat us. Hand me that dry cleaner's bag and the sack on the floor beneath the car seats."

Annie handed over the items. Stacy ripped off the plastic bag that held a Navy blue blazer and put it on over the cerise T-shirt. She took a pair of four-inch heels from the sack and shed her sneakers, transforming herself into a woman of casual elegance with the addition of the oversized sunglasses hooked to the visor. Balling the plastic for disposal, she asked Annie, "Do you have anything in your car you can switch to quickly? I don't think we have time stop by the apartment, and I know nothing of mine will fit you."

"No kidding. I have some clean scrubs, that's all."

"I have a great idea. I'll stop by your car. Get into the scrubs but do it stealthily. If the kids see us, our caper is over."

They executed the plan perfectly and were off to one of New Orleans best restaurants and a Garden District landmark filling an entire street corner with its Commander's Blue—a somewhat aqua color—and white building. Striped awnings in the same colors shaded the pillared porch. A turret with fish scale shingles rose above it. As she and Stacy went inside and out of the June heat, Annie remarked, "This place was built around the same time as Matt's house. They were big on turrets in that era."

"Seems so." Stacy approached the maître d' with her big smile in place. She raised her sunglasses just a peep to show more of her face. "Would you have a table available for Stacy and Annie Billodeaux? It's Take a Nurse to Lunch day. She saves premature babies in a neonatal ICU."

"Absolutely, right this way." Though he peered at Annie's blue scrubs, what else could the poor man do after a speech like that? He personally seated the women, pulling out their chairs and tucking them in. "Your waiter will be with you shortly."

Tourists stared and wondered who the celebrities were. Okay, fine, one woman who looked like a celebrity dining with her personal nurse. The menus delivered, they studied their choices.

"I'm going to have the Eat Fit NOLA lunch: chilled watermelon and lime soup, Louisiana crab and heirloom tomato salad, and the sorbet du jour for dessert. Oh, and a nice glass of Chablis while we wait."

"Make that two," Annie said. Used to following Jude and Stacy's lead, she ate whatever came along with little fuss or bother. Besides, they always chose well. The wine came immediately.

Stacy took more than a sip. "Ah! So refreshing, so much better than chocolate milk."

"It is good but speak for yourself about the chocolate milk. I love it."

"If your children want it every day, you'd get tired of it."

"I guess I might, but I'm not positive about that. It's good warm too. A beverage for all seasons."

Then, Stacy hit her with a not so subtle question, making her suspect Jude might have put her up to it. "How are you doing finding a baby daddy?"

Annie feigned shock. "Heaven forbid that such a thing should happen in the Billodeaux family. MawMaw Nadine is still living and would never let us get away with it. We'd have a shotgun wedding before the announcement got out of my mouth—and Daddy owns several shotguns. He could lend two to Dean and Tom to keep the groom surrounded."

"Our grandmother is rather fierce and totally traditional, but you are evading my question. Any men in your life?" Stacy continued to drink her wine, peering over the rim at Annie.

"Plenty, but they are all three months premature. Really, if no one comes along, I could adopt—or inseminate after Mawmaw is long gone, but she'll live to be a hundred and I'll be too old." Annie wanted a child so badly it always made her a little queasy to talk about it. Usually, she made her longing into a joke like now.

Stacy laughed and changed the subject. "Tell me truly, is Matt's son going to live?"

"He has a great chance. Though he doesn't seem so to Matt, little Daniel is quite sturdy. I suspect he'll resemble his daddy in the long run. It's wonderful seeing Matt interact with him, so sweet and awkward, but lots of the dads are that way. Make sure he goes back to the NICU tonight or even this afternoon. The contact is very important."

Their cold soup arrived, delicious as expected, and was followed promptly by the crab salad. Stacy checked her watch, far more elegant than the one Annie used for her nursing duties. No diamonds around the dial of that one. "We're good. We have time for the sorbet."

This was nice, Annie thought, dining out with a woman other than Jude, not that she didn't love her twin. Stacy insisted on picking up the tab. "After all, it is Take a Nurse to Lunch day, isn't it?"

"If you say so."

Back at the house, Stacy released her nanny to classes after receiving a concise report of the morning's activities: finger painting outside on the picnic table with DJ making tracks with his toy dinosaurs through the crude landscapes Wynn drew, followed by a lunch of peanut butter and jelly sandwiches on whole wheat accompanied by baby carrots, and one half each of those giant chocolate chip cookies. Now, the kids napped. Proof was supplied by the paintings on display on the side of the refrigerator and the diminishing cookies in the bag.

Relaxed, Stacy suggested, "How about I make coffee and we split one of those cookies? Sorbet is good, but really doesn't satisfy a sweet tooth. I figure we've got at least one quiet hour ahead."

"Sounds good. I'm off all day."

About the time they settled at the kitchen table with coffee and cookies, the men returned, loud and smelling of workout sweat and masculinity. Stacy put a finger to her lips. "Hush, it's nap time." Dean raised his brows suggestively at her. "Not for us! I think you're becoming more like Daddy Joe every day."

"I've done the snip like I promised and expect some rewards."

Matt, not accustomed to Billodeaux banter, seemed awkward and embarrassed, not knowing where to look or what to do. He turned toward Annie. "I see you have your scrubs on. Are we going to visit Daniel?"

"Um, we could." She didn't add this was one of her precious off days. "Oh, we brought your suit and suitcase. They're still in the trunk of Stacy's car. We got the clothes to Bultman's too. Missions accomplished." She wished she hadn't said the last

52

words. His face became sad in a second.

Dean stepped in fast as if he protected a ball carrier. "Did the paparazzi give you any trouble?"

"They were verbally obnoxious. Stacy threatened one off the porch and called the cops to give us an escort after we picked up the things Matt wanted. I said Matt had no statement to give during this time of grief and told them the baby was well. Considering, we were mighty generous. I have to say Stacy is a champ at this sort of thing—and has acquired an admirer among the police."

Stacy snorted. "I've had too much practice considering the field day they had with me and Dean before we got married."

Matt apologized. "I'm sorry I put you ladies through that. I should have handled it myself."

"We were happy to help."

Dean offered, "I'll get your stuff. Go ahead and shower, then you can visit your son with Annie."

Matt promised Annie, "I won't be long, but I will be thorough. No germs in the NICU." He rushed for the stairs as if a coach told him to hustle. Annie had time for a second cup of coffee before he returned.

She watched him crunch himself into her small car again. "I promise I'll get my own ride after I get back from Indy. I leave tomorrow. The funeral is on Saturday afternoon. Mellie's family is taking care of everything. I guess I should be grateful."

"You should have some say, but if allowing them do the arrangements keeps the peace, let them."

"They had her taken to Bultman's. Are they good?"

Annie nodded. "The best, almost a New Orleans tradition like Mardi Gras. They took care of Jayne

Mansfield. We picked out a pale pink suit for Melinda with a rhinestone brooch on the shoulder. I hope that is okay."

"Yeah, she looked great in that suit, only the pin is made of diamonds. I gave it to her this past Christmas. Not long after, she told me she was expecting. We held off for a while on kids, getting my career established and all. We were both excited about Daniel, Danielle if it turned out to be the girl she wanted. You will watch over him while I'm gone? Tell him I'll be back soon, okay?"

"I'll give him the best of care." The same care she gave all her NICU babies, but he didn't need to know that either.

Chapter Six

Matt and Annie scrubbed up side by side. He obeyed every rule of the NICU, going at once to Daniel's incubator and seating himself by the port nearest the infant's head, trying to totally ignore the thin blonde woman with the large, black-framed glasses magnifying her gray eyes who nursed her small child in a rocker. The ward lacked the stillness of his night visit. Doctors passed in and out checking charts, consulting with the nurses. Most of the babies had visitors crouched by their side, all murmuring into those tiny ears.

Annie introduced Louella, the day nurse, a black woman with a great grin and sure hands in changing those diapers and feeding the infants. "L'il Daniel's daddy, pleased to meet you. Visit anytime." She went on with her work, and Annie made herself useful. He searched his mind for what to say, then carefully inserted a finger through the port and lightly touched his son along the ribs where no tubes or wires went in or out. "Not ticklish yet, huh?"

"One day he will be," Annie said in passing. She stayed near but did not intrude.

"I think I promised you my life story. I don't know who my real mom and dad were. The Keatons adopted me as a baby from a Catholic agency. They were wonderful parents and would have loved you too.

You'll always know who your parents are, Melinda Ames and Matthew Keaton, even if your mom didn't live to see you. I'll show you pictures."

His eyes strayed to where Annie spoke quietly to the nursing mother. "How well Arielle is latching on now. It won't be long before she goes home. We are so grateful that you kept pumping milk all this time and donated the extra for other babies."

"It's the one thing I could do for Arielle, and if I helped others, that's good. I may seem scrawny, but I have boobs that produce," the mother said with pride in her voice. "Say, is that..." she dropped her voice and whispered to Annie.

Annie nodded. "Remember our privacy rules."

"Oh, sure." She turned her curious face back to her child.

"Let's see," Matt continued. "I had a good childhood, raised Catholic of course. Did the choir boy thing for a while, but I kept getting bigger and bigger. My voice changed early. I had to find something else to do. First day of middle school, the gym teacher asked me if I wanted to play football. My mom wasn't too happy about it, but Dad said to let me try. Turned out I was really good at it. Got a scholarship to Notre Dame, complete with gold helmet, playing under the eyes of Christ. That's where I met your mother. She planned to be an elementary teacher, but we married right out of college, so she didn't need to work, not with my signing bonus and all. Mellie was really beautiful." He regarded his furry, red son. "You don't look like me, but that might be a good thing. Doesn't matter so long as you are healthy."

"Nothing is wrong with your looks, Matt. When

Daniel's hair comes in, I think it will be dark," Annie said. "He'll be a handsome boy. Remember, we all start out this way."

"I'll try to keep that in mind."

The mother across the room buttoned up, raised her daughter to her shoulder, patted and rocked. He'd have to learn to feed Daniel with a bottle. Somehow, that intimidated him more than any opposing lineman, but Annie would show him the proper way. After a while, the new mom returned the baby to Louella who placed her into an open warmer heated with pads and reattached a few monitors. Arielle's mother assured her sleeping baby that she'd be back later and prepared to leave. As she passed, Matt felt compelled to speak despite the rules.

"Ma'am, thanks for donating milk for the babies. My son is going to benefit from that." He stood, offered a hand, then jerked it back. "Guess we're not supposed to do that in here. I'm Matthew Keaton."

"Junelle Wagner. I'm happy to help your poor, motherless babe. I guess I overheard too. Don't worry. In a few months, he'll be as big as my Arielle, bigger, I suspect." Junelle eyed his physique with an appreciation that should have made him blush, but he didn't do stuff like that. Still, the unit seemed warmer than usual.

"Well, thanks again." He sent Junelle on her way with a big smile on her face, why he couldn't say. "I guess I shouldn't have done that, Annie," Matt confessed.

"The nurses can't share medical information, but I know the parents do out in the waiting room. Some join support groups after their children are at home. It's an idea you might consider."

"Maybe. I'd be the only guy there."

"No, fathers are just as concerned."

"Okay." He took his seat again and regaled Daniel with his childhood shenanigans, adding he didn't want his son to do any of those things: toads in the teacher's desk, the joys of whoopee cushions, especially when a nun had a really fat behind, and taking dares that resulted in broken limbs when, say, you jumped off the top of the bleachers.

Annie brought him a water bottle unasked. He gulped it down. All that talk, far more than he usually did, made his throat dry. "I wish I could stay the rest of the day, but I have to get on that plane to Indianapolis and face the Ames family at the funeral. Sorry you have to cart me back to Dean's house. I'm taking up too much of your time, Annie. I'll see about getting a car as soon as I get back. That's a promise."

"It's been no trouble for me. Anything I can do to help."

He believed her. Annie Billodeaux appeared to be a woman who only said things she meant and did not play games with men, unlike another he could name.

Chapter Seven

Indiana was hot in June, but it lacked the steamy atmosphere of New Orleans in more ways than one. No one offered to pick Matt up at the airport. He rented a car, found a hotel room not too far from the funeral home, and checked in for the night. He let Mellie's family know he'd arrived and got the hours for the viewing. With no dinner invitation forthcoming, he went to a drive-up and returned with a sack of hamburgers and fries. He heard Mellie's gently nagging voice saying that kind of diet was bad for his heart. Who cared now if that heart was broken? He tossed and turned all night reliving the nightmare in New Orleans. If only he'd realized the situation sooner, accelerated faster, gotten to the hospital more rapidly. No time to mend her unhappiness with him now.

Breakfast came with the room. Matt showed up to do his duty by his wife from ten a.m. until two p.m. Saturday with the Lutheran church service to follow, and then the burial in the adjoining churchyard. The Ames family sat in the first row in front of the casket. A vacant chair next to Buckner "Bucky" Ames, Melinda's dad, showed him where to sit. Bucky's middle-aged bulk created a barrier between him and her mother, but Matt could see easily over the top of Bucky's thinning gray pate. Marilyn's entire body appeared to be as stiff as her short blonde hair, styled and sprayed to last throughout the ordeal. Bucky had gone to fat, and she to lean over the years. Lean and mean, the words simply popped into Matt's mind.

The two brothers, Buckner Junior, who always went by Buck to distinguish him from his father, and Jordan, the younger one, sat with heads bowed and fingers clenched until the mourners arrived and clasped hands with them. Andrea, his seventeen-year-old sister-in-law, brought up the end of the row. Only she got up, came to hug Matt despite her mother's glare, and asked to see a picture of the baby. Probably just teen rebellion, but he appreciated the gesture. He thought he saw Bucky Ames sneaking a peek and angled the phone in his direction. "I'll send you pictures, Dre," he said loud enough for Marilyn to hear.

"Thanks. He's so tiny and helpless. This is so tragic." Dre dabbed at eyes sporting way too much grim makeup. Despite being born with the same blonde beauty as Melinda, she'd gone Goth lately and died her hair a dead black. No need to buy color appropriate clothes for the funeral. All of her garments were dark from the laced boots heavy enough for Frankenstein to the black turtleneck too hot for the weather and adorned by a thick metal chain. Her face painted white was paler than Melinda's in the coffin. No tats or piercings, though. Matt suspected Marilyn forbade it. She'd once been called by the childhood nickname of Andi. Dre suited her better now she claimed, so that's what he called her. Her mother continued to use Andrea.

Compared to her, the brothers came across as bland, blond Midwestern college students. He paid their college tuition and would continue to do that regardless of their lack of greeting. After all, they had to live with their mother and saw Matt more often on TV than in person. He understood.

The extended Ames clan arrived and trickled through the formalities, pausing to peer at Melinda who resembled Sleeping Beauty with her golden hair fanned out on the satin pillow as if she waited for his kiss to revive her. With her hands folded at her waist and beautifully manicured, her large, diamond engagement ring caught the glint of the mildly scented candles set at the head and foot of the coffin as did the star-like brooch on her shoulder. Some said brief prayers before giving Matt's hand a tepid shake and offering feeble condolences.

Marilyn had gotten to these folks who'd once talked football with him at the annual family reunion and urged him to give pointers to their sons. In her version, he'd taken Melinda to New Orleans to die and had his son ripped from her womb because he was Catholic and cared more for the child than for her daughter, ridiculous and totally wrong. Matt was sure some didn't believe her, but Marilyn organized that family reunion, and none would cross her. He doubted he would be invited again no matter how much he praised her potato salad.

A tall shadow and a firm handshake came between him and his view of Melinda. He raised his eyes to meet those of his former quarterback, Ryan Luke, the man's blue gaze watery beneath his dark brows. "I'm so sorry, so sorry about everything. I wish I could have convinced you to stay here. You were my best ball carrier."

"What's done is done. It's all over."

"Right. I'll go pay my respects." Luke stepped up

to the coffin and bowed his head low.

Matt's former teammates and some with their wives had lined up behind their leader. Matt stood to accept their embraces and manly pats on the back. Their comforting words brought him closer to tears than any other. A few tried to lighten it up by saying they didn't see any of the Sinners here which just proved their team was better. Though they hadn't been happy to have him go free agent, these guys did understand how football worked. You had to seize the best opportunity when it came along because there might not be another in a short career.

"They sent the red roses." A big display bursting with blooms in a black vase bound with ribbons embossed with the word Sinners in gold filled a distant corner of the funeral home. "Most of the team doesn't know me yet, but Dean and Joe Billodeaux offered to come with me. I was afraid…" He lowered his voice. "That someone might insult them. The Billodeauxs have been very kind to me and don't deserve bad treatment."

"Shucks," said huge lineman, Otto Messinger, watching his usual salty language on this sad occasion. "I would have liked to meet the old man. He's a legend. I'd have taken him out for a beer."

"I know you would—and let him pay for it." The brief chuckles that brought also drew a hard stare from Marilyn.

"Excuse me," Otto rumbled and went to take her hand.

One of the team wives pointed out the equally extravagant bouquet of pink roses with the blue ribbons bearing their team's name. Someone had placed it very near the casket. "We knew Melinda and her love of pink. She still looks lovely."

Bultman's had done a wonderful job. The bullet entry wound did not show at all. Of course, it hadn't exited, simply tore up Mellie's brain until she drowned in the fluid and blood inside her skull. Matt felt a dizzy spell hit, not unlike getting up after a hard hit on the playing field. A free breakfast consisting mainly of coffee, orange juice, and a couple of cinnamon buns failed to hold him up. He leaned toward Bucky. "I think I need break." Bucky nodded.

Matt moved down the line being sure to shake hands with all his old buddies and their women. The words, "Tough Break" and "So sorry, so damned sorry," followed him out into the lobby.

A funeral director showed him the way to a side room stocked with catered trays of sandwiches, fruits, vegetables, and cookies. Marilyn had supplemented the offerings with her famous potato salad and other homemade dishes he knew so well from the reunions that he could name the person who brought the baked beans made with dried limas and the slaw studded with raisins. The big, extended family of his dreams had welcomed him warmly and now shut him out in the cold.

Matt took a handful of the little triangular sandwiches regardless of the filling, some pineapple chunks and strawberries, and chocolate chip cookies that reminded him of Annie, the warm-hearted woman who took care of his child like her own. He chugged down two Pepsis and belched at the exact moment Marilyn entered the room. Distaste smeared her face.

"You know we have to take turns. People are

waiting to speak to you while you are back here stuffing your face with our food."

Matt nodded toward the catered dishes. "I think I paid for those. Don't worry; your potato salad is safe. I'm going back right now." He wanted to add, "Coach," but knew he couldn't joke with Mellie's mother anymore. Matt brushed by her, hit the restroom, then resumed his position.

At two, the funeral director told the family he would close the casket in a few moments if they wanted to say a last goodbye. Matt rose, went to his wife, and kissed her lips. He wished he hadn't, cold, so cold and stiff, not a good memory. After he stepped away, Mr. Ames touched his daughter's pale cheek and moved on. Marilyn Ames burst into tears and leaned over the coffin to embrace her child. Her husband and the funeral director raised her up and led her away. The siblings each said their version of "Goodbye, Mellie" and followed the others.

Matt indicated that he'd drive his rental car rather than join the family in the limo. No sense in adding to their misery—and his. The funeral procession lined up behind the white hearse and away they went out into the country to the red brick Lutheran church where Melinda worshiped all her life until she'd married Matt—and fallen away according to Marilyn. Not his fault. Melinda preferred spending Sundays in choice seats at his games rather than at a service. He'd never asked her to convert.

Since the minister who had married them knew her well, he shared stories of Mellie's work with the youth groups and beautiful voice in the choir, how she'd lobbied for pink robes and lost. The people in the pews nodded. Some smiled. Her oldest brother, almost twenty-one, eked out a short piece of praise saying she'd been a nice sister and would have been a good mother. He didn't go so far as to mention Daniel. When Andrea made a move toward the altar, Marilyn pulled her back. Dre's boots made a great thump as she sat again, mumbling "Jesus Christ, I wasn't going to say anything bad, not here." A comment only Matt and a few others heard.

The service ended at the grave, ashes to ashes, dust to dust; in sure and certain hope of the Resurrection to eternal life. Matt dropped the pink rose shoved into his hand onto the coffin. Others followed until the entire top of the casket resembled a flowerbed. The thud of raw earth followed. The Ames family invited everyone to their home for refreshments at the big, square framed farmhouse set in a vast, shady yard down the road. Marilyn's teary blue eyes singled out Matt and indicated, "Not you, murderer, not you."

Dre grasped his arm as he headed toward his rental car. "Come to the house. Not all of us are as psycho as my mom. Shit happens in life. Even I know that."

"No, she's taking this hard. Try not to be too tough on her. I want to get back to Daniel. He needs me."

"Yeah, I guess so. You have my iPhone number. Send more pictures. Tell him Aunt Dre loves him already."

"Thanks, I will." He would have ruffled her hair, but it seemed to be spiked up with some kind of goop. Beneath it lay a pretty nice kid. Instead, he reached into his pocket to give her an envelope discreetly delivered to him as he got into his car. It held Mellie's brooch, engagement ring, and diamond wedding band. He would have let the jewelry go to the grave with her but hadn't thought to tell the funeral director. "Here, I'd like you to take these. I have no use for them. Do whatever you want with the stuff. Keep it, sell it, or use it for something you really want."

Dre snatched a quick look inside the packet. "Are you sure? I'm just a kid."

"A kid with more compassion than most no matter how you dress. Take care, Dre. I don't know when we'll meet again."

His young sister-in-law hugged him hard. "I didn't just do that because you gave me diamonds, Matt. I love you better than my own brothers."

"Thanks. You'd better get back to your family." Matt got into the rental and took the first flight he could arrange to New Orleans. His son waited for him, counted on him, and rested in the arms of a warm-hearted, angelic woman in his absence.

Chapter Eight

Annie neared the end of her shift. One more hour to go. She'd not only taken care of her special charges but moved from unit to unit checking to see if any of the nurses needed her expertise or had questions. They'd gained a screamer on the ward, a drug-addicted preemie who more or less had to go cold turkey while the mother who made the child got Methadone treatments and counseling. One day, she'd have to place that baby in its mother's arms and pray for the best, a very tough part of her job. The infant's thin wails penetrated whenever a door opened or shut, hard on everyone's nerves.

Fairly soon, the nursing mothers trickled in and took over the rocking chairs while Annie signed out and sought her breakfast after a long night. Someone entered the unit and brought with them the tortured kitten cries of the child in agony. Annie wrote steadily on the chart in her hand without glancing up. A deep, masculine voice said, "Hi, Peggy. How's it going?" and she knew Matt Keaton had returned without having to be urged. "I hope that's not my child screaming."

"Nope, drug-addicted preemie. One day you'll recognize Daniel's cries when he really starts to vocalize. Otherwise, same as always: diaper, feed, put to bed, chart, and repeat," Peggy answered. "Your boy is doing well. Tell him, Annie."

If she felt a tiny pang that he hadn't addressed her first, Annie buried it beneath a gentle smile. "One week with us, and Daniel is up to 1,153 grams in weight."

With a furrowing of his broad brow, confusion showed on Matt's face. "Translate, please."

Not the first time she'd been asked this, Annie answered, "That's 2.54 pounds, and he is sixteen inches long which is tall for his age. Takes after his daddy. How was your trip?" She carefully didn't mention the funeral.

"Bad. I'm glad one of us is thriving." Matt sat down by Daniel and, as she turned back to her paperwork, he uttered his usual rapid prayer for the baby's health. "Well, Danny, your mother looked beautiful right to the end. I gave her a kiss from both of us." His broad shoulders shivered for a second in the hot room.

"She's buried on a hilltop not far from where she grew up. We'll visit one day. I didn't go over to the farmhouse afterward but came right back to you on the first plane I could get."

Annie wasn't certain if he was telling the child or her. He went on about giving the diamond pin and Melinda's rings to his Aunt Dre whom he'd meet someday. "Kind of kooky right now, into the Goth stuff, but she'll grow out of it I'm pretty sure. She owns the softest heart in the Ames family and wants more pictures of you. That's brave considering all the tubes and wires."

"Do you want his twenty-eighth week picture taken?" Annie asked.

"Yes, I'm keeping a record."

Again, she delved into his hip pocket for the phone

and got them both in the frame so Daniel would realize someday that his father had stayed by his side. She replaced the phone against the solid warmth of his hip and said, "We've got to stop carrying on this way," as she sanitized her hands. Peggy chuckled.

Matt mustered a brief smile. "Believe me, this is the highlight of my last few days. You get off at seven, right? Could I buy you, both of you, breakfast in the cafeteria?"

"Oh, I like to go straight home, but Annie always eats here. That's because she's single and doesn't have a couple of grandchildren waiting for pancakes. You two go ahead."

Annie moved over to Arielle's warmer and murmured, "Not too subtle, Peggy."

"What? Just telling the truth," the older woman whispered back.

Annie covered their private conversation with a louder remark. "This little girl is going home soon if she can pass the car seat test."

"I think so," Peggy agreed.

"There's a car seat test?" Matt asked, eavesdropping.

"Yes, the infant has to be able to stay upright in a car seat without any breathing issues. We watch for bradycardia events."

"Huh?"

"The slowing of the baby's heartbeat below the normal heart resting rate. You'll soon learn the terminology."

"Just like football jargon I guess, but more serious."

"Very serious."

Matt turned back to Daniel, stroked him softly with a single finger. "You hear that, buddy? Bradycardia is serious. Don't do that, okay?"

Annie took and recorded Arielle's vital signs for the doctor due on his morning rounds. She checked the time. "I go off duty now, Matt, but you can stay if you want. I'm used to getting my own breakfast."

"No, I'll come with you. I need to eat too. Not much but pretzels on those red eye flights."

He bid Daniel goodbye and walked Annie through the ward and downstairs to the cafeteria. She grabbed a tray and considered her options. Matt followed her lead. Annie selected a cup of fresh berries, a bowl of oatmeal topped with brown sugar and slivered almonds, and a carton of milk to pour over it. She filled a cup with hot water over an herbal teabag, no caffeine for her just before bedtime.

She waited as Matt stoked up on scrambled eggs blended with cheese, tomatoes, and crumbled bacon. He added some sausage links, a couple of biscuits, and large orange juice, and then paid for both of them. He led the way to a table. The cashier who knew Annie well gave her a wink. "Dinner date, ah-huh."

"Just breakfast, Leola." She doubted the devastated man would be dating anytime soon.

Taking a seat across from Matt, she unloaded her tray, added some berries to her bowl, and spooned up her oatmeal, glad to see he had recovered his appetite considering the way he attacked the eggs and sausage.

"Oatmeal, I had plenty of that growing up in Indiana. Biscuits are way better down here, hardly ever the refrigerator kind." He slathered the heart-healthy spread and jelly on one.

"We do pride ourselves on our biscuits, but to be honest, my brother-in-law, Junior Polk, makes the best in our family. Have you met him yet?"

"No, a lot of the guys are on vacation, but Dean says he'll be here for the voluntary training days because he's just hanging out in Chapelle with his wife and baby girl, mostly cooking and gaining too much weight that he needs to work off before camp. He's an awesome cornerback. It will be a privilege to play with him and Dean."

Matt hesitated a minute as if pondering what else to share. "My old teammates came to the funeral, and that made it bearable. Otherwise, people barely acknowledged me. Melinda's mother, Marilyn, sure did a great job of spreading the word that I'd killed her daughter. I couldn't wait to get out of there."

"I've never heard anything more unfair. She'll regret it later when Daniel is older, and she passed on helping you. Can't she take any solace in her other daughter, the one I heard you mention, the one with the soft heart?"

"Andrea, Dre we call her, is the anti-Melinda right now. I think she dyed her hair and went Goth to be exactly that. It's a teen emo thing that will pass, but it puts her at odds with her mother all the time. Not much solace there. The boys are home for the summer, but they're guys. They won't be at the house much if they can help it. I think Bucky, that's my father-in-law, will come around faster than Marilyn. Regardless, it's time I man up, move into the house, unpack the rest of those boxes, and get settled since I'm staying here." He loaded the second biscuit with eggs and made a sandwich out of it.

Annie paused in the midst of sipping her tea. "Why not go back to Dean's place and rest first? Really, you shouldn't be alone."

"I came here right from the airport in a rental car that I'm keeping for a few days until I can buy another SUV like I promised—with lots of leg room."

"Do I sense my vehicle is a little crowded for you?" She eked a grin out of him.

"Absolutely, yes, but you won't have to haul me around anymore."

When he bought the new vehicle, she'd be seeing a lot less of him. He'd probably visit Daniel during the day, and Bess would have the pleasure of his company. No more of these companionable breakfasts in her future. She'd be eating alone again.

"I didn't mind. Don't worry about disturbing Dean and Stacy. With young children, they're always up early."

"I like his kids. Wynn is such the little lady, and DJ is a hoot. Lots of good energy in that house. It's the kind of home I hoped to have, wished I'd had sooner, but Mellie thought I had to pursue my career first. She got pregnant just after I decided to go free agent. We might have had two by now if she hadn't held back, two when we were back home near her mother and family—then I had to go and have my way." Although most of the food had vanished, he left some on the plate and abruptly finished his orange juice.

Annie thought rapidly. "Really, stay at Dean's today and get some rest. I come out of my cocoon around four. I'll call, and we can make plans to help you get settled in the house on Tuesday, a whole bunch of us with enough manpower to move furniture and scare off the paparazzi."

"That would be great." He gathered their empty dishes onto a tray and carried them to the window where a conveyor belt moved the dirty plates to the kitchen. Then, he walked Annie to her car as if she hadn't done that alone a hundred times or perhaps needed the protection of his size. Matt opened the door for her, too, and cautioned her to buckle up in a way that caused a tender smile.

"I can see you'll take really good care of Daniel when he's ready to go home."

"He needs you more right now. Be careful driving when you're tired."

Annie allowed herself to wish Matt needed her just as much as his son. "I will. See you tomorrow."

Chapter Nine

Still in her comfy PJs, Annie stood before the open and mostly empty refrigerator. She or Jude really should go grocery shopping, maybe on their Sacred Sister Thursday, though Jude would gripe about getting survival rations on her day off. As Annie turned toward the cupboard and took down a can of noodle soup to nuke, her phone rang. Better not be a telemarketer when she'd newly gotten out of bed. "Yeah, what do you want?" she answered, snapping. "I know what I don't want: a free knee brace, a Caribbean trip to view time shares, or another credit card with way lower interest for one year."

"Good to know. This is Matt, Matt Keaton. I guess I woke you up. Sorry. I worked out with Dean this morning and was down for the count all afternoon myself. You want to come to dinner?"

The second Matt opened his mouth, she knew who called. He wanted to take her out to eat. Her heart gave a slight flutter like a neonate with a valve problem. Too bad he now realized she woke up surly, not full of sunshine and smiles as Mellie probably had. "I was awake and about to heat some soup. I'd love to go out. I can be ready by six."

"Good, I'll tell Dean. He's making pizza in that awesome wood oven he owns. Stacy says we can make plans for tomorrow."

No need to be disappointed as Dean did make a mean pizza. "What can I bring?"

"Stace is putting together a salad and has plenty of wine. You don't need to bring anything, though I sort of hoped for more of those giant chocolate chip cookies. I really didn't appreciate them first time around—if it's not too much trouble. I'll pay for them."

"It's not like I baked them myself. I'll bring some, though Stacy won't thank me between her kids, her dog, and her diet."

"Maybe I shouldn't have asked."

He took everything so seriously. She added a laugh. "Joking. I'll be there at six with cookies in hand, my treat. See y'all then." Driving her own car, toting dessert, wearing the regular jeans and tee, but maybe with a little more makeup than usual.

Annie dashed for the shower to do what she could with her hair and all the rest of her body. She'd be sweaty again by the time she crossed Canal Street to buy the cookies, but her scented shower gel should overcome that. No need to use plain antibiotic soap as she had four glorious days off.

This could be fun with the kids, Stacy, Dean—and Matt. Being petite and wanting to stay that way, her menu rarely included pizza. She chose jeans that cupped her small behind, a stretchy top that made the most of her breasts, and sneakers because the children always wanted to be chased around the courtyard. Annie drew a red ribbon that matched her shirt through her curls and tied it in the back to give her usual mop more shape and interest, best she could do outside of an emergency mission to a hairdresser, and no time for that!

She must get to the coffee shop before all the giant chocolate chip cookies were devoured. As it turned out, only three remained. Annie supplemented them with oatmeal raisin. She and Stacy could eat those. Let the kids share one and leave the others for the men. She slung the bag into her hot, stuffy car and headed to Dean's home where the usual greeting of leg hugs and excited dog awaited. Forgetting to leave a note for her twin of her whereabouts, she'd call after seven.

Stacy gave the usual orders to the children and dog to get off Aunt Annie as she emerged from the kitchen bearing a large tray of pizza toppings. She wasn't much of a cook, but to give her credit, she did know how to temptingly array foods: lines of green pepper rings and thin-sliced red onion ran between the ranks of pepperoni and small chunks of ham. Little bowls held crumbled bacon, chopped mushrooms, black olives, and jalapenos. Shakers of hot pepper flakes and parmesan already graced the picnic table.

Dean ladled tomato sauce onto the dough he purchased from a local restaurant and pressed into three large pans. "Just in time, Annie, or else your half will have nothing but veggies since you're sharing with Stacy. Wynn, DJ, what do you want on yours? Plain cheese as usual?"

Wynn nodded, but DJ questioned Matt who studied the third naked pizza as if he contemplated a work of art. "What you gonna have, Mr. Matt?"

"The works, that means everything. Same as your dad."

"I gonna have the works too." His small, dark head nodded decisively. Obviously, big men ate everything.

"Don't get your stuff on my side," Wynn

complained.

Dean drew a line down the middle pizza and formed a W on one side and a DJ on the other. "Don't cross the line, Deej."

"A good solution, but you know he won't eat all those toppings," Stacy prompted.

"Here." Matt pressed one of each topping generously spaced on DJ's half. "If you bite into something you don't like, pick it off and eat the rest. Watch out for that jalapeno on the tip."

Annie allowed herself an internal sigh. Lucky Daniel to have such a dad, already good with children. "You handled that well."

"Learned from my own father. I wish he were still around to see Daniel. He'd be in the NICU day and night, my mom too."

Again, Matt's utter lack of support struck Annie hard. "We'll organize the team wives to be rockers when Daniel is bigger, and you know I'm there all weekend."

"That's the only thing that keeps me from asking for a cot to remain by his side."

"No need for that unless he goes critical. Like most babies, he sleeps in the early weeks. Soon, Daniel will be on milk, and we'll add eat and poop to his functions. Daily visits are good enough. Some dads rarely make it in."

"No more talk of poop while I am creating the ultimate pizza." Dean, with no regard for design, heaped handfuls of everything on the third pizza and made the shredded mozzarella rain on top. He used a wooden peel like a pro to shovel two pies into his wood-burning oven. "The ones for the women and children first. Real men can wait—and have a second beer from the cooler. Hand me one, Matt, and get another for yourself."

Stacy fetched a large bowl of shredded lettuce and cherry tomatoes from the kitchen, tipped the leftover toppings into the mixture, doused it with Italian dressing, tossed, and *voila*, a dinner salad. Annie and Stacy started with the greens, picking out the tiny tomatoes and sweet pepper rings for the children to eat while they waited. Annie had kept her word about the cookies, left in the car to preclude predinner begging by any except the dog. Mati received a small bowl of chopped ham.

The men stood by the oven making guy talk about the upcoming football season and the merits of various grills. "Stacy could make bread in this oven if she wanted. I mean it's good for more than pizza." Dean repeated his argument for having the oven in the first place.

"As if I want to spend my days doing that in the New Orleans heat when the city has lots of great bakeries." Stacy added more salad to her bowl. Annie did the same to stave off the desire to eat the entire half a pizza.

"My yard is pretty small, but I could probably fit a medium-sized grill on the patio," Matt said, thinking ahead.

"You could get a smoker. Now that my dad is retired he has more time to hunt. Nothing better than smoked game. We'd share with you, Matt."

Stacy rolled her eyes. "And the next addition to our yard is going to be a smoker."

"Great idea, Princess!"

She'd fallen neatly into Dean's trap. Annie laughed, enjoying the moment complete with kids and dogs—and Matt Keaton. Once she'd badly wanted freedom from her family, but now realized how much she missed them on occasions like this.

Dean removed the first of the pizzas, brought them to the table, cut the wedges with a heavy-duty slicer, and admonished his kids to wait until the cheese cooled. The mountainous third pizza made its way into the oven. The men set a good example by eating their salads while they waited.

At the end of the meal, Stacy only had to wrap half of the women's pizza and the slices the children didn't touch. "Be sure to take ours back to Jude."

"I'll get the cookies form the car. I need the exercise after all that cheese," Annie said. She stood, very aware her jeans fit tighter.

"I'd better walk with you in case there are paparazzi around," Matt offered.

"Oh, I'm small, swift, and scandal-free. They rarely notice me anymore, while you are a large target. I propose we meet at your place tomorrow at nine. This time we take Dean. Some heavy lifting will substitute for your usual workout, and I doubt the photographers will harass the captain of the Sinners." She raced out the back gate before he could argue and returned in minutes to dole out the cookies according to plan.

Stacy herded her chocolate-streaked children off to bath and bed while the others enjoyed the cooling of the day on the patio. Annie's phone rang—Jude.

"Where in the hell are you?"

"Sorry, I should have left a note. I'm at Dean's place. We had pizza. Come and join us."

"Too tired for kids and dogs right now. Bring some home. I'll eat it after I shower. Matt still there?"

"Yes," Annie answered neutrally. "Tomorrow, we're going to get his house in order."

"Glad I'm working. See you around…"

"Eight, I guess. Bye." She would have liked to linger longer as the blue hour turned to night.

"You're really tight with your sister." Matt sat beside her at the table as he had all evening.

Annie shrugged. "Twins, you know."

"Twin hellions," Dean added. "They liked to make the boys in our family as miserable as possible. Of course, Stacy played a part in that too. Still, my dad said his worst nightmare was having twin girls who went into cheerleading, then nursing—every man's dream. My folks kept a good eye on them through high school. Believe me, no guy dated our sisters without my dad grilling them like suspected criminals. Once they got to college, Tom and I were supposed to supervise them. It's a big campus, and like Annie said, they were small and swift."

"Not scandal-free?" Matt asked.

"They cut up a lot their first two years away from home. We could warn off the athletes, but not keep the girls out of the frat houses. Too many parties going on any given night." Dean raised an eyebrow Annie's way. "The yellow press claims I'm not the only one in the family with a butt tattoo, but I cannot confirm that."

"Nor will you ever. Really, I have to go before this gets any more personal." Annie stood.

Stacy appeared at the kitchen door. "Time for tuck-in duties."

Dean rose to say nightie-night to his children. "To

be continued. Careful driving home, little bitty sister."

"See, that's why we rebelled. I can handle New Orleans traffic on a Monday night, you big lout," Annie replied, using Stacy's favorite term for her brother. She slipped the wrapped leftover pieces of her pizza into the cookie bag. "I must go home and feed my double."

"It's dark out now. Let me see you to your car. I know, overprotective, but I'd really like to hear the end of that tattoo story." Matt stood up, a big, strong tower of a man.

For once, Annie felt like being protected. "Okay, it's not far."

They encountered no lurkers on the short walk. He waited for her to unlock the car and get inside but leaned over before she shut the door. "About those tattoos."

He had a faint smile on his very masculine lips. If it lifted a bit of his misery to tell, she would. "Jude and I aren't identical twins, but people do have trouble telling us apart. So, in college, we went for tattoos, a red butterfly on Jude's left butt cheek and a black one on my right. No one could see them unless we wore thong bikinis, which we never did at the ranch. However, we participated in some wild spring breaks and Mardi Gras antics. A paparazzo got a shot of us on the beach in Cancun. We claimed those weren't our behinds. You know how those rags fake news."

"Lying to your parents?"

"Of course. Our wild days are long over—behind us you could say. Now our only concern is to keep those butterflies from getting any bigger. Say, have you seen Dean's tattoo? I've always wanted a look, but I'd have to pants him, and he can fight me off too easily."

"Sure, in the locker room. He has two."

"Two!"

"Yep, two hearts with devil tails. One reads Sinners and the other Stacy on opposite cheeks."

"So that's what he gave her for their last anniversary. Stacy would only say it was something special she'd wanted for a long time. I wonder if she has one that says Dean."

"I can't tell you that. Probably shouldn't have divulged the other, but I didn't know it was a secret."

"Wait until Jude hears!"

"Please, you didn't learn it from me. I need all the friends I can get right now. Be safe." Matt shut her door decisively and sent her on her way.

Chapter Ten

The next morning, Annie spotted only one photographer still keeping watch at the little pink palace. He hunched in the doorway of his car, most likely taking a piss into a bottle, when Matt and the contingent of Billodeauxs drove up and parked. With a quick zip, the man turned, camera already in hand and mouth open to shout a question. Before he could spit it out, Dean loomed over him while Matt continued up the walkway with her and Stace. The women turned to watch the show.

Their quarterback wore his game face and spoke in a tone he used for audibles that implied no one was going to mess up the play. "Let the guy alone. Be gone by the time we get the door unlocked."

"I have the right…" The paparazzo made the mistake of taking a picture of Dean's scary face.

Dean ripped the camera from his hand, examined it, calmly removed the photo chip, and ground it underfoot. He returned what he had taken. "Go somewhere else. No story here." Dean strode to the front stoop where Matt worked the keys. As they crossed the threshold, the reporter started his engine and faded away.

"Always great to have my big lout along," Stacy purred, placing a hand on her husband's throwing arm.

Annie had to admit she'd enjoyed the display of

strength and believed Matt capable of the same once he recovered from his loss. "There's a bed that needs to be put together in the small room upstairs. Maybe you two could start there," Annie suggested with a sly smile. She'd like a few minutes alone with Matt.

"Race you to the top," Stacy dared, and darted for the spiral staircase. Taking two wedged-shaped steps at a time, Dean overtook her with ease.

Matt simply watched them at play before saying, "You don't really think they'll use the bed, do you?'

"Not if we're up there too. Stacy keeps trying to get Dean to be more spontaneous. Let's go. You know this isn't the most child-friendly staircase," Annie mentioned as she negotiated the somewhat steep risers to the second floor.

Right on her heels, Matt said, "Mellie said we'd put up a baby gate."

If Melinda said it, she must be right. Annie shrugged, unconvinced. She'd seen her siblings climb over some amazing barriers when very young. She took a minute to check on Dean and Stacy. Stacy's bossy genes had already kicked in as she directed her husband to shove the dresser away from the window as it blocked the light and position the bed across from it along the blank wall. Dean had screwdriver in hand to assemble the bed frame. Stace positioned the more easily moved night tables. "Hey, see if you can find the sheets to fit, Annie. Looks like a double to me."

"Will do." A large, neatly labeled box in the hall said Linens. She sorted through the contents, all white sheets and towels that reminded her of the hospital, but at least they weren't pink or flowery. Unfurling a sheet that looked the right size, she ferreted out the pillowcases, a top sheet, and a homey quilt in a wedding ring pattern that might have served as a spread. Annie took them to Stacy in time to see Dean manhandle the box spring onto the frame.

Matt lurked in the hall, clenching and unclenching his large hands, not knowing what to do with them. Annie gave him a hint. "Why don't you help Dean with the mattress. I'll search for pillows."

As she opened another box, she heard the mutual grunt as the men heaved the thick mattress into place. Pillows found, she took them to Matt and suggested he stuff them in the slips while Dean and Stacy tried to find the right corners on the fitted sheet. On another trip, she supplied them with an armful of throw pillows that matched the bedspread and announced finding a pair of brass table lamps that seemed to fit the décor.

"There," Stacy said. "One guest room, small but cozy. What's next?"

"Help me haul the rest of the sheets and towels to the linen closet in the master bath." Annie distributed a heap into all the waiting arms and led the procession past the empty nursery and through the painful scene in the large bedroom. She couldn't imagine what Matt must feel passing the rows of his deceased wife's shoes and gowns in the walk-through closet. She distracted him by commenting, "Lots of white. I kind of expected pink," as she unburdened him of a tower of towels.

"Mellie's mom told her white sheets and towels matched everything and could be easily bleached for stains. That's why hotels use them."

"Did she always do what her mother said?"

"Pretty much. They were close."

Too close, but Annie shouldn't judge. She still

used the pale gray and lavender sheets Stacy left behind in the apartment. "Here, take a set of towels and washcloths to the small bathroom."

As soon as Matt left, Stacy sidled over with her stack of sheets. "Now there's a well-trained man. He does what you ask."

"Don't I always?" Dean said, offering his load of linens.

"No, or maybe eventually, but Mama Nell did teach you not to be a slob, bless her. Do we ask about his wife's clothes and shoes?"

"I think we must. Simply seeing the stuff has to be hard," Annie whispered as she heard Matt returning. Both Stacy and Dean looked at her, silently nominating Annie to bring up the subject. Not the first time she'd had to deal with delicate subjects in her line of work. Telling parents that a failing infant might not make it through the night never came easy.

"Linens all stowed. Matt, did you want to use the empty boxes to store Melinda's clothes, or should we wait on that?" Give him the choice to decide.

Head bowed, the big man thought a moment, nodded. "Yes, box everything and take it to a charity, the suitcase too. If you find any more jewelry, there's a box in the top dresser drawer. Put it in there. Maybe Daniel's wife will want it someday."

He'd gone from shell-shocked to thinking of the future. Good. But his recovery from grief would take a very long time, Annie suspected. To lose a wife and blame yourself, to be cut off from family because of it, she could not image the hurt he kept contained in that large frame.

"Stacy and I will take care of it. I noticed a butcher

block table obstructing the entrance to the dining room and a couple of matching benches. Why don't you and Dean put that in the breakfast area of the kitchen? It would go well there."

Again, Matt nodded automatically. "Sounds good. Ready to play moving man, Dean?

"Every day of the week."

"Hey." Stacy objected. "I don't change the furniture around that often."

"You say." A quarterback quick on his feet, Dean dodged a pillow she grabbed from the king-sized bed and swung his way. He bolted for the staircase with Matt following.

"Good, now we can really talk," Stacy said as she dragged some large boxes into the bedroom. "This place isn't right for a single man, plus he should be closer to other people and team members. Maybe we could talk him into moving into the building where Tom and Junior keep apartments."

Annie began removing gowns and suits from the padded hangers, folding each one carefully into a box. "You want me to bring up the subject, right?"

"Oh, girl, if he trusts you with his fragile son, he'd trust you on any advice. You have a bond already." Stacy started with the drawers, dumping anything she found there, undies, sweaters, socks from Melinda's side, into the depths of the linens box. She placed a substantial oak jewelry box on the dresser's top and opened it out of curiosity. "Some nice things in here, not my style, but nothing cheap either."

Annie handed her a pearl stickpin with a setting of tiny sapphires removed from the collar a pale blue suit to add to the treasure chest. "Nice that Daniel's wife might someday wear these jewels."

"Or Matt's next wife. He won't be single for long—rugged good looks, big paycheck, and already housebroken. He needs a mother for that baby too."

"That will kill the deal for some women. I doubt he'll even think of remarrying before the baby is ready to come home."

"Wouldn't kill the deal for you." Stacy gave Annie one of those know-it-all smiles.

"Please, that idea is unseemly right now. We'll recommend some good baby nurses when the time arrives. He doesn't need to rush into anything."

Tasks finished, she and Stacy sought the muscle to carry the suitcase and boxes to the Billodeaux family SUV, huge and black with red pinstriping, safer than the red Mustang Dean still clung to for joy rides. They found the men downing a beer from a small cooler and sitting at the table they'd moved

"Dean, it's not even eleven yet," his wife reproved.

"This is thirsty work. What's next?"

"Carry the suitcase and the clothes boxes to the SUV. Use the back stairs. It will be easier. You have anything else in that cooler you brought along?"

"A variety of diet soft drinks, Princess, for your delectation." Dean stood and made a small bow.

Stacy swatted him on the rear. "Get moving. We're here to work." Still, she popped a top on a sugar-free iced tea with lemon. "Let's put some of these appliances under the counters. You know Matt isn't going to use the mixer or bread machine, and probably not the convection oven. We'll leave the coffeemaker, blender, toaster, and microwave up top but plugged into different circuits. We don't want to strain the wiring in this old place."

While Stacy did that, Annie unloaded a box of pots and pans and a block of knives, placing them in logical locations near the stove. She carried a chest of wedding flatware topped with a stack of silver trays and bowls a little too ornate for her taste to the formal dining room where the removal of the butcher block table and stacked benches revealed an antique mahogany table with twelve matching chairs and an enormous Victorian breakfront ready to receive her burden. A chandelier larger than the one in the hall sparkled over the room. She knew Ollie must have thrown in the furnishings with the sale. Somehow, she couldn't see Matt entertaining here. Everything stowed, she returned to the kitchen where the men again sat nursing their beers.

"What's next?" Dean asked.

"Maybe you want to rearrange the furniture in the front parlor, Matt, to make it more Feng shui," Stacy suggested. She possessed strong opinions about design and wasn't afraid to state them, but Stacy hit a sore spot.

"No, that's where Mellie wanted the things. Let them alone." His words came out deep and gruff, edged with sorrow. "Sorry, I know you are here to help, but just leave it be."

Feeling she needed the caffeine and something to relieve a sudden case of dry throat, Annie took a can of Coke Zero from the cooler. "Matt, do you really want a place this big right now? Maybe an apartment would be better. I think Tom could get you into his building if they have a vacancy."

"I think that would be—disloyal to Mellie's memory. She picked this house to raise our child. It's not that big, and I can get a cleaning lady. There's a good parochial school nearby, too. I didn't get a chance to talk to her about that, but I guess it's my decision now." He hugged his beer and took a sip.

Sure, a nice place for a little girl, but not much room for a boy to run, and Daniel would run like the best of kids someday. Well, Annie had tried. She moved on. "I think we should move the fancy china to the breakfront in the dining room and give you more space for dry goods. You won't be using crystal and china like that every day."

"Probably not at all. Move it. I'll save that for Daniel's wife too."

"Hey, man, what about you?" Dean asked. "Where's your man cave going to be? That's important too." Excellent quarterback sneak in Annie's opinion.

"The smoking room, the realtor called it. Not that I smoke. All I really need is a flat screen over the fireplace."

"Plus, a couple of big recliners and a table for snacks. I didn't see any man chairs sitting around."

"Mellie didn't like the way they looked. Too clunky. My mother-in-law used to say a house belonged to the wife to do what she wanted since she'd have to live with it every day while men were out of the house."

Annie bit her tongue before she could say, "It's your house now." Instead, she said, "The Billodeaux men are huge on recliners, literally. The bigger the better. I remember three of us could squeeze into one of them like a pile of puppies. We fought over who got to sit tucked in with Dad in his chair. Fond memories. Sometimes, it's not always about style."

Matt's face softened as if he could imagine Daniel

sharing a recliner with him. She'd made him think. Dean deftly continued the play she'd started. "I know a great place to buy recliners. We need to get you that new SUV too. If the women are done with us for the day, we can go out for an oyster po-boy at Acme, then get started on shopping for man stuff."

"Sounds good except for the oysters. I'm a Midwestern boy and not too sure about them."

"You will come to love them."

"What about us? Why don't we get one oyster, one shrimp, one catfish, and one roast beef and bring them here. We can cut them into samples for Matt. Women also have to eat. Meanwhile, we'll unpack a few more things. Then, you drop us off at home by two so I can let the nanny go before you start on your masculine safari," Stacy suggested.

"Right. Forgot we left your car behind." Dean clapped his hands as if ending a huddle. "To the French Quarter, Matt."

They hustled out before the women added more to the list. Stacy and Annie moved the china and crystal, opened more boxes to find kitchenware to put in drawers, and a chest full of Matt's sports trophies from middle school through his pro career. They lugged the wooden chest into the smoking room and arrayed the trophies on the mantel. A brief search discovered two TVs in the former sitting room. They hauled the biggest into the future den. A nice oriental carpet with a pattern of brown, cream, and tan remained on the floor.

Stacy contemplated the space. "You know, put the wooden chest on the rug and you have the start of a nice man cave. The chest is just beat up enough to have character. Matt wouldn't have to worry about little

Daniel marring the finish either."

"Did you see his name on the end panels? Someone made this chest especially for him." Annie ran her fingers in the chiseled grooves that spelled out Matt.

"Even better, a family heirloom to be. Remind me to tell Dean saddle leather for the recliners. If not, he'll get black."

"I can agree with that."

In less time than figured on, the men were back in the kitchen slicing up the po-boys, spilling bits of seafood on the counter, and mopping up roast beef gravy with paper towels. With plates in hand and a renewal of drinks, they gathered at the kitchen table again to dig into New Orleans delicacies.

Matt nodded in approval. "I could eat oysters this way again."

"While you are out seeking recliners and cars, we'll get groceries," Annie suggested. "Anything special you want, Matt?" she asked as she pushed a fallen shrimp back into her section of the French bread loaf. She didn't indulge often in fried foods, but showed she relished every bite by licking her lips. Winkling out a single fry from the generous shared single serving of Acme's famous Boo Fries covered in gravy and cheese, Annie trashed her diet again, but her simple statement unintentionally struck Matt hard.

"Mellie always bought the groceries." A shadow passed over the shared meal.

"We'll get you the Dean diet. Anything you don't like or want, we can use at our place," Stacy said.

"Sounds good." The shadow passed, and a ray of sun from the garden made its way into the kitchen. "Almost settled again, friends at the table, oyster po-boy in my grasp, and my son in safe hands." Matt favored Annie with a soft smile. "Yeah, it's all good."

Chapter Eleven

Matt had enough beer for the day. He warmed his hands around a large mug of coffee out of habit. In New Orleans, you sure didn't need to, considering the climate but sometimes the air-conditioning blasted like an arctic wind. Not so in Dean's den where they watched a west coast baseball game. Stacy prepared large chef's salads for dinner to offset their fried food and gravy lunch. The apple pie and ice cream Annie added to the purchases at the grocery store went well with the strong coffee. He concentrated on being thankful the women made a meal for him and tried not to dwell on his loss.

Prompted by their mother who said children didn't like sudden changes, he'd told Wynn and DJ minutes ago that he wouldn't be here in the morning since he'd be moving into his own house tonight. Deej said, "Awww," and Wynn pouted, "Why don't you just stay here?"

"I can't remain forever. I'm extra work for your mom. But, my place is only a few blocks away. You can visit." The kids smothered him in hugs, and Stacy hustled them off for baths and bedtime before they asked more awkward questions. Annie went along to help.

On the sleek, black enameled coffee table lay the pictures of the enormous saddle leather recliners to be delivered tomorrow and the dealer's portfolio of the SUV he'd purchased, black like Dean's, and to be detailed in Sinners red and with a devil decal. He'd let Dean take the lead on the vehicle because his quarterback tried hard to integrate him into the Sinners team, and he appreciated that. Matt didn't much care what he drove as long as it wasn't the vehicle with Mellie's blood spilled all over the front seat. Anyhow, he'd have the new car by Thursday. He was learning Sinners got top-notch service in this city.

Annie, her little daisy yellow top splotched with water stains, returned from helping with the baths. In places the cloth had turned almost transparent. Matt chastised himself for noticing.

"I tell you, Dean, your kids are like otters in a tub. No one gets out of there dry," Annie said, but smiled showing she didn't mind. "Your turn to read a book and get them settled."

"More like octopi when you try to pry them out of the water. You'd swear they had suckers on their behinds. Off to do my daddy duty." Dean left, leaving Matt alone with Annie.

"Um, I wonder if you could drive me to the hospital to see Daniel and then take me over to the new house. Don't worry, by Thursday I'll have my own ride again."

She offered him that smile that warmed him as much as the coffee. "Here I thought you just wanted to experience being cramped into the front seat of my subcompact one last time."

"That too." An answering smile crept across his lips but he quickly suppressed it. "I have my bag packed. If we put it in your trunk, you can drop me at my place, and I won't have to bother Dean again. That is, if you have nothing better to do tonight."

Annie simply answered, "I'd be happy to visit Daniel and take you home."

A thought flickered through his mind that she might mean her apartment until he recalled she lived with her sister and wasn't the kind of woman to hit on a man so obviously. "Thanks, that would be great. I'll get my suitcase, say my good-byes, and offer undying gratitude to Dean and Stacy for all they—and you— have done." At least, some things were undying.

On the drive to the hospital, Annie filled him in on the grocery purchases, where they'd stowed his belongings in the kitchen, and how the former toy chest would make a great coffee table if cleaned up and waxed.

"My dad made it. Over the years it went from holding toys to trophies. After Mellie and I married, it ended up in the basement of our house, not nice enough to be seen, too old and battered. I always regretted that." Matt fell silent after making the speech. Once again, he felt disloyal to Melinda simply because she preferred new furniture.

"Around here we venerate the old and battered. That chest is another heirloom for Daniel—or you might want to make one especially for him." Annie certainly knew how to soothe.

"He doesn't even have a crib waiting for him. We were going to buy baby furniture here."

"Stacy and I will be happy to help with that. I do suggest you paint the walls a color other than pink."

"That goes to the top of my list."

Annie handed over a receipt from a charity for the

donation of Mellie's clothes. "They do great work with abused women and the clothing sales support their efforts. It's tax deductible."

Matt took a quick glance at the sum Stacy had written on the slip, surprised by the high amount. He crumpled it into a pocket. No way did he intend to profit from Mellie's death. "We left each other everything in the wills we drew up when we knew a baby was on the way. When my wife's insurance policy pays off, I intend to start a savings account for Daniel." Annie nodded at him as if she expected nothing less.

Arriving at the hospital after another crunched ride, Annie went to change into her clean scrubs, and Matt washed up for the visit. A new tube sprouted from Daniel's nose. He'd wait for Annie to explain. Taking his place by his son's incubator, Matt said his brief prayer and started to talk softly to his son.

"Well, buddy, I'm sleeping in the house your mom picked out for us tonight. Pink is not my color, but I have to say the place is more comfortable than here. One day, you'll be coming home with me." Annie arrived, and he asked immediately, "New tube?"

Annie checked Daniel's chart and gave that reassuring smile he noticed she practiced in the NICU. "Good news. Daniel is starting on breast milk. He's too young to suckle, so we deliver it by a tube into his stomach. In fact, your son is due for an infusion in a few minutes. Preemies are like baby birds that need to be fed often and in small amounts."

"Hey, he's wearing the smallest diaper I've ever seen."

"What goes in must come out. That is also important progress."

"Should I leave while you feed him?"

"No, you can watch and help us afterward by raising him upright to prevent vomiting. Cuddling is so much nicer than being propped."

Matt tamped down his absolute terror at the prospect of holding his fragile infant by putting on his game face, the grim visage that said he had no fear. Annie appeared to see right through his tough façade. "Nothing to worry about. Just hold him gently in the crook of your arm for thirty minutes so the milk stays down. Ignore all the wires and tubes that come with him for now."

Allowing the nurses on duty to carry out the procedure, Annie stepped aside. Daniel writhed with discomfort as his belly filled. "He doesn't like this. Is he in pain?" Matt had to ask.

"Some discomfort. Having food in his belly is a new experience, one he will get used to as we all do when we must." Exactly as he had to deal with the loss of his wife and get used to living alone again, Matt supposed.

While the nurse updated Daniel's chart, Annie carefully removed the baby from the incubator and placed him in his father's arms. "Support his head with your elbow and hold him against your chest. Go ahead and talk to him."

"That wasn't so bad, Danny. Milk is good for you. I still drink milk. Not the same kind though." Matt babbled on until he noticed Daniel's head canted against him. The infant's lips pursed as if he nursed. "Can't really help you out with that. I don't have the right equipment. Say, Annie, if he can do this, why not bottle feed him?"

"Daniel isn't strong enough to suckle yet, but he is practicing for when the day comes."

Yeah, when the day comes maybe his daddy wouldn't feel so guilty, so hollow anymore. Matt held the child very still, afraid of what he might dislodge, but Daniel's heart rate evened out all the same. His arm ached from even so light a burden when Annie at last lifted the sleeping baby and returned him to the incubator. "Who's going to hold him when I'm not here?"

"We have a cadre of volunteer rockers during the day. Mostly older women, and some men. If we are busy at night, we might have to prop him up, but I promise if I have the time, I'll hold him for you."

"I think you'll be better at it than me." Matt massaged his cramped arm.

"Don't worry about that. Try to relax next time."

"I'm keeping you from your own bed. We should get going."

"It's not a problem for me. Glad to help."

Matt waited in the lounge until Annie changed into her street clothes again and returned with the scrubs bundled under her arm. "I'm making more laundry for you."

She shook her head in denial. "I have a dozen of these on hand. You never know when you'll be spit or peed upon. Speaking of laundry, you have a niche under the back stairs at your place where an upright washer and dryer should go. I didn't see any large appliances sitting around." They left the heat of the NICU and walked to the parking garage where the night air proved only a tad less warm.

"The house came with most of the built-ins, and we

99

left ours behind when we sold our place. I promised Mellie she could buy new stuff, anything she wanted, even a new car. I guess I tried to bribe her to be happy here. We gave her sister her old one rather than go to the trouble of bringing it here."

"Generous of you."

"Believe me, Dre needs to escape from her mom some of the time. She just got her license too. Best gift we could give her. Anyhow, I figured I'd send my laundry out."

Annie laughed at his impracticality. "Oh, with a baby in the house, you will need a washer and dryer on site. They go through an amazing amount of clothes and bedding. Lots of leaks with infants from all ends. Your nurse will want to do a load every day."

"Okay, I'll take care of it. I'll put it on my list right after getting cable TV set up."

"Now, that's a male priority if I ever heard one," she laughed. Matt joined in, not minding a much-needed chuckle at his expense.

Dark by the time Annie pulled up in front of the pink palace, Matt heaved his suitcase from the trunk and leaned in toward her open window. "Make sure you lock your doors. I don't want to lose you too."

"I'm not going far. Can't get lost. Sleep well, Matt."

He watched her drive away before entering the silent house, more of a home now thanks to her and Stacy. Regardless, he wouldn't sleep well in the king-sized bed upstairs, used as he was to a woman lying beside him.

Chapter Twelve

Annie carefully disengaged all of Daddy Joe's locks and alarms to keep his girls safe in the big city. He added another layer every time one his daughters had a security problem—if you could call Xochi's kidnapping a mere safety issue. Once inside her apartment, she reset them all again and made her way quietly up the dimly lit staircase to the second floor flat. Perhaps, Jude had a long, tough shift and gone to bed early. No such luck.

Her twin sat cross-legged on the purple sofa with a bowl of ice cream in her lap and *NCIS New Orleans* coming to a happy conclusion with music, dancing, and good food showing on the TV. If only real-life cases could be solved in an hour. Though the police continued to investigate, Melinda Keaton's killer had not been found yet, maybe never.

"You're out late for a Tuesday night." Jude licked her spoon. "There's some rocky road left if you want it, though why I should save some for you when you are gone all the time, I don't know."

So, the mood was going to be bitchy. Annie took a deep breath. Maybe her sister had worked with a cranky doctor or lost a patient on the table. "I left you a note. I went over to Dean's place where I ate well. Apple pie and vanilla ice cream for dessert. You could have joined us."

"Stacy actually baked a pie?" Yes, bitchy.

"I bought it which didn't make it any less good."

"They eat early because of their rug rats. You sat around talking about kids and football until ten?"

Annie suppressed the urge to revert back to childhood and say you're not the boss of me. Jude often had been, still was. "We got a lot done at Matt's house today. He's moving in tonight, though I don't think it's a really good idea. Inside, he is as fragile as his son. He needs to be around people."

Jude pointed the spoon at her as if she held a revealing laser light. "I'll bet you went to the NICU and held his hand all night."

"We did go, yes, but he held Daniel for the first time, not my hand. You should have seen it, that big man and his tiny child—so tense he rubbed his arm afterward. He'll get the hang of it." Annie smiled at the endearing memory, and Jude pounced.

"Do you baby all the parents this way, spending your time off at the NICU instead of getting away from it for a while? The guy should grow a pair."

"Have a bad day, Jude?" She'd take that route instead of defending Matt, which would only make her twin more vicious, as she knew from experience.

"Not particularly. I assisted Dr. Scully with bypass surgery. The patient needs to lose forty pounds and get off his couch, which I will explain to him tomorrow when I present his new diet and rehab schedule. Scully is a brilliant surgeon but lacks even one iota of bedside manner. I have to provide that for him. Sometimes, I wish he wouldn't request me on his surgery team."

"He does because you aren't scared of him, never drop an instrument, or freeze at a critical point. I've observed you in the operating theater, up there with med students. You should have gone for doctor, not nurse."

"You didn't want to go any higher than nurse practitioner."

"I found something I loved to do. You could have moved on without me."

Jude scraped her bowl round and round, gathering enough melted ice cream to prevent her from answering immediately. "I know. You'd take home every one of those babies if you could and devote your entire life to them, leaving nothing for yourself. You nearly do now—and this thing with Matt Keaton can easily get out of hand and hurt you. Me, I don't get attached to my patients like that. It's safer that way."

Jude unfolded from the couch, took her dish to the kitchen sink, and hand washed it. "You'd better not give away our Sacred Sister Thursdays to that man. I'm going to bed."

"I won't. Sleep tight." Understanding Jude too well, Annie let her have the last word. That outburst was as much about Jude as it was about Annie. Only twins know all of each other's secrets.

Chapter Thirteen

Matt called in the early afternoon on Wednesday. "Sorry to bother you, Annie. Busy?" he asked immediately.

Absolutely, doing a big load of scrubs for both herself and Jude. Nice to have an interruption. "Not so much."

"Great. I know this is an imposition, but could you take me to see Daniel today? I worked out with Dean all morning and had lunch with his family again. They're going to the aquarium this afternoon. I'm invited, but I'd rather go to the NICU than butt in on their family time. My SUV isn't ready yet. I swear it will be tomorrow. Can you help me out again? I'm at my place, not theirs." He said the last as if trying to prove his independence.

"Frankly, I think you have a passion for my little car and really don't want a huge SUV."

His voice eased. "Maybe so."

"I can pick you up in an hour, but I have to be back before six."

"Sure, I understand. Maybe you have a date, a cute girl like you."

Good thing he couldn't see her slim, dark eyebrows shoot up, high, high. "Matt, I'm a few years older than you. I haven't been a girl for some time."

"I didn't mean to insult you! I meant you are petite

and pretty and probably have a lot of men in your life."

"True, but most of them are my brothers, the doctors I work with, or little guys the size of Daniel. Don't worry about it. I'll see you soon."

"I can't thank you enough. Say, after I get my SUV on Thursday I should take you for a ride and maybe to dinner for all you've done."

Sacred Sister Thursday, no way. As it was, she'd have to pretend she'd been home all afternoon doing laundry or suffer another bitter lecture from Jude about enabling Matt. Annie regretted deeply what she had to say next. "I'm busy on Thursday."

She realized by his disappointed tone that he'd taken her refusal to heart. "I understand. You have a life outside the NICU."

Not hardly, but better to begin some separation now before he became too dependent on her. Still, she couldn't resist adding. "Any Tuesday or Wednesday would be good."

"Right. Glad to know that. In an hour, then."

"I'll be there." Talk about separation, she almost hated to hang up like some lovelorn teen on the phone. You hang up first, no, you. Annie managed to squeeze out the final word. "Bye."

****

Matt waited on his doorstep and bounded to her car like a huge, eager chocolate Labrador retriever the moment she arrived. As soon as she popped the locks, he crushed himself inside, assuming his usual hunched position of knees practically under his chin. He seemed more invigorated today, another good sign. Cleaving to the NICU rules, he smelled pleasantly of a mild soap, freshly laundered clothes, and a clean shave.

Annie inhaled with appreciation. "Did you sleep well last night?"

Matt's head immediately turned toward the quiet, tree-lined streets of the Garden District passing by. "Not really, new place, new sounds, you know how it goes."

She could imagine the void of the pink palace after dark without the cable TV hooked up. Perhaps, only the trickle of the fountain by the patio provided soothing white noise. He'd probably spent the evening with only an iPhone for company clutched in his big hands. "You'd never know it. You look pretty lively." And handsome, best to keep that thought to herself.

"Dean took me out to the practice field to do handoffs and short catches. He brought along another new player, a kid named X-avier Hopkins. The Sinners picked him up cheap on the low end of the draft from some small college. He's real particular about that X in his name and kind of a showboat, but full of fun. What he lacks in size, he makes up for in energy."

Oh, Annie knew X-avier. "He sang at my brother Teddy's wedding. Quite the character. Dean says he's fast and agile."

"Like a heat-seeking missile."

"What does Dean call you?"

"The Tank. He says he can give me the ball, and I'll roll right over the opposition with it."

Annie had to laugh. "Oh, now you're in trouble. Not only will you have to live up to that, but the whole team will call you Tank. Remember the kicker, Howdy McCoy? He's Tom's stepfather and mentor. He walks into the locker room the first day of training wearing his cowboy hat and greets everyone with a big, 'Howdy.'

Now, no one remembers his real name is Howard. People are big on nicknames around here."

"I've never had one before and don't mind if it catches on with the team, but I'd like you to call me Matt."

Annie took her gaze off the road for a second to meet his. He said those words so sincerely, his eyes sorrowful and deep, deep brown. "I wouldn't think of you any other way." Back to navigating the often crazy New Orleans traffic. Regardless of her straying thoughts, she got them safely to the NICU. No sense in making Daniel an orphan because she couldn't keep her mind on business.

They had their routine down pat: checking in, her changing to scrubs, washing up, her studying Danny's chart while Matt said his prayer and began talking to his son close to the port of the incubator with his hands resting on his knees. Annie requested that Matt hold the baby after his next infusion due in five minutes. On duty, Bess had no problem with it. "Since we added breast milk, that tiny one is growing like a chicory weed. He's at 1,320 grams."

Matt glanced up at the news. Annie did the conversion. "Nearly, but not quite three pounds, a nice gain."

"That is good. Congratulations," said Junelle Wagner from a rocking chair where she burped Arielle. "My girl is almost seven pounds now. We hoped she'd be going home, but she failed the car seat test."

Matt experimented with the new word in his vocabulary. "Bradycardia?"

"Yes." Junelle's usually positive smile drooped. "Maybe next week."

"Hey, I'm going to pray I don't see you here next week, that you'll be at home with Arielle. Maybe when she can have guests, I'll stop by to see how well she's doing."

"Really? My husband, all of us, would love that."

"Absolutely. Annie, would you put Mrs. Wagner's number into my phone? I wouldn't want to just show up and wake the baby."

"I'd be happy to do that." Annie had the pleasure of groping his hip again to get the phone and fulfill his request. She hung onto it. "I want to take a photo of you holding Daniel before I wash again. You can send it to his Aunt Dre—and I'll bet she'll share it with others."

"I'm not certain about that. Who's going to lift Daniel if you're holding the camera?"

"Bess will. I keep telling you we are all competent professionals."

"Yeah, ain't I got two good hands?" Bess teased in mock anger, hands on hips.

"Sorry, Bess," he told the large black woman with the gentle hands who prepared to feed Daniel through his nose tube. "I guess I thought Daniel would know Annie better."

"Should know us all by now as well as he can at this stage, but no offense taken. We get nervous daddies all the time. Won't be long before he can take a bottle, and that will be nice for the both of you."

"It is," Junelle agreed. "Feeding your baby is the best feeling in the world."

Matt smiled her way. "I don't have your equipment, but I'll try."

Again, Daniel squirmed and struggled while the nurse filled his tiny belly with milk, but bundled and placed in his father's arms, he quieted again. The infant's lips pursed seeking that imaginary breast. Annie took the picture. "Give Danny the tip of your little finger to suck. It's good practice for him," she suggested.

Matt complied. "Look at that! He's not very strong, but he is latching on. Good, right?"

"Very good." Annie caught his elation with another snap of the phone's camera. She eased it back into his pocket. With Matt so enraptured, she doubted he noticed her hand on his backside—as it should be. Terrible that she enjoyed it so. She made herself useful to the staff rather than simply stand in their way.

Time ticked by until she noticed they'd be caught in rush hour traffic if they didn't get a move on. Annie reached to tap Matt's shoulder and realized both he and Daniel slept deep in the rocker where they'd settled. "Bess, would you take the baby before I wake Matt?"

"My pleasure. We don't want any wires ripped loose if either one startles." She eased Danny up and out of the way.

Free of the baby, Matt instantly sat bolt upright and clenched his arm to his chest as if he protected a football. "Did I fumble? I mean did I drop him."

"No, no, you simply dozed off. We kept an eye on Daniel. See, he's back in his bed again. You did exactly what you were supposed to do, kept him upright and warm, soothing him with the beat of your heart. However, it is time to go."

He didn't argue, just waited patiently for Annie to put on street clothes again and walk out with her. "I'm aware that I'm taking up a lot of your free time. How about I repay you with an early dinner—that is if you don't have plans to eat later with someone else."

"Someone else would be my sister. I planned to cook for her tonight since she was awfully grouchy last evening."

"How about we get her a dinner to go?"

She shouldn't, she really should not, but Annie succumbed. "Okay, how about The Palace. It's near my place. One of the Brennan's runs it. The food is great like most food in New Orleans. If it isn't, a restaurant will be gone in under a year."

"Sounds good even if I don't know who Brennan is."

"Stay here, and you will."

They parked by Annie's apartment, but didn't go inside. Instead, they walked to the restaurant on bustling Canal Street.

"Indoor or outdoor seating?" Matt asked Annie, being the complete gentleman.

"Inside. There's too much traffic this time of day, and the heat doesn't make it more pleasant. It's a great place to get a drink in the evening and people watch." Better not to be spied by the paparazzi or sighted by Tom or Xochi from their condos across the street, a ridiculous fear because she knew them all to be out of town right now. Why would they care if they saw her with Matt, anyhow? Maybe because the news would spread through the family like water from a broken levee, and she'd get a call from Mama Nell telling her Matt needed time to grieve. Of course, she'd be right.

Possibly recognizing Annie Billodeaux and surmising by his size that she came accompanied by a Sinner, the hostess led them to an excellent table away from the mainstream of customers and waiters. Glad to be out of sight in case Jude returned home early, Annie relaxed and enjoyed the atmosphere of the old Werlein building. She ordered the light Catfish Pecan with rice and veggies. Matt went heavy with a twelve-ounce chargrilled ribeye and potatoes. He shook his head over the prices, but not because of cost. He wondered aloud that beef ran so much higher than good seafood.

"Because the Gulf of Mexico is just down river. Lots of fresh fish available all the time. I'd encourage you to try more of it, though the steak will be good." He was so new to everything, the climate, the city, and fatherhood. Matt needed a project to keep him busy until summer training camp started, and it could not be her.

"Have you given any thought about painting Daniel's room? Pale green or light blue would be nice and calming, even tan. They'd blend with the rest of the house." She didn't voice anything but pink. "My brothers had wallpaper borders in their rooms, football players for Dean and horses for Tom, but you have nice crown moldings that only need a fresh coat of white enamel to shine."

"I haven't thought about it at all. I guess there is plenty of time." Matt sipped his red wine. Annie mirrored him with a glass of white.

"You want to get it done and all the fumes out of the room well before the baby comes home."

"Then, I'd better get on it. How about next Wednesday? I can pick up the paint and brushes and the other stuff I'll need. You paint the bottom, and I'll go high. Maybe Stacy and Dean will help too."

Had she set him up simply to be near him? Annie examined her conscience and thought not, but answered, "Next Wednesday would be great. We should start early before the heat builds."

Fortunately, their food arrived before she dug herself in any deeper. Annie and Matt passed the time swiftly. The traffic lessened. Annie checked her watch and ordered another Catfish Pecan meal to go. They did have enough time for dessert.

"Would you like to have some fun?" That came out all wrong. Nothing like seeing a big man startle.

"What kind of fun?" he answered cautiously.

"Dessert, I meant dessert! How about Bananas Foster with two spoons? I'm too full for one of my own."

"Okay, I've heard of it. Let's do this."

The cart came to their table. The show began as the chef sautéed bananas in brown sugar, added banana liqueur and rum, and flambéed the whole dish in a blaze of blue fire that turned eyes their way. They shared dessert served over vanilla ice cream with two spoons until Annie's takeout arrived, and she noticed the clock had turned to seven. Jude would be wending her way home. She prayed for heavy traffic between Canal and the hospital. Stuffing the remaining heel of their French bread into the go-box, Annie stood up and got ready to run like Cinderella at the stroke of midnight.

"I need to get Jude's dinner home. She'll want to eat right away."

"Just a second while I pay the bill, and I'll walk you home."

"You don't have to do that. It's so nearby."

"This isn't a safe city. I could stop in and say hello to your sister. I haven't seen her since we had dinner with your parents—before Mellie died."

There, a lovely evening ruined. "She's usually tired and out of sorts when she gets home. Some other time."

"I wouldn't want to get on her bad side—but I still need a ride home. Forget that. I can get a cab at one of the hotels or walk. I keep asking too much of you."

"Not at all. Let's walk fast, and I'll get you home."

In the cul-de-sac, Annie tossed the box in the backseat while Matt curled into the front. Mentally, she cursed every red light on the way. Still, Matt didn't hop out immediately when they arrived.

"Thanks, that was a great meal and a nice evening. Mellie would have loved it—except for not being allowed wine," he said with a slight, bereft smile. Annie guessed there would be no good-bye kiss, not even a peck on the cheek.

Matt got out. Annie took off before he'd opened his gate. At least, his parting words had snuffed the romantic glow out of the evening. If Jude found out where she'd been and with whom, her sister would crush what embers remained beneath her heels.

Sweating despite the A/C turned on high, she swerved into the cul-de-sac so glad Jude's car didn't yet occupy its usual space close to the dumpster. Cursing all the devices that had to be unlocked and disarmed before she could get inside, Annie grabbed the takeout and bolted up the stairs. She shoved the box into the fridge and the washed scrubs into their small dryer. By the time Jude worked her way through the security and padded up the stairs on her quiet nurse's shoes, Annie sat on the purple couch sipping a piping hot herbal tea she'd nuked only a minute ago. Casually, she channel-surfed.

"Have a better day, Jude?"

"Not bad. Anything for dinner?" She opened the refrigerator and spied the box. "Good leftovers?"

"A whole meal from The Palace. I had one too. Pecan Catfish."

"Yum." Jude ripped the top of the box off and shoved the bottom into the microwave after removing the bread and slathering it with butter. The microwave dinged. Jude rejoined Annie on the sofa to scarf up her meal. "Thanks, great idea. We usually save a nice restaurant meal for Sacred Sister Thursdays. What's the occasion?"

"Nothing but a craving for good food." Hating to lie to her twin, Annie huffed out a deep sigh.

"Wait a minute!" Jude paused with a forkful of fish and rice halfway to her mouth. "You cheated on me."

"What? I had a glass of wine with my meal." Two actually.

"No, I smell Bananas Foster on your breath. You didn't bring any for me."

"The ice cream would have melted long before you got home. We'll share one tomorrow. My treat. Pick whatever you want to do, and I won't whine about it."

"Sounds like a deal to me. Thanks for the dinner."

"Don't thank me. It's what sisters do, right?"

"Definitely." Jude changed the channel from a PBS show to *Survivor*. "I'll tell you what. We can spend a couple of hours at the aquarium before I drag you through the discount mall. Then, we both have something to enjoy on the agenda."

"Sounds good to me," though Annie knew Matt might like the aquarium far more than her sister.

****

In the stillness of his home, Matt tried to enjoy

114

some sit-coms of happy if eccentric families, not in the mood for the conniving of *Survivor* or anything violent. He was a team player, not an attention-grabber, one of the reasons the Sinners sought him out. Dean cultivated a feeling of camaraderie among the players with Tom acting as his merry prankster and himself as the captain who steered the ship to victory with all aboard. The way he'd taken Matt in after his tragedy and worked with him on his own time made this running back forever grateful.

Bundling his TV, phone, and Wi-Fi, he'd gotten a technician to the house to hook up all forms of entertainment that failed to keep him occupied. His den was small compared to Dean's man cave, and two large recliners filled the space. He leaned back, tried to rest, failed. His gilded trophies on the mantel reflected the flickering scenes on the television mounted above them. Matt leaned forward again and opened his childhood toy chest. Yes, the game balls still resided within its dark interior. He guessed the women found no space for them. Selecting one at random, he carried it to the kitchen, discovered a dishtowel exactly where he thought it should be near the sink, and swaddled the ball. The best sleep he'd had since Mellie's death were those precious minutes in the NICU today, deep and sound with Daniel in his arms. The football was bigger than his son and weightier, but this might work. He turned down the television to a low murmur as if other people, happy, funny people, occupied his house. Footrest up, head leaning back in the deep cushions, he cradled the ball in the crook of his arm—and slept. He woke to the sound of a cheery talk show host Thursday morning.

Chapter Fourteen

Annie and Jude dubbed the day Sacred Sister Thursday early on after their move from Baton Rouge to New Orleans. Though Annie sought peace and separation from her more turbulent twin, she could hardly say no to rooming with her when Jude also landed a job at Ochsner. They'd argued over Annie's decision to work on the weekend night shift. Sure, the pay was great, but Jude considered Annie to be martyring herself to her neonates. "No way would I work hours like that and kill my own social life," Jude let her know.

Their compromise became Sacred Sister Thursdays, the only day they had time off together, to be devoted to their bond as twins. The morning began well enough. They mutually agreed to go to the coffee shop across the street for lattes and a plate of croissants, plain, almond, and chocolate, the last one to be split between them, and all eaten at a leisurely pace since Jude generally grabbed a bowl of cereal before leaving the house early when she was on duty.

After that, a stroll to the aquarium at the base of Canal Street to spend a few hours viewing the silently swimming fishes and feeding the ravenous parakeets in the bird room. "It's like being in a Hitchcock movie," Jude complained. "When you walk out after being pecked and shit upon, you have your screaming kids and tourists jammed up against all the best exhibits. We had to inch along in the steaming jungle room simply to get out of it. I don't know why you have an annual pass."

"I like to come here for some serenity on my days off."

A child reluctant to leave the birds, howled and had to be dragged through the plastic flaps that kept the avians inside. "Serenity, my tattooed ass. Listen to that ruckus."

"Usually, I go to the hall of jellyfish. It's dark there and lovely to watch them float. The new seahorse exhibit is great. Sometimes, the males give birth right before your eyes."

"I wish human males did that. Think about what Mom went through with those multiple births because Dad wanted a big family, and he insisted they use all of their frozen embryos."

Annie disagreed. "Mom wasn't forced. She wanted children as much as he did."

"You say."

"You promised not to complain. Almost time for the sea otter show. We need to hustle to get a good spot."

They arrived too late and ended up smashed behind a tall couple with small children clinging to their shoulders. Jude tapped the man's shoulder. "Could you let us in front. You're blocking the view."

"She meant please." Annie tried to deflect any parental rage.

The daddy turned. His little blonde daughter clung to his black hair like an infant chimp, but considerably cuter. Dean offered them his best teasing grin.

"Anything for my tee-tiny sisters."

Wynn held out her arms. "Auntie Annie."

"Smart girl. It's dim in here. I don't know how you tell us apart."

"You're the one who smiles when you see me."

That made Jude deepen her frown. "You'd better stay put on the big lout's shoulders. With Annie holding you, you won't see a thing."

Leggy, blonde Stacy half-turned, careful not to unseat DJ. "Squeeze in front of us and hush. They're about to start."

"You know this how?"

"Because we were here yesterday. The kids loved it so much, we came back today."

"I don't see your adopted brother, Matt Keaton. He doesn't like to eat fish or see them?" Jude pushed through the narrow opening between Stacy and Dean. Annie followed closely.

"Oh, we invited him both times, but yesterday he went to the NICU with Annie and today he is picking up his new car and choosing paint for Daniel's room. I guess we'll be helping him with that next week."

"Shush!" Annie whispered. "Let's listen to the show." Too late since she felt Jude stiffen beside her.

The trainers ran through demonstrating the sea otters' various behaviors and rewarding them with treats frozen into small balls of ice. The children squealed with delight. Slowly the clot of viewers dissipated and released the Billodeauxs from the blockage. "Penguins, penguins," Wynn chanted, encouraging her brother to do the same.

"Okay, quiet down. Penguins next. You walking or riding?" their daddy asked.

118

"Riding," both offspring declared.

"You want to take her now, Annie, and I'll relieve Stacy of DJ?" Dean said.

Though Annie held out her arms, Jude interrupted. "I've put in enough time here. We're heading for the mall. See you there. Maybe."

Stacy shook her head. "Not likely. Probably Lucky Dogs for us. Go on. I know your Thursdays are sacred."

The air outside the aquarium was no steamier than Jude's attitude. She chugged toward the Outlet Collection at the Riverwalk like a tugboat passing on the Mississippi, pushing Annie before her. As soon as she attained the cool interior of the mall, she turned on her sister.

"Don't you see Matt Keaton is using you!"

"He apologized for taking up so much of my time."

"Users always apologize. After what we went through together, you must realize that."

"He's never laid a hand on me. Still too hung up on his wife to move on yet. After I take him to the NICU, he always wants to buy me breakfast or dinner for helping him."

"Ah-ha! You shared Bananas Foster with that man."

Annie could be pushed, but only so far. She stopped dead in her tracks and folded her arms under her small chest. "Next time you see him, thank him for your dinner too. He didn't have to do that."

"Right, butter up the other sister to stay on your good side. We know how that works." Jude's voice rose and echoed in the vault of the mall. A security guard glanced their way.

Annie replied, "Coffee and beignets on the upper

119

level, right now."

"You can't buy me off with beignets."

"No, but with something in your mouth you might stop shouting at me."

This time, Annie headed off under her own steam, leaving it up to Jude to follow or not. By the time she'd ordered two *au laits* and the square donuts buried in powdered sugar, Jude caught up and snatched a table near the window before two elderly women with a tray could reach the spot.

"See, I always look out for you," Jude gloated. "Best view in the place."

Annie contemplated a cruise ship docked on the river and wished she might sail away, preferably with Matt Keaton, and not her sister. She knew she risked her heart by getting attached to this stricken man and his fragile son so quickly, but the way Matt cared for his infant and remained so clueless about how to handle him made her reach out exactly the way she opened her arms to any helpless child. She must be patient and kind, see how things developed between them.

"You do, but sometimes I have to follow my own path."

"I don't want to see you get hurt or waste your life caring for a child not even yours."

"Caring for a child is never a waste. I think our parents would agree. They've raised several not even theirs."

"Kids take over your life, destroy careers, make you do dumb stuff. Look at Stacy and Xo with their talent for foreign languages. Stacy only does translations at the hospital if they call and doesn't charge for it. Xochi piddles around with prayers and herbs. Mom is just recently immersing herself fully in psychology again."

"Neither Mom nor Stacy or Xochi needs to earn a living. They give back to others because they want to share their fortunate lives. They do a ton of good." The coffee had cooled during their debate, one they'd held before. Annie took a deep swallow. She harbored no appetite for the beignets.

"But, we do. Are you going to throw away a career you worked hard to attain for some needy guy?" Jude shook a beignet in her direction and iced herself with a snow of powdered sugar. She brushed it from her chest and took a bite.

"Listen to me, Jude. I'm going over to Carter's Babies and Kids to get some clothes for Daniel. They carry preemie sizes. Though he doesn't need them right now, the child has nothing. I'm starting a layette for him. Shop where you want and meet me there. Get something to improve your mood. Then, lunch and that Bananas Foster I promised you."

Annie picked up her plate of untouched donuts and carried it to where the two elderly women shared a single order. "I'm not going to eat these. I'm dieting. Please enjoy."

"How kind of you but are you sure your twin sister doesn't want them?" said the one with her cane propped up against a chair.

Annie glanced toward her sister. Jude finished her beignets and sat brooding over the remains of her coffee.

"No, she's had plenty today."

"You certainly don't need to lose weight," the other, who had carried the tray, remarked. "Neither of you."

"Thank you. If you want the space by the window, I believe my sister is leaving too."

"Oh, we're fine here. The young and swift win the race."

"Not always. Have a wonderful day." Annie strode off to indulge herself in buying baby clothes. If Jude wanted to join her for lunch that would be fine.

Chapter Fifteen

On hands and knees, Annie and Stacy washed the baseboards while Matt and Dean prepped the nursery walls for its coat of light blue paint. Sun streamed through the small panes of the semi-circular windows in the tower room. Annie rocked back on her heels and observed, "You'll need custom curtains to darken the space for Daniel's naps."

Looming over her, Matt replied, "I'll add it to my list. Can you tell me where to get custom curtains?"

"We know some interior designers that will help, and I'm always glad to give you my opinion," Stacy said.

"She sure is, all the time." Dean swatted his wife on her backside since she remained on all fours when she made the remark.

"Dean Billodeaux, be grateful I don't bite you in your calf muscle for that and ruin your football season."

Dean backed away. "She would too. Gotta be careful around the Billodeaux girls. Annie seems all gentle, but she bit me more than once as a child. I was practically her teething ring."

"More than half the time it was Jude, not me. Anyhow, Mawmaw Nadine cured us of biting by putting a little hot sauce on our tongue every time we did. I learned my lesson. Jude developed a taste for Tabasco."

"You really aren't much like your sister, are you?" Matt said.

"Not anymore."

Dean wouldn't let the topic go. "Be careful, Matt. They are entirely capable of pulling a switcheroo on people. Jude is quite the actress when she wants to be. Loves drama."

Matt's smile broadened. "Oh, I think I know a way to tell them apart."

"Tell, tell." Stacy insisted.

"Nope, sworn to secrecy. Why don't you give us the bucket, and we'll clean the cornices? Maybe put out whatever lunch you brought in that picnic basket in the kitchen. Bet it will be terrific. We can paint after we eat. You go low. We'll go high."

"Sounds like a plan. My knees are aching anyhow. Coming, Annie?"

Stacy stood and stretched with an arch of her back, so sexy Annie experienced envy of the tall and busty. Her eyes went to Matt's face to gauge his reaction. Nothing. He accepted the bucket she handed him, scaled the short ladder Dean brought to reach the high crown molding, and went back to work.

Stacy led the way down the back stairs to the kitchen. "Great, now we can speak in private. How is the baby really doing? I hope we aren't setting Matt up for more heartbreak by preparing a room that might never be used."

"Daniel is progressing quite well, putting on weight like a lineman. His breathing is still a concern, but we're keeping an eye on that. No reason to believe he won't go home by the end August like any full-term baby."

Stacy opened the refrigerator and eyed the contents. "I see Matt is using the milk, juice, and cold cuts, the fruit too. He's restocked the beer." She opened the freezer and removed the ice bin. "He hasn't touched the prepared meals. They're all heat and serve. No skill required. Do you think he might be drinking too much?"

"No. He usually shows up at the NICU around six a.m. to spend time with Daniel. No sign of a hangover that I've ever noticed. When we have breakfast or dinner together, he eats well, limits alcohol in the evenings."

That drew Stacy's attention away from filling glasses with ice for the lemonade. "Having breakfast and dinner together is a regular thing with you now? I gathered at the aquarium Jude is aggravated by the time you spend with Matt."

"I've made it clear to Jude whatever I do with Matt is not her concern. Yes, breakfast because we leave the NICU at the same time, dinner last Wednesday to repay me for the rides I've given, and last night to show me the paint he got for the room in case I thought it needed to go back. Since I arrived near dinner time, we went out for a bite. I know he isn't starving himself to death for sure."

Annie delved into the picnic basket and removed the sandwiches, two doorstopper-sized ham, roast beef, turkey, and provolone fully dressed New Orleans style with mayo, tomato, lettuce, and a ring or two of red onion piled on sour dough bread, plus two daintier versions for the women. "Wow, did you go to Central Grocery for these?"

"No, my own very modified version of a

muffuletta. We have individual bags of Zapp's chips, the Crawtators or plain in case Matt isn't on board with spicy yet."

"He's beginning to catch on to Cajun levels of heat since most of the food here comes that way but given a chance he'll retreat to steak." Knowing Stacy was just too shrewd, she kept her eyes on the contents of the basket, placed a packet of pickles and olives on the table, and fanned out a handful of individually wrapped pralines for the dessert. When Annie glanced up again, she realized she'd given herself away by avoiding Stacy's eyes. Better to have bluffed by staring her down. She tried misdirection. "I gather we aren't watching our calories today."

"When you make a meal for men as big as Dean and Matt, you simply have to pace yourself with a smaller version of the same. Feel free to skip the chips and pralines. There are apples in the fridge." But Stacy would not be diverted. "It seems you are getting to know Matt awfully well in a very short time. I see why Jude might be concerned."

"Not in that way. We are together in a crisis situation in the NICU, plus I'm trying to help him move forward. That's why I suggested we begin preparing the nursery."

"I don't read auras like Xochi, but your big, brown eyes go all soft and warm when you look at Matthew Keaton while he appears oblivious—mostly."

"He's still grieving his wife of course. What do you mean by mostly?"

"This man gets up at five a.m., showers, shaves, dresses, and shows up at the NICU at six whenever you are on duty. He leaves when you do and buys you breakfast. At least, I'm presuming he pays."

"I've told him not to, but he always reaches the cashier before I do on those long legs of his. I think he and Leola are in cahoots about the bill." Annie's smile peeped out before she could stop it.

"What time does he go to the NICU when you aren't there?"

"That varies. Whenever he has time, I guess. He visits every day according to the guest log."

"Does he buy other nurses a meal?"

"He's offered to take Peggy, but she always turns him down."

"I think I've made my point. You don't know where this is going yet. Don't get hurt."

"Yes, Jude. I mean Stacy. If I get hurt, I'll recover. I've learned that."

The men thundered down the backstairs as if they entered a stadium, but they held out their hands for inspection like grimy children hungry for lunch. "We washed once we finished the cornices. What do we have to eat?" Dean questioned. "Muffulettas?"

"No, I made the sandwiches. It's my own version. I didn't know how Matt felt about olive salad. This will prepare him for the real deal. Zapp's kettle chips, pickles, olives, and pralines."

They gathered 'round the kitchen table, but Matt hesitated for a moment. "I have beer in the refrigerator. I picked up a six-pack of that Turbo Dog you recommended, Dean."

"The lemonade is fresh. I used the juicer to make it." Stacy had already filled the glasses from a thermos jug and set them in place.

Dean, adept at being a husband, said, "Lemonade

now and a beer after we finish."

That settled, they ate, the men concentrating on the food and the women debating toile curtains that would have more longevity versus something like blue puppies for a little boy's room. Since the walls were pale, the furnishings needed to be white or light oak Annie and Stacy decided. "Matt, which one?"

Perplexed, his broad forehead wrinkled, then smoothed. "Mellie would want the light oak. She didn't like dark furniture. Dean, toile or puppy curtains, help me out here."

"Ah, I just play football. I don't know toile from a blue puppy's behind."

"We'll get some samples to help you decide," Stacy assured the new father.

"Oh, I almost forgot." Annie withdrew a large bag she'd stashed under the table and drew out a tiny tan outfit with a cap made perky by bear's ears. "The striped elephant onesie with the beanie is just as cute. There's lots more. I sort of went nuts in Carter's buying preemie clothes."

"Neither of my children would have fit in those the day they were born, but oh so adorable." Stacy gushed.

"Okay, they're using words like cute and adorable. Time we started painting, Matt, before we lose our manhood." Pocketing a few spare pralines for a snack, Dean got up.

Matt moved his hand toward his back pocket. "What do I owe you for the clothing?"

"My gift to Daniel. I've washed everything in Dreft. You can take a few outfits into the NICU when you visit." Though, Annie would gladly have fished his wallet out for him as she did his phone every time he stopped by on her watch.

"You do too much for me, Annie. At least I'm not bumming rides from you anymore. How about dinner tonight to repay you? You, too, Dean and Stacy, for helping out today." Since he kept his eyes on Annie, the rest came out as an afterthought.

"We'd have to get a sitter. Not easy at the last moment," Stacy said, frowning.

"How about a pizza place? Bring the kids. I need to get used to eating with children."

"Mona Lisa on Royal Street? They have great chicken parm and lasagna, too. We need to go early before it gets crowded," Annie suggested.

Dean clapped his hands as if the play clock ran down. "That's settled. Let's paint!"

Annie had done it again, allowed herself to have dinner with Matt Keaton. Leftovers for Jude.

Chapter Sixteen

The breakfast bar offered pancakes today. Matt stacked his high and surrounded them with bacon and sausage. Annie succumbed to having two with bacon, abandoning her usual eggs or oatmeal. She'd given up trying to pay for her meal, given up trying not to enjoy her time with Matt so much.

"Three and a half pounds, my boy is three and a half pounds. That's great, isn't it?" Matt searched for Annie's affirmation.

"Yes, he's ahead of the curve on weight, length, and head circumference." Let the doctor destroy his optimism with the breathing problem, not her. "You got my parents' invitation to come to the ranch for the Fourth of July celebration, right?"

"Your dad called. I said I'd let him know, and he said just to come if I wanted. One more or less didn't make any difference. I'm getting a refill on coffee. Can I bring you a decaf?"

"No, I'm good. You should go to the party. A lot of Sinners will be there, new and old. The food is wonderful, and we have dragon boat races and fireworks. The pool is open and the volleyball and basketball courts. They'll have the horses saddled for those who want to ride. It is chaotic, and my family is overwhelming, but all in good fun."

"Will you be there?"

Simply by looking at him she knew he wouldn't go if she didn't. "Attendance is practically mandatory for me. The only one of the Billodeaux children who gets out of this is Lorena because she's playing volleyball in Australia. Even Mack will put in a grudging appearance and be expected to put up with the razzing about the Sinners outplaying his team, the Cowboys. I do start my shift that night, but I'll be there for the cookout at noon, the races, and to collect my sack of leftovers before I leave. It's a shame to miss the fireworks over the bayou, but you should stay to enjoy them."

"No. What if something should go wrong with Daniel while I'm having a good time?" He crushed a crisp bacon strip beneath the tines of his fork.

"Any crisis will be handled, and you will be notified. After all, once the preseason games start, you won't always be in town. Trust the hospital."

"I trust *you*. How about if we go together? I'll drive you right to the hospital in the evening, spend some time with Daniel, and tell him all about the picnic. I've seen fireworks before, and maybe by next year, he'll get to see them for the first time."

No graceful way to say no, and she didn't want to anyhow. "It's a date." Poor phrasing. She rushed to correct. "Driving to the ranch and back in one day is taxing. Generally, I'd stay overnight if I had off, but if you want to be my chauffeur, that's fine. My mom will pay you in leftovers, and I'll kick in gas money for the new Escalade."

"No need. We're friends helping each other out, but I won't turn down the food." Contented, Matt finished demolishing his tall stack. Not as content to be merely his friend, Annie blotted her lips of syrup, done.

****

Matt arrived in the cul-de-sac at seven a.m. sharp. He followed his instructions exactly to summon Annie from her apartment by ringing the bell twice, standing aside, and waiting as if he were a date she didn't want her parents to meet. A minute later the door slammed open.

"Hi, Annie." The woman scowled at him. "No, you're Jude. Sorry for the mix-up. We've only met once before, Matthew Keaton." He held out a hand she declined to shake.

"My sister will be down shortly. See you at the ranch." She strode to the car that matched Annie's, though hers was red, not the color most small cars came in—black, made a U-turn tight enough to miss the dumpster, but barely missing Matt and his large Escalade as she joined the never-ending stream of traffic moving past their corner.

Matt stared after her as the car's tail lights disappeared. He failed to hear Annie's quiet approach and jumped when she poked him in the back to make her presence known. "I can tell you encountered Jude," she said with a teasing smile on her face.

"Yeah, is it only me she hates or all men? She must have had a really bad experience with some guy."

"You could say that. Mostly she's protective of me. Wait a minute. I have to reset the alarm. I opened the locks and chains earlier since I knew you were coming."

"Jude isn't the only one who is protective, I guess."

"No, my dad seems to add another layer every year." Annie used the keypad to secure her door but nodded toward the fire escape. "Smile, you're on

132

Candid Camera."

Matt finally found the security camera cleverly mounted under a step of the fire escape. He grinned and waved before opening the Escalade door and hoisting Annie onto the high front seat. "It's not a joke," she told him. "That camera helped identify the men who kidnapped Xochi two years ago."

"Sorry, didn't mean it to be. I think Mellie mentioned the kidnapping. Human sacrifice involved, right? She had a weakness for the tabloids. Didn't want to be in them, but she loved a sensational story. Getting into the society pages at a charity event was more her style. I don't enjoy them, but she did. I tried to give Mellie what she wanted. I should have gone with her more often." Regret tinged his voice.

Annie ignored the human sacrifice remark and instead commented, "She certainly had a lot of lovely gowns and shoes to match."

"That was what she liked, along with nice jewelry."

Annie went silent as he nosed the SUV into the traffic and made the turn toward the interstate ramp. The burden of conversation fell heavily on Matt. Oblivious as any man, he continued the topic of his deceased wife.

"I paid for our wedding with part of my signing bonus. Told her she could have anything she wanted. Boy, I did not know what I was getting into. Ten bridesmaids chosen from her cousins and sorority sisters. Besides her brothers, I had to ask members of my Notre Dame team to fill in. The girls didn't seem to mind."

"I guess not. A football player is every coed's

dream."

"Yours, too?"

Finally, she loosened up and chuckled. "Oh God, no. I grew up with football players, had one for a dad, plus all his hulking friends. Not to say they weren't nice to us. If not, they'd answer to Dad, and later Dean and Tom. Jude and I never dated team members because they'd been warned away from us."

"Who did you date?"

Annie wrinkled her cute, little nose. At least, Matt thought of her nose that way. "Frat boys, though we didn't join a sorority. My mom said those girls were snobs who wanted to exclude others—but if we really wanted to join, we could. We didn't."

"Is that where Jude had her bad experience?"

"We both had less than wonderful encounters with fraternity boys, but it's not my story to tell." She switched subjects back to his relatives. "Dre wasn't in the wedding?"

"No, Mellie said she was too young. Honestly, they didn't get along, and that was before the Goth stuff."

"Too bad. I'm close to my sisters, all five of them."

"You'd want them in your wedding?"

"Every one of them. Ignore your GPS, take the next exit and go the back way. We don't want to drive through the Baton Rouge traffic."

Matt made the turn that took them out of the city and over a vast swampy area with cypress trees towering by the side of the raised highway. "Anyhow, we had stretch limos taking us from the church to the house, big, white tents on the lawn of the Ames' home, live band, champagne fountain, open bar, four-course dinner, and a cake big enough to house the family chickens who were locked up for the day. Orchid centerpieces, shrimp cocktails, all that stuff, honeymoon in Hawaii."

"Did you have a good time?"

"Mellie did, and that's what counted. A wedding is the bride's special day Marilyn said repeatedly. My handful of kin from California sort of got swallowed up in the crowd of the Ames family, Marilyn's relatives, and their friends. Not that I had much time to talk to them. We were pushed around by the photographer, the wedding planner, and the emcee with the band. Cut the cake, do the first dance, wave from the limo as we left for the airport. I'll have to show you the album sometime."

Annie didn't indicate she'd enjoy doing that. "So, you didn't have a good time?"

"I did on the honeymoon. Anyone who doesn't love Hawaii has no soul. Have you been?"

"Yes, several times to see the Pro Bowl, once on our way to Adam Malala's wedding in Samoa."

"I should have known. Mellie probably read about that in *People*."

"Probably." Annie went silent again until she told him to make a right that would take them all the way to Chapelle, her hometown. "Watch out for speed traps going through all these small towns. It's a major source of income in Louisiana."

"I'm not speeding."

"I know, but the limit can drop from sixty-five to thirty-five as soon as you cross their borders."

He almost said, "Yes, dear," at the caution, but caught himself in time.

Along the way, Annie pointed out shabby

135

Lynn Shurr

restaurants known for great seafood or a big breakfast. Outside of Morgan City, she motioned toward two bald eagles lurking in the trees and suggested they waited for fresh road kill. His GPS had plotted their new course, but he turned it off, preferring to listen to Annie's soft-voiced directions and commentary. He supposed she used her NICU voice all the time, but nice that she had no need to comfort or issue instructions for a change, and her words were only for him.

After leaving the highway, they negotiated a few rolling hills into the town of Chapelle, passed the modest Catholic church that gave the town its name and appeared to be a great age, but Annie explained it had once burned down and been rebuilt according to the original plans. No, she didn't attend services there. According to a Billodeaux family agreement, the boys and her dad were dragged to Mass by their Mawmaw Nadine and the girls attended the Episcopal service with their mother. Xochi, baptized as a Catholic before her adoption, went with the guys, and Teddy, born a Baptist, balanced things out by going with the girls.

"Everything in the Billodeaux family is complicated," she warned.

He got his first taste at the open wrought iron gate leading to Lorena Ranch where a lean and serious man, hair short and grizzled, stopped the car, and asked his name. Annie leaned around Matt's bulk and said, "It's okay Knox. This is Matt Keaton, one of the new Sinners."

Knox Polk consulted a tablet grasped in his tawny hands. "Yep, he's on the list, Miss Annie." Still, the man's unexpected green eyes narrowed as if he judged Matt to be friend or foe, but he waved them on their way.

"About as friendly as your sister, Jude," Matt remarked.

"Knox is our ranch manager/bodyguard. He's suspicious of everyone. You'd never believe he's Junior Polk's dad because Junior is one of the sweetest men I know. He loved Xochi since childhood and finally convinced her to marry him despite the age difference. I keep telling Knox he can drop the Miss Annie stuff because we are family now, and were like family before, but he is too set in his ways. Ex-military, never relaxes."

They drove along the winding lane shaded by massive live oaks and popped out into the sunshine where the columned mansion referred to as the ranch house despite its verandas, elevator, and movie theater addition, stood. Annie directed Matt to park near the barn, anywhere he could find a space. "Looks like an Escalade show lot," Matt observed.

"A popular brand with the Sinners, old and new. The one with the cross on the back instead of the red devil belongs to the great Rev Bullock who became a pastor after he retired. The rest are sort of interchangeable. Billodeaux relatives usually come in trucks. Jude and I squeeze our little cars in anywhere we can. We're a little late to the party, so start a new row with plenty of room for the behemoths to turn around."

"Yes, ma'am."

"That's the way you should address a woman who gives you an order. You're catching on to Louisiana ways," she teased, giving him a playful rap on the arm.

"Trying. If I stay here permanently, I'll soon

ma'am and y'all with the best of the Southern boys."
He wondered if Annie would like if he became a
permanent resident of New Orleans after he retired.

She let that comment slide. "Okay, get ready to
enter the maelstrom."

By the time they reached the barbecue pavilion,
Matt had met the other Billodeaux twins, boy and girl
adolescents who gave pony rides, and so many gray or
balding former Sinners, he felt as if he walked down an
aisle in the Pro Football Hall of Fame. By the umu oven
where the whole pigs roasted stood the Samoan legend,
Adam Malala, and his assistant for the day, Junior Polk,
who took as deep an interest in cuisine as he did in
football.

Junior stepped forward to offer a hand and
apologize. "Sorry I haven't been around to help you get
settled." He nodded toward a group sitting in the shade
of the oaks a few yards away. "Wife, baby, restaurant
keeps me here, but I'll be at camp. I need to work off
my own cooking." Junior patted his firm belly.

Adam Malala, the former cornerback who had also
been sharing the tricks of playing this position with
Junior as well as recipes for pork and plantains when
they walked up, chuckled. "Too bad you don't live in
Samoa, Junior, where a big gut is a sign of status. You
could let yourself go." Obviously, Malala hadn't.
Though his explosion of dark, frizzy hair had threads of
silver, the rest of him was mostly muscle.

"Not with my wife watching everything that goes
into my mouth—when I'm home—but I enjoy making
and trying new dishes for Down by the Riverside, my
restaurant."

Annie interrupted. "Lots more folks to meet, but

138

let's say hi to Mom and Dad first before we move on. What time will the pigs be ready, Adam?

He checked both his wristwatch and the position of the sun in the sky. "An hour maybe."

"Great, can't wait to eat."

"There's plenty of nibbles already out if you're hungry now. I brought a whole pan of alligator balls," Junior offered. Observing Matt's expression, he added, "The gator meat is ground and seasoned, then fried. Alligators don't actually have balls. Not the external kind anyhow."

Relieved that he wouldn't be subjected to a weird food experience designed to test his manhood, Matt said, "I'll try one."

"Hurry, they go fast around here."

Annie led him into the screened pavilion where vegetable and fruit trays already made the table colorful, placed as they were on either side of the brown, fried alligator balls. Annie hoisted one of the balls onto a toothpick and offered it to Matt. Instead of taking it, he opened his mouth like Daniel accepting a bottle, and let her feed him. "Good, way better than I expected, but not like chicken."

"I've always thought pork, but really, alligator meat is mild and takes on the flavor of whatever you cook it in, red sauce or étouffée, in this case fried."

Their entrance hadn't interrupted a ruckus over by the vast grill covered with various pots and pans. Matt took it all in, the playful struggle, the ease of their long relationship, so different from his parents' conservative ways and vastly different from his marriage to Melinda.

Petite Miss Nell attempted to pull her husband away from a bubbling iron pot of baked beans. Her small but toned arms wrapped around his waist. She dug in the heels of her sandals and pulled as hard as she could. "The beans do not need more hot sauce. They don't need any hot sauce at all!"

The tall, still in great shape and immovable, Joe Dean Billodeaux held the bottle of sauce above the pot, plinked it with a finger, and watched a large, red drop descend into the bean pot. "There, that should give them some kick. I can't abide bland beans, me."

Nell gave up. "One drop shouldn't make too big a difference, but no more. No one else will be able to eat them."

"Oh, Tink," he said, using her pet name. "Joe Dean's Hot and Spicy Sauce always makes a difference." Joe held out the bottle on the large hand that had thrown hundreds of perfect spirals in a long career as if he displayed it in an ad. "Maybe that should be its new slogan, 'Always makes a Difference.' All proceeds go to Camp Love Letter for seriously ill and handicapped children."

Nell snatched the bottle away. "If people don't burn their tongues on it."

"I beg to differ," Joe said. "Want to go inside, upstairs, and settle this argument away from our guests? They won't notice we're gone for a half hour or so." He released the charming grin that had once convinced numerous women to sign his little black book, but that was in the past, way in the past.

"Joe, we have company!"

"Lots of it, so?"

"Matt and Annie are here."

"Oh, Matt and Annie." Joe strode forward to pump Matt's hand. "I'm glad you decided to come."

A well-padded Hispanic woman with thick, gray hair pulled back in a bun bustled over from the stove. "Mr. Matt, with the *muy enfermo muchacho*?"

"The baby isn't sick, Corazon, only premature," Annie corrected. "Junior's mother, Corazon Polk, who helped raise all of us."

"Nice to meet you." Corazon thrust a small package drawn from her deep red apron pocket decorated with yellow rickrack into the hand Matt offered.

"For the baby. I make. Open, open!" she insisted.

Matt parted the tissue paper and revealed a knitted cap shaped like a Sinners black and red football helmet complete with the red devils on its side. "This is great. Thank you."

"Now all will know he is one of the Sinners, a strong boy like my Junior who weighed twelve pounds when he was born." Pride tinged her voice.

"I'll save it always."

Corazon beamed. Joe said, "How about those alligator balls? I think they could be spicier, but Junior says tourists have to be able to eat them."

"I think they were just right."

"Dean is looking for you to row in his dragon boat. Take a few of the balls along to keep you until we get all the food on the table. Tink and I have something to settle upstairs."

"Joe!" Nell protested.

Matt did spear another alligator ball since breakfast without Annie's company usually ran to milk and cereal. "I guess we need to find Dean."

"He'll be the guy with the clipboard and the worried expression. He wants to sign you up before

Tom sees you."

They stepped outside, leaving the food supervision to Corazon, as she obviously preferred by her quick return to the stove. Matt eyed Joe carrying his wife toward the house despite her token resistance. "Are you parents always so—affectionate."

"You mean horny? Pretty often. Used to make us cringe with embarrassment as teens, but now I think we'd all like to have that much passion for our spouse after years of marriage."

"My marriage wasn't like that, more—formal I guess."

"Every marriage is different." Annie patted his arm, whether in sympathy or sadness, he couldn't tell and had no time to decipher. Dean descended gripping the predicted clipboard.

"I need you for the center of my boat to balance Junior when we row. Annie, you are the lightest. How about drumming for us?"

"Isn't Teddy doing that?"

"No, he and Jessie are rowing for Tom this year. Jude is their drummer."

"Then, sign me up for your team."

"I knew I could count on a little sisterly rivalry. Matt, come with me. I'll explain the strategies of dragon boat racing."

"Is Stacy around?" Annie searched for her tall, blonde sister-in-law.

"I think she's gone to sit with Teddy, Xochi, and the babies. Matt, you coming? This is important. Tom almost beat me last year."

Matt allowed himself to be parted from Annie, but he craned his neck to watch her small form join the group under the oaks.

****

Annie took a seat on a folding chair next to Xochi, her adopted Mexican sister, the one who could see auras. Xo held her five-month-old baby girl in her lap. Since giving birth, she'd taken on a Madonna-like sheen and softness that deserved a halo all its own. Not that Xochi couldn't fight if she wanted. She'd come into the family as one tough little girl and hadn't made life easy for her kidnappers either.

Stacy's children played in the bouncy house, and Stace perched next to Teddy in his wheelchair. His adopted daughter, Lizzy Jane, black curls bouncing, blue eyes alight, toddled between his chair and that of his wife, Jessie, never letting go of her hold on a knee or an armrest until she raised her hands and uttered one of her new words, "Up." Teddy raised her onto his lap using his strong biceps. No wonder Tom had claimed him for his rowing team. "Glad you could get here with your work schedule, Annie."

"I'll have to leave early, but I wanted Matt to come and enjoy the day. He needs to get out."

Xochi's little Pilar started to fuss and burrow into her chest. Discreetly, she lowered her top and nursed the baby under a bright Spanish shawl. Stacy's kids, still full of bounce, raced over to them, hollering and screaming, and circling the chairs. Lizzy Jane applauded their performance with delight. Under cover of the noise, Xochi leaned Annie's way and quietly observed, "You're in love."

"Stop reading my aura!"

"I can't help it. You've always had the green aura of a healer like me. Now it's glowing with love—for whom?"

Despite Xochi's whisper, Jessie heard. Hazel eyes bright with curiosity, she cocked her blond-streaked head their way. "Yes, spill, who's the lucky man?"

Like a game of telephone, Teddy repeated, "Annie's in love. Who could it be?"

Stacy, used to the noise her children created, answered. "Easy, she loves Matt Keaton and his baby."

"I'm so happy for you," Jessie said. "Who knew I'd find the best man I've ever known after I became crippled? Glad you didn't have to go through that to discover yours." She squeezed the hand Teddy rested on his lap and ignited his wonderful smile, two people in wheelchairs, deeply in love with each other.

How Annie envied them despite their handicaps. "It's not that simple. He's still grieving for his wife and worried about his son who will probably have to undergo a procedure soon. He regards me as a friend he can trust. I have no idea of his feelings other than that."

"Let me take a peek at him," Xochi begged.

"He's off somewhere with Dean, but don't. It's bad enough all of you have figured me out. Nothing may come of it. Please keep this to yourselves."

"You are asking a lot of the Billodeaux family, but we'll try," Stacy said. "It's pretty obvious though. That's why Jude is jealous. For once she can't control your life."

"What, she doesn't have a healing aura like me?"

Xochi shook her long, dark locks, and her baby reached to grasp them. "Jude has always been hard-edged orange, full of ambition and herself." She untwined the tiny fingers from her hair. "I can't help what I see, so if Matt happens to come my way—I'll keep my observations to myself."

Annie convinced herself she really did not want to pry into Matt's emotions. "Good."

Attempting to turn the attention away from herself, she focused her eyes on the pavilion where Adam and Junior raked away the earth and leaves from the roasting pigs and transferred them to planks. "Looks like we're going to eat soon."

In what had become a custom, they raised one of the planks to their wide shoulders and trotted off to display the centerpiece of the picnic by circling the pool and summoning the swimmers, volleyball players, and other guests to the feast. The second pig was carried to the table by other volunteers, and Corazon rang the iron triangle vigorously, letting everyone else know the food was on the table.

"We'd better get in line before the first pig returns and draws the crowd," Teddy said. "Hang on for the ride, little monkey." He wheeled off with Lizzy clinging to his shoulders and his wife right behind him.

Xochi transferred her sleeping baby to a sling made from the shawl and followed them. Stacy herded her kids ahead but lingered a bit to wait for her to join them. "Annie, aren't you the least bit curious about what Xochi can tell you concerning Matt?"

"I am, but I believe we should let this play out in its own good time. Daniel isn't out of the woods yet. It's no time for romance." Still, she searched through the crowd for Matt until her gaze found him. He approached with Dean and X-avier, plus a few others of the current Sinners team. They let women and children cut ahead, waiting their turn like gentlemen. She'd probably be finished eating before he got to the table.

That's the way it should be, Matt finding his place among the men of his team, not clinging to her.

Annie didn't see him again until the dragon boat races began, and she took her spot in front of the big drum on the prow that she'd beat to keep the rowers on pace. Dean placed the heavy weights, Matt and Junior, in the center of the craft and filled in with the lighter rowers. He, of course, would steer in the stern.

Tom organized his own team, positioning his people here and there. "Teddy and Jessie toward the middle. Mack, I'm pairing you with Alix since you are both strong strokers."

"Yes, I am." Mack, the reprobate Billodeaux brother, leered at Alix and caused a blush to climb her pale cheeks.

"Since she's my wife, on second thought, Alix and X-avier, you sit together." He motioned one of the teen boys eager to row next to Mack. Not equally matched, but that move kept Mack away from the woman Tom adored.

"What's the matter, Tommy? Afraid I'll steal her away?" Mack jeered.

"More afraid she'll kick your balls back into your pelvis," he returned. Everyone knew she could too.

X-avier gallantly handed Alix into the boat. "My pleasure, Miss Alix." He bowed with a flourish, and caused Alix, the Sinners' Amazonian punter, to blush again. Annie just shook her head at all this byplay taking place in the next boat, the Billodeaux family in full action with more to come.

Jude hopped into her high seat behind the drum. "We have the stronger team," she smirked.

"We have Matt and Junior."

146

"Dead weight in the water."

No more time for trash talk. The fully loaded boats made their awkward way to the starting line. Her dad blew the whistle to start the race. The long oars cut into the brown bayou water, knives through melted chocolate. Froth formed. Dean gave Annie the nod to increase the pace now that his team had the rhythm. Jude matched her. True, Matt and Junior added a great deal of weight, but with each heave of their shoulders, their boat shot forward. Dean had wisely filled the rest of his crew with the lithe and wiry. He signaled for a more rapid drumbeat. Annie obliged, really getting her back into it. They flew along like the great white egrets spooked from the shallows, but as usual, Tom's team did not lag behind. The curve in the bayou that signaled the end of the race loomed ahead. They ended in an apparent dead heat. The boats circled and returned to shore to await a decision.

"A tie," Adam Malala declared.

Mack Billodeaux jumped from Tom's craft, nearly dumping his team in the river. "That's a pile of shit. We had them."

His father arrived in time to hear. "Eliminated by poor sportsmanship. The prize goes to Team Dean."

"Sure, doesn't it always." Mack stalked off and left his fellow racers shaking their heads.

Matt and Junior moved ashore much more carefully. Suddenly, Matt plucked Annie from her place behind the drum and twirled her around. "We won! What did we win?"

No matter that her muscles ached from pounding the drum and her skin burned from her stint as lifeguard at the pool before the races began, she experienced a burst of happiness like no other in her life before he allowed her feet to touch the ground again. "Adam always provides the prizes, small tokens, really. We do this for fun—but we won!"

Annie caught a glimpse of Jude, her expression almost as sullen as the one Mack habitually wore. She couldn't help herself and mouthed, "We won" in her sister's direction, but to Matt she said, "Most of us do it for fun. Sorry to say we need to shower and get on the road shortly. Really, I should have brought my own car and let you enjoy the evening leftovers and fireworks."

Her dad moved up the award ceremony to accommodate her and Matt's departure. Adam presented leis of fragrant tuberoses to the women and green-leaved maile to the victorious men, plus small hand-carved tiki statues as trophies. Tom led the good-natured applause to make up for the disgrace Mack brought on their team.

Annie moved toward the pavilion again. "We can't leave without our sack of leftovers." The large shopping bags literally had their names inscribed on them in black marker. Corazon presided over the dispersal of the food.

"What, no Mawmaw Nadine making sure we get our share?" Annie joked.

"She gets old but won't admit it. Fell sleep in the shade. I make sure you get some of her bread pudding." Corazon handed over a heavier bag to Matt. "You drive safe and take care of our little Annie."

"I swear I will."

They were the first to leave and hit the road to New Orleans. Matt admitted, "I had a great time. I didn't think I'd ever feel like having fun again, but this beats anything the Ames family did."

"It's hard to beat the Billodeauxs en masse." Annie yawned. "If you want to come to the nursery tonight, we can do something special with Daniel." She yawned again. "Too much sun, and all that rowing. Sorry, I think I'll nap on the way back."

Matt watched Annie curl into the cushions of the Escalade. She offered him a sleepy smile. Her lei exuded the scent of the tropics as her dark head drooped and her eyes closed, the white flowers encircling her like a halo for an angel. His angel.

Chapter Seventeen

They swung by Matt's house to leave the leftovers since Annie insisted he take her share, then headed for the NICU. Annie reluctantly left her lei behind in his car. "You don't need to change?" Matt asked.

"I always have clean scrubs in my locker. You never know when you'll be peed or barfed on in this job."

They both knew well the routine for entering the NICU and completed it swiftly. "So, something special is going to happen tonight?" Matt probed.

"Yes, I think we are overdue for kangaroo care. The nursing mothers experience it sooner. Tonight, it's your turn. Relax, you'll enjoy it," Annie assured him. She wanted him to have this special moment with Daniel before his next challenge as a NICU parent. One she couldn't tell him about yet.

"It's been a big day for new experiences, but I'm game. Just tell me what to do."

Daniel's unit lay quiet and still as the babies in the incubators. One bassinette stood empty. Matt noticed immediately. "Little Arielle is gone." His voice held a tinge of dread.

"Yes, she passed her car seat test yesterday morning and went home to her family," Peggy, already on duty, said.

"Hey, maybe my prayers do count for something."

His face relaxed into a smile.

"All prayers count, my Mawmaw Nadine would say. Sorry I ran a little late, Peggy. It's hard to escape the ranch. All right, Matt, take a seat in the rocker and strip off your shirt," Annie ordered.

"Sounds a little kinky, but okay." Matt stripped his fresh Sinners tee, the one he'd put on after showering at the ranch since the Billodeauxs kept a supply in all sizes at hand and his was sweat soaked through from the race. Peggy, taking in the sight of the broad expanse of his chest, gasped a little. Annie hadn't figured Matt for a man who shaved his chest, but he did. Every delineation of his muscles showed in clear definition. The sight was worth a gasp and maybe a little drool.

She forced her thoughts back to business. "We're doing skin-to-skin care tonight, Peggy. Matt, the baby will rest on your chest for an hour, listening to your heartbeat, your words, a lullaby. We've found the babies cry less and sleep better after such contact. It stabilizes their heart rate and breathing. The benefits are endless."

"I'm ready." Matt held out his arms for his son.

"Let me fit you with a kangaroo shirt. An hour is a long time to support an infant and the stretchy material will help with that." Annie checked out their supply of the garments and held up the largest, clearly too small for the football player. "Maybe we'll make a sling with a blanket instead. Would you like a privacy screen?"

"Killjoy," Peggy muttered.

Matt's deep laugh filled the room. The babies stirred. "Sorry, that was loud. I've been in so many locker rooms I have no modesty left. Just set me up."

With Peggy's help, Annie did, settling Matt with

some cushions on his lap and transferring Daniel stripped to his diaper, tubes and all, into to his embrace and nestled against his chest, soft frail body against hard muscle. They arranged the blanket to cradle the child if Matt's arms tired and to keep both warm.

He gazed down on the small head and murmured his brief prayer for his son's health before starting to describe the Fourth of July celebration in great detail. "The Billodeauxs had pony rides and rock walls and bouncy houses for the children. One day, you'll love all of those things. We had a whole pig to eat, two pigs. That's a lot of pork. Maybe next year you can taste some."

Annie slipped out to walk the ward and see if her advice or help was needed elsewhere. Matt didn't need her right this moment, though she would gladly have stayed and listened to his deep, soft voice commune with Daniel for the next hour. She trusted Peggy to keep an eye on Danny's vitals in her absence. When she returned, it appeared Matt had run out of words because he crooned the song *Danny Boy* to his baby in a deep baritone voice that she suspected might be quite powerful if unfettered.

Of course, she'd heard the lovely melody before with its aura of sadness, the pipes calling, the roses falling, and Danny Boy going away. The singer vowed to wait for his return in the sunshine or the shadow because he is so loved. She'd overlooked or never heard the last two verses about the lover dying and waiting for Danny in heaven. Maybe, he'd meant the song as a tribute to Melinda. Her heart twisted a little in envy to be so loved.

Matt glanced up from his sleeping baby. "Sorry, I

don't really know any lullabies and that song was one of my dad's favorites. He taught history at the university and loved to tell those of Irish descent that an English lawyer wrote the song—but that didn't take away from its beauty or shouldn't. I'll have to look up something better if we do this again."

Peggy, changing the baby in the second incubator, sniffed as if she held back tears. "You can sing it for me anytime. Even this young man settled down at the sound of your voice, and he's been restless all evening."

Annie delivered the news as gently as she could. "You don't have to change a thing, Matt. Daniel's vitals are so strong right now, but we have to put him to bed and let you go home and get some rest. Dr. Brown wants to speak with you early tomorrow around seven. I'll stick around until he comes."

"Sure, then we'll go to breakfast like always. Do you know what he has to say?"

"That's between you and the doctor." Annie lifted the baby, and Peggy prepared the incubator for his reception.

Matt shook off the blanket and stretched his shirt over his wide chest again. "You were right, Annie. This was a special day. Thank you." He moved toward the door.

She wished she could send him off with a kiss but settled for a warm smile. "Yes, in many ways. Don't worry about tomorrow."

****

Matt arrived at six and had his chat with Daniel before Dr. Brown showed up with a clipboard full of forms and a serious expression on his kind face. "Mr.

Keaton, stay seated. Do you recall my talking about PDAs previously? The tube in the heart that needs to seal as the baby grows?"

"Yes, sort of. A lot was going on after Danny's birth. It's supposed to close by itself, right?"

"And usually does, but in Daniel's case the hole has remained larger than we'd like at this point. It does impact his breathing. We've been making sure he has adequate oxygen, but feel surgery is necessary. We'd like to operate on Monday if you will give your approval."

Matt nodded, but his eyes never left Daniel. "Will you do the surgery?"

"No, our hospital has an excellent pediatric surgeon who specializes in neonates. Annie and I will see to your boy's recovery. The procedure is in his best interest. If you will give your approval, sign these forms where the check marks indicate."

Matt took the clipboard and scrawled his big, bold signature over and over again. "What time Monday?"

"Eight unless we have an emergency."

"I'll be here waiting."

Annie touched his shoulder. "So will I. Let's go get coffee and that breakfast you promised me."

"Not much appetite all of a sudden."

"Hey, you trying to get out of feeding me? I'm famished." She nudged him toward the door since her shift had ended half an hour ago.

"No, I enjoy having breakfast with you."

She'd prepare a plate for him, convince him to eat whatever she left on hers which she planned to overfill, and tell him how the cells in Daniel's tiny body were primed for growth and healing. His son would survive because he had the heart of a Sinner, exactly like his dad.

Chapter Eighteen

After they took Daniel away for his surgery on Monday morning, Annie and Matt went to the cafeteria as usual. This time, neither displayed an appetite, but both managed some scrambled eggs and biscuits. Rather than her regular decaf, Annie accepted two large cups of full strength coffee which truly meant something in New Orleans. The amount of caffeine in the brew could keep a flight crew wide awake on an eight-hour trip.

Another infant had come into her care at four a.m., and the adrenaline rush of hooking up all the monitors, inserting the IV into the tiny arm, and adjusting the oxygen feed until the baby stabilized carried her through the next hour. She'd also counseled and reassured the shocked parents, laying out for them the procedures and what they might expect in the months to come. When Matt arrived at six, all that extra energy had worn off, but she stayed by his side until the surgical staff wheeled his son away. Dead tired, she intended to stay alert and be there for Matt for the duration of the procedure. Of course, nine o'clock came and went before the surgery actually started, but once Danny returned to the NICU, she'd go home and sleep as long as she needed.

After loitering in the cafeteria far longer than the food on their plates required, they retired to the NICU waiting room and waited—and waited—until Dr. Brown, who had assisted, came to tell them the ordeal was over. Daniel did well as expected. "He should be on track for release at the end of August if all goes as planned, and he meets the criteria to go home."

"Good, great." Matt's enthusiasm dimmed. "That's the start of the regular season. I'll be gone a lot. Next week is training camp, and I'll visit no matter how fatigued I am. After that the preseason with two away games." He fretted his way through a football player's schedule.

"Daniel will be fine right here in the NICU with me and Peggy and Bess caring for him until he can leave." Annie squeezed his arm. "By then, we will have found the perfect baby nurse to care for him."

They both scrubbed in again and went to the side of the incubator where Daniel was splayed out and hooked up to so many tubes and wires he resembled a bizarre science experiment. The small chest rose and fell evenly despite the dark row of stitches running down his breast bone and holding his fragile flesh together.

"He looks so ill." Matt sank into a chair and murmured his prayer, longer than usual.

"No, he's already improving. I know just what he needs to improve his appearance though." Annie found the knitted cap, carefully washed, that Corazon had made for the baby. She reached in through the port and settled it on Daniel's head with his dark hair finally starting to come in a bit. The red devil applique winked up at her as if they shared a secret. "There, now he is officially one of the Sinners like his daddy."

Matt nodded, a faint smile on his lips. "I'm going

to stay a while, but could you take a picture before you go."

Again, Annie had the pleasure of rooting the phone from his hip pocket and taking several, not all full length with the apparatus attached, but close-ups of Daniel's peaceful face topped by his jaunty cap. She returned the phone and announced that she'd be going now.

"Yes, get some sleep. Promise you won't nod off at the wheel, Annie. We can't afford to lose you," Matt implored.

"I could probably find my way home with my eyes closed, but I won't try it." She left him there, worried, hunched by Daniel's side much like those first days in the NICU.

Back at the apartment, Annie slept past seven p.m. When Jude arrived home cranky about no dinner being on the table like a spouse from the 1950's, Annie offered her explanation. As her sister picked up a phone to order Chinese takeout, Jude waggled a finger at her. "Getting too close to your patient, not a good idea."

****

Matt held off two full days before calling Annie. He knew she deserved her days off, knew he leaned heavily on her, though he shouldn't. Regardless, he punched in her number and prayed she'd answer, not just let it go to voice mail because she'd gotten tired of holding his hand, metaphorically if not physically. If Annie wished he'd go away, it didn't show in her voice as she picked up.

"Anything wrong, Matt?"

He wished he could say, "No, I simply wanted to hear your voice", partly true, but that was not the case.

"Annie, Daniel is running a low-grade fever and not eating much. He's losing weight. He's losing ground."

"Perfectly normal after surgery like his. He'll bounce back soon."

"Yeah, that's what the nurses told me, but isn't there anything we can do now for him?"

On the other end of the phone, Annie took a deep breath. "I don't know how you feel about this, but Xochi and Junior and the baby are in the city right across the street from me in their condo since training camp is starting soon. Um, Xo is an herbal healer, a *traiteur* the Cajuns say."

Not what he wanted to hear at all. "I don't think the hospital would allow her to dose Daniel with herbs. Who knows how that would affect him?" Matt clenched the phone tighter in his hand, deeply hoping Annie had something better to offer.

"Xo would know, but that's not what I am suggesting. She also practices the laying on of hands and has special prayers to endow strength. Would you like to try that? It's a matter of faith, not science, but surely harmless. I've seen her make a difference before in the NICU."

Matt took his own deep breath. "Some of the guys at the picnic mentioned having your sister treat them. They claim they mended faster. Can't harm, might help. Okay, let's try that."

"I'll set it up for Thursday morning."

Matt remembered. "Don't you always spend that day with your twin? Will that cause any trouble between you and Jude? She's not fond of me already."

"She can sleep in if she wants. We were planning to go to lunch with Xo. It's still on. How about nine at the NICU?

"That's a date." He truly wished it were a real one and not a matter of life and death for his son.

Chapter Nineteen

Though the NICU had a one guest at a time policy, Annie took advantage of her status to remain in the room while Xochi did her thing. For that, Matt was grateful. Once, her healing sister had dreaded coming to the hospital with so many sickened souls around her, Annie told him, but since her training with an elderly *traiteur* she'd learned calmness and balance. Matt studied the woman placing her hands through the ports of Daniel's incubator.

She had the dark curls he'd come to associate with the Billodeaux women but worn long and pulled back on this occasion. Her eyes, large and brown as Annie's, gleamed with empathy. She stood taller and had features and a figure more lush and rounded than the twins. Her skin of toasty brown Xochi owed to her Mexican mother, any Billodeaux traits to a cousin of Joe's who'd fathered her, then died with his wife in a drug deal gone bad. Xochi had found a home at the ranch until she'd left to study healing in the old French ways and marry Junior Polk.

Now, Xo laid her fingers gently on Daniel's head and torso. She murmured a prayer Matt couldn't understand despite a required two years of high school French. Didn't sound anything like what little he'd learned. Annie said the prayers were passed along from *traiteur* to *traiteur*, never shared. And oh, he was not to offer Xochi payment for her service, a gross breach of etiquette. Nothing for nothing?

Yet, as the *traiteur's* beautiful, full lips moved, he swore his son's color improved and the small limbs moved more than they had the last few days as if the baby gained strength and energy. No one seemed amazed except Matt. Nurse Bess beamed and declared, "They always get better after Miss Xochi comes. I've witnessed this before. Between her praying and your singing, this boy is going to get better fast."

Xochi withdrew her hands. "Daniel might seem frail, but he has inner strength. I merely gave him a boost. What do you sing to your son?"

Bess raved, "His *Danny Boy* brings tears to your eyes, and that one about all the pretty little horses makes the babies quiet down and listen. If this man was a Baptist, I'd recruit him for our choir."

Annie arched her dark brows at him. "You've added to your repertoire?"

"Yeah, over the weekend I looked up some lyrics. *Toora, Loora, Loora* is easy, but I keep forgetting all the verses of that mockingbird song." He felt as if he should stare at his toes and scuff his shoes in embarrassment over how soft the tough running back Matt Keaton had become.

"Daniel doesn't care if you get the words right. It's the tone of your voice that matters. I think you are wonderful for learning lullabies."

"Well, mothers usually take care that, but he doesn't have one, so I'm filling in for Mellie."

Annie's warm regard faded away and went back to business. "We should leave now and let you visit with Daniel."

Matt turned to Xochi, "I want to th…" Then he remembered not to thank the *traiteur* and switched plans. "I'd like to take all of you to lunch. Name the place."

Xochi's soft brown eyes lighted. "We're going to Middendorf's for lunch, the twins and I, then antiquing in Ponchatoula, our strawberry capitol. Since I'm nursing Pilar, I seem to be hungry all the time. I can't wait to get there. The restaurant is about twenty miles from New Orleans. Do you have the time?"

Matt gave himself credit for not flinching about the nursing remark. Spending so much time in the NICU, he'd become inured to conversations about breast milk and seen plenty of women with babies tugging at their nipples. "It would be my pleasure. I'll stay with Daniel for a while and meet you there. Annie deserves her day off to with spend with her sisters."

"Maybe I should stay. You might get lost," Annie protested.

"The new SUV has GPS. I'll see you there around eleven-thirty since Xochi is hungry already. No worries." Matt took Xo's vacated seat and leaned in to talk to his son.

****

"Matt is running late," Xochi said. She had already attacked the hush puppies after asking that they be brought out early.

"He'll be here soon," Annie answered. The twins were finishing a second glass of wine by the time she spotted his big build and rugged, handsome face attracting the attention of other diners. His appearance brought a wide smile to her face and a warm flush to her cheeks. Already lit with too much wine, she quelled her reaction.

Not that the women had minded his tardiness. They'd had plenty of time to dissect Matt in his absence with Jude doing most of the probing and cutting.

"Did you get a good read on him this morning, Xo?" she asked. "I only want the best for my sister."

"Stop it! I told you I didn't want to know," Annie protested.

Xochi swallowed her third hush puppy. "I saw nothing bad, Annie. In fact, I think we've got another white knight like Dean and Teddy, a guy who always wants to do the right thing. He is suffused with love for his son, but also conflicted by other emotions." She held up a tawny hand. "You know I don't see the future and can't tell you what his problems are. Still, he's a good man. Does that satisfy you, Jude?"

"I guess it will have to because here he comes." Jude raised an impatient hand to attract his attention in the large, rustic interior of Middendorf's with its open beams and cheerful banners hanging from the ceiling. They'd taken a four top rather than one of the picnic tables that dotted the floor.

"Sorry I'm late. I did get a little lost." He took the empty chair, overwhelming it with his size.

"No surprise there," Jude murmured to Annie and got a well-deserved crushing of her toes in their open sandals.

"Have you ordered yet?"

"No, we waited and waited for you. We need appetizers." Jude declared.

"Quickly," Annie told the hovering waitress since her twin had bottomed out her second glass of wine and ordered another. She tried to dismiss Jude's rudeness as too much alcohol on an empty stomach.

"How about the frog legs?" Jude challenged, staring directly at Matt.

"I heard you ate those things down here. Why not?" he said, staring her down.

Annie tried to reassure him and mute Jude's combativeness. "They really do taste like chicken."

"I'm up for anything. Daniel's fever went down right after you left." He sent Xochi an appreciative glance since thanks were off the table. "What else is good to eat here?"

Xo placed her order and gave it her endorsement. "The cut thin catfish is the specialty. Large portions, comes with French fries, coleslaw, and hush puppies—although I think I've already eaten mine."

"We'll get you some more. I'll have the same," Matt said to a waitress only too happy to comply with increasing the tab. Annie ordered broiled shrimp with lemon butter, along with Jude, and sent her on her way.

Matt eyed the model train circling the building. "Danny is going to love that someday. Junior didn't want to come?" he asked, showing a tad of discomfort dining with three women and no backup.

"He's giving me a mommy's day out before training camp starts. I left plenty of bottled breast milk for Pilar." She glanced wistfully at the wine glasses and the beer the waitress sat in front of Matt before scooping up another hush puppy.

"Since Daniel is on the mend, maybe you should decide on whether to go with breast milk or formula when he comes home." Jude poked at him again, obviously trying to embarrass him.

Annie crushed her toes once more and said, "He

has plenty of time to decide that."

Matt countered her sister again. "I think we should go with a breast milk service. It provides extra immunity."

The frog legs arrived, deep fried and golden. He took the first one and sucked it off the spindly bones. "It does taste like chicken. Dig in before they get cold."

Perhaps, Annie had bruised Jude's tootsies enough after the frog leg dare because the rest of the meal proceeded with civility. The mammoth plates of fried catfish arrived along with the shrimp. Xochi swore she'd take some home for Junior, but Matt ordered another to go for her husband. Since all of the women had been raised among football players, they discussed the hardships of training camp and the prospects for the upcoming season.

With Dean Billodeaux as quarterback, reaching the playoffs was a given, but Annie felt compelled to add, "Dean believes Matt and X-avier will give the offense exactly the boost they need to go all the way to the Super Bowl." She allowed a little pride to seep into her voice.

"I hope he's right," Matt answered with becoming modesty. "X-avier would say hell, yes! You think there will be any hazing at camp?"

"With Tom, you never know, but it will be the funny kind, nothing cruel," Annie admitted.

"Okay, I'll brace myself."

"You're a seasoned player. He might give you a pass."

"Humpf," Jude said, expressing her scorn for Tom's antics. "Do you plan to go antiquing with us in Ponchatoula too?"

Truce over.

"No, that was Mellie's idea of entertainment. I'm going to do some weight work at the training center. With camp coming up, I want to be in peak condition."

Xochi sighed. "I wish I could say the same for Junior. He spends too much of his time sampling new recipes for his restaurant. He'll need to sweat off those extra pounds."

"Besides testing the rookies, that's why they have training camp. Not everyone arrives buffed up from the off-season." Matt finished off his mound of catfish.

Annie couldn't help herself. "That certainly won't be your problem." Okay, she'd spilled to her sisters about Matt's impressive bare chest and wonderful singing voice like a schoolgirl with a bad crush. "I mean, you've done all the voluntary training sessions."

"Glad you think I'm ready to play. Hey, anyone for dessert? I see they have a white chocolate bourbon pecan pie and something called chocolate indulgence." The waitress had thoughtfully left a menu with the desserts exposed.

Xochi patted her stomach. Only one portion of fish and a handful of fries remained on her plate. She added that to the takeout box their server left at her side. "I think I am finally full, but you go ahead, Matt."

He laughed so deep and good-natured it went straight to Annie's heart. "I'm in training, remember. Annie—and Jude—can I get you anything?"

"We're planning to have a coffee break and strawberry pie in Ponchatoula, aren't we, Annie."

"Yes, that's what we decided. Besides, I've eaten as much as I can hold." She'd left most of her fries untouched.

"I'll take care of the check, then, so you ladies can start shopping."

"Mostly we look. Our apartment is too small for extra stuff and neither of us wants to dust it anyhow. Only Xo has a place large enough to house more." Annie loathed to leave his company.

"If I find any interesting old cooking tools or signs, I get them to decorate the restaurant," Xochi added, giving Annie a few more seconds with Matt.

"Let's get going. I need to hit the restroom first," Jude said, shoving away from the table and grabbing her straw bag from beneath the table. "You coming, Annie?"

"In a minute. I just want to thank Matt for the wonderful meal."

"Yeah, thanks. Don't get lost on your way back." Jude strode off as if she had to dig a latrine by herself.

"No thanks needed," Matt said as he signed his credit card bill and pocketed the receipt. He directed the comment toward Xochi, who nodded. He understood her restrictions as a *traiteur*. "Can I walk you to your car? I hope that food for Junior doesn't spoil in this heat."

"Oh, I'm driving since I can't drink, and we always have a cooler in the back. You never know when Junior will find perfect peaches or fresh shrimp along the roadside. As for walking us to the car, believe me, you do not want to wait on three women to finish in the restroom. Return safely to New Orleans, Matt."

Annie and Xo watched Matt's broad back move toward the exit along with most of the other women in the place. As they turned to join Jude, Xochi leaned close to Annie's ear. "He has feelings for you. The second he set eyes on you, his white aura flushed pink, exactly the way it does when he speaks to Daniel. No need to share that with Jude. She'll only hassle you about it."

"I think Matt has her figured out. He's starting to fight back—and that's very good for me. Jude will be Jude, no matter what, and does exactly what she wants."

"Yes. That bothers me, but I'm already thinking about strawberry pie. Off we go."

Chapter Twenty

Daniel Keaton thrived after his surgery, putting on weight on a daily basis. Annie made sure father and son had lots of kangaroo time. She encouraged the singing of lullabies that appeared to benefit all the nursery occupants, even the mother with straggly brown hair and a hunched posture whose child arrived six weeks early, but still weighed more than Daniel.

The songs interrupted her litany of apologies whispered at the port of her baby's incubator. "The doctor told me not to smoke, but I ignored him. Mama's got a nicotine patch now, see. No more cigarettes for me." This gladdened Annie who saw too many babies released into the same atmosphere that contributed to their premature arrival.

Unfortunately, nothing much changed between her and Matt. Encouraged by Xochi's reading, she'd purchased a strawberry pie crowned with whipped cream in Ponchatoula to take over to Matt's place once they returned to New Orleans. Jude had sulked when she discovered the pie wasn't meant for them to share, so Annie merely bought two. At a time that seemed ripe for dessert and any fantasies that might go with whipped cream, she ventured to Matt's pink palace and rang the bell during the balmy blue hour before dark. "Out back," he shouted loud enough for the neighbors to hear.

Balancing the pie box, Annie made her way carefully along the narrow path nearly obscured by aspidistra leaves running alongside the house and hoped nothing like a startled garter snake caused her to drop it. She emerged from the foliage to find Matt bent over the patio table left behind by the previous owner and fiddling with his phone.

"You shouldn't just invite anyone in. I could have been a paparazzo hoping to catch you doing nude meditation like Ollie."

Matt rewarded her with a grin. "They don't bother me since Dean had a talk with them. Besides, I could tell it was your car. Most of the players drive vehicles with much bigger engines. Yours purrs like a kitten full of milk." He eyed the box. "Is that pie?"

"Straight from Ponchatoula. Want a piece?"

"Absolutely." The way he said that word encouraged her to think of something other than pie. Then, he added, "I could make coffee."

"No, still too hot out, but iced tea would be nice if you have any." Annie fanned her hot face.

"Got some canned stuff if that is okay."

"Fine with me." Annie sat in the garden chair opposite his as Matt went inside to return with two cans of lemon-infused tea cold from the refrigerator, paper plates, forks, and a knife to cut the pie. The size of his grip impressed her. He could probably cup both her breasts in one palm. Good that the slowly fading heat of the day might account for the blush she felt rising.

"Were you talking to someone when I arrived?" Annie did the honors with the dessert, carving out a piece twice the size of hers for Matt.

"Just hung up. Dre, my sister-in-law. She's fighting

with her mother again. I listened, which is all she wanted. Told her she could visit for a while if they needed a cooling off period, and then sent her the latest pictures of Daniel. She heart-liked the one of him in his Sinners cap."

"Who wouldn't?"

"Marilyn. Seems they argued over her carrying photos of Danny around in her phone and showing everyone. She wanted them deleted, and Dre refused. Marilyn threatened to cut off her cell phone service. That's life blood to a teen. I don't know how it will turn out, but I'll keep sending the photos."

Though she thought "cruel bitch." Annie didn't speak the words. "Do you think Dre will visit? We could take her to see him in person."

"Hell, no. Marilyn won't let her. I only wanted Dre to know she'd be welcome anytime."

"You're a good man, Matt Keaton."

"All I can do is try. Great pie, really great."

They finished the treat as the mosquitoes came out for their own sort of feast. Matt walked her to her car and bent over in a way she hoped might lead to a kiss. Instead, he ran his thumb along her upper lip. "You have a little whipped cream right there." He licked it from his finger before closing the door and sending her on her way. By the surge she received from his touch, it might as well have been an embrace.

Annie returned to her apartment where Jude lurked, also eating strawberry pie. "You get to second base or anywhere near a home run?" Her sister scooped a dollop of the topping onto her finger and sucked it suggestively. Her gesture lacked the innocence Matt displayed.

"That would be none of your business. I'm taking a bath and going to bed early."

"I'll take that as a no," Jude shouted after her. "If you truly want something, you have to go after it with more than a piece of pie."

Chapter Twenty-One

Yes, nothing much changed as Daniel moved closer to discharge from the NICU. During training camp, Matt visited the unit around eight at night and stayed until the fatigue from two-a-days in the heat caught up with him. On Friday night, he told Daniel all about running the bleachers, doing push-ups and squats in abundance, lots of ladder sprints, and then the drills in carrying the ball, catching the ball, stripping the ball. Enthralled by each spoken word, the baby's now wide-open blue eyes watched Matt's face intently from his blanket kangaroo pouch. Thoroughly familiar with the demands of training camp and not as enchanted, Annie went to visit another unit where premature twin girls had been checked in. Might have been her and Jude so many years ago.

Matt noticed when she returned. "Daniel, I've saved the best for last so Nurse Annie can hear, too. Tom is her brother, the kicker, and the funny man on the team. We have this guy called X-avier, good rookie player but sort of full of himself. They call a person like that a showboat sometimes. What does Tom do to welcome X-avier to the team? He rents a small Mardi Gras float that looks like a riverboat. The guys hike X-avier up on the top of it and push him around the field. Is X-avier embarrassed? Nope. He starts belting out *Ol' Man River* with lots of dramatic gestures. His voice is a little light for that song but turns out he played the part of Joe in a high school musical."

Annie shook her head. "That's fairly typical of Tom's hazing jokes. He nicknamed one guy Beef and challenged him to tow a livestock trailer the length of the field, which the man did. Earned him lots of respect. I imagine the team appreciated X-avier's good-natured performance. Is Dean still calling you Tank?"

"Yep. I hope Tom doesn't find one and ask me to push it."

She made a mental note to call her brother and tell him to go easy on Matt, who had enough problems. She gazed at Daniel so content against his father's chest. "Looks like his eyes might stay blue, though there's still a chance they will turn brown like yours.

"Doesn't matter if he has blue eyes or brown," Matt said as if defending the child.

"Naturally, then he'd have eyes like his mother." Perhaps, she preferred the baby to favor Matt and gave that away in her voice.

"Right."

She'd irritated him. "About time to put Daniel to bed. Why don't you sing one of your lullabies?"

"Which?"

"I'm partial to *Danny Boy*." The sweet melancholy air about parting suited her mood. In not too many weeks, Daniel would be fit to leave the NICU, and who knew how often she'd see either of them after that? A hired baby nurse lay in the infant's future, and the football season approached to claim all of Matt's attention.

Peggy, who changed the new baby's diaper, agreed. "Maybe it will settle this little stinker down

175

while I give him a bottle."

Matt complied and left soon after with the parting words, "When training is over maybe we can share breakfast again—until the preseason games start."

"I'll look forward to that."

As soon as Matt cleared the NICU, Peggy said, "You know I wouldn't mind having breakfast with that man either, but I've left you a clear field to be with him after your shift. Better let him know you're interested before he goes public. Nothing is more appealing to women than a big man with a bitty baby."

"How do you know I'm interested?"

"Honey, we all do."

Annie completed her rounds again with no masculine company for breakfast in her near future. She took a break to call Tom, hoping he wasn't already in bed, but then the kickers didn't work out quite as hard as the rest of the team. She reached him and asked he not embarrass or torment Matt.

"Torment? I don't torment anyone! No, we have something nice planned for the Tank—a baby shower, but with beer and barbecue. We're chipping in for the most elaborate baby stroller we can find and one of those carriers men wear on their chests."

"Are the wives invited?"

"Sure, as long as the women don't ruin the party by making it all girly."

"Not girly. I'll pass the word. Please have it when I can attend."

"Sis, you got it."

****

Tom worked in the baby shower on a Thursday evening midway through the preseason games. Easy enough to lure Matt over to Dean's house for a cookout, especially as he'd enlisted Annie's help in the timing.

"Make up an excuse for Matt to pick you up, then phone us when he arrives at your place. The guys are parking in back of the house. We're putting traffic cones in front of Dean's where we want Matt to park and will remove them when you call."

"What if someone slides in there while we're in transit?"

"No worries. One of our biggest linemen is going to stand in the space until he sees you coming."

"Sounds like a plan. See you there."

Matt accepted her feeble excuse not to use her own car without question. "I need to have my brakes checked tomorrow. I don't trust them."

He didn't suggest she ride with Tom or Junior, both living right across Canal Street from her apartment, either. He did ask, politely but not happily, "Does Jude need a lift, too?"

"Oh, she has other plans." In fact, Stacy had recruited her sister to help with the decorations. She'd be there in the thick of things.

"Great! I mean okay. See you at quarter to seven."

Punctual as always, Matt showed up on the dot. Annie made the call in his presence. "We're on our way. Put those ribs on the grill."

As Matt parallel parked into the fortuitous space, he asked Annie if she'd noticed a big man run around the side of Dean's home. "Do you think it's a paparazzo?"

"I didn't notice. Whatever, Dean can handle it."

As they went up the walk, Wynn and DJ's shrill, childish voices screamed, "They're here," with even more exuberance than usual through a crack in the door.

Annie believed that was when Matt caught on to something fishy, but he walked stolidly into the net—and a hallway sporting garlands of blue crepe paper and dripping streamers from the chandelier. In the crowded living room, the team wives and girlfriends shouted the required, "Surprise!" and surged after him as the children grasped his big hands and dragged him toward the patio, past the formal dining room with a table mounded with gifts, and outside where most of the team waited with upraised beer bottles. "To Daddy Matt."

The late afternoon sun glinting off his red hair and turning it into a fiery wick, Tom stood before the fountain and announced, "Welcome to your baby shower, Matthew Keaton. Before we dig into the eats provided by our chefs, we want to present you with two special gifts from the team."

Off to the side, Junior Polk manned the grill, flipping racks of ribs and adding them to a heap already sitting on a tray by the sauce bar providing Joe's hot and spicy, Connor's sweet and mild, and a mustard concoction of his own design. Dean cranked out pizzas from his oven in the most popular combinations: cheese and pepperoni, sausage and mushroom, and everything on it, jalapenos optional. Both men grinned ear to ear despite the trickles of sweat running down their faces as if they worked out instead of cooked.

"The first gift, your very own Baby Björn to be worn around town." He beckoned to Matt to descend from the porch and try it on. "This one has a waist strap and back support. We don't want you to hurt yourself lugging Daniel around. Alix, help him into that contraption."

His wife and punter arranged the baby carrier over Matt's big shoulders and asked him to inhale when it came to fastening the waist strap. "You might want to add an extender," she suggested.

Tom signaled to Wynn and DJ who came forth hauling a fuzzy blue teddy bear by its arms. "From us!" they cried. Tom popped it into the carrier bear-face out.

"Hey, I think it goes in the other way," an experienced father called out from the crowd.

Tom studied the tag. "Says either way is okay. All bases covered. Which brings us to our next gift—a deluxe stroller that converts into at least four kinds of things like a transformer. You'll figure it out. Accessories include a built-in speaker for an MP3 player, a pocket for a tablet in case Danny wants to watch videos, a rain cover, a bug net absolutely necessary for strolling in Louisiana, a parasol…" Tom paused for the team to do a coached Oooh-Aaah. "And best of all, cup holders.

"Bottle holders," a wife on the porch corrected.

"I'd say one for a bottle and one for your beer," Tom countered. "Here, take it for a spin around the fountain. See how it corners."

Shaking his head, Matt seized the handles and maneuvered the stroller in a circle with the blue bear still bobbing on his chest. "Look at that. I'd say he's a natural," Tom claimed and led a round of applause.

Matt took a bow, almost dumping the stuffed bear on the patio tiles, which drew some laughter. "Really, thanks guys. You've gone out of your way for me and Daniel. Tom, if you ever need to borrow these things, just let me know."

Alix sent her blonde hair flying as she shook her

head. "I still have a few years on my contract. You might wear them out by then." Having mercy, she helped Matt out of his Baby Björn and rested the bear in the stroller.

Tom took over again. "Time to eat. We have pizza and ribs and all sorts of sides from avocado toast to zucchini strips and dip lined up on the tables on the porch, all made by the fabulous women of the Sinners. We could have had it catered, but they wanted a family affair. Welcome Matt, to our team family."

The applause broke up fairly quickly as lines formed. From her spot on the porch, among the wives and girlfriends, most of them model perfect, Annie watched as Matt received plenty of backslaps along with a rack of ribs and a slab of pizza. How well his Mellie would have fit in with these polished Sinners women who had all the time in the world to work out and get their hair and nails done.

She felt shorter, darker, older, and definitely more tired than the rest of them, knowing her shift started again tomorrow night. Jude stood somewhere amid the tall blondes and bodacious black women so beautifully dressed but wouldn't give a damn of course. Someone put an arm around her shoulders—her mom, just as petite, dark, quite a bit older, but still married for years to the legendary Joe Billodeaux. Her presence gave Annie hope.

"I think Tom handled that well," Nell said. "Just enough comedy and some real sincerity, but I think we've lost Matt to the men until after dinner when the women take over with gifts and cake. Come sit with us in the meantime. Your dad has a table staked out over there."

Annie swore sometimes her mother could read minds—or Xochi had slipped and told her everything. Still, a few secrets never reached Nell's ears, especially those between Jude and Annie.

The party continued with the slicing a huge cake appropriately decorated with all things baby boy and football combined, plastic storks and a goal post, blue booties and brown footballs. Undoubtedly, Tom had ordered it. Afterward, Matt endured the endless opening of gifts: mountains of diapers, drawers full of cute outfits from size zero to two, blankets and quilts, two humidifiers and three wipe warmers plus an engraved silver cup and noise cancelling headphones especially for Daniel to wear to games. He held up each item and said, "I appreciate whatever this is," a few times when he was stumped, which earned him good-natured laughter. Then, he passed the presents around the dining room to be oohed and aahed over like the stroller, but uncoached this time. As the guests departed, he shook each and every hand and offered his thanks again.

Dean showed him how to collapse the stroller into the SUV, and Tom helped mound the gifts onto the seats. Annie remarked, "There's barely room for me in the front seat."

"I'll always have room for you, Annie. You're so tiny."

"Great, more short jokes, as if I don't get enough of that from Dean." But she smiled to let him know she didn't mind a little bit.

"Would you mind going to my place first to unload this loot since it's close? I've been thinking I don't need it all and might take some things to Arielle Wagner since I promised to visit—if you'll help me pick out what she could use."

"Definitely a wipe warmer. I doubt if Junelle invested in one of those. It did occur to me that I didn't bring a gift tonight."

"You've given me so much already. Set up Daniel's nursery and got him all those preemie clothes. Now that he's in an open warmer, the nurses dress him all the time. I never know if I'll find a little bear or a Sinners fan when I come to visit. I have a picture of every one. Besides that, you've given me so much support. I don't know how I would have weathered these months without you."

Annie might have enjoyed hearing more praises, but they arrived at Matt's house, all lit up with spotlights left in place by Ollie to highlight his former home. They hauled the gifts inside, dumping them in the right-hand parlor, which had a smattering of furniture that wouldn't fit in the living room and sat arranged in no particular way. Unpacked boxes sat on tables and stacked on the floor. The gifts merely added to the clutter.

"You should do something about this," Annie suggested. "Finish unpacking, really move in."

"It's mostly Mellie's knickknacks and family pictures. Things I don't know how to handle yet."

"Once the season begins and Daniel comes home, you won't have much time to deal with it and should take it on soon. Matt, he could be released in two weeks or so. Another item you haven't taken care of is selecting a baby nurse. I wish I could get our Nurse Shammy to come. She took such good care of the triplets and loves babies, but she is getting older and is caught up with Xochi and Teddy's children right now. I also think she doesn't like to leave her husband since he's getting up in years, but everyone on the list I gave you is excellent. Have you interviewed any of them? If you procrastinate, some won't be available anymore."

"I only want the best for Danny."

"Of course, you do, but you have to make up your mind and choose soon."

Matt took a deep, chest-expanding breath. "Annie, I want to ask you something."

"Anything." Her heartbeat kicked up and her breathing with it. Could this be happening now, amid the debris belonging to his late wife and the piles of gifts from his new team family? Not a setting she would have chosen, but anywhere with Matt would do.

He took her hands and looked into her eyes, brown meeting brown. "Annie, I want you for my baby nurse."

Chapter Twenty-Two

The sharp disappointment took her breath away. Her hands slipped from his grasp. She slumped onto a boxy chair stacked with gift bags and crushed them exactly the way she felt in her heart. He valued her support and her help in setting up the nursery, probably her company at breakfast and her connection with the Billodeauxs, too, but he wanted a nurse, not a new wife.

"I'm sorry. Am I asking too much? I mean I'll pay you twice what you make now, and you'd have every evening I'm home off if you wanted. Maybe not weekends during the season, but after that."

He wanted a live-in babysitter, not a person to share his life and Daniel's. She gathered the pieces of her shattered pride. "I'm very well paid and have a career I love. Really, until or unless I burn out, I have no intention of leaving the NICU."

"I understand that, but you endure a lot of stress and don't have much personal time. This could give you a new life with only one child to care for. Three times your salary, name your price."

His desperation touched her. "I wouldn't do it for the money, only for Daniel." And you, and you, and you.

"For Danny then. Please!"

Annie pushed from the unattractive chair sturdy enough to support her wobbling legs. Is this how football players felt when they'd been blindsided, the unexpected coming from out of nowhere and taking them down? "I believe all the gifts are inside. I should get home."

"Annie?" His deep voice pleaded.

"I'll think about your offer. Take me back to the apartment now." She flicked off the spotlights as she headed for the door just in case their sheen highlighted a few tears she wiped away with her fingertips.

Matt lumbered behind turning on the porch light. "Be careful. Don't miss your step."

She'd already gotten to the gate and swung it open.

"Annie, are you angry with me?"

"No, simply unprepared for your offer. I'll give you an answer shortly." Once she got over the shock of what he really wanted from her.

Men of Matt's type rarely babbled, but he did tonight, all the way across Canal Street and into her cul-de-sac. He reviewed the baby shower, how he appreciated Tom's joke and being welcomed by the team, the torture of opening all those gifts no matter how well meant. Matt tried hard to elicit her laughter at his own expense, but Annie remained quiet in her corner of the front seat until they arrived.

"Yes, it was a nice evening," she said, getting down before he could jump out of the SUV to help her. Until that last part. She went through the unlocking ritual which Matt watched from the car, then raced up the stairs where Jude waited.

Her sister stuffed her face with leftover baby shower cake, all the plastic ornaments cast aside on the kitchen table. A glass of milk, half downed, sat nearby. "Want some? All those skinny babes barely touched it.

They have to exercise it off at the gym while we run our tails off at work. It's too late for coffee now. You sure took a long time getting home and had plenty of time to do it. Did you?"

"Jude, please. We had a lot of gifts to carry inside—and he wanted to ask me something."

Jude's fork clanged against the side of the plate. "No shit! He really asked you to marry him? I figured he'd pine for his wife at least a year."

"No, he asked me to be Daniel's nurse at twice my current salary." She'd held it in all the way home. Now, the tears came in a flood complete with quaking shoulders and hiccups.

Jude sprang from her chair, oversetting it, and embraced Annie. "I didn't like him before and now I hate him. Tell me you said no."

"I—I said I'd have to think about it."

"Don't. Call him right now and tell that bastard you are not going to be the hired help."

"He thinks of me as the best nurse for Danny, not hired help. If I were there in the house with them, he might come to see us as a family."

Jude let loose with a harsh laugh. "Don't fool yourself. When he gets over his wife, he'll start dating models, and you'll be the babysitter waiting for him to come home from being with them. Why set yourself up for more hurt?"

"Because I do think he cares for me, but simply can't act on it yet. Maybe that's another reason he asked me to move into the pink palace."

"Idiot! Go take a hot bath and add some lavender oil to the water. Get a good night's sleep and make a decision when your mind clears."

"Good idea."

Annie followed her sister's directions, but she didn't rest well until nearly dawn when fatigue overtook her. She stayed in bed because she needed to prepare for her shift at the hospital she told herself, but mostly she didn't want of face Jude.

Annie couldn't escape. Her sister stayed home and was in the midst of making chicken noodle soup when she went downstairs as if she had an invalid in her care. Like ripping off a bandage, Annie figured she might as well do it fast.

"I've decided to take Matt's offer."

Jude turned from stirring the steaming pot. "You were there to pick up my pieces when I fell apart, and I'll be here to gather yours."

Chapter Twenty-Three

Annie handed in her two-week notice to much shock in the NICU, though Peggy said with a wink she understood completely. Annie doubted that. Daniel passed his car seat test with no bradycardia incidents on the day of her brief going away party.

As the regular football season approached, she and Daniel were ready to move into Matthew Keaton's pink house. Lovingly, Annie placed the now seven-pound-two-ounce baby into the crib of the pretty nursery she'd helped create and attached a monitor to detect any physical irregularities before moving to the small, comfortable guest room next door where she'd be staying. Other than her clothes, she hadn't brought much with her except pictures of the family and numerous shots of her and Jude, arms around each other in various locales. Personal items went into the bathroom at her end of the hall, though Matt told her to feel free to use the luxurious master bath anytime she wanted.

Their first full day passed awkwardly with Matt trying so hard not to wake the baby when getting up early for team meeting and practice. His efforts didn't matter as Annie was already in the nursery giving Daniel a six a.m. bottle. Wearing a simple cotton nightie and a bathrobe, she sat in the rocker attending to his son's needs, having gotten up while Matt showered.

He apologized profusely. "I'm so sorry. I didn't hear him cry over the sound of the water."

"That's why I'm here," Annie answered.

He made his own breakfast and offered to bring her a tray. "Only coffee right now," she said. "He'll sleep again fairly soon, and I can go down to the kitchen and get what I want."

"I stocked up on oatmeal and eggs. Got scones from the bakery. Anything else you want, let me know."

"Don't miss team meeting," she prompted. "There are fines for that."

"Right." Matt kissed Daniel's cheek, coming so close to her own she felt the brush of his freshly shaven chin, and took off for the Dome.

He returned tired, but clean and showered, spent some time talking and singing to Daniel before both went down for a nap. With free time on her hands, Annie assembled dinner, though it wasn't exactly in her job description. She fried a four-pack of seasoned pork chops purchased at a Cajun butcher shop, made a large portion of instant mashed potatoes, nuked a sack of mixed vegetables, and shook salad from a bag. Not haute cuisine, but Matt sat down to eat it without complaint.

Somehow, they'd lost the easiness they'd had in the hospital cafeteria with dozens of people around where they'd celebrated every ounce the baby gained and even his first normal poop with a meal of pancakes or omelets. Relieved when Daniel began crying during the meal, she had an excuse to leave the kitchen table and trotted up the backstairs to attend to him. She spent much more time changing, feeding, and soothing the infant than she had in the NICU. When she returned, Matt had shown his appreciation by eating three of the four pork chops, clearing the table, and setting her plate on top of the microwave for reheating. Annie offered a rueful smile and an observation. "Babies—don't expect to get through a full meal uninterrupted for a while."

"I won't. I do have ice cream if you want dessert."

"No, thanks."

Matt scooped out a bowl of chocolate for himself and took it to his den. She finished her dinner and retreated to her room to watch TV until Daniel cried again. All of them went to bed early.

Around midnight, Daniel's alarm went off. Annie darted from her room to run smack into Matt's bare chest in the hallway as both desperately tried to reach the baby. She hadn't paused to put on a robe over her modest but rather flimsy nightgown, and he wore only pajama bottoms, not that either noticed until the crisis passed.

Daniel had kicked off his monitor and only wanted attention. "Best not to give in during the night or he'll want playtime at all hours," Annie warned. She reattached the monitor, wrapped him tightly, and turned out the light again.

"Hard not to." Matt lingered in the doorway before returning to his room. Next morning, he was gone before either Annie or the baby woke since they'd been up at four for a changing and bottle.

Though technically three months old, Daniel was developmentally a newborn still in the eat-sleep-poop cycle. He had yet to smile but watched his mobile of blue teddy bears swirl above his head with bright eyes. Movement and color interested him and when awake,

Annie took him downstairs in his carrier to see the wider world, mostly her stuffing the scrubs she still wore into the washer and dryer or sitting near the garden window while she had a cup of coffee or figured out what to make for dinner. She knew enough to take an afternoon nap when he did to store up energy for his night feedings.

Used to caring for multiple babies and being on her feet, she found her new pace too slow. As she wasn't recovering from childbirth as most new mothers were, she had an excess of energy. She would have loved to take Daniel out in the super stroller in the early morning, but for now thought it best to keep him away from the germs of the curious and the pollen that filled the air.

Taking on the project of sorting the baby gifts, putting away what they would keep, and making a pile of things she thought Junelle Wagner could use helped pass the time. She didn't dare dispose of Mellie's things, but organized the boxes against the walls of the parlor after peeking into each one to see what they contained and labeling each with a marker. She shoved the chairs into a grouping around a table and sat down, admitting she was curious about only one container, a collection of pictures and albums. Surely, Matt wouldn't care if she looked through them.

Right on top, Annie withdrew a framed photo of an ascetic older couple with their arms around Matt garbed in a high school graduation gown too short for his size. His adoptive parents were proud as could be, probably acknowledging that their son looked nothing like them as he rose head and shoulders above their slender frames and graying heads, but not caring a bit. That made her smile as she ran a finger down Matt's tall form until she recalled their tragic death only a few years later when they died in that car crash on their way to one of his college games. She set it up on the table and took out a pristine white box containing the fabled wedding album.

Yes, the affair had been grand and documented step by step from Marilyn arranging her daughter's veil to the cutting of a lavish five-layer cake by the couple and numerous shots of the bride and groom with various family members, especially his new Ames in-laws who lined up with Matt towering in the middle like a prized athletic trophy. Buckner and his boys stood on one side while Marilyn leaned into her eldest daughter and slightly away from a much younger blonde girl, the now Goth Dre. Would she want such fancy nuptials? No, she didn't think so.

A stunning portrait of Matt and Melinda with his arms around her willowy waist in their full wedding regalia, his smile so happy, hers so pleased, was duplicated by a framed version for dresser top decoration just beneath the album. Annie had to admit Melinda had the height to carry it off while she imagined herself in the same picture, so small people might assume she'd been a child bride. There would be no striking contrast of blonde and dark since both she and Matt were brown and brown as the cops said. She set that one on the table to further remind herself of the kind of woman Matt had lost and carefully replaced the album in its tissue and box.

She excavated five years' worth of Ames reunion pictures, all labeled by date and with a varying cast except for Marilyn and her family always dead center, first row. Matt appeared standing behind them, again a man so unlike the other relatives, the cuckoo in the nest. The rest of the contents spilled out: his baby book, every page filled in with events like "first tooth" and "first steps" and "first word"—dada like most babies— and album after album of photos from newborn to college student. Caught up in reviewing Matt's life, Annie jumped when her phone buzzed in her pocket. Jude.

"Hey, Sis, you bored with playing mommy yet? You on for Sacred Sister Thursday? If Matt really meant what he said about letting you have evenings off when he's home, we could go to Mariah's Place and do some dancing. Meet some guys, have a few drinks. What do you say?"

"I'd say I don't want to leave him alone with the baby this soon."

"What, he can't change a diaper or give a bottle? That's all on you?"

"No, he does those things. I trained him before Daniel left the NICU. Even though I'm here, he keeps getting up nights whenever the baby cries. The alarm sounded the other evening, and both of us rushed to the nursery. I think we need more time to establish our routine before I go drinking and dancing with you."

"Spoilsport. How about only going out for dinner?"

"I just said…"

"What if I bring dinner over there tomorrow night, enough to feed the giant, too. Does a pan of Mona Lisa lasagna sound good with plenty of bread sticks? You make a salad. I'll bring the wine."

"That would be very nice of you. I'll admit I am experiencing some cabin fever, staying inside most of

193

the day while Matt is gone. Let's make it around six. We tend to go to bed early."

"Too bad it's not with each other." Jude's laugh had a cutting edge to it. "If I wanted a man that badly, I'd go for it."

"You most certainly would, but I am not you. We need more time. See you tomorrow around six."

Involved with her conversation, she missed Matt's arrival until the front door slammed. Maybe the vibration woke Daniel because he started to howl. Here she was pawing through his past while his son cried for attention.

"Annie, I'm home…" he began before he spotted her in the parlor sitting at a table dotted with framed photos and an album from his childhood open before her. His happy, relaxed features hardened.

She jumped up. "Really, I wasn't prying. I sorted the gifts and boxes and this one caught my eye. You might want to put some of the photos out here and there."

Matt's gaze went to his wedding picture and the faces of his deceased parents. "Not right now. I'll clean this up. Daniel needs you."

"Yes, sir," she answered in the same way she'd addressed doctors who gave her orders. Annie scampered toward the doorway and ducked under his arm since he stood balanced in the frame. "Oh, by the way, Jude is bringing us dinner tomorrow. Lasagna from Mona Lisa. Isn't that nice of her?"

"Yeah, can't wait." His tone said he could wait until the end of time for Jude to show up at his house whether she brought excellent food or not. "Go take care of Daniel."

She raced down the hall and up the spiral stairs. She'd caused him pain and bother with no way to fix it. Daniel squalled as if the service had seriously deteriorated since he left the NICU as she changed him, put on a clean outfit, and warmed a bottle taken from the mini-fridge they'd put in the nursery to ease going down the narrow stairs at night. Annie settled in the rocker to let him nurse. Holding Daniel close, rubbing a light finger across his shock of dark hair, she let the baby soothe her instead of the other way around.

Chapter Twenty-Four

Jude arrived earlier than Matt for their Thursday dinner which did not make Annie particularly happy. Just more time for Jude to criticize and make snarky remarks. After Jude popped the lasagna into the oven to warm, she leaned against the kitchen counter as Annie prepared the bagged salad with additions of sliced mushrooms, olives, green peppers, thinly sliced red onions, and anything else in the fridge to make it more special. Daniel watched the activity from his carrier stowed in a safe spot, accidently hitting the toys that dangled above his head from time to time. His avid eyes seemed to be attempting to make sense of two women who looked so much like Annie.

Annie topped the salad with grated parmesan and sat it on the kitchen table already set for three this evening. She checked the clock again. Matt rarely ran so late. After training, he nearly always came directly home unless Annie asked him to pick up his dry cleaning or some groceries. Jude filled the time with chatter about her cases at the hospital which made Annie a little homesick for her old job of saving tiny lives.

She had little to add to the conversation but disliked when Jude turned the comments her way with sharp, hurtful observations. "Why are you still wearing scrubs? That's no way to turn a man on."

"I'm used to them. They're comfortable and easy to wash when a baby boy gives you a good squirt in the chest or misses the cloth on your shoulder when he spits up. Besides, Matt has seen me in street clothes often enough to know I have a female shape under them."

"Have you figured out his type of woman yet? His wife fell into the tall, blonde, and beautiful category, short, dark sister of mine."

"Matt hasn't shown any interest in women yet. The other day, I unearthed his wedding album and took out a portrait of the two of them together. He caught me at it and asked that I put the photos away. He finds them too painful to view right now."

"Maybe he doesn't think he looked handsome enough."

"Not a possibility. They were a beautiful couple, well-matched in height."

"Which means you aren't? Consider Mom and Dad if you want an example of an odd couple that worked."

"I tried to do that but couldn't manage to put myself in the picture."

"You are hopeless. Where is the big brute anyhow?"

"Don't know." Annie accepted a glass of wine.

When Matt did show up, he carried a bakery box and a sheepish expression. "I, ah, stopped off for a beer with some of the guys and picked up a cheesecake from the Cake Cafe on Chartres since it wasn't all that far from Mariah's. Sorry if I'm holding up dinner."

"At least you're learning your way around the city," Jude sniped. She'd insisted on opening one of the three bottles of wine she'd brought and was well into draining her second glass while Annie's first sat half full by the basket of breadsticks. "Nice to have someone to take care of the kid while you stop off at the bar."

"Matt, you have every right to some social time, and I love cheesecake," Annie countered.

"'Yeah, since you aren't working as hard now, you'd better go easy on it. Matt needs to allow you some gym time. Planet Fitness is open all night. Let's eat." Jude removed the lasagna from the oven and transported it to the table. She shoved a serving spoon through its cheesy layers, topped off her wine and Annie's before taking a seat.

Matt also sat and splashed some wine into his glass. It occurred to Annie that the main reason he'd run late and missed his usual time with Daniel could be summed up in one word—Jude. Well, she'd allowed her to come over and had to help them get along. She steered the conversation to the training sessions, and Matt supplied some interesting stories to move the evening along. Usually, they discussed Daniel, another safe topic, but one Jude would scarcely be interested in hearing.

When the baby began to turn red and grunt just as they were about to cut the cheesecake, Matt jumped up and grabbed the handle of the carrier. "I'll take him upstairs for a change and a bottle. I'll see if I can get him down for a few hours. You visit with your sister, Annie." Quick on his feet on and off the field, he pounded up the stairs with his son as if he needed to make a big score for the team.

"Thass nice. He lets the hired help eat dessert in peace." Jude tipped the second wine bottle over her glass, found it empty, and opened the third.

"I don't want anymore," Annie said. She'd had a glass and a half, Matt probably two. The rest had been absorbed into Jude's petite body.

"But I dooo!"

"I'm making coffee to go with the cheesecake."

"None for me." Jude carved out a sizeable chunk of the pecan, chocolate, and caramel turtle cheesecake and toted it to her seat.

Annie cut a small portion for herself, all too aware of Jude's comment about her possible impending weight gain. Both had finished by the time they heard Matt's voice singing the lullaby about the pretty little horses in the nursery.

Jude sniffed with sudden sentimentality. "Mom and Dad used to sing that one to Dean and Tom and us—but not so well. I guess Matt's not so bad." Jude laid her face cradled in her arms on the table.

"No, he's a considerate man with a very good voice, though babies really don't care as long as you sing to them." Far more considerate than her sister was currently being—her drunk sister who appeared to be asleep or passed out just to the left of the remains of her cheesecake. At least, she hadn't gone face down into it.

Upstairs, the singing stopped. Annie imagined Matt easing Daniel into his crib, attaching the monitor, covering him with a light blanket. A moment later, he tiptoed down the stairs and took in the sight of Jude collapsed at his dinner table. He held up the green wine bottle to the fading summer light. Half gone, and all of it in Jude.

"My turn to apologize. I'd drive her home, but I couldn't get her up the stairs."

"I'd be happy to do that for you," he offered.

Lynn Shurr

"No, no. Jude can be hard to handle when she's drunk. Believe me I know. Could you carry her upstairs and put her on my bed? We shared a bunk often enough when we were growing up. If she gets sick in the night, I'll take care of her, and get her back to the apartment tomorrow."

"What about Daniel if I'm gone?"

"He passed his car seat test, and we both have bases for it in our cars. I guess we'll go for a ride and visit Aunt Jude's place."

Annie knew Matt wasn't happy about that, but he didn't argue. He scooped Jude from her chair and started for the kitchen staircase. She roused enough to nuzzle his shirt and say, "I dream of a big man carrying me upstairs to the bedroom." Jude stroked his cheek. "Not so bad."

Matt rolled his eyes. "Dream on. Here we go."

He handled her easily. Annie also dreamed of a scene like that, but with one specific man. Now, her sister got to live it—and wouldn't remember a thing in the morning. Disgusted, she poured coffee and cut a generous serving of cheesecake for Matt. He deserved it for his labors.

Returning, he joined Annie at the table where she had her second cup of brew. One of them should be alert and sober tonight. He inquired carefully, "Does Jude have a drinking problem?"

"Not really. She put away a lot of booze in college, and I had to haul her back to the dorm more than once, but she settled down junior year, got into nursing, and really put that behind her except for the occasional Saturday night overindulgence when she's out with her friends. Her job is more stressful than mine was. I guess she needs the relief sometimes. Also, though I hate to admit it, something about you gets under her skin."

"I understand she doesn't like your living here. I guess I got between you and that explains it."

"Yes, probably does. She likes to run my life as well as her own."

"You can't allow that. You're two very different people. I could never mistake one of you for the other."

"Try telling her—but not tonight."

Matt regarded the last wine bottle again. "Two glasses left. Want to go out into the garden and relax?"

"Why not?"

Matt took the bottle and the two glasses. Annie grabbed the baby monitor. They shared the wine, talked as the last of the light faded, more comfortable with each other at last having faced another crisis together. With Jude sleeping in her bed, Annie knew nothing else would happen tonight other than Daniel's midnight feeding.

Chapter Twenty-Five

Matt went to bed full of heavy food and more wine and beer than he usually indulged in at any time. He'd walked Annie to her room, wishing he could step inside and be with her for the evening, but it wouldn't be tonight. With the door wide open, he saw Jude had ransacked her dresser drawers while they were outside and now slept as deeply as Daniel under Annie's quilt with only two thin black spaghetti straps of a nightie showing against her lightly tanned shoulders beneath her riot of dark curls.

Annie sighed. "I guess she helped herself to my lingerie. I was saving that one for a special occasion."

"Any occasion with you is special." This one called for a soft kiss, but Daniel whimpered in his sleep, and both of them dashed to his crib. He'd kicked his blankets off and didn't rouse as Annie wrapped and secured them again.

"He was awake a lot today. I don't think he'll cry for a bottle until midnight. We both need to get some rest."

Matt nodded. What else could he do? Shove Annie into the rocker and have his way with her? Ten o'clock—both of them would be out cold until Danny stirred again. He went to his big, lonely bed and lay on the side near the baby monitor. The football he'd used as a surrogate Daniel sat next to it. Now that he had the real thing in the nursery, he didn't need its comfort anymore, but oh, how he needed Annie. With that thought in mind, he hit the pillow and slept deeply for a couple of hours.

Something woke him, and not his son crying for attention. Annie teased him that he'd developed mother's ears, able to hear if Daniel so much as drummed his feet against the mattress. He sat up trying to detect what was wrong. The door to his room opened. Backlit by the hall light they always left on to illuminate their way to the nursery, Annie's petite, delicate form stood silhouetted in the opening. She pushed the straps of a short, silky, nearly transparent white nightgown edged deeply in black lace top and bottom from her slight shoulders and let it pool to the floor. Annie had come to him.

For a few seconds, he believed it because he desired her so badly. He'd wanted to give her time to adjust to a permanent place in his home, his life, before rushing her to a commitment which might have been made out of sympathy or simply friendship. Or could have repelled her that a man had forgotten his dead wife so soon and moved on to another.

She turned to close the door and in the last beam of light before darkness, he saw the tattoo on her hip, a butterfly, a red butterfly. Before he could react, she'd launched herself onto the foot of his bed and crawled toward him like a tigress stalking a water buffalo. Her small white breasts attracted his gaze whether he wanted them to or not. She got as far as kneeling between his legs and laying a hand on his bare chest. "Nice, so nice," she whispered.

Matt shoved her hand away and flung her onto her

back.

"Yes, yes!" she said. "Now! Take me."

His voice boomed out far louder than intended. "Get the hell out of here, Jude!"

The baby monitor must have picked it up. Daniel began to wail. He heard Annie's light footsteps, not stopping at the nursery, but rushing on to his room. She'd find him in bed with her sister, dear God help him. He jumped from the covers to put distance between them. As he had since Annie and Daniel moved in, he wore pajama bottoms. Aroused when he thought Annie had come to him, he'd deflated fast enough when he noticed the red butterfly, but who would Annie believe—him or Jude, her twin sister? Not likely him. She'd leave tonight, tomorrow, forever.

Annie not only flung open the bedroom door, she turned on the overhead light, took in the scene, Jude naked on her back, legs splayed, Matt pressed against the wall, Daniel screaming over the monitor in the nursery. Without glancing his way, she marched to the bed and rolled her sister off its side, making no attempt to break her fall to the carpet. She heaved Jude who landed on hands and knees upright and turned her toward the door.

"I can't believe you'd do this to me. Trying to seduce a man you know I love—in my best nightgown." Annie stooped to gather the delicate fabric in her fists. "Put it on." Jude obeyed, not saying a word. "Go back to my room and get dressed. I'll call a cab if you can't drive."

"You don't understand. I'm not that drunk. I did it for you."

Annie shoved her sister in the right direction and

prodded her down the hall. Matt followed but veered off to console his son who had never heard two women shrieking at each other in his short life. He gathered the baby into his arms, laid him on his bare chest over his heart, rocking Daniel slightly.

"I know, I know. It's a shock to me, too. I've never had two women fight over me either. But, Danny, Annie loves us. She said so."

The infant quieted as if he understood, but more likely the heavy thud of Matt's heart did the trick. He felt his son wet through his diaper and knew Daniel wanted his bottle, judging by the way he rooted, seeking a nipple. The angry words raged on in the next room. Time to take charge and end this.

Carefully supporting Daniel's head, he strode into the hall and entered Annie's room without knocking. Jude stood, defiant, but clothed, hands on her hips, and in Annie's face. Annie wasn't backing off. "You've never done anything for me. It's always about you! You wanted Matt all along and tried to take him!"

Matt held Daniel tight and covered his ears to prevent him from startling when he raised his voice and dominated the shrill argument of the women. "Take this outside. Don't wake the neighbors. They will call the cops. Once you get it all out of your systems, Jude goes home one way or another. Annie, you can see your sister on your own time, but she isn't welcome in this house anymore."

Annie turned tear-filled brown eyes, a wounded doe, on him and the baby. "Poor Danny, I'm so sorry. Jude, move your ass outside. Let's finish this."

"You don't have to ask me twice. I hate this place and what you are doing—or not doing to my sister."

Jude stomped toward the staircase. Annie put on her robe and followed.

Matt took Daniel back to the nursery and changed his diaper, sat in the rocker, and fed him a bottle. All the while, he talked to his son, low and steady. "Don't worry, Danny. We're going to keep Annie with us, I promise."

Chapter Twenty-Six

Annie faced Jude by the fountain, whose pleasant trickle should have eased their tension. It did not. Though their voices were still strident, they did try to keep them down.

"I tried to see if he had any interest in you. All cats are black in the dark, right? If he thought I was you and made love to me, then you could take over next time, the ice broken so to speak. I have to admit after I got a good look at his body, it wouldn't have been such a sacrifice. That trip up the staircase in his arms—hot."

Annie resisted the urge to push Jude's butt into the small pool where the water collected and recirculated, but not by much. "That should have been me."

"Exactly, but when were you going to let him know how you feel? A year from now or never because he hooked up with someone else while you took care of his kid?" Jude appealed to her reason, arms held out to receive a hug of forgiveness.

Too soon for that. "When did you come up with this grand, self-sacrificing scheme—the minute I told you I'd take the job and leave you alone in the apartment?"

Jude hugged herself instead. "No, about three glasses of wine in at dinner when it seemed to make perfect sense. I didn't drink that third half bottle. Every time you got distracted by Matt's singing or the

207

cheesecake, I watered those houseplants you have by the window with it. If they die, I'll replace them."

"Like you tried to replace me tonight, so easily?"

"No, like you offered to replace me once upon a time when I got knocked up with a frat guy's baby. You took the pill and got chlamydia. Birth control pills made me nauseous and bloated, so I relied on condoms. Get drunk enough, and a girl forgets to tell the guy to use them, or in your case, didn't bother to insist he put one on at all."

Annie's voice dulled with the worst memory of their sophomore year of college. "Mom and Dad would have been so ashamed of us."

"Nope, Mom would have understood and coped. Dad would have made sure both fellows were kicked out of LSU, and he'd do the kicking personally."

That comment drew a very faint smile from Annie. "Maybe. We'll never know since we vowed to handle the situations ourselves." Recalling painful times, Annie sank into one of the patio chairs. Jude took the one opposite and seized Annie's hand before she could snatch it away.

"The jerk paid for my abortion, and you came with me here to New Orleans, stayed by me until it was over, and never told a soul. But before that, you begged me to have the child. Let's skip a semester and go home to the ranch, you said. Your Mardi Gras madness baby will be born in October. I'll say it's mine if you don't want it. We can go back to school at the local university, and no one will know the difference. You offered to make that sacrifice for me."

"Not a sacrifice. I believed I'd be sterile for life from contracting a venereal disease. Thank God, a former girlfriend turned that ass in to the health center people who made him list all his sexual contacts. I was only one of half a dozen he infected. So easily cured with antibiotics, but did I get treatment in time? The fear still nags at me."

Jude squeezed the hand she'd captured. "The doctors said you'd be fine, and I can still have kids if I want them—which I don't. But, I always did think that's why you are so nuts for babies. Perhaps, I was selfish, but I wanted to keep my life on track, not sidetracked, and I didn't want you to have to pay for my mistake either. Those crises certainly sobered us up, and look at us now, saving lives on a daily basis. At least, I am. You gave that up."

Annie jerked her hand away. Thinking of the past when they'd stood together almost dissipated her anger. "I'm starting on a new course, Jude—if you haven't burned down the bridge to it tonight."

"I admit my boozy idea sucked. Seemed wonderful at the time. Just so you know, Matt rejected me rather forcefully the second he knew I wasn't you. I was so sure I could fool him."

"I told him about the butterflies."

"Okay, a minor betrayal. Our sisters know because they've seen us naked, but we still have Dad and our brothers in doubt. I know my mistake tonight was huge, but it did accomplish its goal. Matt knows you are in love with him."

"Really? I don't see how when I was having a screaming fit with you and left him to care for Daniel."

"Annie, you said the words, that I tried to seduce the man you love, right in front of Matt. I also noticed you didn't blame him one bit for the situation. If that isn't love, I don't know what is."

Annie pressed her fingers to her lips. "Oh, no. In my anger I let it slip out. I don't see how I'll face him now." She eyed her sister with suspicion. "Was that part of a plan to get me to leave here?"

"You said it, not me. I think you should go upstairs and deal with him now. I'll drive myself back to the apartment. Nothing sobers a woman up like a shouting match with the person you care the most about in the world."

"Oh, Jude, Matt has banned you from the house. I don't know when we'll see each other again. I guess it could be soon if he asks me to leave too."

"I doubt he will. You are the best baby nurse in New Orleans after all. If he does, my arms are always open to you, and you still have your keys." Jude stood and leaned to embrace her twin. "Are we good now?"

"As much as we can be. I won't say thanks for what you did, but I guess I can forgive you."

"That's all I want. I'm sure I'll be seeing you, sis." Instead of leaving by way of the house, Jude took Matt at his word and choose the narrow side path to the front yard, lurking snakes or not.

Moments later, Annie heard her car leave the quiet, elegant neighborhood. She remained alone by the fountain, listening to the burble of the falling water, trying to figure out what to do next. A storm brewed in the distance turning the balmy evening she'd shared with Matt into a steam bath of humidity. Her thin cotton nightie stuck to her skin beneath the robe, and the mosquitos fought to dine on her ankles.

She must go inside and face more turmoil, but if she were lucky, perhaps Daniel and Matt had both gone back to bed.

No such luck. She heard the slap of Matt's bare feet on the flagstones before he placed gentle hands on her shoulders. "Annie, come upstairs with me."

Chapter Twenty-Seven

Silently, Matt escorted Annie to her room. All the while, he searched for the right words to put her at ease and take the tears from her eyes, to say what lay deep in his heart. He lacked the facility with language that his mother, the English professor, possessed. He'd had no chance to inherit it from her. Undoubtedly, a big, dumb jock conceived him. He felt it keenly now.

Annie had restored order to her space after Jude ransacked the dresser drawers seeking nightwear before going to bed herself. Only the white silk and black lace nightie lay crumpled on the floor, the single sign of the tempest that had taken place. Annie reached down and balled it into a waste basket.

He spoke the first words that came to him. "Don't do that. I'd like to see you wear it, not Jude."

Annie's eyes grew big. "What?"

"That came out wrong. I meant if you had come to me instead of your sister, we'd be in bed together right now." Everything that came out of his mouth made it worse.

"Really?" Her brows raised. Her cheeks flushed.

"Even without the butterfly tattoo, I knew she wasn't you, the aggressive way she tried to seduce me. You have to believe I didn't encourage her." Still stumbling.

"You don't think I can be aggressive in bed?"

"You are kind and loving—but I guess you can be anything you want to be anywhere. Please say you'll stay here with me and Daniel. You said you loved me. You screamed it during your fight with Jude. Probably, you'll think I'm a big douche for telling you that I have feelings for you so soon after my wife's death."

He placed his hand on his bare chest where his son lay not long ago, where his heart thundered. "The heart wants what it wants, someone famous said." Certainly, his mother would have known who and helped him out in this situation. Maybe, somewhere, she did. "I want you Annie. I love you no matter what you think of me for bringing this up so soon." There, he'd made the leap across the goal line and finished the play no matter how ugly and awkwardly.

Annie moved away from him. Possibly she'd leave tomorrow, afraid of being rushed, afraid of his size. She turned her back and dropped her robe. She stretched, taking the damp nightie over her head. The black butterfly on her rump appeared to flutter as she withdrew white silk and black lace from the basket and let it slither down her back. Annie turned to face him.

"What do you think?"

"That it looks better on you." Not a man of words, but one of action, Matt closed the distance between them in one long stride and lifted her into his arms. Annie's hands moved around his neck. Close to his ear, he heard her soft sigh. They passed the nursery where his son slept and rounded into his bedroom. The sheets were still disturbed from his rejection of Jude. He laid her down as gently as he would Daniel and joined her there, bringing her into his arms again and kissing her as he'd so often wanted to do.

He meant to take his time, sliding his tongue along her lips and pressing lightly, but Annie opened for him immediately and took him in with a twining of tongues. Her fingers raked through his hair and his tangled in her curls. His urgency grew faster than he intended. Annie felt it and shoved the pajama bottoms out of the way. She took him in her hand and stroked. He disposed of the nightie and massaged her breasts, small, perfect in his hands. With one finger she moved him onto his back and mounted his erection. He thrust upward, completing their joining. Matt tried not to hurt her with his size, but Annie wanted none of that. She told him so with the pace she set and the open pleasure on her face revealed by light in the hall beyond the door they'd failed to close. He helped her along with his hands splayed over the cheeks with the black butterfly.

Nothing like Mellie who withheld any sign of enjoyment in the last year and hadn't really participated avidly before that. Sometimes he wondered if he'd fallen in love with her family and not the woman herself, a tragedy for both of them. Annie gave this moment her all, while the first time he'd been with Melinda was clumsy and soon over, college kid sex. He'd improved since then, holding back until Annie came, and then, he matched her, letting go like a celebration of a long-desired event.

Annie came to rest over his heart. Her small hand smoothed his hard muscles. "And you thought I couldn't be aggressive," she said. With a fingertip, she circled his nipple, making it pucker tight again. "When I first imaged being in bed with you long before I should have, I thought you'd have a hairy chest. Kangaroo care proved me wrong."

214

"I did. I shaved it for Daniel. I thought he'd like that better, and it would be more sanitary. But, if you enjoy the naked chest, I'll keep doing it."

"I think I'd love you either way."

"My angel."

She laughed at that. "Haven't I proven I'm not? I just ravished you!"

That's how I've thought of you for months, but maybe a little devilish too." He stroked her back over and over much as he did when holding Daniel, both his special beings. His thoughts roamed and suddenly hit a wall. "Annie, I should have asked before—are you on the pill? With you being a nurse I figured…"

That broke the spell of her languor. "I'm not on the pill because I haven't been sexually active for a while. I'll see about getting some."

"I should have remembered to use a condom. It's my responsibility too. Annie, I want you to know if you if I got you pregnant, I'd do the right thing and marry you."

She didn't respond immediately, and he thought she'd fallen asleep, but she did finally offer a comforting if awkward answer. "Don't worry. I had a period recently. We should be fine."

Her head drooped against his chest again. She went to sleep, right there, curled on his body, as small and precious as his son. The long-awaited storm struck, shook the windows with its fury and passed rapidly like the fight between Annie and Jude. It woke Daniel, but not his emotionally drained nurse. Matt rolled Annie to the side and tucked in the covers before getting up. "I'm coming, Danny, and I've got good news."

Chapter Twenty-Eight

Annie woke at six to the sound of Matt's shower. At first, she thought rain pattered against the window and the wind howled around the corners of the house. But no, it rained only in the bathroom and the howl came from the baby monitor. She searched the bedclothes for the lingerie hardly worn and soon discarded, put it on, and went to tend Daniel. Before Matt appeared in shorts and a T-shirt, ready to go for practice, she had the infant changed, dressed in a clean onesie, and suckling his bottle. He didn't hesitate to come forward and lay a kiss on both their heads.

Annie savored the sweetness of the moment. "It appears Danny slept through the night. I didn't expect that so soon."

"Actually, he didn't. He woke when that storm came through. I took care of him." Matt punctuated that statement with a wide yawn.

"I vaguely recall the rain, but you should have wakened me. It's my job to do those night feedings."

"You were worn out by more than your fight with Jude, and you know I always wake up when Danny cries anyhow."

Annie felt her face go warm. "And I tell you to go back to bed. All is well."

"It certainly is. Love you in that nightie. I'll put some breakfast together for both of us." Matt left with a grin on his face that said he had no complaints about last night.

Annie stared down at Daniel's dark head blissfully cradled against the silk. She really should have put on her robe or her scrubs. Jude's mocking voice sounded in her head. "Why are you still in scrubs? That's no way to turn a man on."

After she nestled Danny in his covers, she changed into jeans, a clingy tee, and sneakers. Annie caught Matt devouring a piece of last evening's cheesecake as he sat at the table. "Is that the breakfast you planned to make for me?"

"Nope. Coffee is ready. Eggs are in the pan and the whole wheat bread is ready to be toasted. I cut up a cantaloupe too. I got hungry waiting for you, but I'll work it off today. I like to get to practice as early as Dean, but he's hard to beat."

Annie pushed the button and watched the sliced bread disappear into the toaster. The eggs lay congealed in the pan, but still warm. She plucked a piece of cantaloupe, sweet and cool, from the bowl. When the toast popped, she made up plates for both of them and sat down.

"About last night…" she began.

"Don't tell me that will never happen again. It was great—after Jude left. I hope you'll sleep in my bed again tonight. I'll be gone tomorrow and back late on Sunday after the last preseason game, thinking of you and Daniel all the time I'm away. Are you sure you can handle him alone? At the hospital, there are dozens of people around to help, but not here."

Annie appreciated his concern, but what resonated with her was his desire to have her in bed with him tonight. "We'll be fine. Best baby nurse ever, remember. If I do need someone, I can always call…"

"Not Jude."

"Not Jude. I wanted to say Stacy or Xo. And yes, I want to sleep with you again tonight." Annie swore she'd never seen a happier man—or one who'd shoveled down his meal faster and rose to leave while she still piled scrambled eggs on her toast.

He kissed her on the lips, briefly but with warmth. "Give one to Danny for me. Got to go."

His huge presence left a void behind that she filled with another cup of coffee and a tiny sliver of the cheesecake. Should she call Jude and confess that in some weird way, her plan had brought them together. Nope. Let her stew slowly in her own juices for a few days.

****

Saturday morning, Matt, looking remarkably handsome in coat and tie but a little tired around the eyes, left to travel with the team for that last preseason game. Coach Buck insisted on professional dress for his players and fined any who wanted to be more comfortable in sweats or hoodies. Since she'd be alone with Danny all weekend, Annie wore her scrubs, then regretted her fashion choice. She certainly didn't leave Matt with a sexy image to lure him home again. Frankly, he didn't seem to notice as he kissed her and his son goodbye.

A twinge of guilt pinched at Annie. She'd been responsible for those tired eyes. Friday night, they made love vigorously after Danny went to bed, and she convinced Matt she would not be crushed if he took the upper position. Considerately, he kept his weight on his knees and arms as if doing a training exercise, but it worked for both of them. The man had stamina. Seemed he could keep that stance all night long. Later, after Daniel's three o'clock feeding, they went at it again. Six o'clock arrived way too soon.

Other than taking a nap when the baby slept, she debated how to spend her day. Laundry featured big in her morning. Danny sat in his carrier watching her sort out the colors on the kitchen floor and load the clothes into the washer. Daniel fussed for his bottle just when she'd put her lunch on the table. Annie held him in the crook of one arm with her hand twisted around to feed him and ate her toasted cheese sandwich and cubes of cantaloupe with the other. Nap came next on both of their agendas.

She'd just gotten Danny down when the doorbell rang. Surely not Jude hoping to sneak back into Matt's house. Maybe Stacy or Xo, and she'd welcome their company, but asked them to call first. Whoever it was had no consideration and hit the bell again. She practically slid down the bannister to the front hall to stop the racket. A quick peek through the peephole told her nothing as the person had leaned aside going for the bell again. Warned by Stacy to be cautious of anyone coming to the door, Annie opened the door only a crack. "Yes?"

"Is this Matt Keaton's house? Looks like his place from the pictures."

She didn't open the door any farther, but took in the Frankenstein boots, the dark, shapeless dress hanging just above them, the white face, and the dead black, spiked hair of the young woman. One of the groupies who often threw themselves at football players? "He's not home. Can I take a message?" Annie prayed it wouldn't be, "Tell him I want to have his baby." Matt already had one of those.

"I'm Dre, his sister-in-law. I came to help with Danny. You must be the nurse Matt always talks about. Say, it's frickin' hot out here. Can I come inside?"

"Oh yes, Dre." She should have guessed from Matt's description. But how had the teenager gotten to their doorstep from Indiana? A silver Lexus that didn't seem to jibe with the girl's appearance sat in Matt's usual parking place. Could belong to anyone, Annie guessed. She opened the door wider and stepped aside. "We didn't expect you."

Her loose black dress flapping around her legs, Dre swooped in like a vampire who had been invited inside to feast on their blood. She surveyed the hall with blue eyes outlined with kohl. "Cool staircase. Can I see Daniel?"

"He's sleeping. Where are you staying?"

"Here. Like I said, I came to help. I had another big fight with my bitch mother, so I threw my stuff in the car and started driving to a place where I'd be wanted. Two and a half days. No big deal. Tell me where to put my suitcases, and I'll haul them inside myself. You're tinier than I expected."

Annie drew herself up, but she could not compete with Dre's natural height jacked up by her three-inch thick soles. "I have to think about that. It's a fairly small house with only three bedrooms, and I'm in the guestroom next to the nursery. Matt will be out of town until Sunday night. I suppose you can have his bed for now. I'll have to change the sheets."

Dre shrugged her shoulders like a crow ruffling its

feathers. "Okay. No matter what my mom says, I'm not picky. I'll get my bags." She clomped outside again and headed for the Lexus.

Annie raced upstairs, glanced into Daniel's room to make sure he still slept, then dashed for the master bedroom to strip the sheets reeking of two nights worth of sex. She shoved them into a hamper and shook out one of Mellie's many sets of linens. Two thuds in the hallway told her Dre had returned with the suitcases. The girl shouted from the base of the stairs, "You up there? Should I bring the suitcases?"

Annie darted to the head of the steps. "Please keep it quiet. I just put the baby down. Go through the kitchen in the rear and use the back stairs. Spiral staircases might look romantic but aren't so great for hauling." She returned to putting on a top sheet and pulling up the bedspread. By the time she heard Dre thudding down the hall, she'd changed the pillowcases and fluffed the pillows against the headboard.

The girl appeared in the doorway, dropped her bags, and surveyed the suite. "Awesome!"

"Wait until you see the master bath. Anyhow, this will do for the night. Would you like something to drink? I was just going to make fresh coffee." Untrue, but what did Dre know about new baby weariness?

"Something cold sounds great, but you drink coffee in this heat?"

"It is New Orleans. Everyone does."

"Can I see Daniel before we go downstairs?"

"I guess. Be very quiet." Annie led the way to the closed nursery door. The soothing waves of a white noise machine greeted them. Danny was used to people moving all around him, so a little quiet background noise seemed appropriate.

Dre loomed over the crib like a wicked witch about to snatch the child and place it in a tower, but her black-slathered lips softened into a smile. "He looks like a real baby now."

"He's always been a real baby. He'll be down for a few hours. When he wakes, you can hold him after you wash up." Dre sniffed. "You don't have a cold, do you?"

"Nah, maybe a little hay fever."

"That won't get any better being in Louisiana. Plants and weeds bloom all year round. Everyone has a sinus condition."

"Between that and the heat, you don't make it seem very inviting here."

Maybe Annie had sabotaged her native state subconsciously. Having Dre in the house changed the dynamics between her and Matt yet again. She couldn't sleep with him when a teen stayed with them observing their every move. Oh well, the visit had to be brief since school started in the north after Labor Day. Locally, kids had already begun classes. "Let's go to the kitchen. There's cheesecake if you're hungry. New Orleans does have wonderful food."

"I got Burger King in Baton Rouge for lunch, but cheesecake sounds great."

Dre accepted one of the canned iced teas and a chunk of the cheesecake, almost gone after Annie took another sliver to eat with her nuked coffee left over from breakfast. Dre watched her nibble in an attempt to make it last longer. "I guess short people like you need to watch their weight," the Goth girl observed.

Oh, the unfiltered mouths of teens. Annie retorted,

"I'm done growing up. You're not. Have you called home to let your family know you arrived safely? That's a long drive alone." Then, she considered Marilyn's bias against Matt. "Do they know where you've gone?"

"I left a note." Dre stuffed her mouth with cheesecake, apparently to avoid saying more.

"Give them a call right now. They'll worry." No matter what Dre's problems were with her mother, Annie knew her own would want to know. She received a sullen glance for her advice.

"This is Matt's house. You can't tell me what to do."

"Well, Matt isn't here. That leaves me in charge. Call your folks or collect your baggage and drive back to Indiana." She hadn't dealt with NICU crises for years without becoming assertive when she needed to be. Some people had to be told what to do.

"Matt will be pissed that you threw me out. I'm going to call him right now." Dre withdrew her cell phone from a pocket of her scarecrow dress.

Annie snatched it away. "He's on a plane right now and preparing mentally for a game. Do you want to make more trouble for him with your family?" Annie turned on the phone and handed it over to Dre. "You have lots of messages. Pick one and tell them you are here and well."

Grudgingly, Dre sent a swift text and let Annie take a glance at the answer. "I'm at Matt's house." She turned it off again. "There. Satisfied?"

"I guess that will do. Now, tell me how you managed to finance this impromptu visit? I see you have a reliable car. Did you use a credit card for lodging along the way or sleep at roadside rests?"

"Hell, no, that's dangerous, and my parents say I'm too irresponsible to have a credit card yet. They're pretty stingy with the debit card, too, no more than fifty dollars at a time, but it paid for my lunches if I kept it cheap. Matt gave me Mellie's car and some of her jewelry. Told me I could do what I wanted with it. I hardly need a diamond wedding band." Dre fingered the leather dog collar she wore around her neck as if it were all the adornment she desired. "I hocked the ring for travel money and stayed in decent motels. I have a lot left over, but Matt can reclaim the ring if he wants. I saved the ticket."

Matt had given this kid his wife's wedding ring? Something to ponder at a later date. Annie issued a compliment. "You're very clever."

"Yeah, I am. Can I have the rest of the cheesecake?"

She'd considered saving it for Matt, but said, "Sure, polish it off." It gave them an excuse for not talking.

Dre's stare wandered to the window and the garden beyond. "Cool, it's like being in Hawaii or someplace tropical with the palm trees and all those weird plants stuck in the fountain. Really humid, too."

"The plants are bromeliads. Hawaii isn't very humid. The breezes blow from the sea all the time. Now, Samoa down by the equator is humid."

"You've been to those places? Wow!"

"Yes, Hawaii when my dad played in the Pro Bowl more than once and American Samoa for a wedding. Interesting and beautiful places."

Dre went wide-eyed. "Matt always called you

Nurse Annie, but now I recognize you from Mellie's trashy magazines. You're one of the Billodeaux family. Celebrities."

Good, maybe being star struck would make the teen easier to handle. "Well, my dad is, but we did get to travel a lot. Want to hear about Hawaii and Samoa?"

Dre swilled some more iced tea from the can and nodded like a kid who hadn't been anywhere or done anything yet but wanted to in the future. Annie poured more coffee. The travelogue filled the time until Daniel made fretful sounds in the baby monitor. He'd be in full wail soon.

"That's our cue. Let's wash up." Annie led the girl to the sink, rolled up her long sleeves, and insisted she scrub to the elbows with antibiotic soap.

"Is this really necessary?" Dre complained.

"For now—if you want to hold the baby."

Dre obeyed. She followed Annie meekly to the nursery where Daniel kicked and fussed. Annie deftly moved him to the changing table and had Danny stripped, changed, and into another cute outfit before the baby reached full demand cry for his bottle. As she warmed the milk, Dre watched in awe.

"You're really good at this. His diaper wasn't nearly as icky as I thought it would be."

"He's still on breast milk. It will get worse and much more stinky when he starts on solids. Sit in the rocker and hold your arms like this." Annie draped a flannel baby blanket over the drab dress and placed Daniel in the crook of Dre's arm.

"You're going to let me feed him? I don't know how."

How many times had she instructed new mothers

in both breast and bottle feeding? Annie had lost count. "Keep his head up, make sure the nipple stays full to keep him from swallowing air. If you rub the nipple on the side of his mouth, he'll find it and latch on."

"Look at him go!"

"Yes, he's a strong sucker now that his heart is mended."

Dre snickered at the word sucker but sobered immediately. "I saw the tiny scar. Poor thing."

"He's fine now, a great big boy like his daddy."

"Would you take a picture of the two of us with my phone, here in my pocket?"

Finally, Dre appeared to be the nice kid Matt claimed she was. Annie did that favor and began to give her the benefit of a doubt. Maybe she would be helpful during her short stay.

Danny nursed with his eyes closed but opened them wide as he slowed down. He spit out the nipple, regarded Dre's black lips and spooky blue eyes. Not Annie, not Daddy, he appeared to register, and let out a piercing scream.

"Oh, he doesn't like me. Take him. Take him quick!"

Annie covered her shoulder with a soft cloth and talked softly to Daniel as she patted his back. He emitted a big belch and a little milky spit. With a contented sigh, he settled against Annie's cheek.

"Gross," said Dre. "Maybe I shouldn't hold him again."

"You know how some kids are afraid of clowns? He's never seen a person who looks like you—not that you're clownish," Annie hastened to add. "He only knows me, his dad, and the nurses in the NICU. He'll get used to you, but maybe lose the black lips and all that kohl while you're here." She didn't dare suggest Dre wash the gelled spikes out of her hair, too, but maybe she'd do that voluntarily during her stay. One could hope.

"Take him downstairs. He likes to watch the birds that come to the fountain. Maybe you could keep an eye on him while I take a short nap. I'm up a lot at night." Doing what she didn't need to say.

"You'd trust me to do that?"

Actually, the idea scared her a bit, but Annie gave the girl a firm nod. The monitor sat right by her pillow, and Dre was cautious enough with her nephew not to do anything stupid. Somewhat rested after an hour, she went downstairs to find Dre gently rocking Daniel in his carrier with her foot and bending over to jingle his toys. Danny still regarded her with suspicious eyes but didn't cry. Maybe this brief visit would work out once Annie figured out where to put her.

Chapter Twenty-Nine

Annie resisted the temptation to call Jude and instead dialed Stacy from her room after telling Dre she'd go to bed early in order to be up with Daniel. She left the girl watching TV in the den.

"Help me, Stace."

"Is something wrong with Danny? You'd know more about that than me."

"No, Matt's teenaged sister-in-law showed up today. Basically, she ran away from home to visit the baby. I figure she has to leave when school starts up north in a couple of weeks, but where do I put her and what do I do with her while she's here? I don't want to drag Daniel all over town to entertain the kid and certainly won't let a seventeen-year-old wander the French Quarter alone. Any ideas?"

"What are your plans for tomorrow?"

"Watch the preseason game even though Matt won't play very much."

"Same plans as mine. I'll call Xo. We'll bring the food. And before you ask, my kids aren't snotty and neither is Pilar. Monday, we could take her to the aquarium. My two never get tired of that."

"Sounds good. That will give Matt some time to decide what else we can do. Big favor—could you ask her to stay overnight with you? Right now, I have her in Matt's bed, but he'll want to hit the sheets as soon as he gets home."

"Really?"

Annie could envision Stacy's coy smile. "I meant he'll be tired and want to sleep. You are as bad as Jude."

"Speaking of whom, Xochi ran into her at the coffee shop and said her aura is diminished, whatever that means,"

"We had a falling out, but I think we'll get over it."

"Good. See you around eleven tomorrow."

Sometimes it was great to have sisters. Sometimes not.

****

Annie's sisters came to the rescue bearing a pot of spicy chili, a large salad, a huge bag of corn chips, and their children. The usually outgoing Wynn stayed locked to Stacy's side while DJ clung to one of her long legs as they peered at Dre.

"Is she a witch?" Wynn queried.

"Witch," echoed DJ.

"No, this is baby Daniel's Aunt Andrea," Annie explained. "There are no such thing as witches."

"*Snow White* has a witch. *Rapunzel* has a witch. *Hansel and Gretel* has a witch," Wynn insisted.

"Sometimes, I wish the Brothers Grimm had never taken up collecting folk tales." Stacy pushed the children forward. "Say hello."

Dre made an effort to befriend them. She squatted down to their level and issued a friendly smile still encased in black lipstick. "Hi, you can call me Dre. I'm a Goth, not a witch. I don't eat little children or put them in towers." Still, the children backed away.

Amused, Xochi said, "Don't worry about it.

They'll get used to you. New Orleans does have its share of Wiccans and voodoo priestesses. You'll fit right in. Here, hold mine. She's at the loves-everyone age."

While Pilar didn't babble and smile for Dre, she did take an interest in the thick, dangling chain that had replaced the dog collar. Immediately stuffing it into her mouth, the baby girl began to teethe and drool. Xochi took her back and offered a paper napkin in exchange. "Sorry about that."

"The chain is stainless steel and won't hurt her. At least she likes something about me."

Meanwhile, Annie bustled around the kitchen putting bowls, plates, forks, and spoons on the table, and sticking a pair of tongs into the salad. She nuked hot dogs and buns for the children and laid out toppings for the chili: grated cheddar cheese, chopped onions, sour cream, more jalapenos than it already possessed, and a variety of bottled salad dressings. "Are you sure this meal will be good for Pilar?" she asked Xochi.

"She'd better get used to it since Junior cooked a huge vat of the stuff to make sure we wouldn't starve while he's gone. With our backgrounds, chili is in her blood already."

"Okay. If she gets gas, you're the one who will be up all night with her. Grab whatever you want to drink from the fridge and fix your chili and salad any way you want. Only ice cream for dessert, but Matt does love it so we have four different half gallons to choose from, or you can mix them up. We'll take our chili into the den since the game is about to start. Our men won't be playing long. We might as well enjoy them."

Dre latched onto the term "our men" like a baby to

a breast. "Is Matt your man?"

Annie deflected that question easily. "I have two brothers and a brother-in-law playing, and Daniel and I are definitely rooting for his daddy."

They moved into the den with its two big recliners, the old toy chest serving as a coffee table, and little else but the TV over the mantel festooned with trophies. "Xo, since you have the baby, why don't you take one of the recliners? They have two cup holders and arms wide enough to rest a plate."

"If you take the other. Daniel won't want to be in his carrier all the time."

"Stacy are you all right on the floor? I can bring in a chair."

"We'll be fine if you get me a tablecloth. Indoor picnic, might get messy," Stacy said as Wynn demanded chili on her dog and of course, DJ followed.

Annie set the carrier containing Daniel by her chair and faced away from the screen. No overstimulation for her little boy. She fetched the tablecloth and spread it out. Stacy sank down cross-legged on her yoga limber legs. Wynn sat beside her taking ladylike nibbles of her chili dog, while DJ rolled onto his stomach and stuffed his face with corn chips and hot dog. Dre in dark skinny jeans, a bulky black cotton sweater accessorized by her chain, and oddly, ballet flats, sat on the floor by Xo who appeared to accept her the best. The game began.

"Go Tom!" Stacy shouted as their brother kicked off, sending the football into the end zone, and forcing their opponents to take a knee. The Sinners' defense polished off the other team in three plays and forced a punt. Dean trotted onto the field and orchestrated a touchdown in six plays. Even better, Matt carried the ball across the goal line after a run that clearly showed how he'd earned the nickname Tank by shoving some players aside and running over others. He simply kept going until he reached his destination.

Annie scooped up Daniel to watch the replay. "See Daddy run!" She clapped his tiny hands together. To DJ's delight, Daniel farted. "I think we need a diaper change. Be back in minutes." Not wanting to miss a second of watching Matt play, she was.

Matt did his job in the second quarter, blocking for a long run by X-avier resulting in another score. Junior punched the ball out for a fumble on the return and gave the Sinners the ball again. Xochi applauded and prompted her daughter. "Daddy made them fumble." Pilar, who roamed the room on hands and knees, getting into the corm chip bowl taken from DJ until he ate his carrot sticks and playing with Daniel's dangling toys, plopped on her fat behind and clapped too, though her big, brown eyes searched for the huge man who threw her into the air and made her laugh. Daddy on the TV meant nothing.

During halftime, Annie gave Daniel a bottle, and Xo offered Pilar a breast. They put both babies down for a nap while Stacy released Wynn and DJ into the backyard with ice cream cones and a couple of toy boats to float in the fountain. None of "their men" played the second half, and only X-avier was able to make another touchdown, proving himself to Coach Buck. The Sinners won. Annie felt like a real team wife sitting there among her sisters, cheering on the team, tending to their children together. Maybe someday, she would truly be one.

To her surprise, Dre did her share of the work

cleaning up, rinsing bowls, and putting them in the dishwasher. After a nod from Annie, Stacy sidled up to the girl. "Say, would you like to come home with us since we have plenty of room. I brought the SUV because of the children, but our place is within easy walking distance of here."

Immediately, Dre's kohl-rimmed eyes turned on Annie. "Are you trying to get rid of me? I'm going to call Matt." She drew her phone like a weapon.

"No. He's probably in the showers right now. Then, he'll be on the plane and the team bus, plus the drive home. Matt will come in late and want his bed. I just don't know where to put you. The alternatives are sharing a bed with me or stretching out in one of the recliners. Take your pick." Annie wished she could simply give her bed to Dre and sleep next to Matt but knew that to be impossible. "We'll discuss how you can stay with us tomorrow."

"Okay, I guess. Probably should have given you more warning, but I thought you might tell me to turn around and go home."

If only. Bad enough she and Matt would have to come up with a plan to house Dre for her brief stay and seem happy about it. The girl went off to gather some overnight gear and returned to announce pointedly, "I'm only taking enough for one day," before leaving with Stacy and her family. Xochi lingered behind under the pretext that she didn't want to wake Pilar. She made some herbal tea and sat with Annie who slugged down coffee.

"I'm going to need this to stay awake for Matt's return. Dre is a problem, short-term, but a problem."

Xo sipped her tea and eyed Annie over the rim of

the cup. "Because you and Matt are sleeping together?"

Annie shielded her face. "Can you tell from my aura or just figured it out?"

"You are absolutely glowing with love, more so than before, but I could have guessed from Jude's unhappiness. You won't be coming back to live with her again."

"No telling yet, it's all so new, but she brought it on herself. She tried to seduce Matt by pretending to be me on Thursday night. He kicked her out permanently, but afterward he confessed he had hoped the woman trying to crawl in bed with him was me. Then, I made sure of it."

"*Loco*," Xochi commented. "Was Jude drinking?"

"Yes. She tried to convince me she did it to bring me and Matt together. I'm still not positively sure she wasn't jealous enough to try to take him away from me."

"She is suffering for her actions. Might do her some good to reflect that she can't run your life anymore. However, I see another problem looming. Dre isn't a bad kid for all the gloomy makeup and attitude, but she is keeping something from you. Beware."

"Great. Let me get another cup of coffee to deal with it—and maybe a large bowl of rocky road. How about you?"

"Extra calcium is always great for the baby. Two scoops."

As they finished scraping their bowls of chocolate, nuts, and marshmallows, Pilar, whom they had put down in a corral of pillows on Annie's bed, began to cry. "That's my cue to do a diaper change and take her home. Annie, this will all work out."

"Xo, I wish you really could tell the future."
"That's what everyone says."

Chapter Thirty

Matt let himself into the house a little past midnight. He tried to tiptoe up the stairs, almost impossible with his big feet, but neither Daniel nor Annie stirred. He'd hoped to find Annie curled in his bed and Danny sprawled on his back sound asleep for the next few hours. Disappointment reigned when he carefully opened his bedroom door to find his bed neatly made and no Annie. He hadn't turned on the lights and nearly tripped over a couple of suitcases in his way. What the hell? Was she leaving after all?

Matt pounded toward her room. No Annie. At the thought that he'd lost her, his heart thudded as it did at the end of a ninety-yard run down the field. Had she gone back to her sister's apartment and taken Danny with her? Or, had the baby gotten ill and been returned to the NICU in Annie's arms? He opened the nursery door and found them both oblivious to the world. The white noise machine covered the sound of his breath as he huffed out a hefty sigh of relief. Both were here and well.

Ensconced in the rocker and wearing her usual nightgown and robe, Annie seemed to sense his presence. Her dark lashes fluttered open. "I tried to stay awake for your homecoming but didn't succeed."

"I'm glad you got some rest. I caught up with sleep on the plane. Let's go to bed, my bed." He failed to keep his grin tamed.

Annie, still groggy, muttered, "I should change the sheets again."

"Don't worry about the sheets, honey. We are only going to mess them up." Since she seemed slow to stand, he offered, "Let me carry you."

"No need..."

But, Matt already had her in his arms, trying to move with stealth from Danny's nursery. She didn't object. So far, so good. He laid her tenderly on his big bed and began to strip out of his suit, tie already loosed, and a few buttons of his shirt opened on the way home.

Annie propped herself up on her elbows. "Not that I don't enjoy a good striptease, but we have to talk."

That caught him with his pants down literally and his eagerness exposed. "Condoms, I've got condoms." He took off for the bathroom and commenced opening and closing drawers. "Here they are." He stood by the bed holding the treasures from his quest in his hands.

"That isn't the problem." She eyed the suitcases that had nearly tackled him. "Your sister-in-law, Dre, arrived unexpectedly. She wants to stay here and help with Daniel."

He turned around as if someone approached his blindside. "Where is she?"

"I pawned her off on Stacy for the night. She slept in here after her arrival. But, what are we going to do with her next?"

Matt sank down on the side of the bed, felt the mattress give beneath his bulk, and tossed the two condoms on the night table. "School starts up north in two weeks. I guess we could put her in the closest hotel and bring her over every day."

"A teen alone in a hotel near the French Quarter, I think not. Maybe she could stay with Jude."

"No way."

"It's not fair to ask Dean and Stacy to keep her."

"Yeah. How did she get here anyhow? I can't see Marilyn giving her a plane ticket."

"She drove Mellie's car."

"I should have recognized it, but being tired and in the dark, I was just pissed that someone had taken my spot and I had to hike down the block."

"There are plenty like it in New Orleans. I did make her call home to say she arrived safely, but she only left a message. I'm getting bad vibes about the whole thing—or at least Xochi is. Maybe Dre will confess to you. All I got out of her was a desire to see Daniel and help out."

"Any other ideas about what we can do with her?"

"We could clean out the front parlor of all the boxes and odds and ends of furniture. Put that stuff into storage and rent a basic bedroom set for her stay."

Matt brightened. "Then, we'd be upstairs, and she'd be down there away from anything we might want to do."

"We're going to have to cool it while she's here or risk her tattling to your mother-in-law who would make something ugly out of it."

"I guess." He turned his hunched shoulders to her, deeply disappointed.

Annie shifted on the bed. Her small hands began to rub his shoulders. "We still have tonight."

"Better make it last then."

Matt kept his promise, adoring her body with his touch until Annie in her urgency begged him to enter.

Even then, he measured every stroke. The condom helped him maintain control to bring her home twice before he succumbed. He tore open the second condom just before dawn after tending to Daniel's needs. Now that they'd finally begun a relationship, two weeks apart seemed like an eternity to him.

Chapter Thirty-One

Annie got the girl back sooner than she'd wanted. Matt had a nine o'clock team meeting and a light practice to attend. Mostly, they'd be analyzing the preseason games and working on improving weaknesses. Of course, he was gone when his sister-in-law reappeared looking as ghastly as usual while Annie downed her second cup of coffee. Apparently, Dre had taken her makeup and hair gel with her. Her clothes were different but still black on black, an oversized tee featuring a glowing skull, and leggings.

"Stacy gave me breakfast and wanted to drive me here, but I thought I should learn the neighborhood," Dre told her.

Why, Annie wanted to ask, but held it in. Generally, people who looked like her roamed the Quarter, not the Garden District. "Matt will be home early afternoon, but we worked out a plan you might like for your stay. We'll rent some bedroom furniture and give you the use of the front room downstairs. There's a powder room off the hall that used to be a closet. It's small, only a commode, sink, and mirror. Let me show you."

Annie led the way to the almost hidden door under the spiral staircase and showed the bathroom to Dre like a realtor, switching on the light and stepping back. "Voila. Your private ladies' room."

Dre took in the décor. "I've never seen a pink toilet seat before and hope to never see one again. I feel like the wallpaper is vomiting cabbage roses on me. I'm not surprised Mellie loved this place."

"We concentrated on getting the upstairs finished for Matt and Daniel. Mostly, we live in the kitchen and the den down here, but I have to agree with you. It's a bit much, but only temporary. We can go look for some furniture today after Matt gets home. In the meantime, you might help me shift the things in there into the hall and the living room until we can find storage."

"That's exactly what I want to do. Thank you, thank you!" Dre embraced her with wild enthusiasm.

Wiping a smudge of white makeup from her cheek, Annie wondered at the exuberant acceptance of their short-term plan. Better than sulking and sneering, she supposed. "Say, I haven't had a chance to shower today. Would you sit with Daniel while I freshen up? Or you can stay down here near one of the monitors as long as you don't obstruct your hearing." Annie gestured toward the girl's dangling earbuds. Evidently, she'd marched home to her own music, listening to a different drummer from the rest of the world.

Dre eagerly accepted the assignment. "What do I do if he wakes?"

"Comfort and rock him. You'll have to unclip his vitals monitor before you pick him up. I'll show you how we change him and warm his bottles as soon as I get out, but he should be down for a while."

Annie wasted no time washing in the smaller bathroom and shoving herself into scrubs, both meant to mask that she and Matt were up to any hanky-panky. She did put on light makeup and lipstick to welcome him home. When she got to the nursery, Dre held Daniel in the crook of her arm. Her bizarre face did keep his attention focused.

"Did he cry?"

"No, but I could tell he was awake, so I took the thing off his foot and picked him up. He hasn't made a peep."

"Danny isn't a big talker yet. His repertoire is fret, cry, burp, and fart mostly. Is he wet?"

"I think so."

"Okay, this is how you change him." Dre had a chance to practice because when exposed to the cooler air, Daniel sent up a fountain that immediately soaked the new diaper and the front of Annie's scrubs. "Little boys do that. Got to be quick." While she changed, she let Dre pick a newborn outfit from the piles in the drawers, and they took the baby downstairs to watch them move boxes and lug furniture to make room for his aunt.

By the time Matt returned, they sat at the kitchen table eating strawberry ice cream to put out the fire of Junior's leftover chili. "Great to see you again, Dre. Got enough of that for me?"

"Plenty of chili remains, recommended in small doses. We polished off the strawberry, but you still have your choice of mint chip, rocky road, and butter pecan." Annie swore he nearly kissed her but swerved away from her cheek to pluck Danny from his carrier instead.

"Great. I already had a training meal, but no dessert."

"How was it?"

"Healthy. Hi, Danny. I hear you've met your

Auntie Dre, the one we sent all the pictures to while you were in the NICU. You're very bright-eyed today. Daddy is going to take care of you while the girls shop. We're going to have a manly afternoon. I planned to move the stuff out of the front room, but you women beat me to it. I guess I can put the boxes in the Escalade and move them to the storage place we found. Daniel might enjoy a car ride. I still haven't kept my promise to visit Junelle Wagner and take her the stuff we put aside. How about it Danny? Want to visit your old NICU girlfriend, Arielle? I'll bet she's pretty cute by now."

Though Annie smiled, she wished she could go with them on the visit, but she had another kind of babysitting to do. "We'll try to get delivery of the furniture today. Let me put on street clothes and off we go." Annie raced up the stairs to change and returned dangling her car keys. The sooner they got this settled the better.

At the rental store, she let Dre pick what she wanted, predictably a black lacquer bedstead, dresser, and night table with Chinese fixtures, less so the lamp with the rearing bronze dragon as its base. "Could I have the desk and chair too?" she begged.

"I suppose." Annie wondered why the girl didn't use the laptop she'd brought along on her bed like most teens, but Matt had said to get her whatever she wanted within reason. Annie signed the papers for the minimum month's rental and a guaranteed by four o'clock delivery. Doing her duty as hostess, she took Dre to Café du Monde for café au lait and beignets. Both came home still brushing the copious powdered sugar of the donuts off their fronts. The skull on Dre's shirt appeared to be drifting in snow.

Matt emerged from his den. Again, Annie sensed he wanted to kiss her and most likely whisk her upstairs for a quick romp while Daniel slept, but not with Dre around. "Judging by your clothes, I see you experienced one of the best things about New Orleans. I am happy to report Arielle is thriving, and her mom appreciated the gifts. I threw in a check to help with their medical expenses since I really didn't pay for any of the stuff— and Junelle cried. Crying women, I'm not good with crying women. Anyway, how did the furniture selection go?"

"Great, really great. It gets here at four. I tried to tell Annie I wouldn't change my mind on the style, but she only took out a month's lease. I'll be here way longer than that."

"What?" both Matt and Annie blurted out.

"Don't you have to be back in Indiana for the start of school?" Annie said with caution not to expose her dismay.

"I'm not going back. I'm here to stay, to help out, since no one else in my family will."

"But you'll miss your senior year: homecoming, the prom, graduating with your friends, being in the yearbook, searching for colleges in Indiana." Annie pulled out every plus about the last year of high school she could recall.

Dre's fierce black eyebrows drew together. "Do you honestly believe I'd go to anything as douchey as homecoming and the prom? What friends? All those Mellie-type cheerleaders and prom queens think I'm a weirdo. Just sitting in Café du Monde watching the people go by I can tell I'll fit in better here than I ever will up north. Besides, you're only the baby nurse. You have nothing to say about it. Right, Matt?"

Annie's argument and Dre's diatribe must have given Matt a moment to organize his own play. He ran it now to Annie's relief. "You were always my favorite in the Ames family, and I'm glad you came to see us, but I doubt your parents would allow you to stay here under any circumstances. Also, if you ever disrespect Annie again, I'll bodily put you on the next plane out of here, and you'll leave the car behind. It's still registered to me."

Dre's kohl-rimmed eyes rolled with dramatic desperation. "If you force me to go back, I'll run away again and live on the streets. I might commit suicide. You don't know what it's like since Mellie died. Even worse than before."

Annie, who had stepped slightly behind the girl while she argued with Matt, mouthed his way, "Bluffing," but she could see he was unwilling to call his sister-in-law on such serious threats.

"I'll tell you what, Dre, let's see how things go the next two weeks. After that, I'll be gone a lot with training and game travel. If you can't get along with Annie and be a help rather than a hindrance, you'll have to go, like it or not." His voice emitted the same authority he had on the field.

"You'll want me to stay in the end."

The doorbell rang. Dre dashed for the door as if making an escape from a blazing fire. "My furniture is here early. Wait until you see what I got."

Matt frowned after her. He took a chance and hugged Annie to his side for a stolen kiss that Annie felt she had to break. Shaking his head, he said, "Is that normal, the mood swings? Maybe Dre really is unstable."

"You grew up an only child. I had five sisters and having been a teen girl myself, I can tell you that's absolutely normal right down to the rebellion. Xochi checked her out and didn't see anything dark about her despite her outward appearance, but said she had a secret. Now it's out. You bought us a two-week reprieve on how to deal with it. We'll have to be very careful in front of her."

"She'll be downstairs, and we'll be up."

Annie hated to crush his desire. "Your room is directly above hers. Any noise we make…"

"I could come to your bed. Or we could do it in the shower with the water running. She'd never know. I can almost feel your body slick with soap." In the shadow of the staircase, he slid his hands up and down her sides.

"Cut it out. I'm getting wet simply listening to you. Two weeks isn't that long after waiting all summer."

"You say."

Chapter Thirty-Two

All four of them survived the first few days without mishap, though Annie gritted her teeth more than once and held in words she wanted to say. Dre did go out of her way to prove her usefulness, even offering to babysit for Stacy and Dean, though they didn't take her up on it. She begged to paint the walls in the parlor any color but pink and offered to do the work herself. Matt vetoed black, deep purple, and red from the outset, and told the girl that Annie had final approval.

"Why? I'm family, and she's just the help. She'll leave long before me, I promise."

"Annie did a great job decorating the nursery and making the upstairs livable. Plus, she's not just help. She saw Daniel through his most dangerous hours. That makes her a heroine in my playbook. Don't forget that."

In the end, Annie steered her toward a pale gray, no cheery colors for Dre. It went well with the furnishings and didn't make the girl want to barf. She could have called a professional painter now that Matt had less free time but thought a little sweat equity would do the teen some good, and after all, she had volunteered for the work. Dre's pervasive attitude seemed to be that Matt would buy her anything she wanted, but she held back on asking during this supposed trial period.

Annie summoned Stacy to reach the high parts of

the walls and also called Xochi to borrow their oriental screen to set in front of the large window for temporary privacy as Ollie's lace curtains did little to block the view from the street. She'd deal with new curtains once Dre left. Soon hopefully. Xo arrived with the baby and Junior on Sunday afternoon. Her husband carefully unloaded the screen from his Escalade and set it in the living room out of harm's way. Dre inhaled deeply when she saw it. "That is the most beautiful thing ever."

The trifold screen framed in black portrayed a Japanese garden gone wild with poufs of gold and silver flowers on lavender stems harboring imaginary beasts and fantasy butterflies. Annie had seen it many times when visiting Xo at the condo and always marveled when she found some new detail catching her attention. That Dre admired it, too, said she did have some inner sensitivity despite her deadpan exterior. However, the girl's next words lowered that assessment a notch or two. "Can I keep it? I know Matt would buy it from you."

"A friend made this. It's not for sale," Junior rumbled like an annoyed giant bear. "She made Xo jealous and helped bring us together. It's a special piece."

"No, she didn't," Xochi denied.

Junior sounded a deep laugh. "I can give you her name and number if you'd like to see her work. She also gives a great foot massage and is very nimble if you are interested, Matt." Evidently, Xo hadn't revealed Annie and Matt were now intimate.

Xo elbowed him in the side. "I caught them in the act of massaging each other's feet. What was I supposed to think?"

"Nothing, that's what." Her husband gave her a squeeze.

Annie looked on with envy of their closeness but also with some concern that Matt might want that foot massage too. As it was, he lurked nearby shaking his head. "Not my style." Whether he meant Japanese artists or foot massages, she wasn't certain.

"Good thing you came along, or I'd have to move the furniture away from the walls myself. Dean got out of this somehow," Matt told Junior.

"Hey, he's watching the kids so they don't come here and make a mess," Stacy defended her husband. "Xo can still stash hers in a playpen."

"Got it in the car. She did mention we should stay and help." After Junior retrieved the pen for his daughter, he and Matt hefted the bed and shoved the dresser to the center of the small parlor. The desk and chair took less muscle. Annie began putting the painter's tape around the baseboards. Stacy and Xo followed suit in other areas of the room. They tackled the window, and elegant white fireplace that took up one wall. Between the five of them, they had the first coat on in an hour and took a break with cold drinks and snacks in the kitchen. Annie counted herself as grateful for all the help.

"I think we can finish before dinner, but I guess Dre should sleep with me until the fumes clear," Annie said, following that with a long swallow of iced tea to cover her reluctance.

Dre had no trouble expressing her distaste. "Holy crap, it's latex paint. The fumes won't kill me. I'll leave the door open for a couple of nights. I want my space."

She certainly had created one, selecting an

unopened set of red sheets for the bed from Mellie's array of linens even after Matt told her they'd been a gag gift for her sister's wedding shower. "Even better," Dre replied. After draping the tall bed frame set up to support a canopy with gray gauze she insisted on buying with some of her travel money, she'd sat cross-legged against the red pillows like a spider in her web. Truly, Annie didn't hate her, but resent the kid, yes, for showing up exactly when she and Matt had finally admitted they cared for each other. Now, they needed to go undercover again.

The second coat applied, Chinese takeout with enough white cartons to satisfy everyone's taste ordered for dinner, and furniture moved into place again by seven, Dre exuded triumph. "See, it looks great. We need to get together again to strip that disgusting wallpaper in the hall bathroom. Bet we could get a black toilet seat tonight."

"Not tonight. Junior and I have team meeting and practice tomorrow. If you're happy with the room, great. We could put a TV in there for you if you want," Matt offered. Annie suspected he thought that might give the two of them more privacy. No such luck.

"Don't need one. I can stream whatever I want on my laptop anywhere in the house. You have fantastic Wi-Fi."

"Good for us," Annie said. Maybe if they discontinued the service, Dre would go home. She and Matt had a looong week and a half ahead.

Chapter Thirty-Three

Matt struggled with sleep. Like holding Daniel or the surrogate football in bed, having Annie near his heart relaxed him, especially after sex. He heard her get up in the night with Daniel and forced himself to stay put, letting Annie do her job alone just in case Dre suspected more went on than bottle feedings at three a.m.

He'd tasted the sweetness of Annie Billodeaux and wanted more, and like the impatient teen below, wanted it now. Sure, being a football player, he'd had a few women, but from the time he'd met Melinda he'd been faithful to her. Did he compare Annie to her? There was no comparison. Mellie had made it clear from the start that making love to a beautiful woman like her constituted a privilege. She allowed it, sometimes indicated she enjoyed it, but rarely participated to any extant, while Annie threw every ounce of her small body into the act. How he craved her.

Daniel and his own alarm went off at six a.m. He stayed in bed, envisioning Annie in her robe taking care of his son, rocking him back to sleep, getting ready to return to her bed. Matt shoved the covers aside and walked down the hall. Sure enough, there she was swaddling Daniel, laying him in his crib, attaching his monitor. His son's blue eyes remained alert. Annie wound the mobile above his head where it played a gentle tune and hypnotized with spinning teddy bears. At his entry, she said, "You should be in the shower by now."

"So should you—in my shower. I promise a quickie and can skip my shave. I'll still be on time. Please, come with me."

"Awfully tempting, but Dre…"

"She still thinks she's on summer vacation. Have you ever known a teen that didn't sleep in when they have the chance?"

"No, but what if…"

Matt took her hand and led her away, a thick finger to his lips like a man cautioning her to keep a secret—which they were. He planned to put that finger deep inside Annie as soon as he could, prepping her for more to come. He drew her through his bedroom where he made a brief stop for a condom, and into the vast shower stall. He turned on the water to warm while he stripped her of her robe and prim nightie. Annie toed off her slippers before he lifted her inside the clear glass box.

The bath gel sat in a nearby caddy. Matt lubed his hands with it and applied it to every inch of her body, especially the slope of her breasts and the sensitive crevice between her legs. She reciprocated, washing thoroughly behind his balls, over them, and along the rigid penis. Matt fumbled with the condom, and Annie giggled into his chest while the water rained down like an early morning thunderstorm. He lifted her slick body, pinned it against the wall, and entered. With her arms around his neck, her legs around his waist, shielding her face from the droplets in the protection of his vast chest, Matt quickened the rhythm, not wanting to rush, but needing to. He couldn't wait much longer. Nor could Annie. She came like a water nymph taken by the waves.

Matt leaned his head against the tiles and slowly withdrew. In arching his back, he somehow lost his hold on Annie's slippery body. She slid down the wall and thumped against the tiles. He gathered her up at once and turned off the water. "My God, are you hurt!"

"Only my dignity, as they say. Might be some bruises on the buttocks. Next time, whenever that may be, I'll need to be on top."

"That's a promise."

Annie stepped out of the shower, wrapped herself in one of the lush white towels, and swathed her wet curls with another. "You'd better get dressed. I'll make you a breakfast to go."

"I'd give up breakfast every day if I could feast on you," he said and meant every word.

"Methinks a poet lies beneath all that muscle." She poked his pecs fondly.

"Maybe my poetry loving mother had something to do with that. Tomorrow, same time? I promise I won't drop you again."

Annie simply smiled and shook her head. "We really need to be careful around Dre."

Sauntering away, Matt tried to get a better view of her backside butterfly, but the man-sized towel enveloped Annie better than her robe. Tomorrow morning for sure.

****

Though her legs felt wobbly and her backside throbbed, Annie checked on Daniel, now deeply asleep in his crib. She finished toweling off, shrugged into her

253

scrubs, and briefly dried her curls, not that it helped much. Wanting to make sure Matt did not leave unnourished, she shoved some thick slices of whole wheat bread into the toaster, quick fried an egg, and topped it with a slice of cheese. All the while, the coffee brewed, filling the kitchen with the scent of dark roast. As Matt pounded down the backstairs, she handed him a tall travel mug of coffee and the sandwich wrapped in a napkin.

He grinned. "You take good care of me and Daniel." With a furtive glance over his shoulder in case the troublesome teen lurked, Matt kissed her goodbye on the lips and headed out to the team's usual routine.

Annie gave a sentimental sigh. It might be like this every day if they were married. Would that come to pass, or did he need her now only to care for them both? She poured coffee for herself and made another egg sandwich. Before she sat down, Dre showed her face in the kitchen doorway. Without her makeup, her spiky hair askew, her wrinkled, oversized cotton pajamas bearing a rubber duckie print, she seemed less like an annoyance and more like a lost and confused child.

"That smells good. You got one for me?"

About to tell the kid to make her own, Annie relented, handed her plate over to Dre, and went back to fry another egg. "You're up earlier than expected. Help yourself to some juice."

"Can I have coffee?"

Annie considered. Lots of Cajun kids were raised on coffee-milk, and she'd been allowed coffee at seventeen. "Sure, but it is fairly strong. You might want to add milk and have it *au lait* like we did at the café."

Dre filled a big mug to prove her toughness, took a sip, poured half out, and went for the milk. Annie made certain she didn't laugh, simply sat beside her, and ate in companionable silence finally broken by the girl.

"I thought I heard Daniel cry around dawn."

"Yes, he's gone back to sleep now."

"And a big thud. I was afraid you dropped him. I almost got out of bed to be sure he was okay."

"Believe me, if I'd dropped Daniel he would have shrieked like a five-alarm fire bell—and I never would. Matt probably let something slip in the shower." Annie ducked her head behind her own mug, hoping any flush might be mistaken as a caffeine rush.

"You didn't hear it? It was loud."

"I was engrossed with Daniel."

Dre finished her breakfast and took her dishes to the washer. "I think I'll take a shower."

"Or you can have a luxurious bath. Matt has quite the huge tub he hardly uses unless he has bruises to soak. It's beneath a stained-glass window, and I think there are some bath bombs and gels in a basket if you like." Annie didn't add that the bath accessories had been Mellie's choices placed there by Stacy when they set up the bathroom. "You are welcome to use it."

"Do you?" The girl seemed to imply Annie might have used it with Matt. Maybe one day since the bathtub had the potential to hold two.

"Not so far. I'm more used to grabbing a shower. That's how it is when you have a baby to care for."

"Me, too. All that bath gunk was more Mellie's kind of thing. I wonder if she would have sacrificed her beauty baths once Daniel was born."

"We'll never know. I believe she wanted to nurse

255

Daniel his first year."

Dre emitted a harsh laugh more in tune with her usual appearance. "Until she noticed her breasts sagging is more likely. Of course, Matt could always buy her a boob job. He got her whatever she wanted. Mellie and my mother used him. I don't want anyone else to do that to Matt." She stared at Annie with a sharp blue gaze scary enough without the kohl liner and totally oblivious that she was also taking advantage of him.

Annie agreed. "Matt is a wonderful guy." She let it go at that, not adding loving father and considerate lover to the list. "Why don't you get that shower now? I'll clean up the kitchen."

She took care of the frying pan and her dishes, then went upstairs to see if Daniel wanted to begin his day. She'd heard a few peeps coming from the monitor, the opening throes of awakening, as well as the thunder of a shower being taken in the smaller bathroom. Changed, fed, and outfitted for the day, the baby sat by Annie's feet in his carrier ready to go downstairs when Dre burst in, her face outraged.

Annie used the quiet but firm voice of the NICU. "Did you have a pleasant shower?"

"I used the small bathroom, the one that is supposed to be yours, out of respect for Matt. The tub was dry, and your hair is wet."

"Yes?"

"But, I wanted to see that stained-glass window you mentioned, so I went down the hall to Matt's room. Yeah, that bathtub is really something, the shower too. I know guys beat off in the shower. I have two older brothers, but I found this in the bottom by the drain.

They don't need a rubber if they're in there alone." Dre held out a shriveled condom wrapped in toilet tissue. "Small, wet foot prints led from the shower, way too tiny to be Matt's. You are screwing my brother-in-law."

Annie considered denying the accusation, but her parents had taught her to own up to her actions and accept the consequences. Lies seldom made situations better. She'd go with no contest. "Aren't you a Nancy Drew?" That came out more glib than she intended.

"Her?" Dre sneered. "I always figured out the plot before she did. I'm more *Harriet the Spy*."

Annie remembered reading the book as a kid about a girl who spied on people and wrote down the honest, brutal truth in a journal, that when found, cost her all of her friends. No wonder Dre had none if that's who she took as a role model. Annie drew on the inner calm she summoned when distraught parents wanted to blame each other for their child's premature birth or the staff if their baby had a defect. "Matt and I care for each other."

"So what? If you don't let me stay here, I'll call my mother and tell her how you desecrated Mellie's memory only a few months after her death. She'll sue for Daniel's custody because neither of you are fit to take care of him."

Annie remained unrattled. She set her eyes on Dre and spoke directly to her. "First, what Matt and I do does no harm to Daniel. Second, if we are unfit to care for him, we are also unfit to have you live with us. Marilyn will demand you come home. If you want to play this card, go ahead and do it."

Annie didn't expect the gush of tears from Dre's naked eyes. She wasn't sure if they sprang from anger or desperation. The girl turned and ran. Downstairs, the front parlor door slammed as Dre returned to her web. Daniel startled.

"You know what, Danny? We'll stay up here for a while and give your aunt time to cool off and think. Why don't we read a book?" Annie reached for one of the chubby board books on a nearby shelf and placed Daniel in her lap. "It won't be *Harriet the Spy*."

Chapter Thirty-Four

When Annie went to let the cleaning lady in, she passed Dre's closed door without disturbing the girl. She noted the silver Lexus still sat on the street, so the teen hadn't made good on her threat to run away again. Lunch time came for Annie and Daniel. No sign of Dre. Both took naps, a good way to pass the time until Matt came through the door to help her deal with the sister-in-law situation.

By the time he did return, she sat in the garden next to the trickling fountain with Danny at her side, taking in the sights and sounds of nature filtered through a sheer piece of netting hung over his seat. "Where is my son and my girls?" she heard him call as he entered the kitchen. Annie waved to get his attention. His girls, he'd had the sensitivity to include Dre, but she felt a little less special. Shame on her for that.

"There you are." Matt joined them in the garden and immediately fished Daniel from his carrier and into his arms. He did that furtive glance around again before kissing Annie and taking the seat next to her.

"No need for that. We have been found out by *Harriet the Spy*."

"Who?"

"Dre. She saw the condom in the bottom of the shower and added all the clues together in a very calculating way. Followed that with a threat to call her mother who would sue for custody of the baby, which I highly doubt, if we didn't let her stay with us. I pointed out that if we aren't fit to take care of Danny, we aren't fit to chaperone her."

Matt groaned. "Sloppy play on my part. After you fell, I forgot about the condom." He cradled Daniel in his arms. The baby studied his face with wide blue eyes showing no sign of turning brown. "I love this kid so much, I don't know what I'd do if I lost him. I don't even care if he's not mine."

"What?" The very inference jolted Annie.

"Mellie and I were having problems with our marriage. After a couple of years, we seemed to have nothing much in common. I wanted a big family. She was reluctant to have a small one. She loved being the star of a society event. I stayed home. Last December, it seemed like she went to a fancy affair every weekend while I played out the season before my contract ended. Otto Messinger, one of my teammates, got dragged to some charity gig by his wife. Afterward, he told me Melinda and our quarterback had shared a table, gotten pretty friendly, and disappeared for a while. He thought the move to New Orleans might be a good idea. I did too."

Matt gazed into his son's eyes, not Annie's. "Wasn't long after that Mellie said she was pregnant. I think she tried another ploy to stop our move because she wanted to stay close to her mom, but I can't be one-hundred percent sure Daniel is mine. Maybe she wanted to continue her affair with Ryan Luke. I didn't confront either of them, just made it clear we were moving to New Orleans together."

Annie leaned her head on his shoulder. "There are

tests we can do. Heck, my dad was accused so many times of fathering illegitimate children, he kept his DNA profile with his lawyer. The only one that panned out was Dean."

Matt shook his head. "I don't want to know about Daniel. I was adopted, and where I came from made no difference to my parents who couldn't have given me more love. After they died, I did put my name in one of those data banks for women seeking the children they'd given up, but I don't care if I get a response. At the time, I'd taken Melinda's family as my own."

"You know nothing about your origins?"

"Pretty sure she was a Notre Dame coed, maybe a girl in one of my parents' classes. As for my biological father, I could probably pick him out in a Notre Dame yearbook if I tried from my looks. He either didn't know about me or didn't care. Either way, I don't want to meet him. A man should stand by a woman who carries his child. Anyhow, it doesn't matter to me at all. I was loved. Daniel is loved by me, and I hope by you."

"Yes."

"He'll be my son, no matter what."

Though the breeze didn't stir the trees on a day thick with humidity, the foliage at the side of the house rustled. Annie always imagined snakes hiding among the thick leaves and seldom took that path. Dre emerged as dark and sinister as a water moccasin. She struck. "I heard everything."

Annie refused to be threatened again. "Still spying, Harriet?"

"I was waiting to catch Matt alone, away from your influence."

"Time for you to go home, Dre." Matt said the

words with finality. By the way Dre stood rooted before them, Annie knew the girl thought she'd found solid ground this time.

"If you send me back, I'll tell Marilyn you aren't Daniel's dad. She'll want her precious Melinda's baby if he has nothing to do with you, the man who got her daughter killed."

The guilt remained, Annie could tell, by the stricken look on Matt's face. He held the baby closer, Daniel's small head cupped by his large hand, as if never wanting to let go. She stood and got between him and the teen viper.

"We don't know the truth, but I'm familiar with the law concerning paternity. It came up from time to time in the NICU. If a man's name is on the birth certificate, he is legally the child's father. If DNA proves otherwise, a court case can drag on for years, and that's only if the birth father wants to press for custody. I doubt that would happen. Dre, think of all the people you'd hurt—Matt and Daniel, the family of the birth father, your parents who would learn something ugly about their deceased daughter."

"What about me! It's always Mellie, Mellie, perfect Mellie, all day and all night from my mother's lips. I'd like her to know her prized child sinned big time—because Mom doesn't care what I do." Dre let loose with all her venom.

Annie tried a softer approach. "She's still grieving. We hope in time she'll want to be Daniel's grandmother, and you will always be his aunt. Be reasonable. Go home, finish school. Maybe you can go to college here if you want."

"I can't. I can't. I'm pregnant. Marilyn doesn't

know. You think my life with her will be any better when she already hates me, the daughter who didn't turn out so well?" The venom turned to tears, great gushes of them. Dre crumpled into the third chair and buried her face in her hands.

The nurse in Annie kicked in hard. "How far along are you? Have you gotten any prenatal care?" Far too often she'd tended babies born to very young women who'd neglected themselves or kept up bad habits and given birth to low weight infants. Sometimes the mothers disappeared after the birth. In other cases, they started on the long path of struggle trod by many single parents with no support.

"A little over three months, I think." Dre mopped her eyes with the hem of the oversized tee and exposed her white, vulnerable belly for a second. Annie assessed the girl as barely showing.

"This guy, a senior, told me I was special, unique, exciting. We were doing it in the backseat of his car, not for the first time, when Mellie died. I turned off my phone and didn't realize until he took me home. Up 'til then, Mom thought how great that a boy took an interest in a weirdo like me. I didn't see him again after that night. He used me for sex. It's not like he showed me off me off in public." Dre sniffed hard and wiped at her smeared eye makeup.

"Oh, Dre, you didn't use any protection?"

She shrugged. "My mother said the best protection is not to have sex before marriage. Maybe I wanted to defy her by being careless. Perfect Mellie did it before you married, right Matt?"

He stood, towering over both women, and still clutching his son. "Not as often as you want to believe.

But this guy, where is he now?" Matt rumbled as if he wanted to wrap his huge hands around the boy's skinny neck. Not used to any but a gentle tone in his father's voice, Daniel squirmed and fretted.

"College. I don't want him in my life, our life. I had it all planned. I'd come here and learn to take care of a baby from your nurse. Then study for my GED and go to college in New Orleans. The nanny watches both our babies. I'd live with you, and we raise our kids together. I didn't think you'd fall for *her*." She jerked her head in Annie's direction.

Matt sucked in a deep breath of forbearance. "I promised I'd send both you and your brothers through college. I'm making good on that promise to the boys right now regardless of how things stand with your parents. Sure, you can go to school down here once this mess is straightened out, but you will not blackmail me or treat Annie poorly or that deal is off. Understood?"

Dre gave him a grudging nod.

"There's more. You must tell your parents the situation. If they say to send you home, you go."

"But, but the high school will put me in a class for pregnant teens where all they do is learn baby care. Everyone will see me swelling up!"

"If your parents allow you to stay here, we'll take responsibility for you and your baby, but you live by our rules."

Annie doubted anyone argued with Matt when he wore that grim game face. Even she felt a trifle intimidated, and she didn't stand in his direct glare. Daniel began to cry. Matt put him to his shoulder and patted his son's back.

"Mom won't want the shame. She'll let me stay.

Dad doesn't have anything to say about it. I guess I don't have to tell her about Daniel now." The sulk returned to Dre's voice when she asked, "What are the rules?"

Annie couldn't help herself. "No more coffee for you. Or black hair dye or all that makeup. Any of it might be bad for your baby."

"Oh, come on. Matt?"

"That's just the beginning of the list, Dre. Number one is to call your parents."

Chapter Thirty-Five

Matt held out his hand for Dre's phone. She slapped it into his palm like a surgical instrument. "I'd use mine, but I don't know if they'd pick up the call." He turned the baby over to Annie, selected the number from her contact list, and let it ring. His luck held because Bucky answered. He put the phone on speaker.

"Are you all right down there, Dre? You need to come home. School is starting soon, and we haven't heard a word from you."

"Bucky, it's Matt. We're all well. In fact, that's Daniel crying nice and strong. Time for his bottle, I guess. Here's Dre. She has something to tell you."

"I'd better get Marilyn."

"Nooo!" Dre wailed. "Daddy, I got myself pregnant. Matt says I can have the baby and stay here to go to school if it is all right with you."

Her father answered loud and clear. "No one gets themselves pregnant. It was that damn boy who hung around you. I should have known. He'll answer for this if I have to…"

His wife entered the conversation. "You slut. No wonder he wanted to date you. You were giving it away for free." Marilyn's voice was no less shrill and ugly than it had been in the NICU when her first daughter died.

"Maybe I should have asked for money for my

services. Besides, Matt and Mellie had sex before marriage," Dre blurted, attempting to hurt her mother as her mother's words must have hurt her.

"They were engaged adults. Get rid of the baby. Matt can pay for that. Then, you come home and obey our every word until you graduate."

"I'm keeping my baby. I am. My baby will love me."

Matt's deep voice took control. "I'll see she gets to college, but I won't be paying for any abortions, Marilyn. We'll take care of her here if you give your consent. We'll make it legal."

"Who is we?"

"Annie, the nurse who cared for Daniel in the NICU and is seeing to him for me."

"Are you sleeping with her? Are you replacing Mellie already?" Marilyn's voice broke slightly.

Matt declined to answer. "I made an offer to help your living daughter. Do you accept it?"

"Keep her and her bastard!"

Bucky finally asserted himself. "Marilyn, go lie down and let me handle this." His wife must have left the room because he went on to say, "Matt, she's been on the edge of a nervous breakdown all summer. This might be the last straw. Send any papers you need to become Dre's guardian. I'll sign them. And Dre, my Andi Pandi, I love you, I truly do. One day…"

"Yeah, it's always one day. But thanks for saying the words." She disconnected from her father. "I guess I'm all yours, Matt. They didn't put up much of a fight."

"This should be about what's best for you and the baby. It's not a game to win or lose."

Now that the shouting ended, Daniel rested in the crook of Annie's neck, comforted by her familiar scent and soft voice. But he nudged against her, still wanting that bottle. "I'm taking Danny inside for a feeding. Dre, come along and help. You have lots to learn." The pregnant teen followed without protest.

****

Matt sorted through all that had happened. First, he needed to get guardianship papers drawn up and sent off to Indiana. He'd consult with the Billodeauxs who had dealt with all sorts of adoption and foster care issues. Like having Joe's DNA profile available, they must have a good lawyer to take care of such matters. He pondered Dre's education. Private school or a GED test? She was smart enough get to New Orleans unscathed and implement her plan. A GED and early admission to college might suit her better. The baby would arrive in six more months, probably in time for Super Bowl Sunday.

Meanwhile, he had to find an ob-gyn for the girl, get her on vitamins. Annie would know how to go about that. He wanted Annie by his side and in his bed. No need to hide that fact from Dre anymore. The kid wasn't nearly as innocent as he'd assumed. Sweet Jesus, he'd barely learned how to be a father to an infant and now he'd have to figure out how to deal with a rebellious teen way before his time.

Well, sitting among the pink begonias wouldn't give him any answers. He stood and went inside to find what appeared to be a happy domestic scene. Her face washed clean of tear-stained makeup, Dre gave Daniel his bottle. She held him properly and angled the bottle exactly right to keep the nipple filled, Annie's doing, no doubt. With her complexion natural and pink from a scrubbing, her blue eyes unlined, the baby studied her face with less anxiety.

The woman he loved put together a large salad for dinner. She smiled his way. What the hell. He kissed the back of her neck and made his first pronouncement as a surrogate father.

"Dre, you obviously know what men and women do in bed. I'll be sleeping with Annie from now on. Do you want to take over her room or stay where you are?" Treat her like a two-year-old, give her a choice, don't back her into a corner, he seemed to remember from hearing the older guys talk about their kids.

Dre appeared absolutely repelled. "Oh, yuck, no. I don't want to be upstairs where I can hear you doing it—and her room is so sweet with all those homey quilts and family photos and stuff. I'd want to barf every day when I woke up. Hey, I was doing that anyhow, but my stomach settled down just before I made my escape," she said, way too pleased with herself.

"Tomorrow you'll see a doctor and get the vitamins you need, young lady. This is not a joking matter." Had he just used the term young lady like a middle-aged man with a dad bod? He caught Annie's quick smile out of the corner of his eye. They were in this together for better or worse.

Chapter Thirty-Six

Of course, getting Dre to a doctor fell to Annie. She'd known the football player's life since birth. With the first league game coming up on Sunday, Matt's practices ran long and hard. He came home tired—but he volunteered to take the girl if she scheduled a late afternoon appointment. Annie also knew about doctors' hours. They'd work Dre in if she called in a few favors from her time in the NICU, but the wait time might be substantial. Annie let Matt off the hook.

She'd spoken to the nurse of an obstetrician who worked out of Ochsner and wrangled a checkup for nine a.m. She and Dre sat in the waiting room until eleven surrounded by women mostly in their thirties who had delayed having children until their careers were cemented into place. They dressed in stylish maternity clothes for the most part, but one or two went for cute with tops declaring "Baby on Board" or the sex of their issue proclaimed with "Son" and an arrow pointing down.

Except for telling Dre to wear something easy to take off, Annie hadn't come down hard about her clothes. She'd already fought the battle of the makeup that morning. "None of that chalky white stuff on your face. You know makeup like that scarred the faces of geishas. Who knows what's in it."

"Yeah, hundreds of years ago." Dre did the eye

roll, somehow less effective without the kohl liner which Annie also nixed. She enforced a freshly washed face and maybe a little lip gloss.

"As if I own any lip gloss," came the snarky reply. No argument about the hair style. As if defeated, Dre didn't bother to spike her locks with gel. They lay around her pretty, natural face like a black picture frame.

Now they sat among these tailored women with Dre dressed in her skull T-shirt, leggings, and flats, accented with a studded dog collar. The conversations clumped around how far along are you and due dates. One blonde, still wearing dangerously high heels at around six months, politely eyed Annie in her slim dark skirt and red blouse. "Must be your first appointment. You aren't showing at all."

"Oh, I'm not here to see the doctor." That shouldn't have caused a pang in her heart, but it did. "Only an escort."

The woman mouthed, "Stepchild" and inclined her head toward Dre who held a *People* magazine in front of her face as if someone from back home might recognize her. "I have two of those, but this is my first."

"Sort of," Annie answered and felt relief when the nurse called the woman's name. Another arrived with a new infant in a carrier which she sat down next to Daniel in his, taking the open space.

"How old is yours?" she inquired.

Annie decided not to explain that Daniel was over three months or that she was his nurse or whatever. She answered, "A couple of weeks" as if he'd been born in late August as he should have been.

"Well, you look great. Took me months to get my

shape back after the last one."

A snicker emerged from behind the *People* magazine. "She's only the nanny."

"Oh, sorry. Is the baby yours?"

Dre dropped her cover. "Nope, mine is still in here." She poked her belly.

Sufficiently embarrassed, the woman backed off and called up a game on her phone. Dre did the same.

They waited and waited and were finally summoned into the room with the stirrups on the examination table. Dre eyed it like a filly about to be ridden for the first time. Annie sat in a corner while Dr. Garner kept up a pleasant, relaxing conversation as he peered, poked, and palpated. She waited outside the door for Dre to dress and followed her to the doctor's consultation room where the obstetrician went over the rules of pregnancy, dispensed prescriptions, and handed over pamphlets on childbirth methods and breast feeding, all of which Dre declined to pick up. Annie shoved the printed material in her purse. Perhaps, that is why he addressed her instead of the girl next.

"No use of drugs, alcohol, or cigarettes. No new tattoos or piercings. That's all good. Miss Andrea is in fine health and should have a routine pregnancy with a due date of…" He fiddled with an app on his tablet. "February seventh. We'll take good care of her."

Annie rose and shook his hand. "Thank you for working us in, Dr. Garner.'

"Anything for the Angel of the NICU. You are sorely missed there. This little fellow stole you away from us." He nodded toward Daniel who, so far, had behaved better than Dre.

"An offer too good to refuse."

"Make your next appointment on the way out and be sure to fill in the forms for a payment plan."

"That won't be a problem. Dre is Matthew Keaton's sister-in-law. He's footing the bill."

A quick look of concern crossed the doctor's face. Annie read it as a question about molestation. She shook her head vehemently. "No, only another teen pregnancy." She said it in the same tone as Dre had called her just a nanny and got a hostile glance from the girl in return. She chided herself for sinking to that level. "Some family problems. We'll take good care of her."

"I know you will." The doctor dismissed them.

"Wow, that was really invasive," Dre said of her first internal examination as they moved to the exit. "I mean like Dr. Garner is kind of good-looking, not a McDreamy, but handsome enough to make that situation embarrassing. He admires you. Why don't you chase after him instead of sinking your claws into Matt? And, couldn't you find someone older to look at my privates?"

"First, the older doctors often aren't accepting new patients. Second, Dr. Garner is married with three children. He sees a dozen vaginas a day. Yours is nothing special to him. As for claws, NICU nurses don't have them." Annie displayed her stubby nails. "We don't want to scratch the infants, and they're easier to keep clean."

That shut Dre up for a few blocks on the way home, though she brightened again when Annie pulled up to The Company Burger. They both deserved a reward for getting through this morning. As she passed the bags to Dre, she felt compelled to say, "This is okay once in a while for a treat, but you need to eat healthy for the baby."

"Yeah, now it's all about baby."

"Yes, it is."

Dre wolfed down most of the fries on the road home while Daniel began to fuss in the backseat. She did, however, help get the baby out of the car before diving into the juicy double patties of the cheeseburgers. Annie raced upstairs to change Danny and heat a bottle before the toasted bun of her burger went soggy with the juices. Upon her return, Dre had already finished and rummaged in the kitchen cabinets. Yes, definitely in the ravenous second trimester, but she wasn't foraging for more food. "Here it is! Olive oil."

"For?" Annie seated herself and twisted her wrist around to feed Daniel with one hand while taking a bite of burger with the other.

"My hair. I want to remove the black dye naturally, not with harsh chemicals. They say online soaking your hair with olive oil for a long time, then washing it a lot will take it out. I want to get started. See, I do care about my baby."

And she was gone, a large bottle of extra virgin in her hands, leaving Annie to struggle with Daniel and her lunch. She managed and comforted herself with the knowledge that by the third trimester, the thin sliced onions and pickles buried beneath the patties would give Dre heartburn when the baby pressed against her stomach. Still, she felt a trifle envious of Dre's condition in bearing her own child.

Worn out by his active morning, Danny fell bonelessly into a deep sleep after emitting his post-bottle burp. Annie laid him carefully in his carrier. One thing Dre couldn't have, but she could. Annie made herself coffee and took one, deep reviving sip before her phone rang.

Though it clearly said Mom, her mother started out as she always did by saying, "This is your mother calling."

"Yes, Mom. I kind of recognize your voice by now."

"Checking in to see how the new job is going. I remember very well feeling so isolated when I was sitting in your father's bachelor pad with Dean in my arms and him on the road or at practice. Of course, I didn't know half of what you do about babies."

"We're doing all right, and I'm not alone. Matt's sister-in-law is visiting. She said she'd come to help with Daniel."

"Oh, good, the northern ice is starting to thaw." Leave it to Mama Nell to see this as a plus.

"Mom, she's seventeen—and expecting a baby. She wants to stay with us."

"Our family seems to attract pregnant teens like honey does bears. I had to deal with Cassie, and Teddy with his sister. Now you and…"

"Andrea, Dre for short. She wants to keep her baby, but I think she has this ideal vision of remaining with Matt permanently and raising the child alongside Daniel. She's made it fairly clear that my role is the nanny. That's not why I left the NICU."

"You left because you care deeply for Matt and Daniel. She's in your way, and you are in hers." Her mother always reaped top scores in perception. Annie supposed it came with being a psychologist, but she'd applied her skills to raising her children as well.

"Yes, you see Matt and I have—become intimate lately. It's awkward with her here."

"I'm not surprised about you and Matt."

"Did Xo or Stacy tell you?"

"I could see it coming at our Fourth of July bash. I'm glad for both of you."

"Thanks, that makes one person."

"Nonsense, we all are except for your guest. Oh, I forgot why I called. Isolation. With Matt's first game coming up, I convinced your dad to get a luxury suite at the Dome instead of our usual fifty-yard line seats and dinner afterward. I know you don't want to expose the baby to crowds and eating out with an infant is tricky. We'll have food and just family up in the box. I've already told the others if they have the sniffles to use our regular seats. Your guest is welcome too."

"Will Jude be there?"

"She usually is. Xo did mention you'd had a falling out. Mend it or you won't be happy."

"That's going to be hard. She tried to seduce Matt. He rejected her."

"I see. But, his rejection means he prefers you."

"Loves me, Mom."

Her mother's voice softened. "Even better. I'm sure Jude didn't put much effort into it as she usually gets what she really wants."

"She was drunk—and has the nerve to claim she brought us together."

"You're both adults now. Deal with it, Annie. I'm counting on you. See you Sunday."

Yes, she'd deal with it for the sake of lying in Matt's arms every night, taking in his warmth, his gentleness, his care for her needs even when tired. She should pity Jude who had nothing so wonderful.

Chapter Thirty-Seven

From the kitchen, Annie heard a loud rap on the door announcing the arrival of Papa Joe and the white fourteen-passenger van he'd used to cart his large family around for years, not glamorous but practical. She finished loading the clear diaper bag given by one of the wisest team wives. No fancy baby clothes or silver cups for her. It came with baby blue noise-cancelling headphones. "You'll want to take the baby to the games. These will protect his ears and get you past security." VIP or not, only clear bags were allowed. Annie stowed her own personal items among the bottles and diapers and wipes to cut down on baggage.

She hurried toward the noise, hoping to get there first, but Dre had already emerged from her lair by the entrance. The girl, bedecked in her combat boots, black jeans, and a big red tee with the hideous version of the Sinners' devil on it, opened the door. Papa Joe did what he did best since retiring from football—offered a dazzling smile and a warm handshake. "You must be Andrea, Matt's sister-in-law. Happy to have you come with us."

Instead of a gracious reply, Dre said, "I guess you know all about me." She gazed at the toes of her boots, head bowed under a black knit hat pulled down around her ears. Despite ruining a half dozen of Mellie's pristine white towels and using several bottles of olive oil, her hair had turned a drab light brown, nowhere near its original blonde. Only a fringe could be spied around the edge of the cap.

"I think we'll get to know you much better by the end of the game. Annie, is the little guy ready to roll? I knocked instead of ringing the bell in case he was sleeping."

"No, he's wide awake. Do you need to put the car seat into the van?"

"*Mais*, no. Don't I have grandchildren? We have a baby seat and child seat installed." He clapped his hands as if releasing the team from a huddle. "I want to get to the Dome in time to give the team a little pep talk before they go out for warmups. We're playing Atlanta. We can't mess this one up."

"I'm sure Coach Buck will appreciate that." Like he did all of her dad's exuberant interference—with gritted teeth. Annie retrieved both Daniel and the diaper bag from the kitchen, and they were good to go.

"I see we have another Sinners' fan in the making." Daddy Joe nodded with approval at Danny's red onesie with the happy devil on the pocket and Corazon's knitted cap. "Let me." He relieved her of the carrier. The group moved to the van with Dre clomping behind them. Using practiced hands, her dad, the father of many, strapped the baby in the car seat next to the excited Lizzy who babbled, "Ba-be!"

"Dre, why don't you sit in the back with T-Rex and Edie. They're around your age," he suggested, but it came out sounding more like he'd called a crucial play. Dre parked her boots next to Edie, a smaller, younger version of Annie. T-Rex, a teen clone of his dad who hadn't mastered his charm yet, greeted her with an indifferent "Hey" and stretched out his long legs as far as he was able.

Edie held out her hand. "Just ignore my brother. He's such a guy. I'll be your friend."

Annie, seeking her own seat, nailed Dre with a glare for letting her sister's offer hang in the air. Finally, Dre accepted the hand and presumably the friendship that came with it.

Annie introduced her mom, Corazon, who sat with the babies, and Teddy's wheelchair-bound wife, Jessie. All the rest would meet them in the suite.

Nothing like the VIP treatment her dad always received—special valet parking and a service representative dubbed Whitney to see them through security and up to the four-hundred level in the stadium. The very attractive young woman led the way into the box and pointed out the amenities: a floating bar already set up and the buffet soon to be stocked with barbecued shrimp skewers, Buffalo chicken wings, fried oysters wrapped in bacon, and assorted other goodies to see them through the game. "If there's anything else I can do for you, Mr. Billodeaux, you just let me know." Their blonde service representative dimpled at him.

"You can call me Joe, sugar." Whitney received his legendary smile. At this point, Annie figured the woman would either melt at his feet or shout, "Me, too!" and smack him across the face.

Before either happened, Mama Nell came to the rescue. "Where is the best place for a diaper change? Three of his grandchildren are going to need it during the game."

Joe's smile faded, but reignited when he faced his

wife. "You always know what we need, Tink." She kept him on the straight and narrow path of matrimony. As far as Annie was aware, he'd never cheated on their mom and didn't plan to in the future. That's what she wanted, a rock-solid marriage that could withstand minor slips without rancor. The representative took the hint and guided Nell to nearby facilities. She returned shortly without the young lady.

A lounge area with high-tops and white armchairs peppered the area above the tiers of seats overlooking the field and offered flat screens on the wall for those wanting close-ups of the game. Xochi and Jude already occupied two of the seats. One greeted their group with a wide, white smile, the other a black scowl.

Xo got up and hugged Joe. "Thanks so much for doing this. Now the children can roam around, and Daniel is out of the crowd and noise. But, Dad, you shouldn't go around calling women sugar anymore. They might misunderstand."

"Why not? I call you sugar sometimes and Lizzy and your mom and Miss Lolly at church who must be near one-hundred. I call all females sugar. Doesn't matter if they're pretty. Anyhow, I'd do anything for my girls. You know that." But his Billodeaux brown eyes flicked longingly toward his usual box on the fifty-yard line occupied with friends who had been given tickets.

Annie knew what this sacrifice meant to her dad. He loved being in the thick of things right where the refs could hear his criticisms. "I think we're all settled. Why don't you go speak to the team, get their spirits up? Say, isn't that Trinity sitting in the box?" She pointed out her unathletic computer geek brother, easy to spot with his black-framed glasses and unkempt curls. "Looks like he's saving you a seat."

Her mother smiled and gave her father a light swat on the backside. "Go. We'll be fine. Come back at halftime and have some food."

T-Rex, realizing he was about to be abandoned with the women and children, said, "Uh, yeah, I need to talk to Trin about some problems with my laptop." He left the suite on his father's heels.

"Looks like we have a testosterone-free zone if we don't count that baby." Jude went to the bar and helped herself to a large white wine.

Starting too early, Annie thought as she met Nell's eyes and followed the nod of her head in Jude's direction. "Here, would you watch Daniel for me?" She turned the carrier over to her mother and went to join Jude at one of the high tops.

Her sister turned on her immediately. "First a babysitter, and now you have a weirdo pregnant teen to oversee," she hissed. Her dark, resentful eyes followed Dre as the girl went down the stairs, slumped into a front row seat, separating herself from the others, and plugged in her earbuds. "She's the serpent in your pink paradise, I'll bet."

"Did Mom tell you Dre is expecting?"

"Yeah, trying to drum up sympathy for your situation is my guess, but you won't receive mine. Matt certainly is getting his money's worth, a live-in mistress who will have three children to raise, one of them a surly teen."

Annie tamped down the desire to throw the wine in Jude's face. "All of them need me, even Dre though she won't admit it. It's my choice, not yours. Mom wants us to make up, but you aren't making it easy."

"Not trying to. You take your road. I'll take mine." Jude tossed back the remainder of her wine and headed toward the bar again.

Annie placed a hand on her arm. "Don't. Drinking isn't going to solve our problem. What is your path—alcoholism and one-night stands when you have the urge?" Good thing Jude had emptied her glass, or she might have been the recipient of the same treatment she'd considered a minute ago judging by her twin's ugly twist of the lips. To her surprise, Jude returned to the high-top stool.

"It's only you who drives me to drink. I *have* decided on another path to take alone. I'm enrolling in med school at Tulane to become a full-fledged doctor. I should have gone into it right after college but didn't want to leave you behind in nursing school."

Annie softened toward her sister. "I didn't have your ambition. That's a good path for you since you hate taking orders from others. Now, you'll give them. Of course, if you plan on doing surgery, you'll have to stand on a stepstool." She'd almost gotten a smile out of Jude. "You have my full support, and I hope I have yours however my life turns out."

"Yeah, yeah, I'm always there for you. Got your back." Jude waved a dismissive hand in the air. Annie guessed they'd made the peace Mama Nell wanted.

The door to the suite opened, and Stacy appeared with her two kids who ran to meet Pilar crawling up the stairs and Lizzy who slid from Jessie's lap to join the ruckus. The noise level rose considerably in a second. Jude wrinkled her nose. "Now I do need more wine. Any chance those noise-cancelling headphones you got for Daniel would fit me?"

"I don't think so, but I know what to get you for Christmas."

Jessie flicked on the flat screens to the pregame show which her husband hosted along with the great retired wide receiver, Connor Riley, a famous former coach, and a long-time sports commentator. As Teddy's mellow voice sounded, giving his opinions on the upcoming game and joking with the guys, Lizzy shrilled, "Da-dee!" to almost everyone's delight. Jude got her wine, and Dre stayed put in her isolated nest.

Annie made sure Daniel's headphones were in place before the team entered the stadium, spewing from the inflated red devil's mouth emitting the smoke of dry ice. The crowd began to cheer along with everyone in their box who moved closer to the window. After warmups, Tom performed the perfect kickoff, driving the ball into the end zone, and took his seat. The Sinners defense slugged it out with Atlanta for seven plays before getting the ball.

When Dean handed off the football to Matt, Annie dropped Daniel peacefully sleeping into Jude's lap to race to the window and press herself against the glass. "Go, Tank, go!"—which he did with straight arms and kicks that freed him from lunging defensive players and a final leap over a man on the ground to get to the ten-yard line before stumbling.

Jude held Daniel out to Annie. "Quick, take him. He's waking up. I think he's wet." She regarded a damp spot on her white slacks. "Very wet."

"A little baby pee won't hurt you." Annie took Matt's son to the window and clapped his tiny hands together. No telling if Matt could see, but he did glance their way before taking his place behind the line. She waited to seek the changing table despite the soggy diaper until after the next play.

Dean did a fake, drew his opponents off to the left, and ran the ball across the goal line himself. The people in their suite roared along with fans from the cheap seats way up top where the air was thin, to the row of men who always dressed liked popes and those who took the devil theme a little too far, way down to Joe's box where Annie's dad did a little victory dance of his own.

Daniel got his dry diaper and a bottle. Xochi settled next to Annie and Dre. She pulled out a plump, tawny breast to feed Pilar. "Nursing, it's so good for the baby," she said loudly enough to overcome whatever music absorbed Dre. She earned a shrug.

"Matt gets his supply from a breast milk service. That's the way to go." The girl adjusted the volume upward.

Unfortunately, that was the only score in the first half except for a field goal by Tom matched by Atlanta. The Sinners went to the locker room tied. Mama Nell called out, "If you haven't eaten yet, grab a plate before the men get here, or there won't be much left."

Annie plucked out Dre's earbud. "Better get something to eat, but the food will be spicy, so go easy or you'll get heartburn."

Another shrug as if that were the only gesture the girl knew. "Haven't so far." She sloped off to the buffet table and piled her plate high with shrimp and chicken wings, forgoing the oysters. Annie left Daniel in Xo's custody and followed her in line. She selected modest portions of everything and chose an icy Coke Zero to wash it down. Still, she found the food spicier than usual and experienced a little of the heartburn she'd cautioned Dre about. The girl wolfed down wings and saucy shrimp constructing a mound of shells and fragile bones the size of a small pyramid. Must be nice to be so young, so thin and tall, and so cocksure you knew everything.

Edie, trying her best, sat at the high top with Dre. "If you need me to explain anything about the game, I'm your gal. Dad says I teethed on a football."

"I know enough." She licked barbecue sauce from her fingers and glugged down a bottle of water.

The thunder of male footsteps sounded in the hall. Nell herded the children out of the way and down to the window to watch the marching bands. Joe burst in with T-Rex, Trinity, and the horde of friends he'd invited from the box. The catering containers emptied fast. Their representative checked in, and Joe ordered refills. "*Merci beaucoup*, sug…ah, Miss Whitney."

Jude put a plate of petite fours, mini-eclairs, and napoleons on the table where Annie finished her meal. "I'll bring coffee."

"Tea for me. Thanks for getting dessert before T-Rex and Trinity empty the trays. I can understand how Rex packs it away at his age. He's a growing boy. But Trin is so slim, and he bends over a computer all day. You'd think he's a competitive eater."

"High metabolism. We failed to get that gene. Women never do." Still, Jude stuffed an éclair into her mouth before bringing the beverages.

Annie's tension eased. She and her twin were finding balance again. No telling when Jude would be welcome at Matt's house, but she'd work on that.

Maybe the custard and puff pastry of just one napoleon would ease her mild indigestion.

Jessie shushed everyone to watch Teddy on the halftime show. The game resumed, and the men departed for their box again. Babies full of milk and children replete with petit fours napped in the cushy seats. The women gathered near the window to view the end of the game, hard fought until the end, but the Sinners triumphed seventeen-fourteen. Annie felt no little pride that Matt had scored the second touchdown by bulling through the Atlanta line.

When Whitney approached as the clock ran down, Nell asked her to have the leftovers boxed and sent to the van. She announced another variation on their game day plans. "We're going to Dean's house instead of a restaurant tonight. Our players will join us there after they celebrate with the team at Mariah's Place."

The van awaited along with T-Rex and Daddy Joe to see them home through the post-game traffic, but not without some blaring of the horn and a few insults shouted at other drivers. "Eh, *couillon*, you don't know you let every other car into da line, no?"

The *couilllon,* or nut case, seemed more thrilled than angry to be cursed out by Joe Dean Billodeaux and made space for the mammoth white van to merge with traffic. Unscathed by road rage, they reached the Garden District safely, much to Annie's relief since they had Daniel in the car. With the leftovers laid out in the kitchen, Mama Nell and her sisters went to sit beneath the porch fans stirring the still-warm September air with cold drinks in their hands. Daddy Joe, armed with snacks, said he and T-rex intended to retreat to Dean's man cave to listen to the postgame interviews. Only Annie hung back before she joined the others.

She grabbed Dre's elbow, almost spilling the girl's second helping of chicken wings. "Just a minute. My family has gone out of their way to make you feel comfortable. Our Samoan friend, Adam, says they have the spirit of *alofa,* a giving kind of love they have extended to you. You can be as rude to me as you like because I don't care about your opinion, but you will end this evening with a smile on your face and a thank you coming out of your mouth. I shouldn't have to teach you manners as well as baby care. Do you understand?"

Annie expected another shrug but received a stunned expression and perhaps an inkling of tears in Dre's blue eyes. "You're pretty tough for someone shrimp-sized, but yeah, I can do a smile and a thanks. It was kind of neat being treated like football royalty. And your dad is totally hot." Dre exited the kitchen. Annie followed. The girl plunked down beside Edie on a lounge. "Want to share some chicken wings?" Despite the shrimp slur, Annie considered her job done for the evening. She took her place on the porch.

Her eyes scanned for Matt as soon as the garden gate opened. To her disappointment, Teddy came in the lead working his armband crutches toward Jessie and Lizzy dozing in her lap. The perpetual newlyweds, Tom and Alix followed with arms around each other, then Junior and Dean. Finally, Matt brought up the rear and shot the latch. Two tired children hugged Dean's legs, and Stacy went to give her big lout a kiss. Junior bounded up the steps to embrace Xochi and kiss the top of Pilar's nodding head. Annie wished Matt would do the same. Instead, he paused to pat the excited, white pouf of a dog jumping at his feet, then stood there all alone with his big arms hanging at his side, seeming a little lost about his next move.

Annie couldn't take it anymore. She wanted to declare that she and Matt were a couple loud and clear, at least in front of her loved ones. Moving carefully around Daniel's carrier, she bolted down the steps and flung her arms around his waist. "You were wonderful today." Standing on tiptoes, she brought his head down for a kiss. He smelled of a recent shower that brought back memories, and his lips had the tang of the beer he'd shared in victory with the team. Though he returned her affection, he cut the embrace short, tucking her under his arm. She looked upward and realized his gaze locked with her father's eyes across the courtyard. Every person on the patio went quiet, even the yapping dog.

"Well?" her dad said.

"Joe, I love your daughter—and we're together now. We've kept it quiet out of respect for the Ames family, but it is a fact."

"No surprise there. But, let me tell you, me. Don't you hurt my little girl, or I'll come for you."

"No, sir, I'd never hurt Annie in any way," Matt swore.

"Oh, Dad! That isn't necessary." Annie hoped not. Her father maintained excellent health, but leaning against the bulk of Matt, she doubted he could take her lover in a fight—though there was his gun collection. That would be the worst nightmare of all—if the two men she loved most, not counting Daniel, came to blows over her. Wouldn't happen. The world might not know yet, but she and Matthew Keaton were a permanent item.

Chapter Thirty-Eight

Despite Annie's assurances that she understood a football player's life during the season, Matt tried to hold up his end. On Monday after team meeting when the men were given a day off to cope with their sprains and bruises, he went to Joe's lawyer and had the papers drawn up to become Dre's guardian for a short time since his sister-in-law turned eighteen in March. Hard to believe she'd be a mother by then.

He had the document mailed express and included a request to Bucky for his daughter's school and medical records. His original plan to enroll her in the same parochial school he'd chosen for Daniel sank like a tug in the Mississippi when Dre revealed her pregnancy. The nuns would not want her around corrupting their virgin students, though from what he remembered of Catholic school girls, most of them weren't by graduation, a form of nun defiance, he guessed.

Getting Dre her GED seemed like the way to go. Maybe, she could start college early after the birth of the child—but that would put more of a burden on Annie to care for two infants, though she said, "No sweat." Yet, he worried about her. She seemed tired but had to be ordered back to sleep when Daniel woke at three a.m. for a bottle, and he said he'd take care of it. Regardless of her fatigue, whenever she settled on his chest with no more weight than a dove on a nest, and he became aroused, her small hand found its way to wrap around his penis and give him pleasure. He'd never met a woman more giving, certainly not his wife. Annie would never deceive or betray him.

Matt thought she and Dre were getting along better, but maybe his SIL only behaved in front of him, and he wasn't around enough to tell. When he'd asked Dre to help out more with Daniel in order to give Annie some down time, she'd replied, "If she'll let me."

He laid down the law to both of them. "Annie, you need to take longer naps and allow Dre to sit in the nursery and take care of the baby's needs. No reason the girl can't do a load of laundry or help with dinner either. We are a team in this together to achieve the best result possible." Jesus, now he knew how Coach Buck felt trying to coordinate the efforts of eleven men on the field all at once. He had only two women to deal with, perhaps the harder job.

Matt headed directly home after consulting with the lawyer. He could give them both a break from each other and watch Daniel since he was back earlier than usual and not as tired. Naturally, someone had snagged his parking place in front of the house. He parked down the block and hoofed it toward home. Damn, intercepted by one of the neighbors, a lush busty redhead walking her Shih Tzu on one of those leashes that let the dog roam, then jerked it back at will. The small animal didn't stand a chance. Neither did he as she positioned herself in the center of the sidewalk and used the leash to cut off any escape to the right. To the left, a huge azalea bush overgrew the path. This encounter not being a football game, he couldn't simply run over her. *Ambushed.*

"Hi, neighbor, I'm Kimberly Walet. Kim to my friends, and I hope you will be one. I have the center hall villa on the corner, at least for now, but I plan to get it in my divorce decree. So sorry to hear about your wife's death and your struggles with your son." She switched the leash to her left hand, offering a long-fingered hand with nails lacquered in bronze that caught the sun to Matt. Her dog raised the skirt of his long hair and watered a nearby live oak.

Having no choice, he gave a short, business-like shake. "Thanks. Daniel is doing well."

"So glad to hear that. As a mother of two boys I know I'd be frantic to lose one of them. Both are at boarding school right now, but I'd love to have you meet them. Perhaps, we could go to one of your games and get together afterward. But, tickets are so expensive, and at the moment, I'm having cash flow problems. Their father pays for their education. However, he isn't very involved in their lives. They could use a role model like you."

Okay, she wanted free passes and a second husband. He could supply the first, no sweat. He had no intention of doing the second. From her red hair to her voluptuous breasts and overall tan, Kim was as fake as could be. Not like his Annie, so good and genuine. How to extricate himself?

"Nice meeting you. I'll mail you some passes for the next home game in three weeks. I came home early to spend some time with my son, so I'll be moving along now."

"Certainly. Sun Tzu, I call him Sunny for short, and I are done with our walkies and going back your way. We'll just tag along." She turned aside and reeled in her dog. Matt increased his stride, but Kimberly was long-legged enough to keep up even on her wedge-heeled espadrilles with the ankle-breaker straps. The dog broke into a trot. Sunny panted with relief when they reached Matt's gate and came to a standstill.

Matt considered vaulting over the fence to make his escape but remained polite. "I'll see you get those tickets."

Kim put a staying hand on his arm. "That would mean so much to my boys. I have to say this house is a strange choice for a man of your machismo. I mean perfect for Kingston and Ollie, but pink, really? You'll have to come see my place. It's painted white and much roomier. How about tonight?"

The lace curtains in the front parlor window moved. Dre the Spy at work. "Sorry, I need to turn in early. We have a heavy practice tomorrow. Some other time."

Kim pouted with lips pumped up by collagen. "I do get lonely in the evenings with my boys away from home. Are you sure…"

"I don't have much free time during the season and like to spend it all with Daniel." And Annie.

She drew her lips back over beautifully whitened teeth. "It's an open invitation. Ta-ta for now."

"Yeah, ta-ta right back at you." Matt fumbled with the gate latch, but once open, strode in giant steps to the safety of his pink palace and his Annie.

****

Annie cherished this moment alone, along with a cup of hot tea in her hands and two macaron cookies on a nearby plate. From the kitchen table, she watched

Matt carry Daniel around the garden, pointing out the birds and flowers, though the infant had eyes only for his dad and ears cocked toward his father's deep voice.

Dre entered and snatched the chocolate macaron Annie had been particularly ready to relish. Why couldn't the girl simply stay in her room like other teens glued to her laptop and social media? Instead, she devoured Annie's treat, spilling crumbs on the top of her still very tiny baby bump and brushing them off on the floor.

"Always so hungry. Anyhow, Annie, you'd better get your game on. I saw Matt talking to a redhead out by the gate. She's stalking him. She left her car in his place, a red Jag—can you believe it—and has been walking that mop of a dog up and down the street for the last hour. Poor thing, it's still hot out there. I mean, that woman is leggy and really glam, so not like you."

How Annie appreciated being reminded that her scrubs were wrinkled because she'd forgotten them in the dryer and her eyes were underscored with dark circles. "I know who she is, our neighborhood cougar in the midst of a divorce searching for her next prey. Kimberly Walet has ten years on Matt. You took my cookie."

"Jeez, there's a whole box on the counter." Dre added a lemon, a strawberry, and another chocolate to the plate and poured herself a glass of milk. She took a seat next to Annie. Both observed Matt turn Daniel toward the fountain to view the fall of sparkling water. "So cute, a big man with a tiny baby. Honest, I only wanted to warn you. I can tell this Kim is mostly ornamental, like Mellie. You, you're useful, utilitarian, you know."

"Thanks a heap for that compliment. You'd better be cheering for my team. Kim sends her boys to boarding school. She'd have you in a home for unwed mothers before they left for the honeymoon at some Sandals resort." Annie nibbled her cookie and sipped her tea. So tired.

Matt brought Daniel inside. "I think the fountain turned on his own sprinkler system. He's wet."

Annie rose to take the baby. Matt waved her back to her chair. "I'll take care of it. He's due for a bottle and nap. You two enjoy your snack and conversation." He headed up the stairs to Daniel's room.

Dre dunked a pink macaron into her milk. It disintegrated. "Now I have a strawberry milkshake. Can we get some Oreos instead of this fancy stuff?"

"Put it on the grocery list."

In the nursery, Matt began to sing *Danny Boy*. Annie envisioned him holding Daniel close while giving him a bottle and rocking back and forth. Back and forth. Her eyes closed. She fell asleep at the table with Jude's warning about being cast aside for a model or starlet playing and replaying in her mind like a hurricane storm warning.

Chapter Thirty-Nine

The doorbell woke Annie from her afternoon nap. It sounded again. Where was Dre? Oh yeah, tending Daniel and studying for her GED in a patch of garden sunlight as she strove to regain blonde highlights in her hair with the help of lemon juice. Not that the girl needed much study. Her educational portfolio showed straight A's in all her advanced placement subjects junior year. She lacked only three more classes to graduate, one each of history, English, and math. The rest of her senior year choices had consisted of electives ranging from art to political science. Annie credited Dre for having more depth than she'd anticipated.

She credited the person at the door for sheer persistence as she made her way, still groggy, down the spiral staircase. Finding Kimberly Walet on the other side of that door woke her up entirely. "Yes, yes, can I help you?"

Kim stared over Annie's head, searching the hall. "You must be the nanny. Is Matt at home?"

"Nurse," Annie corrected. "No, he is not. Still at practice."

"When does he usually get home?"

"Depends. Sometimes, he gets a beer with friends afterward." Rarely, but Annie wasn't about to share that information.

"Hmmm, well. I brought him a little treat. I simply

love to bake, and I figure a big man like him needs all the calories he can get when he's training." Kim held out a charming basket of cupcakes ensconced in a red cloth napkin—the kind of container that had to be returned.

"Thank you. I'll see he gets them."

"Be sure to say Kim sent them just for him."

"I couldn't possibly forget. Have a nice day." Annie shut the door decisively and turned the lock. She carried the basket to the kitchen and plunked it down on the table. Summoning Dre and Daniel from the garden, she said, "Hey, want a special snack?"

Dre peered at the contents of the basket, cupcakes with a slick of dark chocolate frosting. "What kind are they?"

"Doberge. Kimberly brought them for Matt. Hinted she loved to bake. As if. These are from Debbie Does Doberge over on Annunciation Street."

Dre's blue eyes widened, and a hint of drool appeared in the crook of her smile. "There's such a thing as doberge cupcakes?"

"Yep, in New Orleans they exist as do most of your heart's desires."

"That's why I love it here. Can we have some right now?"

"Well, she said they were for Matt—but yes. Pour two glasses of milk for us."

Dre eyed the empty coffee carafe that Annie usually kept full. "I'll make you some coffee since she interrupted your nap."

"No, I'm good. The chocolate will wake me up."

They'd had two each when Matt arrived to claim his share. He offered Daniel, nestled on his lap, a tiny smear of icing on his finger tip. The baby latched on immediately and seemed a little upset when the bottle replaced the frosted finger. "These are so good even Danny wants more. Were you out and about today buying baked goods?"

"No, Kim brought them for you, but we figured you'd share. If you want more, you can get them at Debbie Does Doberge." In that short sentence, she told him she knew about Kim and dissed her baking abilities. "I'll have Dre return her basket tomorrow with a polite note saying how much we all enjoyed them." With that action, she would mark her territory.

Matt devoured half a cupcake in two bites. "Nice of her, anyhow. These are great. No coffee? Should I write the note?"

"Nope, I'll take care of it for you. Let me make that coffee." Annie moved to the other end of the kitchen and began setting up the coffeemaker.

Dre followed for a refill of milk. "Nice moves. Go Team Annie. He doesn't get it, does he?" she murmured.

"Men rarely do."

****

Kimberly kept them in baked goods: blueberry muffins, a variety of bagels, the identical oversized chocolate chip cookies Annie had purchased for Stacy's kids months ago. Matt recognized those. "I remember DJ sharing his with me. You sat right beside me and squeezed my arm. I was in pretty bad shape back then, but you steered me out of the fog like a guardian angel."

Annie marveled that such a rugged face could own such as tender smile. She returned it. Take that

Kimberly. Still, she couldn't help feeling glad Matt had two away games coming up, one on the west coast and one on the east. The team would fly out Friday for both, get a practice in, play Sunday, and return on Monday. She'd have scant time with him between those games, but Kim would have none no matter how hard she tried.

Annie elected not to go to either game as she didn't want Daniel exposed to plane travel yet. Most of the Billodeauxs would follow the team, all except Xochi who also preferred not taking her baby anywhere by air yet. Annie told Dre she could accept the invitation to attend with the family, but the girl turned down the opportunity.

"Hey, I know you want to travel. That will be hard once the baby arrives. Why not see some of Los Angeles and Philadelphia? You can room with Edie."

"No, thanks. I mean I like Edie, but you might need me."

Annie doubted that but refrained from an eyeroll or sarcastic comment. Lately, Dre had gone quiet and did as Annie asked—like returning Kim's containers and providing a full report on the encounter.

"Her maid answered the door. Can you believe she has a maid?"

"Many people in New Orleans do."

"I'm glad we don't have one. That would be weird." Dre thought for a moment. "Or maybe fantastic. Kimberly shouted at the woman to ask who was there. When the maid said someone returning a basket, she bounced right out. Those boobs can't be real, huh? At her age, they should be sagging by now. Real disappointed to see me and not Matt. Asked who I was. Told her Matt's sister-in-law here to help with the baby.

She didn't need to know the rest. Better we double-team her than you take her on alone, right?"

Annie agreed with that strategy, though she felt sure Matt had no interest in the pestiferous woman. However, men fell unwittingly into traps set by females all the time. Look at what had happened to Dean, the straightest of the straight arrows. He loved his son by Ilsa but must live with the huge mistake of having gotten involved with the mother. She didn't want that to happen to Matt.

For the first game against the Rams, Annie and Dre hosted Xochi and Pilar for a pizza party. For the second, Xo entertained them at her condo and provided fresh, spicy salsa, homemade tortilla chips, and a meal of cheese enchiladas made by her mother-in-law, Corazon. Junior and Xo definitely had the largest TV, one where Annie could see Matt's every expression when he sat on the bench while the defense played. How she wished to be there in person, but Daniel's well-being had to come first. The Sinners took their Los Angeles opponent easily, the Eagles not so much. Matt returned battered but uncomplaining, having scored a touchdown in both games. Ah well, two home games approached, more rest for him and time for them together, then a blessed bye week.

October arrived with its mild mornings and warm afternoons, the first month to stomp on the back of summer's intense heat. While she rested, Annie let Dre take Daniel out in the super-stroller to return the latest baked goods pan from a batch of great double-chocolate brownies Kim's maid probably created. Dre returned full of indignation.

"Annie, that—that slutty cougar put her hands on

Daniel. She didn't even ask, just grabbed him up like she wanted to eat him. She didn't hold him right either, and then Danny started to cry, and she dumped him back in the stroller like he was a toy, not a real baby. I told her not to touch him again, and she laughed at me. Said she'd had two babies of her own and wasn't too old to have another in case this one didn't survive. I came right home. Is Danny okay?"

Annie checked for any signs of acute distress and found none, but clearly, the baby hadn't enjoyed his encounter with Kimberly as he continued fussing until his bottle and nap time. Annie went down for rest, too, and the ever-energetic Dre parked herself in the rocker to study. How long Annie slept she didn't know when Daniel's monitor sounded. She dashed to his room and found Dre bending over the crib.

"Annie, he's not breathing! I put him on his back to sleep. I didn't do anything else, I swear! Is it SIDS?"

"No, no, probably an A & B, apnea and bradycardia." She raised Daniel and patted his back to remind him to breathe. No luck. "Dre, get the mask and bag out of the bottom dresser drawer, stat!"

Annie affixed the mask on Daniel's face and gave the bag several squeezes. The blue tint of Danny's lips faded. His eyes opened again. Crisis over. She removed the gear and took him to the rocker to rest against her shoulder. "We're okay now, aren't we, Danny?"

"Do you think he really is? Did I bring this on? Did Kimberly? Will this happen to my baby?" For the first time, Annie noticed Dre lay a hand possessively on her belly.

"Unlikely unless you give birth prematurely. That's why we have to be sure his monitor is on when Daniel naps. That's why I'm here—to handle these spells. And no, I don't think you caused this, and though I'd like to blame it on Kim, probably not her either."

"Annie Billodeaux, you really are something. I didn't see it before, but you are."

"Thanks, but any NICU nurse could do the same. Look, I'm going to take him to the hospital just to make sure this has nothing to do with his heart surgery. Will you stay here and intercept Matt, tell him where we are? He's due back from practice in an hour or so. Be sure to say Daniel is fine. This is simply a precaution. We'll be home soon."

Annie gave Daniel a diaper change and a cute new outfit for their visit, proud as any mother showing off her child. She left Dre still looking stunned in the doorway and passed Kimberly forever walking poor Sunny up and down their street on the way to the NICU.

****

Matt returned home to his worst nightmare, maybe two of them since Kimberly Walet intercepted him by the gate to thank him physically for the game tickets by wrapping her arms around him and giving him a hug that mashed her silicone breasts against his chest, plus kissing his cheek, leaving a slick of coral lipstick behind that he erased with his thumb. The dog, as if trained, tangled his leash around Matt's feet. Matt fought free exactly as if a tackle grabbed his ankle and another his torso to bring him down but avoided kicking the Shih Tzu by an inch or two.

"No need to thank me. I hope your boys enjoy the game."

"Why not come over to my place and meet them

afterward? They'd love that."

Did women still bat their false eyelashes at men, he pondered. Evidently, some did, but not Annie. "Sorry, I have other plans. Have a good time with your sons." He sprung the latch and escaped once more.

Inside, the house had a stillness about it that he hardly recognized. No baby squalling or women in the kitchen talking over coffee. "Annie, Daniel, Dre, I'm home." No answer.

Perhaps, they'd gone somewhere and gotten caught in traffic. Maybe, they'd had an accident. Memories of his bloodied SUV with Mellie slumped in front seat flashed in his mind. He checked his phone. No messages. With a panic he never showed on the playing field, he raced to the kitchen and searched for a note of any kind, tore up the backstairs to the nursery, and found an empty crib.

"Annie, Dre!"

His SIL appeared with swollen blue eyes still tearful. Matt tried to be gentle, but he grasped her shoulders harder than he meant and gave her a slight shake. "What happened?"

Without her black lipstick and former attitude, Dre's lips were pale and shaking. "Daniel had a spell, an A & B. He's fine, Annie said, but she took him to the hospital to be checked. She really is amazing, Matt, the way she handled it. I thought the baby died. He wasn't breathing, so awful. Maybe my fault because that woman…" Dre jerked her head toward the window, and Matt had no doubt whom she meant. "Kimberly grabbed Danny out of the carriage when I went to return the brownie pan. I should have stopped her, but she was so quick—cougar-like. When he started to cry, she said an ugly thing, that if he died, she could still have kids. I came right home. Annie said not likely that caused the problem but..." Tears spilled.

Matt drew her in and gave Dre a hug much more sincere than the one Kimberly offered. He nudged her to sit in the rocker and reached for the phone in his hip pocket. No, if Annie went inside the NICU, she'd have hers turned off.

"She said they'd be home soon." Dre sniffed and cleaned her face with a handy baby wipe. "I can make coffee while we wait. We have Oreos. Annie got them for me. She's nice, she really is."

"I agree. Okay, coffee it is. Milk for you."

They waited in the kitchen for the phone to ring, for Annie's car to return with Daniel. Neither happened.

Dre said, "I was going to ask you to be my birth partner, but now I think I want Annie to help me." She dunked her cookie and sucked in the soggy wafer like the child she wasn't far from being.

The very thought that he'd have to see Dre's private parts at a birthing paralyzed Matt for a moment. He withheld an answer until that appalling thought passed. "Yeah, Annie would be better."

"You think she will after I was so snarky to her?"

"I don't think Annie holds grudges. She forgave her twin for...never mind. Something far worse than being snarky."

"Good, because I mean to do better. Matt, I think my baby is starting to move. This is so for real now, and I'm scared."

"Don't be. We both have Annie." He gave in to a childish impulse and dunked his Oreo into the coffee made nice and strong the way Annie drank it. Better with cold milk. Someday, he'd sit with Daniel and show him how it was done.

A car door slammed. It had the light, tinny sound of Annie's subcompact. He got halfway down the hall before Annie entered, her arms devoid of Daniel.

Chapter Forty

"Is he…?"

Annie recognized the anguish in Matt's deep, dark eyes, the same pain she'd seen in the NICU the night Daniel came into the world. She went to him immediately, cupped his face. "Daniel is fine. They decided to keep him overnight for observation and have his surgeon look at him in the morning to be certain his heart is functioning well. This may not have been Danny's first spell. Remember that night we collided in the hall when the alarm went off?"

Inside the tender cage of her hands, he nodded. "It could be that the alarm startled him out of an A and B, and he kicked off his monitor. Whatever it is, if he needs more surgery or just requires careful watching, we'll get through it. Daniel has the heart of a Sinner you know." Annie lowered her hands and rested her head against his own hard thudding heart.

She jolted when Dre joined the embrace by hugging them both with her baby bump firmly planted in the small of Annie's back. How unexpected. "I'm so glad Daniel is okay," the teen burbled, her voice choked with tears again. Their huddle broke up.

"Dre made some pretty good coffee, strong the way you like it. We've broken into the Oreos too. Come sit down. You look tired." Matt led her to the kitchen table and went to fill a mug.

307

Annie waved the offer aside. "I had some at the hospital. Since I have the chance for one full night of sleep, I'll pass on more caffeine, though strangely, some doctors are using it to counter these A & B incidents now. Nearly dinnertime, and I haven't given food a thought."

"No problem." Matt waved a sheaf of takeout menus they used far too often. "Chinese okay? Whatever you want." He dialed the number and ordered Mongolian beef and pork fried rice for himself. "Annie?—chicken lo mein. Dre?—an order of pot stickers, a Four Happy with white rice, some shrimp toast, and let's get a triple order of egg rolls. A half hour. That's good."

Annie waved her hand. "No MSG!"

"Tell them not to forget the fortune cookies," Dre added. "Maybe they will tell us all is well."

"I wouldn't put my faith in them. I'm going to make a pot of green tea. You are all welcome to share." Annie rose to start the water.

"A beer for me. I earned it in training. You should see the bruise on my back. Junior took me down harder than he meant to. Maybe I'll show you later." Matt grinned at Annie and helped himself from the fridge.

"I'm tired of milk. Can't I have a Coke, please, Annie?" Dre begged.

"Get her a Coke, Matt. After the day we've had, we should all get our heart's desire."

Within half an hour, the surface of the kitchen table sprouted white boxes like a garden of Chinese mushrooms. Annie put out plates and dug spoons into each entree, no eating from the boxes if they wanted to share. Matt dumped his entire helping of Mongolian beef onto his plate and added some of the fried rice plus two egg rolls. He shoved two shrimp toasts on top of the pile. Good, no repeat of his loss of appetite when his tragedy occurred. Annie spooned out a modest portion of lo mein, claimed an egg roll, two pot stickers, a shrimp toast, and considered herself done. She watched Dre hoover through box after box.

"What, you thought we didn't have Chinese in Indiana? I'm leaving some for lunch. Ah, here are the fortune cookies. One for Matt, one for me, one for Annie, and a leftover. I guess we ordered enough for four."

"More like six," Annie noted.

Dre popped the cellophane wrapper on her cookie and broke the crisp outer layer. She read her fortune aloud. "Sometimes we don't get what we want, but what we get is better." She mumbled, "In bed."

Annie choked on a mouthful of noodles and spit them into a paper napkin. "Dre! Where did you learn that game? Jude and I didn't hear about it until college."

Matt grinned. "Sounds like the Rolling Stones are writing fortune cookies now. Mine reads, 'Good things lie ahead'—in bed." He leered at Annie. "Read yours."

"A road paved with lies makes a rocky path to follow. Somehow, I don't think adding in bed will make that any more amusing."

"You need a better fortune. That one doesn't suit you." Matt handed her the last cookie.

"Deceit will lead to a downfall. In bed." She tried to make a joke out of it, but her stomach, unstable lately, churned.

"I think we've already been there, done that. Save

it for Jude," Matt told her with an edge to his voice.

They finished eating, packed the leftovers into the fridge, watched TV, and turned in early as they did every night, but tonight Annie wanted to make their evening a little more special. Much as she loved Daniel, uninterrupted time to make love and simply sleep held huge appeal for her.

She started as soon as they hit the sheets, her hand moving over Matt's chest, teasing his nipples, heading down to the region he didn't keep shaved. Some fondling, and he didn't need much more to spring erect. He turned on his side to give her a kiss. Annie wrapped her arms around him, and he flinched. Ah, the nasty bruise. "Let me see. Yes, that is pretty ugly. You get to be on top tonight. I promise not to claw you."

"Aw, one of my favorite parts. When we get going, I don't feel a thing but the pleasure. I'm ready but let me make sure you are too."

Just thinking about making love with Matt made her ready, but she didn't protest the kisses down the side of her neck, his massage of her breasts, his teasing of her sensitive nipples that sent tiny sparks through her body. His hand moved between her legs, finding that pulsing point and testing her with a finger. She writhed beneath him.

"Just a second while I suit up." He reached for a condom.

Annie wanted to scream, "Just do it! Now!" Tonight, she could scream if she wanted without waking Daniel. Dre would simply have to put on her headphones downstairs if she had a problem with it. They might not have this opportunity again.

Then, she took his power into her body with every

thrust and let it build to the explosive point. She shrieked like the gulls on the waterfront, like the trumpet solo in a New Orleans jazz club. Matt, his sweat dripping on her heated skin, said, "I hope that wasn't a cry of pain."

"Not pain! Here it comes again."

He joined her this time with a deep bellow of his own. When he rolled to the side and cradled her, he said, "I didn't know either of us had so much volume inside us to let loose."

"We've schooled ourselves to be quiet for the baby and Dre. But not tonight."

"Just think, a full night's sleep ahead too." Matt, who'd had a hard practice and the emotional stress of worry about his son, went out like the light Annie had turned to extinguish.

Both woke automatically at three as Daniel had trained them to do, but instead of getting up to heat a bottle of milk, they warmed each other again. She should have gone back to sleep easily, but she lay awake with the truth of the fortune cookie tormenting her mind. "A road paved with lies makes a rocky path to follow."

Chapter Forty-One

Annie woke as tired as if she'd been up all night with the baby. She feigned sleep when Matt went to shower, slipping out of bed while he was occupied, and downstairs to start coffee for him. Nuking a cup of tea, she moved far from the dripping pot with its nauseating aroma and stilled her stomach with dry toast while lavishly buttering some for Matt. She managed to scramble the eggs and prepare bacon in the microwave. There, juice and milk poured and in place by the time Matt thundered down the stairs.

"Aren't you eating?" he asked, shoveling in the food as if last night left him in need of an energy boost.

"I had something earlier." True enough if dry toast counted.

"Maybe I should skip practice and wait until we hear about Daniel. Tough as he is even Coach Buck would consider that a good excuse."

"No, go for training. No telling how long they'll have to wait for the surgeon. I'll leave a message on your phone as soon as I know, but my guess is he'll be home waiting for you by the time you arrive."

Matt finished his food and tilted her head up for a goodbye kiss. He paused. "You still look tired. I should have let you sleep at three a.m."

"No, I woke same as you. Don't make Coach Buck mad by being late."

She added a playful swat to that rock-hard behind as she'd often seen Stacy do to her brother, keeping it light. The moment he left the house, Annie stopped holding it in. As she rushed to the sink, the smell of the coffee hit her nostrils again. Her once go-to remedy for lack of sleep turned on her. Tea and toast came up and splattered against the porcelain.

"You're knocked up, right?" Dre observed from the kitchen doorway.

Annie swore the girl had cat feet encased in the yellow duckie slippers that matched her pajamas. She didn't answer until she'd rinsed her mouth with cool water. "Yes. You're up early."

"I have my October prenatal checkup at nine. You forgot? Believe me, I know the symptoms. I had to hide them those first three months before I could escape Indiana. Not so hard as I spent most of my time in my room and my mother pretty much ignored me when she wasn't finding fault. Won't be as easy for you sleeping with Matt. The kid must be his since you never go anywhere or do anything. He isn't aware yet, or he'd be coddling you like he did Mellie. Jeez, you two were loud last night going at it."

"Thank you for your insights, Dre the Spy. I slipped up, not him."

"And you a nurse. Tut, tut. But, what my dad said, you didn't do it alone. Well, I guess a woman can now with artificial insemination, but the natural way is more fun."

"Dre, please don't tell him. I want to wait until the bye week so he has more time to take it all in and consider what he wants to do. Meantime, could you make your own breakfast while I shower?"

"Sure, I'll just have cereal. I'll bet eggs and coffee and that good bacony smell makes you want to barf again."

Annie swallowed hard as she cleaned the sink of the evidence of her lie to Matt. Two more weeks to hide her situation from him, then face that she'd deceived him like Mellie, only this baby was definitely his.

****

The sorta handsome Dr. Garner arranged for Dre listen to the rapid lub-dub of her baby's heartbeat. Annie watched as his technician prepared her slightly protruding belly with gel for the ultrasound and searched for the fetus within the womb.

"I hear it! Annie, look at the little fingers and toes," Dre exclaimed.

"Yes, they're all there." Her own baby—only the size of a lentil and hardly recognizable as human right now. "Notice anything else?"

"I hope that's the umbilical cord looped between the legs. Please tell me it is, doctor."

Dr. Garner grinned. "What you see is a tiny penis, Dre. It's a boy."

"Oh, no! Oh, no! I need to have daughter. One I can teach to be independent and herself no matter what. A boy, how will I raise a boy alone?" Tears gathered.

Annie squeezed Dre's hand. "Matt and I will be around to help every step of the way. Boys need to learn independence and their identity too."

"You'll be my birth buddy, won't you? I was going to ask Matt, but I'd rather have another woman, especially you."

Annie didn't suggest Dre's mother might fill the role better. They'd had no contact since the dreadful phone call. As for Matt, he might not be around for the birth if the Sinners went all the way this season. Good practice for herself. Maybe Dre would be hers if Matt decided to stand aside and not be involved. "I'd be honored to do that for you."

After they marveled over the child a while longer, the technician shut down the machine and handed Dre a towel to wipe her belly. Dr. Garner assured his patient that all looked normal and taking Annie aside, confirmed her pregnancy established by the test she'd taken after leaving the NICU the previous day. He handed her a sheaf of prescriptions for prenatal vitamins, folic acid, and basic care information. "Annie, if you need help of any kind, ask me. You've certainly given your all for my smallest patients."

"Thanks. I'll be fine." Maybe on her own, but fine. Didn't she have the world's greatest family—unlike Dre? Among the Billodeauxs, no one raised a child alone. She'd cling to that.

Dre, dressed again in her partly zipped jeans and baggy tee sporting a red dragon belching yellow flames on the usual black background, joined them. "I don't suppose you'd be in the mood for a burger topped with grilled onions, huh?"

"No, but maybe a milkshake." Annie fought down the nausea awakened by the very thought of fried onions. "After lunch, we could see about getting you some maternity clothes. You're pushing toward five months, and that baby is going to start growing in leaps and bounds." She received the typical Dre shrug.

"Lots of women make do with unzipped jeans and big shirts. Besides, I don't want any of those *I Love Lucy* tent tops that scream preggers."

"I doubt they are still in style, but if you want to remain discreet, stay away from the knit dresses designed to show the bump that Hollywood stars favor."

"Okay, okay, we'll shop. How about if I get a cheeseburger with no onions?"

The deal struck, Dre wolfed her burger and fries while Annie sipped a thick chocolate shake. They decided on jeans and slacks with a pouch for the baby and soft, pastel tees made to accommodate a growing belly. Not a single one had a devil or other grotesquery on the front, but no puppies, kittens, or cute slogans. Annie added in two high-waisted floaty dresses, one long and one knee-length. Because they were near a hairdresser who took walk-ins, she guided Dre to a chair and asked the stylist to trim and blend the light brown, natural blonde coming in from the roots, and the lemon juice streaks into an attractive pixie cut that framed Dre's face and made her appear considerably less sullen, rather pretty and glowing, a fact Annie would not mention. She could have described the morning as a perfect mother/daughter sort of day if her mind hadn't constantly shifted to Daniel and the possibility of further surgery for the boy.

As she paid the hairdresser, Annie's phone buzzed. She shared the good news with Dre. "Danny is ready to come home. The doctor believes, though he's a big boy, his respiratory system is still maturing. We'll have to keep an eye on him and an ear out for the alarm sounding."

"Glad you know what you're doing, because I don't." Dre checked her new hairdo in the mirror. "I look lots better, but I'm still me inside."

"And always will be. Let me call Matt and tell him we'll all be waiting for him at home."

Chapter Forty-Two

Annie wished she could say the next two weeks simply flew by. They did not. Each day crawled along like a three-legged turtle trying to cross a road in heavy traffic. At least, Daniel suffered no more A & B events. Matt, in heavy training for the two home games, slept deeply, not noticing her larger and more tender breasts or the persistent morning sickness she hid as well as she could. To her surprise, Dre colluded to keep the secret, often getting up to make the coffee and breakfast for Matt, giving Annie time to worship at the porcelain throne in the small bathroom where she'd stashed her prenatal meds.

Her dad continued to provide the suite for women and children but spent most of his game time in the favored fifty-yard line box. The only change Annie noticed concerned the food served which now tended toward the blander fare the children favored: chicken nuggets with dipping sauces, hamburger sliders with a choice of topping on the side, and the ever-favored pigs in a blanket, or itty-bitty hotdogs as Wynn called them. Annie wondered if the change of menu might also mean her mom had caught on to her condition. If so, she didn't bring up the subject.

Dre hung out with Edie who raved about her new haircut, saying, "I wish I could go straight and streaky, but I'm stuck with these messy, black curls just like

Jude and Annie. Personally, I think they are genetically linked to all the short Billodeauxs, girl or boy like Trinity. Mom won't let me bleach my hair or get it straightened. She claims Dad and Dean have the same hair but keep it really short so you can't tell. My brother Mack has curls down to his shoulders, but they look sexy. Just so not fair to women."

In what became their new custom, the family retired to Dean's house after another victory and waited for their players to return. After the first game, Annie wanted to openly greet Matt with a kiss, but he failed to enter the rear gate with the rest.

"Where's Matt?" she asked Dean as he filled a plate with a mound of kiddie food and tossed the begging dog a hamburger slider minus the bun.

"He got hung up at Mariah's Place, mobbed by fans who wanted to buy him a drink for those two touchdowns he scored."

"Maybe I should go get him."

"Hey, he can handle himself. Besides, this redhead, what's her name—Kim from our neighborhood—dragged him out on the dance floor a couple of times so he didn't drink much. He's not too bad a dancer, way better than Tom, but I should show him some of the Cajun steps and my salsa moves. We could double date sometime when the two of you are ready to come out as a couple."

Mati danced on his hind legs, performing for another treat. As Dean selected a hotdog to toss, Stacy's voice cut through the air, "Don't feed that dog anymore snacks!"

"Yes, Princess. Your wish is my command." Instead, he handed Annie the pig in a blanket and whispered, "Sneak that to Mati when she isn't looking. I hate to disappoint him."

Eventually, Mati got his hotdog, and Annie got her wish. Matt came through the gate to join their party. Some time had passed, enough time in Annie's inflamed imagination for a fast stop at Kim's house and a quickie with a slightly drunk football player. She shoved that idea aside and went in for a hug. "Nice perfume," she remarked, inhaling a heavy scent not his and some beer on his breath, but nothing stronger.

"Kim is one of those close dancers, and she wears a lot of scent. Almost made my eyes water. She leaches right onto you. She asked for tickets to the next game because her sons had to leave with their dad and didn't have time to meet me. I'll get her the tickets, but I'm skipping Mariah's and coming right here. Want me to get you some wine?"

"Ah, no. An iced tea would be good. In a minute." Annie relaxed against his chest, held back the repulsion caused by the strong perfume, and steadied herself with the rhythm of his heartbeat. Only one more week before she must confess her unintentional sin against him.

****

Annie did not get that time to prepare the words that rolled over and over in her mind like a player hitting the turf hard—"Matt, I'm pregnant."

On Monday, Matt set out for the team meeting while Dre cleaned up the kitchen and Annie started her day in the usual way, barfing in the upstairs toilet. She heard Dre's warning, spoken extra loud and bright. "Hey, Matt, you're back early. Seems like you just left."

"Forgot my wallet."

"I'll get it for you." The girl did her best to stop him, but he'd hit the back stairs too fast.

Annie tried to repress her heaving, but her stomach refused cooperation. *Damn.* She hadn't bothered to shut the door. She heard Matt before she saw him.

"Annie, are you all right, my angel?"

Gagging complete, Annie got off her knees and turned on the cold water tap. She rinsed her mouth and hid her face with a damp washcloth. "Some of those game leftovers must have gone bad."

Behind her, Matt flushed the toilet and put the lid down with a bang. "I don't think so. Dre and I had plenty of each, far more than you, and we're both fine."

"Maybe just a bug I picked up somewhere."

His large hands circled her waist and lifted her to a seat on the commode. "Is there something we need to discuss?"

Annie studied the tips of the white nurses' shoes she still wore around the house and dabbed at a splatter of vomit on her blue scrubs with the washcloth clutched in her hands. "You'll be late for team meeting. Better hurry."

"I'll pay the fine. I'm not so self-centered I haven't noticed the signs, your being tired, drinking tea instead of coffee, avoiding wine, now this." He gestured toward the toilet where the water still trickled into the tank. "It's not my first time around, Annie."

"Okay, yes, I'm pregnant." She raised her gaze to meet his and saw the flicker in their deep, brown depths—distrust and disappointment in her. Annie rushed to explain. "I didn't do it intentionally! That first night we were together, so caught up in each other we both forgot about condoms, I didn't want to add to your worries. I was closer to my fertile period than I said, but exactly like many a woman has fooled herself, I thought one time won't do it."

"If you'd told me you weren't on the pill right away, I would have been more careful." His voice seemed heavy and sad to Annie, that she'd lied to him.

She rushed on. "Also, I had reason to believe I might be infertile. No sense in alarming you for no reason."

His steady, dark gaze became unreadable. Annie figured he showed her the visage his opponents saw beneath his helmet just before he hit them hard. No malice, only taking care of business. She jumped to conclusions and might as well have sacked herself.

"I don't want an abortion. I told you that my sister and I were fairly wild in our early college years."

He nodded. "Frat parties, butterfly tattoos."

"Far more and far worse than that. I'm not the angel you believe me to be. I contracted chlamydia from a guy I dated. He'd infected several young women. A public health nurse contacted me and got me on antibiotics. It's easy enough to cure if caught early—but was it early enough? She counseled that I should be sure to tell my personal ob-gyn because the disease could cause scarring that leads to fertility problems. I didn't for fear my parents would find out. Since then, I've doubted if I could become pregnant. The few men I've been with after that, mostly med students and doctors, were careful, and so was I. Jude always accused me of working the weekend evening shift to avoid dating. Maybe she's right. But Matt, I want this baby."

"Good, because abortion isn't a possibility, just as I

told Marilyn about Dre. I said that night I'd marry you if you conceived a child. Name the date."

She hated the flat tone of his voice. How many times had she fantasized his saying those exact words? Countless, but never in a bathroom cramped by his size. Never with vomit on her breath and streaking her clothes. Never in a forced situation.

"No," she answered.

"No?" His big hands came toward her shoulders.

Annie raised her knees under her chin and bunched on her precarious throne like a fairy on a toadstool. "I didn't try to trick you into marriage. I'm not going to force you to marry me now. Both my dad and Dean faced this kind of situation and neither married the woman. I'd always wonder if you really wanted me to be your wife or simply felt obligated."

As if suddenly aware of this threatening size, Matt dropped his hands and instead raked his hair with his fingers, a gesture Annie remembered well from the NICU. "I'd never hurt you. I've said I love you."

"Love can be temporary. Right now, you and Daniel need me, but not forever. Marriage should be permanent. You haven't mentioned getting married since that first night when we slipped up."

"Because I wanted to wait a decent time after Mellie's death, maybe next June for us. I did have the thought in my mind, but don't know how to convince you. I don't have the words." He held his hands out, imploring.

"Ahem." Dre stood in the doorway. "I found your wallet. You'd better get going. I'll look out for Annie."

Matt's dark brows drew together. "You knew, you knew before me."

"Dre is sharp. She figured it out before you did. No wonder she had a perfect score on the GED test. We must discuss her future. We need to…" Annie's attempt to deflect his anger failed miserably. His fists balled tight.

"Discuss ours. Tonight. Annie, I hope to change your mind by then." Matt snatched the wallet from Dre's fingers and thundered down the stairs. He slammed the front door with enough force to crack the glass panes—and awaken Daniel in his crib.

"Mad much?" Dre commented. "I'll get the baby."

"I think I need someone to hold me close right now." Annie relaxed her limbs and stood.

Dre held out her arms. "Bring it in. It won't hurt Danny to fuss for a few minutes."

Strange how she felt like the mixed-up child now as she released her tears against Dre's brand-new maternity top, the yellow one with the innocent trim of appliqued daisies. No innocence between them, not so much as a petal's worth.

Chapter Forty-Three

Coach released the team early after the usual meeting and watching the film from the last game, dissecting the plays that worked, the ones that failed. Ordinarily, Matt headed home when he had the rare free afternoon to bask in the balmy October weather with Daniel and Annie, maybe take everyone out to dinner. Today, he sought out Dean, who stayed behind to watch the game tape over and over as he often did, always trying to improve, the quality of a topnotch quarterback.

"You got a minute. Could I talk to you?"

Dean froze the screen. "If it's about that fumble you had in the last game, you got hit hard enough to pop that ball halfway down the field. You more than made up for it with the two touchdowns. Matt, you're a great fit for this team."

"Um, not about football." Yeah, he noticed the "oh, shit" expression cross Dean's face.

"Personal problems? Annie?" Dean switched off the monitor and prepared to listen the way good team captains did.

Matt felt a surge of gratitude. He couldn't imagine talking to his old QB, Ryan Luke, about something like this, but then, Ryan had been part of his marital problems. "Yes, Annie. She's pregnant. We got careless one night."

If he expected anger, he got understanding. Dean

nodded. "You know I had a son out of wedlock. I loved Stacy, not Beck's mother. I keep the boy in my life. I know Annie. She won't give up the child, but our whole family will be there for her no matter what you do."

"Dean, I want to marry her ASAP. She turned me down. Says she doesn't want to force me." Matt gave into the urge to pace the room as he often did the sidelines when a game failed to go well.

"You love her? Stacy said positively, but I'm not as good reading these things as she is."

"Absolutely. I told her so before I knew. She says love can be temporary."

"Lust sure is, but love, true love, is devotion." Dean wrinkled his brow. "Did I just quote some sappy Fifties song?"

Matt shook his head. "I think that's *Young Love*, but not exactly. My Mom liked the really old oldies from her middle school years. Doesn't matter. How do I convince Annie to marry me?"

"The twins were stubborn and hard-headed from birth, though Annie is the softer of the two. We couldn't bribe them with a candy bar or anything else to stop them from ratting on me and Tom when we were doing stuff we weren't supposed to do. Being so small, they could hide anywhere, up a tree, behind a hay bale"

"Interesting but not helpful." Matt paused in front of his quarterback and held out his big hands as if waiting for an answer to be tossed into them.

"Me, I had to grovel, really grovel to get Stacy back after I messed up with Ilsa."

"Grovel? Neither of us did anything wrong— except forget the condom."

"Hey, Stacy did all sorts of things to make me

jealous, most of them lies, yet I had to get down on my knees and beg. We both have big shoulders. You and I can handle some private groveling."

"I don't think she'll buy it. I'm willing to shoulder the blame. She won't let me. Did Tom and Alix hit any bumps in the road. How about Junior and Xochi?"

"Alix thought Tom wasn't treating her as an equal as a kicker and teammate. Xochi and Junior had an age difference problem. They overcame their issues."

" 'The course of true love never did run smooth.' Neither of those things works for my game plan."

Dean did a double take as Matt paced past him again. "Ah, Shakespeare?"

"My mom taught a class in it. I picked up a little."

"So, maybe sonnets and flowers?" Dean shrugged as if he'd given it his best try. "I also got Stace a big, honking engagement ring. If you need one, ask for Leslie at Schifferman's. He won't steer you wrong."

"I think I'd need something more than poetry and posies to convince her. Melinda could be soothed with expensive jewelry, but I've never seen Annie wear any at all. We met under dire circumstances and got to know each other over breakfast in the hospital cafeteria, not with fancy dinners and champagne. Nothing about our relationship has been traditional."

"I could ask Stacy. They're tight, especially since Jude tried to break you up, but Jude does know Annie best."

"Jude claims she wanted to bring us together by making moves on me. I still stay as far away from her as I can." Matt raked his hair but wanted to pull some of it out at this point. "Don't tell anyone else yet. Give me some time to work on it."

"You have my word, but my mom might already suspect. The menu for the suite has gotten a lot blander. Stacy noticed, too, but Mama Nell said she was catering to the children. Our mother won't be your big problem. Dad is the one with the temper."

"Yeah, I promised not to hurt Annie, and now I have."

****

Matt carried his woes to Mariah's Place, the Sinners' hangout, open at eleven a.m. to serve curious tourists with their guidebooks in hand and closed by two a.m. because the owner he'd met said she needed her beauty rest in the apartment over the establishment. Mariah, what a character. He sat in the deep shadows at the far end of the bar and lunched on stuffed potato skins washed down with beer, make that three beers. None helped solve his problem, and he couldn't go home to Annie without a plan. When he ordered a fourth drink with a whiskey chaser, a woman slid onto the seat beside him. Not Kimberly, thank God, but the famous and flamboyant Mariah herself.

Tom's step-grandmother resembled no elderly woman he'd ever met. An outrageous white wig topped her head and stage makeup puttied away any wrinkles. She showed off a cleavage deep as the Grand Canyon in a bright red dress that matched her lipstick and high heels way too dangerous for a person of her age.

Tom had introduced them on his first visit to the watering hole. She'd pulled his head down for a kiss on the cheek that left a vermillion brand behind and declared him "one of my boys now." Matt spent less time in the place than most of the team and had rarely spoken to her since that evening, though he thought she'd cast a green-eyed, disapproving glance his way when Kim dragged him onto the dance floor the other night.

She got down to business right away. "Problems, big guy?" Mariah motioned to her bald bartender to take away the shot glass. "I think you can handle four beers, but this isn't going any further. You and Annie Billodeaux having trouble?"

"How did you know?"

"Can't be your game. I don't miss a one. You're doing great. That slutty redhead getting between the two of you? I can tell you, Annie is the one you want. Tom said you'd declared yourself, then I see you with another woman."

"I thought the family was going to keep quiet about me and Annie."

"Son, the Billodeauxs do consider me family being Howdy McCoy's mother, and then there's Tom. I may not be a shrink, but I have life experience, lots and lots of experience. How can I help you?"

Matt gulped half his beer. "I don't think you can. I want to marry Annie. She doesn't want to marry me." He couldn't, wouldn't reveal the news about the baby to this much older woman who wore perfume more seductive than Kim's heavy choice and who rumor said had run through so many men that Howdy's parentage had been in doubt for years. At least, he knew Annie carried his.

"Because of the redheaded bitch? I used to be one of those, so I know the type, persistent and pushy. I can take care of her for you, point her in another direction, and if she won't go there, I'll ban her from the bar. My boys should be able to come here and be comfortable.

Bring Annie sometime. Jude shows up now and again, but I haven't seen the nice one in a while. Those twins are close. You might try to get Jude on your side."

"We aren't on the best terms, but thanks. Getting Kim out of the way might help a little." Matt stood and received one of her full-bosomed hugs. Mariah clipped along with him as if gauging his ability to walk a straight line to the door. No problem. His mass absorbed liquor like a dry desert. He'd learned that in college, but seldom put it to the test anymore.

Outside, he blinked in the sunlight and checked his watch. More time had passed than he'd thought. Not too long and the blue dusk of autumn would throw its magic cloak over the taller buildings and sink down into the deep and dirty crevices of the French Quarter. He started for home but found himself turning into the cul-de-sac where he'd often picked up Annie. Nearly seven, he'd do the unthinkable and wait for Jude whom everyone thought had the answer. Think broad shoulders, think tough and fearless. Get ready for the snap. It came quickly.

Jude's small car pulled up alongside his. "Hey, asshole, get out of my parking space."

"We need to talk."

"Look, I just got off my shift. I'm tired and hungry. Since you carried my sister off to your palace, there's no dinner waiting for me, and you are the last person I want to hang out with."

"The feeling is mutual, but I'll buy you dinner at The Palace Cafe right around the corner. This concerns Annie."

"Okay, but at some secluded table. I don't want my sister to think we've got something going on. Why aren't you at home, sweet home, with her and the kid?

"We hit a snag. Let's walk. She'll be wondering where I am."

Jude glanced at her wrinkled scrubs and shrugged. "I don't think they'll throw me out, not with a Sinner beside me."

They went the short distance to the restaurant where the wait staff addressed her as Miss Jude and provided the table she wanted. "Okay, so I'm a frequent diner, especially since Annie left."

She wasted no time ordering the most expensive item on the menu, the twelve-ounce ribeye, medium, with smashed fingerling potatoes and foie gras butter. Bring the red wine now. Matt ordered the same, well done, skip the wine. Jude broke open the crusty loaf of French bread on the table and slathered it with one of the butters provided. Her wine arrived. She took a deep draft.

"Now talk."

Matt scanned the dining area and lowered his deep voice as far as he could. "Annie is pregnant with my child. She won't marry me."

"Which shows her good judgment. You don't have to tell me—she won't agree to an abortion either."

"I didn't ask her to get one." Already, Matt wished he'd ordered the wine or something stronger.

"Right, you're super Catholic. It's her choice to do what she wants with her body, not yours."

"This isn't an argument about the ethics of abortion. She doesn't want to force me into marriage."

"Annie is simply too good. She could marry you, have the kid, divorce you, and live on your riches. That's what I'd tell her, but she won't. Your best bet might be letting her have the baby single, then proposing again to show you aren't being forced."

"That doesn't work for me. I want the child to have my name."

They volleyed back and forth, each one hitting hard in the face of the other. The wait staff stayed well back from the intense conversation. Even the water boy failed to refill their glasses.

"Too bad. When Annie makes up her mind, it's hard to change. She certainly didn't take my advice when she insisted on moving in with you to babysit."

"She does far more than babysit. She saved Daniel's life only days ago, and she's helping Dre cope with her circumstances."

"That's Annie through and through. Too bad you knocked her up. If you'd proposed without duress, she'd agree in a minute. Too late now, so sad. Tell her I've saved her room."

Their waiter approached. "Would you like your second glass of wine now or with dinner?" he inquired of Jude.

"With dinner."

Matt balled his napkin in his fist. "Could you bring the bill and make mine to go?"

"Certainly, sir."

"If you think I mind eating alone, you'd be wrong. I enjoy my own company."

"Because no one else does." Matt scribbled his name on the tab. He seized his go-box when the waiter delivered it, crushing its edges in frustration.

Jude offered him a last casual suggestion tossed like a cheap Mardi Gras throw. "You can try to get our mom on your side. Dad, I'd be careful there."

"So I've been told. Thanks for nothing." Fuming, he strode from the restaurant and bumped into Tom and Alix, arm-in-arm as usual and making a double barrier.

"Hey, you here with Annie and the baby?"

"No, with Jude. You can eat with her if you want. I'm leaving."

Only on the way home did he remember he hadn't asked Jude to keep quiet about the baby.

Chapter Forty-Four

Annie waited and waited for Matt's return. She'd thought out her plan during the day, began to worry when he missed his time with Daniel before she put the baby to bed, fantasized that he'd spent the afternoon with Kimberly just down the block. Ashamed of herself, she tried to reach him elsewhere—Mariah's Place, left earlier, Dean's house, not there, not at Junior's apartment or Alix and Tom's though he'd passed the couple on his way out of The Palace Café. Could they offer congratulations? No, they could not!

Shortly after disconnecting with the family lovebirds, she heard the growl of his huge SUV and another rattling slam of the front door. Matt dominated the doorway into the den where she and Dre watched a movie and devoured popcorn. Dre grabbed her bowl, spilling a few fluffy kernels on the rug in her haste, and said, "I'll watch the rest in my room, give you some privacy. 'Kay?" She ducked under her brother-in-law's arm and scampered away. Annie turned off the TV.

Having complete faith that he'd never hurt her physically despite the scowl on his face, Annie rose to face Matt. She went to him, close enough to smell another woman's perfume on his clothes. Damn this pregnancy for making her nose so sensitive. Blurting the words without thinking, she said, "Did Kimberly change her scent? This one isn't nearly so musky."

His large hands gripped her small shoulders—and folded her against his chest. "Not Kimberly. I spent some time at Mariah's Place where I failed to drown my sorrows. Mariah sent me on my way before I reached that point."

"You told her!" Annie's protest came out muffled he held her so tight.

"No, she thinks all this is about Kimberly, and I let her believe it. Kim means nothing to me, I swear. I wish she'd let me alone."

She wouldn't admit she'd called Mariah's and tried to track him down. That came across as clingy and weak. Annie needed all her strength now. "You've been at Mariah's this whole time?"

"No, I humbled myself and asked Jude to help me. Some help. Cost me an expensive dinner, a women's rights lecture, and a tribute to your choice not to marry me." He loosened his grip a little. "There's a steak dinner in the car. You and Dre should split it. Both of you need red meat, lots of iron."

"Thanks, we have pills for that and already ate. I think you should sit down and have a meal, then I'll explain what I want to do."

"Not hungry. I want to hear this now." He released her. She took one recliner, he the other. Neither put their feet up.

"I'm not very far along, Matt. In fact, I won't be showing much until the end of December. I can see Daniel through his first four months at home and find an excellent replacement, then I'll discreetly move to the ranch and have the baby there—sometime in May. Sorry, it's not your luckiest month."

Dre burst in from the hall where obviously she'd

been listening. "No. You promised to be my birth partner."

"You could go to the ranch with me and give birth in Lafayette, or when you start birthing classes, I might move in with Jude again until your baby comes."

"Dre, this isn't about you. Go to your room." Matt rose to make sure the girl did as he told her. He turned back to Annie almost swallowed by the huge recliner. "Great that you have all this worked out, and I have nothing to say about it. Why, Annie, why?"

She took a deep, deep breath. "On the playing field, you never hesitate. When I told you, I saw that moment when you did, as if you thought both Mellie and I betrayed you. That's no way to begin a life together—with suspicion in the back of your mind."

"We have a life together now. We only need to make it legal. Jesus, Mary, and Joseph, any man will hesitate when told he's going to be a father unexpectedly. St. Joseph planned to send Mary away and needed an angel to convince him to marry her. Do you think Mary said 'no thanks' to his offer? Annie, you are my angel and this child is mine."

She'd grown up with Catholics, lots of them. That he'd called on the Holy Family for help wasn't lost on her, and in that context, his argument was powerful. She could almost hear Mawmaw Nadine in her mind saying, "Don't be so *tetu*. You marry dis man." Her father would say the same. Thank God, he didn't know yet.

"Times were very different then. She might have been stoned otherwise—while I have a way to make a living and raise a child alone."

"Not alone. Even if you persist in this plan, I want

the child in my life like Dean has his illegitimate son." Matt winced at the words. "You don't have to do this!"

"I'm sorry. I'd always wonder if you truly wanted me."

"Hell, I want you now."

"I think it would be best if I moved to the small bedroom again."

"No, I can be gentle. We can cuddle. Whatever you want. Don't leave me and Daniel."

"And Dre, don't forget Dre," his SIL said, having crept back to eavesdrop.

Annie needed to retreat before she lost the battle. "I'm going upstairs now. I'll take the three o'clock feeding."

"No, you won't. I had no Daniel time today, and you need to rest. At least count on me for this one thing."

She conceded. "Please have some dinner before you go to bed."

Her mind rolled back to coaxing him to eat after the death of his wife. So hard not to give in as much as she loved him. Once he nodded, she left.

****

Daniel took a bottle at midnight but didn't stir at three a.m. When Matt woke at six, he pounded on Annie's closed and locked door. "Annie, Annie, I didn't hear Daniel all night. I'm afraid to go into the nursery. He might be…"

Coming to the door in her old, homely nightgown, she said, "The alarm would have gone off. You know, he's been home six weeks now. He's starting to sleep through the night. Let's see."

They stood over the crib of a baby starting to

awaken for the day. His blue eyes opened and focused. His mouth opened too. Time for a change and a bottle.

"Get ready for practice. I'll take care of him."

"Annie, we can't do without you. Please."

"Don't be late." She turned her attention to the baby, and he went away. Hard, so hard to resist.

Chapter Forty-Five

The long week got no easier. Matt came home late a couple of more times, always saying he'd had dinner elsewhere, not elaborating, but he didn't neglect Daniel. He insisted on giving the last bottle of the evening and rocking his son to sleep while Annie "rested" in her room. As if she could. Every night he sang *Danny Boy*, a song of longing and loss so soulfully it tore at her heart. Once, returning from the bathroom, she'd heard his deep voice gone soft saying to the infant, "You'd like a baby brother, wouldn't you? You'd be close in age like Dean and Tom, best buddies. Danny, we can't lose our angel."

It took all her resolve not to rush in and say she'd stay with them both forever. In fact, she should leave sooner than December. This weekend, she'd see her mother and ask for her advice, which would be good since mom probably knew the circumstances already. But when Sunday came, all seemed normal in the van. Dre settled in with Edie and T-Rex who raised his head from his phone long enough to say, "I like your hair," before returning to a fantasy football game he had on the screen. Corazon fussed over the babies, her mom serenely rode shotgun while her dad cursed out other drivers in the traffic crush around the Dome. Jessie sat by Annie for a change and squeezed her hand a time or two—the only indication that news of her pregnancy had reached the ranch.

At their suite in the Dome, the menu had changed again to food with an oriental twist: mini-eggrolls, shrimp toast, sweet and sour pork skewers laced with pineapple chunks and green peppers, plus a soothing egg-drop soup Annie truly appreciated. Jude said nothing snarky but cast her twin superior I-told-you-so glances from time to time. Annie decided to sit by Jessie's wheelchair instead of with her sister. The babies, oblivious to any tension, cried, crawled, and clambered around the room with Xo watching over them.

Matt failed to score any touchdowns, fumbled once, and received a penalty for unnecessary roughness when clearing the way for X-avier's run toward the goal. Taking an opponent down by the collar and then running over him with his cleats, not good, and that not good cost the Sinners fifteen yards. Warned that another infraction would get Matt expelled from the game, Coach Buck took him out voluntarily and let him pace the sidelines. At halftime, her dad mentioned Matt's play was off today. Annie concluded that her father didn't yet know the situation. Matt never played dirty but had shown that he could. What would he do next to convince her to stay?

The Sinners won, not by as wide a margin as when Matt played, but good enough. The family retreated to Dean's house with their leftovers to await the victors once more.

Stowing Daniel with Corazon, Annie took her mother aside in the formal dining room since they'd laid out the food on the picnic table this time and the crowd gathered there.

"I guess you know."

"Know what?" her mom said a little too innocently.

"The bland foods, Jessie holding my hand in the van, you figured out I'm pregnant."

Shock replaced coy on Nell's face. "No. It's Jessie who is expecting. She's past the first three months now and didn't want to tell the whole family before she reached that mark. She'll be a high-risk pregnancy, but she and Teddy are so crazy about Lizzy, they wanted another child right away. Their new house out at the ranch will be ready by January, and the baby is due in March. They planned four bedrooms so I'm thinking this won't be the last—but you, no!" Her voice went higher and louder.

Annie wanted to hang her head like an erring teen, though Dre had been defiant, unrepentant. "I'm sorry, of all the girls I'm the one who messed up, and I'm a nurse. I should have been more careful. My baby is due in May, and I thought I'd come home to the ranch to give birth." She raised her eyes to Nell's and found no anger or judgement there. Her mother embraced her, but suddenly dropped her arms to her side.

Annie didn't have to turn to know her father stood in the doorway. "What's going on back here? Everybody okay?"

"Oh, Joe, we're expecting two new grandchildren next year. Isn't that wonderful?" Her mom could put a positive spin on anything.

"Xo is pregnant again so soon?"

"No, it's our Annie. Matt and Annie are going to have a baby."

He had only one question for his daughter. "When is the wedding?"

"Dad, we're not getting married."

"The hell you aren't!"

Jude appeared behind her dad and ducked into the room under his arm as if he were no more than an ignored rail crossing gate. "Hey, Annie, I thought you should know Matt is the first to arrive—with Kimberly Walet hanging on him like he's the last train out of Dodge before the gunfight. Her two boys are trailing her like a posse."

"Oh, there will be a gunfight before that train leaves town." Joe surged from the room with the quickness of his playing days as if evading a tackle. The women pursued him. All arrived in the courtyard in time to hear Kim's shrill voice say, "We went over to Mariah's Place so the boys could meet you and thank you for the tickets, but that—that crone in a white wig told me I had to look for another dance partner or stay out of her place. I knew you'd be coming here eventually. We waited outside the gate. My boys, Foster and Franklin. Thank Mr. Keaton."

The elder, around fourteen and stippled with acne, didn't raise his eyes from his phone. "Yeah, thanks."

The younger, maybe twelve and wearing glasses, said, "Our private school doesn't have a football team. We play soccer so our brains won't turn to mush. You got thrown out of the game today, didn't you?"

Stacy, ever the perfect hostess, took in her hard-charging father, the redhead, and her spawn. She removed Kimberly from Matt's arm and turned her and the boys toward the food laid out on the picnic table. "Won't you have something to eat?"

They barely got out of the way before Joe Billodeaux bellowed with all his Cajun surfacing, "I asked one t'ing of you, *fils de garce*, that you don't hurt my little girl. Now you give her a baby and won't marry her, no!"

"Stop, Dad, please!" Annie shouted, several steps behind, but she saw Matt tense his muscles for the coming punch.

Her father's fist landed squarely in Matt's middle and seemed to bounce off with little effect. The next swing went for the jaw, but Matt deflected it with his massive forearm. He made no attempt to fight back. This could not happen. Annie slipped between them and caught the next hard blow on her shoulder. She went down, saved from hitting her head on the slates of the patio by Matt's strong arms and fast action.

"Annie, are you all right? The baby, is the baby okay?" Matt stared up from his knees at Joe Billodeaux. "I want to marry your daughter. Here's proof." He found the ring in his pocket and offered it to the recumbent Annie.

The gate opened letting in the rest of the family. Vaguely, Annie heard Dean's voice. "Groveling and a big, honking diamond, that's what I told him."

Then Stacy, polite but firm, said, "This is a family matter. I'm afraid you'll have to leave. Here, take this basket of egg rolls and call again." She escorted Kimberly and her kids onto the street and locked the gate.

"I told Leslie I needed an engagement ring for an angel with small, loving hands. He said, 'Five karats, flawless blue-white set in platinum.' I asked for two smaller stones on either side to represent our babies. He had it made up for me. May I put it on your finger, Annie?"

With the pain in her shoulder spasming through her body, Annie answered, "Who is Leslie?"

Dean cast his shade over her now. "The jeweler. Say yes, and we can welcome Matt to the family."

Her father bent down, taking a knee. "I'm so sorry, *cher* heart. Matt, it's my Cajun temper. I jumped the gun, and I'm really glad I didn't have one on me or it could have been worse."

"Make way for the nurse!" Jude butted in. "She doesn't want to marry him. Annie, do you think anything is broken?"

"What's wrong wit' you, girl? The man is offering you a ring," her father insisted.

"Not sure, Sis. Maybe just dislocated. No X-rays or drugs, the baby…" Annie felt herself floating in the air. No, not floating, rising in Matt's arms.

"We need to get her to the emergency room right now."

Jessie wheeled up. "I'm the athletic trainer. Let's get her on a bench facedown and let me have a look." Matt obeyed. With no thought for modesty, Jessie removed Annie's red Sinners tee and unhooked her bra. "Yes, I can see the bulge. It's a dislocation of the shoulder. Annie, if you can bear it, I'll pop it back into the socket, the sooner the better before it swells. I've done it before and being in this chair has made my arms stronger than ever."

"Do it." Annie gave her consent and gritted her teeth. Jessie did the rotation, and the pain ended, but not before one blinding moment.

"We need a sling, an ice pack, and a loose top to put on her."

"I've got scrubs in my car. Don't I always?" Jude

darted off to retrieve them. Stacy rushed to get the other items.

Jessie leaned close to Annie's ear. "Now what's this about a baby?"

"In May."

"Me, too, but March. I wanted to tell you in the van, but with Teddy out of town I thought I should wait. Exciting for both of us."

Annie's dad cleared his throat which might have been clogged by emotion. "Sugar, again, I'm so very sorry, but you haven't answered this fine man's question. Will you accept his ring?"

"I don't want to force him to marry me."

"Honey, when a man offers you a ring like dis, ain't nobody forcing him."

Who started the chant of "Say yes, say yes!" Annie couldn't tell with her face pressed against a picnic bench, too embarrassed to sit up half clothed. Most likely Tom, but it didn't matter. The Billodeaux family, supportive and always in your business, formed a scrum around her. Jude returned and ordered them to turn their backs while she worked her sister into the top of the scrubs, but the chant continued, going on and on while Jessie fashioned a sling to support the injured arm and applied the ice pack.

Annie raised her voice. "If you'd just be quiet a minute. Okay. Yes."

Cheers rose to the high blue heavens. Again, she felt as if she floated there when Matt scooped her up.

"Sorry, folks, we have a date at the emergency room."

"But, Daniel?"

"We are all here to care for him. Go, go, go," her

mother urged.

Not the romantic moment Annie had dreamed, but certainly memorable.

Chapter Forty-Six

While the emergency room doctor commended Jessie's fast treatment, the three weeks in a sling prescribed and then some PT made Annie want to gnash her teeth. How was she going to change an increasingly active baby with one arm out of action? On the positive side, no harm to her baby. Dr. Garner listed some painkillers she could take without damaging the fetus but told her to get to the hospital immediately if she had any bleeding. She didn't, only the ongoing morning sickness she could take as a good sign if it weren't so miserable.

By the time she and Matt returned to the pink palace, Dre had gotten Danny to bed, and her mother had moved into the smaller bedroom—for the duration of her recovery, she said. Annie rested, truly rested, in Matt's arms again.

There had been a time when she and Jude wanted nothing more than to shuck off the oversight of their parents and get away from the interference of family. Now, as Annie sat drinking tea with her mother, she found great comfort in having an older woman around, one who had experience with her situation.

Nell sipped the peppermint brew. "I wondered the same when your dad whisked me to Las Vegas for a quickie marriage—if he only needed a mother for Dean. Here we are twelve children later and still in love. I believe it will work out that way for you. But, we should discuss wedding plans. What are your wishes?"

"Nothing that will attract attention. I thought maybe the first weekend in December at the ranch. I know you'll have the house decorated for Christmas, and it's always lovely. Whatever you want to do for food and drink. That doesn't matter to me."

"Oh, it will to Corazon. We'll work up some suggestions and send them to you."

"Do you think old Father Ardoin could do the ceremony? It would mean so much to Matt to have a Catholic priest preside."

Nell began making notes. "I'm sure he would. Saves you having to get married twice like we did because Mawmaw Nadine didn't approve of the elopement. Who do you want for attendants?'

"My sisters and brothers. Matt has no one, but if he wants any of the Sinners, that is fine with me too."

Dre, silent, abandoned her tea and walked to the cupboard. "We're out of Oreos. I'm going to the store. Need anything else?"

"The list is on the fridge. Thanks," Annie said and dove back into wedding planning, hardly knowing when the girl left. "A simple short dress, I think. Stacy can help me with that and coordinating the bridesmaids and matrons."

"Jude or Stacy for maid of honor? I always thought you'd want Jude but realize things are still rocky there."

"I'm not sure Matt would tolerate Jude, but she must be in the wedding. We need to ask Jessie too. What about Lorena off in Australia. Can she get here?"

"I doubt it. When a volleyball great like Maisie Morton asks a player to be her partner, a person can't just walk out on her for a wedding. It will be summer there, prime beach volleyball season. How about including Dre? She'll be pretty far along by then but isn't going to have a wedding of her own.

Annie went to the cupboard to fetch some saltines. "We have Oreos. I think all the wedding talk upset her. Yes, let's ask her to take Lorena's place when she gets back here."

If Dre wasn't upset when she left, the girl returned with tears coursing down her cheeks and denial on her lips. "It wasn't me! I swear it wasn't me."

"Did Kimberly get in your face? That woman! Oh, and we have Oreos."

"You can't have too many." Dre set down the bags on the kitchen table and wiped her cheeks with her sleeve. A tabloid poked out of the top of one of the sacks along with a bunch of celery. She handed it to Annie. "I found this at the checkout."

"*Keaton forced to marry pregnant nanny*." Annie showed her mom the photo of Joe driving his fist into Matt's middle with a smaller shot of the attempted blow to the jaw. "I'm a nurse practitioner, not a nanny. How many times do I have to..."

Nell shook head. "The press always called me a nurse, not a psychologist. If that's all they got wrong, be grateful." She skimmed the article. "The reporter did get around to mentioning that you're Joe's daughter. Don't worry. The Billodeauxs have had worse said about them. They once implied your dad dated an underage girl—simply because I'm short."

Dre flopped into a chair and gulped her abandoned cold tea. "I didn't take those pictures. You can check." She offered her iPhone. "Maybe T-Rex. He had his

349

phone in his hand. Look, it's all over social media. You and Matt are trending."

"No, Joe won't allow that kind of behavior. Billodeauxs stick together. All the children learn that from birth. I can't think of anybody in our group that would…"

Dre in the process of ripping open a package of Oreos interrupted. "Kimberly's oldest boy had his phone out. Wanna bet he did it?"

"Sounds about right. We'll let Matt handle this. Dre, would you like to be in our wedding?" Annie waited for the reaction, expecting snarky or bored. She garnered excitement.

Dre nearly choked on cookie crumbs trying to get the words out. "For true? I'll be seven months by then and pretty tubby."

"Lorena won't be able to get here from Australia. I need a substitute sister."

"I'd be like your sister? I'm all in."

The three women plotted and planned the rest of the day. When Matt came home, they handed over the tabloid and shared their suspicions of the source. Matt tucked the paper under his arm. "I'll take care of this."

****

That Kimberly had exposed his precious Annie to this kind of trash made the back of Matt's neck sweat with anger, and no, it wasn't just the afternoon heat of Louisiana in October. He rarely lost his temper. Only dumb players did, and he'd been dumb in his last game, full of the need to take out his frustration on someone paid to take his crap. When he reached the corner and turned up path to the—what did she call it—a center hall villa, he'd calmed some. That didn't prevent him from both ringing the bell hard and pounding on the front door. A maid, wide-eyed and uncertain, answered. "I need to see Mrs. Walet immediately."

"I see if she in, suh."

"If that's Matt Keaton, I'm in. Bring him back, Delia." Kimberly's voice wafted down a central hall both long and broad. She stood braced in a rear door that opened onto a lawn. Obviously working on a tan, she wore a bikini so small it was difficult to tell the color except for the two triangular patches of gold fabric covering her nipples.

By the time Matt reached the rear of the house, she'd resumed her place on a lounger and flipped her sunglasses over her eyes. Sunny snored nearby in the shade, no walkies today. "Did your nanny refuse your offer? Come looking for something better?" Kim stretched, arching her back.

Matt tossed the tabloid onto her oiled stomach. "I know Foster took these pictures—and you sold them to the press."

"His mommy needed the money because his evil daddy will let me keep the house but won't provide the mortgage payments. Since you didn't come through for me, I had to think of another plan."

"By embarrassing me and the lady I love?"

"As the kids say—whatever." Her exaggerated shrug hoisted and lowered her heavy breasts.

"How much do you want for the place?"

That got her attention. Kim popped from the lounger and swathed herself in a leopard print coverall. "Two million-five-hundred-thousand and worth every penny. Six bedrooms, six baths, this spacious outdoor entertainment area and landscaped lawn. Privacy walls on all sides. Let me show you around."

Rather than go anywhere near a bedroom with Kim, Matt said, "Just give me a card for your realtor. I'll make a fair offer if you agree to leave the neighborhood and not return."

"As it turns out, I have my license. That's what I did before I married the bastard."

"Relax. I'll walk around by myself and make an offer before I go."

"Suit yourself. I have to catch the last of summer rays since I can't afford St. Bart's anymore." Kim unbuttoned her coverall as if she did a strip tease and coiled onto the lounger again. "Maybe once we make a deal, we can have a celebration."

"No, thanks. Loved ones are waiting for me."

He did his own survey. The staircase in the hall went straight to the second floor without a single spiral. Only a messy master suite strewn with discarded clothes, fashion magazines, and bottles of nail polish showed any sign of occupancy. Except for the two bedrooms her sons must sometimes use, the other three were vacant, devoid of furniture. Matt gazed out a window over the lawn, large for New Orleans, and imagined three little boys running its length in pursuit of a football. From his quick glance at the outdoor entertainment area, it offered amenities as good if not better than Dean's space. He returned to Kimberly. "Two million even, and I'll want to have the place inspected before we close the sale."

"Done!"

"Yes, I am. I can find my way out."

He passed through the house trailed by the maid. At the door, she whispered. "I ain't going wit' her.

Place like this needs a maid. I'd be pleased to serve you and your family."

"Delia, I'll keep that in mind."

Matt strode down the path and through the wrought iron gate. He turned to view the house he'd just purchased. The Greek revival columns were a bit much for him, but oh, that lawn.

At home, the women and Daniel waited. First, he kissed Annie, then he picked up his son.

"What happened! What did you do to her?" Dre blurted.

"I bought her house. She's leaving the neighborhood. Works for all of us. She needs the money. We want more room with the babies coming. Six bedrooms, six baths, and a big, private backyard where our boys can play. Comes with a maid."

"Yes!" Dre pumped her fist.

Annie placed her hand on her belly. "This one might be a girl. Too soon to tell."

"Nope. An angel came to me in a dream and said we'd have a boy."

"Right, as long as it isn't Jesus come again." Annie laid on the skepticism. "I don't think I could handle that."

"Not a messiah, but he will be a great football player."

Annie and Nell exchanged smiles. "If you say so."

Men never knew what they were talking about when it came to babies.

Epilogue

And lo, it came to pass...

But first came the press conference and the wedding. At Joe's urging, Matt took charge and requested the Sinners' PR department to set up a press conference with the reporters. On the raised dais where many a player had answered questions before yet seldom so intimately, he stood behind the mic flanked by Dean and Joe and supported by the massive Junior Polk standing behind him.

"I am announcing my engagement to Ann Marie Billodeaux, daughter of Joe and Nellwyn Billodeaux of Chapelle, Louisiana." Urgently waving hands tried to attract his attention for a question. "Please wait until I finish speaking."

"Annie and I met in a time of crisis in my life. She worked as a nurse practitioner in the NICU where my premature son spent the first three months of his life. His mother having passed away, Annie gave Daniel the care and love he needed to thrive. She lifted me from grief and guilt and taught me how to care for a baby so small I was scared to touch him. When the time came to take Danny home, I asked Annie to come with us and continue to see to his well-being."

An impatient journalist shouted out the question they all wanted answered. "Is Annie pregnant with your child?"

"Yes. We expect the child in May."

"Is it true that you and Joe came to blows over this?"

Joe turned the mic his way. "A slight misunderstanding. By the time I tracked him down, the man already had an engagement ring in his pocket. Too bad no one photographed the proposal, only the very brief quarrel."

Matt reclaimed the mic. "If you will let me finish. Both Daniel and I fell in love with Annie in the NICU and she with us. This angel won the heart of a Sinner. We'll be married in December."

The women in the audience issued soft and envious sighs. The men demanded the date and place.

Dean leaned in to help his less press savvy teammate. "Both are undisclosed."

Another shouted out a question, rude, intrusive, and good-vibe killing, a member of the yellow press, naturally. "Hey, Tank, is it true you have another pregnant and very young woman at your house? Does the baby belong to you too?"

"She is a relative in need of a place to stay. The child is not mine. I think we're done here."

Junior cleared the way. Dean and Joe flanked him. Matt walked out as if he'd mow down anyone in his way. The crowd parted for him and did not follow.

****

The hardest part in planning the wedding came in finding a time during football season to fit it in. Annie and Matt settled on a Friday evening a week after Thanksgiving at seven p.m. with Father Ardoin presiding at Lorena Ranch. Not a single word leaked to the press.

Exactly as she'd envisioned it, Annie stood before a ceiling-scraping Christmas tree festooned with shining balls and every ornament Nell's children ever made for her, in Joe's den stripped of its huge couch, recliners, and floor cushions for the occasion in favor of rows of white chairs. Banks of red poinsettias covered every surface. Not a single one was pink. She exchanged vows and the simple, engraved platinum rings she'd requested from Matt, all the while marveling at the family who made this possible at such short notice.

Stacy had helped her with the dress, street-length and not fussy, ecru rather than the stark white that didn't flatter her dark coloring. No veil, only matching ribbons and pearl-headed pins keeping her black curls in place. Somehow, Stace had cajoled all the women in the wedding party to wear deep red velvet, each dress unique but blending well together, right down to the little outfits sported by Wynn, Lizzy, and Pilar. When she chose Stacy as her matron of honor for her efforts, Jude began to protest, blaming Matt. To which Annie replied, "You will be my maid of honor. I'm pairing you with Mack and expect you to keep him in line." Both women stood beside her while the rest fanned out making half of an impromptu aisle.

Annie considered that in any wedding, the men had it easy. Being athletes and/or members of the Billodeaux family, they came equipped with custom-made tuxedos. Dean acted as best man and the rest formed the other half of the aisle. Only Trinity grumbled a little to her at being paired with Dre in a dress that also had to be custom-made to accommodate her belly.

"Annie, you know Josee is here. What if she thinks the kid is mine?"

Annie threw a friendly smile and wave at his dream girl, the model Josee Riley, sitting beside her father in one of the white chairs placed for the few guests while her mother, Stevie, known for her photography skills and completely trusted not to sell them to the tabloids, took the wedding photos. She answered her nerdy brother. "Everyone knows the baby isn't yours. Perhaps, Josee will be attracted to your kindness and compassion, and not to muscles and athletic prowess. She has brains as well as beauty, Trin."

"You think she'll admire me. All right then." He took his place opposite Dre.

At the end of the ceremony, Annie enjoyed the sheer abandon of Wynn and Lizzy strewing the contents of their little baskets full of red paper rose petals with abandon, carpeting the floor and landing on the special guests as they fell. Nurse Shammy held Daniel wearing the world's tiniest tux and delighting the wedding party with his first smiles. Mawmaw Nadine had the placid Pilar on her lap, but the child kept staring at the huge breasts covered in crimson sequins worn by the person beside her. Having gotten word of the wedding, Mariah donated the champagne and liquor, more or less inviting herself, but always welcome at the ranch. Annie hoped Stevie had gotten pictures of them all.

The same might be said of X-avier Hopkins, the Missile to Matt's Tank. He promised a sound system and appropriate recordings for both the processional and recessional, plus a moving Ave Maria which was out of his range. Having provided entertainment at Tom's wedding, he got an endorsement and an

357

invitation on one condition, that he'd learn the lyrics to an oldie, *Angel Baby*, as requested by Matt for the first dance on the tiny space cleared for it. The words made Annie cry and burrow her face into Matt's shirt. "Hormones," she sobbed. "Happy, not sad."

In the large dining room, the butler Brinsley carved a ham and turkey to order, thin slices requested by the women, great slabs for the men playing football on Sunday. Side dishes filled the space around an all-white, three-tiered wedding cake decorated with icing lace and topped by an angel that Annie and Matt had chosen to be used later on their own Christmas trees in years to come.

As the wedding party filled their plates, Matt bent to tell DJ he'd done a fine job as ring bearer, a compliment that meant little to the boy who had his *bouder* lip out because of a lack of cookies on the table. "I understand that cake has crushed Oreos between the layers."

"It does?"

"Yes," said Dre, standing nearby. "My idea."

"And a good one it was." Annie hugged her substitute sister's shoulders.

All around her warmth and love, but in two days most of the men would be at the Dome for the next game. The Sinners, undefeated, headed straight for the playoffs with home field advantage, taking them through January and probably on to the Super Bowl. No time for a honeymoon, not during the season, only a night in a luxury suite at the Hilton while Nurse Shammy cared for Daniel. Annie knew the truths of being married to a football player, and she'd signed on for years to come.

****

Dre's baby got the message and arrived on a week night between playoff games in January so Matt could haunt the waiting room while Annie coached her birth partner. With the resilience of the young, Dre gave birth to an eight-pound, seven-ounce boy after nine hours of labor and made it look easy. Matt and Annie by her side, Dre announced the baby's name, "Andrew Mathias Ames, the An in his name to stand for Andrea and Annie, and the Mathias is variation on Matthew, but I plan to call him Drew." Dre and Drew, a very small new family. The girl had learned a lot about the meaning of that word in the last few months, Annie believed.

Annie wished she had been so lucky in her delivery. The first week in May, Dr. Garner induced labor for the off-season baby whom he feared grew too big for Annie's tiny frame. She had no objections, not wanting the child to be born too close to Daniel's birthday and all the tragedy that implied. The doctor let her try, but after hours with no progress, told her a C-section could not be avoided. Jude, who popped in and out to give her dubious comfort and spell Matt and Dre, said, "I told you his baby would be too big for you."

She received a firm, "Shut up" from Annie.

At her request, Matt went with his wife into the operating room and did not pass out, even though he could probably see over the drape. After Annie got to see her son, the nurse placed the prophesied boy, all eight pounds, eleven ounces of him, into his father's arms for the walk to the nursery. She smiled to see the confidence with which he held his second son because she'd had a lot to do with that. Before long, he'd be singing about pretty horses and mockingbirds again in the nursery of their new house to Gabriel Jude Keaton. Oh, there had been some debate over the middle name, but Matt conceded to Annie that St. Jude was a powerful namesake, despite it also being the name of his least favorite sister-in-law. "I figure that balances out by using the messenger angel Gabriel for a first name"—the one who may or may not have sent him a dream concerning their son.

****

With Annie still recuperating from surgery when Daniel's first birthday arrived, her family insisted they'd do the planning. "A small celebration," she implored. "Just cake and ice cream.

On the day of, she watched her dad lead two new ponies he'd brought from the ranch into the backyard, a dapple for Danny, a pinto for Gabe. All the pretty horses. She listened to him rationalize the purchases. "I tell you me, Tink, we need more horses with all these grandchildren arriving, especially with Xochi pregnant again."

And heard her mother fussing, "But we don't have to buy them all in their first year. You got Lizzy that little palomino. There is a virtue in sharing, Joe."

Annie couldn't have been happier sitting amid the current crop of babies lying in their carriers in the shade near their mamas. Gabe was dark of hair and eye already. Dre's Andrew had a head of baby chick yellow fluff and her big, blue eyes. Jessie's petite girl, May, named after Teddy's deceased birth mother, Maydell Wilkes, possessed hazel eyes and hair so blonde she appeared to be bald. Daniel crawled among them conversing in gibberish with one or two recognizable words emerging now and then. He paused to study Jessie's wheelchair, always fascinated by it since both she and Teddy often gave him rides. All of them so beautiful and loved she thought.

She turned her attention to the Billodeaux family at its best. Out on the lawn, Tom clowned for the older kids and created huge soap bubbles using nothing more than Dawn detergent and a big loop of knotted string. They delighted in bursting them in his face and chasing each other with wands that trailed tiny, luminous bubbles behind them. Beck, Dean's oldest son, led the pack that included his half-sisters, Princess and Duchess Dobbs. Pilar brought up the rear on chubby legs. The women not minding babies tried to keep some order before any fell and got hurt but ended up joining in the fun catching bubbles on their hands and releasing them into the air again.

Dozy with the heat ramping up for the start of summer, Annie said to Stacy, "Do you think Prince Dobbs will ever marry Ilsa? He claimed he would when his Church of the Dreadlocked Jesus was completed but didn't follow through."

"He's holding out for a son, and the child she's carrying now is another girl already named Countess. She says he's jealous of Beck and wants his own boy. As if I have any sympathy when she tried to steal Dean."

Matt turned from the nearby built-in grill where he flipped hotdogs and hamburgers and warmed the buns with Junior and Dean's assistance. Their new Super Bowl rings, worn for the occasion, caught the sun with every twist of their wrists. "The food is almost ready. I made sure your dad didn't slip hot sauce into the baked beans," he called to Annie.

"Good. There's bottle of his pepper sauce on the table for anyone who wants it." Annie yawned. "I hate being so tired"

Auntie Jude, who hated being called auntie, handed her an icy lemonade. "Keep your fluids up. You lost a lot of blood giving birth to the big bopper."

Annie drank deeply, sucking up the sour of the lemon and the sweet of the sugar used to flavor it. Deep in the house, the doorbell rang. "I thought everyone was here. I didn't expect Mack or Trin, but they both sent gifts. T-Rex had a baseball game and Edie a swim meet."

Delia appeared. "They's a Mr. and Mrs. Ames at the door. Said they were invited, but I never seen them befo'. I ain't fallin' for any fake reporters. Still, I said welcome to our happy home like I always does jus' in case they're legit."

"Yes, they were invited." Not that Annie had expected them to make the trip to see their grandsons. Annie pushed up from her chair cushions to greet them, but Matt insisted she sit. He scooped Daniel into his arms. Dre sat cross-legged on the grass, plucked Drew from his carrier, and settled him on her lap protective as a mother hen with her wings wrapped around him.

Annie smiled pleasantly as the couple emerged from the house too overdressed for the occasion, Bucky in a suit and tie and Marilyn in a deep cerise skirt and jacket with matching heels. Both appeared hot and wrinkled from their journey. "Sorry that I don't get up. I'm still recovering from the surgery."

Marilyn eyed her as if comparing Annie to her tall, blonde, and deceased daughter and finding her wanting.

"I suppose it's a good thing Matt didn't kill another woman having his baby."

Bucky dove in to soften her words and quell his wife. "Marilyn, we spoke about this. Be quiet if you can't say anything nice. Matt is that my grandson you're holding? May I?" He held out his arms to receive Daniel and rest him on the belly hidden by the nicely tailored suit.

"Well then, I see the other one resembles the Ames family. Andrea, I'd forgotten how pretty you were before you went Goth. You look very nice for a change and more filled out."

"Gee, thanks, Mom. Having a baby will do that to you. You want to hold him?"

"No, he'll drool on my jacket."

"Didn't think so."

Daniel pushed against Bucky's chest, wanting down. His grandfather released him with reluctant hands. He crawled immediately to Annie's knee and pushed up against her leg. Marilyn made a judgement. "Is he backwards? Shouldn't he be walking by now?"

To Annie's relief, reinforcements arrived. Joe and Nell lined up behind their daughter. Dean sidled over from the grill, tongs still in his hand. Jude with a ferocious gleam in her black eyes took a spot beside her twin.

"These are some of my premature children, Dean, the Sinners quarterback, and my two nurses. This one is studying to be a doctor." Nell squeezed Jude's shoulder. "As you can see, they all turned out very well."

"That doesn't mean this one will."

Annie mustered the patience she'd developed in the NICU. "While Danny was born a year ago today, developmentally, he is only nine months old since he came into the world three months premature. He is just where he should be and is in fact starting to speak early. Every time he sees Matt a Da comes out of his mouth along with a big smile. Matt is such a good father to all our boys." She included Drew in her gaze.

Marilyn pinched her mouth shut, but only for a minute before she turned on Matt. "I suppose you'll teach him to call this woman Mama."

"No, he already has a name for Annie." Attracting Daniel's attention away from the strangers, Matt pointed to his wife. "Who is this, Danny? Who is she?"

"Ange," the boy said and hugged Annie's knee.

"He calls her Angel as best he can because that is what she is—our angel."

"Damn right she is. Daniel couldn't have a better mother. Bucky, how about a beer? Marilyn, something cold for you?" Joe asked, taking charge, hooking Marilyn's arm, and leading her away.

Throughout the afternoon, Annie observed her family shield her from Marilyn, heard her praises sung even by her brothers who normally preferred to tease her, and let them wait on her so she didn't lack for a thing. No need to do the same with Bucky. He passed his phone to others to get pictures with both his grandsons and one that included Gabe, his arm around Dre, standing behind Annie's chair and urging her to say cheese. Leaning down, he whispered his apologies to her for his wife's behavior. "She's getting help. Hard to tell, I know, but coming here is the next step in her recovery—acceptance of things as they are."

"No need to apologize to me. Daniel should know his grandmother and especially you."

The party ended with the promised ice cream and cake, all Annie had asked for: a small one with a single candle for Daniel to destroy and a larger sheet cake free of drool for the guests. Danny disdained going head first into the frosting, rather scooping out a handful of chocolate icing topped with a yellow rose and shoving it into his mouth.

"See how smart he is, Marilyn?" Bucky said, snapping another photo.

As Daniel's grandparents prepared to leave, Annie did her best to look pleased. In some ways, she was, glad they'd seen the wonderful children they'd rejected, happy and healthy. That included Dre. "So glad you came. Feel free to visit again tomorrow."

"Oh, we're flying out tonight. I promised Marilyn we would. But next time, we'll be visiting longer."

"We have plenty of room if you want to stay with us."

Annie held Gabe in her lap. Matt stood behind her with Daniel on his shoulders. Dre took her place at their side and waved Drew's hand at her father who promptly snapped another photo, though his wife had long since clipped down the hall toward the rental car.

"Now there's a happy family!"

"Yes," Annie thought. They were and always would be come what may.

A word about the author...

Once a librarian, now a writer of romance, Lynn Shurr grew up in Pennsylvania Dutch country. She attended a state college and earned a very impractical B.A. in English Literature. Her first job out of school really was working as a cashier in a burger joint. Moving from one humble job to another, she traveled to North Carolina, then Germany, then California where she buckled down and studied for an M.A. in Librarianship.

New degree in hand, she found her first reference job in the Heart of Cajun Country, Lafayette, Louisiana. For her, the old saying, "Once you've tasted bayou water, you will always stay here" came true. She raised three children not far from the Bayou Teche and lives there still with her astronomer husband.

When not writing, Lynn likes to paint, cheer for the New Orleans Saints and LSU Tigers, and take long road trips nearly anywhere. Her love of the bayou country, its history and customs, often shows in the background for her books.

You may contact Lynn at lynn.shurr@yahoo.com, www.lynnshurr.com or visit her blog:
http://lynnshurr.blogspot.com/
She would love to hear from you and have you review her books.

Thank you for purchasing
this publication of The Wild Rose Press, Inc.

For questions or more information
contact us at
info@thewildrosepress.com.

The Wild Rose Press, Inc.
www.thewildrosepress.com

To visit with authors of
The Wild Rose Press, Inc.
join our yahoo loop at
http://groups.yahoo.com/group/thewildrosepress/

www.ingramcontent.com/pod-product-compliance
Lightning Source LLC
Chambersburg PA
CBHW050029030726
47506CB00001B/178